Ann Firth lives in the south of England with her husband Jim. They have a son called Darren who is happily married to Lisbeth. The author has worked for many years in the world of hair, beauty and fashion, becoming a successful businesswoman. She loves people and life and always has time to listen. Always longing to write but too busy to do so until now.

# LAURA

To my husband for loving me and being my best friend.

To Darren our son and Lisbeth his wife for their support.

To Alan Urwin, an incredible 97-year-old writer himself for his encouragement.

# LAURA

---

## BY

# ANN FIRTH

Copyright © Ann Firth

The right of Ann Firth to be identified as author of this work has been asserted by her in accordance with section 77 and 78 of the Copyright, Designs and Patents Act 1988.

All rights reserved. No part of this publication may be reproduced, stored in a retrieval system, or transmitted in any form or by any means, electronic, mechanical, photocopying, recording, or otherwise, without the prior permission of the publishers.

Any person who commits any unauthorized act in relation to this publication may be liable to criminal prosecution and civil claims for damages.

A CIP catalogue record for this title is available from the British Library.

ISBN 978 1 84363 535 6

www.austinmacauley.com

First Published (2014)
Austin Macauley Publishers Ltd.
25 Canada Square
Canary Wharf
London
E14 5LB

Printed and bound in Great Britain

# Preface

Laura was the daughter of a doting father but a cold and distant mother. When she was just thirteen her father died, and the relationship with her mother became even more difficult until such time as she was thinking about going to University. Then her mother became interested and helpful in finding her a place to live, even giving her a monthly allowance until such time as she qualified. Laura enjoyed this time but, in her ignorance, didn't realise her mother planned to move to South Africa and remarry, cutting all ties with England and her daughter.

After qualifying as a lawyer but unable to get the attention of the man she was so in love with, a friend in Canada persuaded her to go over to visit her to help to get him out of her head. Reluctantly she decided to go, liked it so much and found work had no shortage of men friends, resulting in two quite serious relationships, only to return to England some two years later. Now married, she and her husband moved to the south of England. She got a part-time job at a local solicitors office working for three elderly brothers.

Never could she have believed how this was to change her and her husband's lives forever.

# Part 1

# Tom and Laura

# Chapter One

Laura woke and looked at her bedside clock. It was eight a.m. and Sunday. Nothing much on today she thought, and slid back under the sheets hoping to catch up on the sleep she had missed.

She had got into bed about two thirty a.m. and just could not sleep, so at six a.m. she decided to make herself a mug of hot chocolate hoping to clear her mind and make herself see sense of the totally ridiculous situation she had found herself in. Yet as she held the warm mug against herself for comfort, she felt the tears rolling down her face.

The whole reason for her miserable feelings was she was hopelessly, madly and besottedly in love with Tom – to whom she was just another one of the girls. In fact on Friday when Mr Dill, her boss had come out of his office to ask who his next client was, she had said Tom.

"Tom. Tom who?" he asked.

"Oh, so sorry," Laura replied. "I wasn't thinking. It's Mrs Raymond."

Mr Dill gave her a wry smile, disappearing back into his office.

Laura had been thinking, thinking of Tom. Tom who never left her mind, Tom who she would see at Jake's party tomorrow night. Tom. Tom who made her feel sick, unable to eat when she hadn't seen him. Tom, who kept her awake at night.

Tom was one of her group of friends, always full of fun. All the girls loved him and all the chaps liked him, after work they would sometimes meet for a drink or coffee and if anybody had a barbeque or friends for dinner, or perhaps a joint takeaway, Tom was always there. So as a group Laura would see a lot of him, he always chatted to her teased her and laughed with her, but she knew to him she was just one of the crowd.

He had danced with her last night. She had danced with him last night at Sarah's party. The very reason for her state of mind now she wanted to hate him with his good looks, his super fit body, the flirt, the perfect charmer.

When he was dancing with her and holding her close she thought she would die and he said to her, "Laura you don't have to be so jumpy. I'm not trying to get into your knickers although I wouldn't mind, in the nicest possible way of course." He held her away from him and said, "You're just like a beautiful frog and that's what I will call you." He squeezed her tight.

She pulled herself back from his hold and said, "And you I will call a 'pig'."

She felt embarrassed at what she had said and now she was blushing. He roared with laughter and pulled her closer whispering in her ear. "'The Stud' would be better."

She wanted to scream slap his face, little did he know the effect he had on her, his every touch was like an electric shock going through her whole body and maybe he wasn't trying to get into her knickers, but she sure wanted to get into his pants.

Laura's father had worshiped her and she him. They always had such fun together, he loved sport and he often took her to rugby matches at Twickenham during the season and they would go to watch a local cricket match in summer. He always tried to encourage Laura's mother to go to but she was not interested. Laura was always secretly pleased, not that she didn't want her mother to go with them, but it was always more fun with just Papa. They would have a big fatty bacon roll and a coke, cheer like mad and jump up and down when their team scored, all things her mother would have disapproved of.

Sometimes he would take her to his office in the city on a Saturday morning when he just had something small to see to, which she loved, and afterwards they would go to the shops and he would indulge her in a little gift but, always insist they found a little gift for Mummy. Then perhaps they would go to the ice cream parlour, or have a pizza before going home.

Then one terrible night Papa was taken ill. Laura remembered her mother waking her up to say the ambulance was coming to take Papa to hospital and that she was to be good and stay with the Yatleys at the house next door. Laura didn't mind. Mrs Yatley was such a nice lady, they had no children but they did have a wonderful dog called Jakey, who Laura often went round to play with and sometime she took him for a walk.

"Now hurry," said her mother, "put your dressing gown on and go round they are expecting you." She did as she was told but before leaving she went to kiss Papa goodbye. She would never forget how grey he looked, his arm hanging limp over the side of the bed. When she took hold of it, it was so cold and lifeless she wanted to cry. She wanted to stay by his side until he was better, never to leave him.

"That will do," said her mother, "now run along."

Mrs Yatley was stood with the front door open. She gave her a hug and said, "Come now my little love, let's pop you into bed. I will stay with you and I think your furry friend would like to come and keep you company."

"Oh yes please," said Laura, trying to raise a smile.

She eventually fell asleep and when she woke the sun was shining through the window. She turned her head and realised where she was: Mrs Yatley was still sitting beside her and Jakey was still fast asleep on the end of the bed. Then she remembered why she was there and sat up very quickly.

"How's my papa? Can I go home and see him, is he better?"

Mrs Yatley gently took her hands. "No my darling, Papa has gone to the angels."

Laura put her hands over her ears. "No! No! He can't. I need him, he's my best friend."

Mrs Yatley held her close for a very long time until her sobbing stopped. Jakey came and licked her face, as if he wanted to comfort her too.

Laura stayed with the Yatleys for the next three weeks. They were so kind and nice to her and they tried to explain to her that her mother had a lot to see to and so it was best she was with them. She cried a lot, especially at night when she would bury her head in Jakey's fur for comfort. As she grew up she reflected that her mother didn't come to see her in all that time. There must have been the funeral, but she didn't get to go.

When she went home she found it so hard; no fun, no laughter with Papa. She truly was so unhappy, then one day her mother said to her, "Laura for goodness sake pull yourself together and get on with your life. Stop moping around, your father is dead and frankly I'm sick of your drama."

She was just thirteen years old. Needless to say she and her mother where not close.

Some three months later there was a ring at the front doorbell Laura was up in her bedroom where she spent a lot of her time. Her mother didn't seem to object so perhaps it was best for both of them, although Laura's heart was always sad. She heard her mother go to the door and stepped out onto the landing.

"Hello Emily," she heard a man's voice say. "How are you, may I come in?"

She recognised who it was immediately. Daddy's best friend who she knew as Uncle Jerry. They had been friends since their early schooldays and she knew her mother disliked him immensely. Whenever he had come to see her father her mother was always so rude to him, leaving the room as soon as he arrived. Laura had never understood why, he seemed such a good person. In fact Laura thought so very like her father that, one day, she asked him why.

"Oh, Mummy always has so much to do you know, looking after us is a big job my darling," he had said.

"What do you want?" she heard her mother ask in a hostile tone which made Laura stand back so as not to be seen.

"Well, now the will is all settled and of course you are both well taken care of, I thought it only right I should come and see you both particularly as I am to look after Laura's trust as her solicitor until she is eighteen. I understand completely Emily that I would have been sacked by you the minute poor

Ted drew his last breath, so unless you have explained everything to Laura which I very much doubt, and I am satisfied she understands her father's wishes, I would like to speak to you both."

"No, for your information Jeremy I have not said anything to Laura, for God's sake she is a child."

At that point Laura made one of the bravest decisions of her life. She felt scared but she wanted to know what all this was about .She made out as if she had just come out of her bedroom by closing the door, and walked down the stairs knees knocking. "Hello Uncle Jerry," she said. "Have you come to see us?"

"Yes I have," he replied.

Laura's mother gave her a look of death and reluctantly let him in.

"Shall we go into the lounge, Mummy?" Laura asked already leading the way, her hand out to Jerry. She didn't want him to feel unwelcome and she wasn't sure what her mother would do – come in or storm off as she normally did when he came to see Papa. She sat down on the sofa and Jerry sat beside her. Emily sat on the other side of the room with a scowl on her face.

"Jeremy, I hope this will not take long. Laura and I have a lot to do today."

News to me, thought Laura, and he didn't even bother to reply. Good for you, thought Laura.

Well it transpired that Laura's father had been a very successful businessman and had amassed a small fortune. He had left about ten million pounds, his shares and the house to his wife but he had placed one million pounds in trust for Laura for her education, her university, her travel, her marriage and to buy her first flat and later to buy and furnish a home. She was to have pocket money now and an allowance from it for her teenage years for books and a small car at first then something better later. Uncle Jerry had been given guardianship of her.

Jerry had read all these details out from the file he was holding. He paused and said, "I hope you understand Laura, and you too Emily, there is more to read you may not want to stay," he said looking at her.

"And why not may I ask? Laura is my daughter too, you may have forgotten."

"Very well I will continue."

Looking straight at Laura he said, "This is a letter that your papa made me promise to read to you in the event of his death before mine or before your eighteenth birthday.

*"My dearest Emmi and Laura,*

*I am sorry to have left you so soon, but I know I have left you well cared for and that in my absence, dear Laura, Uncle Jerry will take care of you. I adored you from the moment you were born and you in return gave me so much fun on our trips out and our similar interests. I know right now you will be sad, but I want you from now on only to remember our good times and please one day find a husband who will care for you and love you as I did, but always remember you must always give more than you take and he must be not only your lover but your best friend.*

*And now Emmi, I'm sure you are cross with me still right now just as you were when you found you were pregnant, but I thank you for our beautiful daughter. I am sure you will one day perhaps remarry and I wish you every happiness and for this reason everything I have left you is yours alone. (Apart from the tax man). I know it is the norm in these circumstances if the wife remarries the house must be sold and the proceeds shared with the children but I feel I have provided for Laura and with Jerry's advice I think she will be o.k. I hope you will lose some of your bitterness now but I did love you and I hope you will find forgiveness of me in time."*

Jerry closed the folder and placed a hand over Laura's.

Emily got up walked out without a word.

Laura looked at Jerry. She didn't even want to cry that letter explained so much. That day she grew up and actually felt sorry for her mother.

"Would you like me to stay with you Laura?" Jerry asked.

"No thank you Uncle Jerry, I'm fine. I understand so much now and I realise how Mummy and I have got to come to terms with the situation."

Jerry was quite amazed by these words from such a young girl. At that point he knew he need not worry, he would try to take the place of her father with guidance and he was sure she would go far.

"I think I should go to your mother before I leave," he said. "Here's my office number and my mobile any time day or night, call if you need me." He kissed her on the top of her head and hugged her.

He found Emmi in the hall, stood with the front door open.

"Get out!" she said. "I hope I never have to see you again."

The next few years passed until Laura was fifteen. It was true they lived in a beautiful home with everything they could wish for, but without warmth and love.

Laura spent a lot of time with school friends, Pauline and Caroline, and also with the Yatleys and Jakey who became her soul mate.

The three of them went on to sixth form and she decided she would like to do law. If she could get the grades, she wanted to go on to university.

By this time she had become a pretty dark red-haired girl full of fun and ambition. She was very popular with boys and girls alike.

One day her tutor suggested she should try to get a holiday and Saturday job in a local solicitor's office to have a taste of what she would like to do at uni and it would help with her studies.

The next morning Laura phoned Uncle Jerry to see what he thought of her tutor's advice. She always liked to ask him any questions she had about anything new or that she was unsure of.

"Hi Bun, what's up?"

Bun was his nickname for her ever since that day sitting in the lounge reading her father's letter to her and her mother.

"Nothing Uncle Jerry, but my tutor thinks I should get a holiday job in a solicitor's office. What do you think?"

"Yeah good idea, but not here in my office. Two reasons, one the staff here would treat you with kid gloves knowing who you are and, two, it's too far to come on your bike."

Laura laughed. "I know all that! You are silly Uncle Jerry."

"But actually Bun there is an office in the town by you, Dill & Dill. I think try them, they do homicide law, if that's what you are still thinking; a bit hard going in my book but I wouldn't try to put you off."

"Thanks a lot, speak to you soon. Take care."

It always amazed Jerry how warm Laura was, she certainly didn't get it from her mother. He hoped she would always stay the same and, if she became a lawyer, that it wouldn't make her hard.

The next day was Saturday and Laura planned to go into Dill & Dill. She woke early, jumped out of bed and was surprised to see it had snowed. Never mind it wasn't that much, she would tog herself up and after breakfast she would get going. While eating her toast she told her mother her plan.

"As you will," Emily replied. "I'm out most of the day, there's plenty of food in the fridge but no doubt you will be with friends, or with that awful creature next door."

"Yes Mummy," Laura replied.

If only once she showed more passion. What a terrible life poor Papa must have had.

It was cold as she walked but her excitement kept her warm. She had a rough idea where the office was and soon found it. She pushed open the very heavy glass door and stepped inside. She saw it said *Reception* and approached the desk where a friendly looking lady was sitting.

"Can I help you?" she said with a smile.

"Yes," said Laura. "I'm looking for a holiday and Saturday job. I'm hoping to do law and my tutor thinks it would help me to have an insight to office life *et cetera*."

She started her job one week later – filing, tidying and making lots of tea. She loved it and everybody was so nice to her, something she had not expected.

Some three months later when she was working through the Easter holidays, Mr Dill, the owner of the practice, called her into his office.

She opened the door very nervously and walked in thinking, this is the end.

"Hello Laura," he said, "I hear you want to do law, is that correct?"

"Yes," she replied, "but only if I can get the right grades and go on to uni."

"From what I've seen of you and the feedback from my staff I would think with hard work that will not be a problem."

"Thank you," she said with heart pounding.

"I was thinking. Would you like to come to court sometime with me?"

"Oh, yes please," she said, hardly able to believe her ears.

"Right then that's settled, you need a smart suit, neat shoes, tight lips and big ears. Shall we say next Monday? I'm starting on a new case at the Crown court. Be here eight thirty a.m. prompt it will take about forty-five minutes to get there, go and see Pipa my PA and she will brief you, that's all, off you go."

So that was the beginning of Laura's journey into law, she got her good grades and went onto Uni.

One day in the Easter holidays when Laura returned home from the office, her mother, much to her surprise, was in the front hall. It was normal for her to go straight to her room, which resembled more of a big bedsit now she more often than not fixed her own food in the kitchen and took it upstairs to eat. Mostly her mother was out in the evening. They did have a DIY breakfast at roughly the same time in the kitchen but it was almost as if they were lodgers in the same house. Emily never asked her what she was doing, or how her job or college was going.

Laura always made a point of saying hello and Mother would just nod or sometimes reply, but that was the extent of the conversation.

So Laura was shocked when her mother said, "Laura, I've just taken a stew out of the oven. Shall we eat together this evening?"

A look of shock came over her face she paused for a few moments. "All right. I'll just take my things upstairs and freshen up, say ten minutes." Once in her room she realised her heart was pounding she felt almost nervous, what did her mother want? What did she have to say?

She went downstairs rather cautiously. She could see the table was laid in the smaller of their two dining rooms, a bowl of pretty flowers in the middle of the table, wine glasses, napkins, the lot.

Heading for the kitchen her mother was coming out with the stew, she placed it on the table and said, "Come Laura dear, this will be nice. Come sit down."

Which Laura obediently did.

"I'll just get the wine and the potatoes." Mother opened the wine and poured them both a glass, she sat down and said, "I've been thinking that when you go to university it will be much more convenient for you to have somewhere close by to live in. I assume you will choose Oxford?"

"But Mummy I don't even know if I will get the grades yet."

"Of course you will," replied her mother. "So I think it would be a good idea for us to start looking for something now so as you can be well settled by the time term starts. It's far too far for you to travel every day, particularly on cold winter mornings and dark evenings and we will get sorted on you learning to drive. You have your Trust set up by your father so I suggest you should buy an apartment, or better a small house. There are some very nice mews cottages in that area and they will increase in price if in time you want something larger. I will pay for the furnishings, so what do you think?"

Laura jumped at the idea. Even if she didn't get into uni it would be better for both of them. She knew her mother would be pleased to have her freedom, giving her the feeling there may be a new man in her mother's life.

## Chapter Two

After many trips to Oxford looking for a suitable place to buy Laura and her mother decided on a pretty little mews house. It had a garage which fitted the bill as Laura had set her mind on having a bright red Mini once she could pass her test.

This was a time when she and her mother got on better than ever before. The weeks screamed by, Laura made lots of phone calls to her Uncle Jerry and took him to see the place, although she never got in to conversation about this with her mother: she didn't want to open up old wounds.

The contracts were eventually signed and true to her word Emily paid for the carpets and curtains and all the furniture. They actually ate together quite often now when they got home from a hard day's shopping, deciding what would fit, what would look good and what was practical for this new adventure. Sometimes Laura would cook and sometimes her mother. It was such a change.

When the big day arrived to move in Laura could hardly contain herself. Her mother went with her and after a short stay said. "I'll leave you to settle in now. I've decided to make you an allowance of a hundred pounds a week, that will help to pay the overheads here and help to run the car and pay for new clothes and books you will need."

"Oh Mummy, that is so good of you. Are you sure you can afford it? You have already spent a fortune on me."

"Yes of course I can, only until you graduate and get a full time job, and it will mean you are not forever asking that dreadful Jerry thing for advice and help with money from your trust. Now get on and live your life. You are of course always free to come back to the house, but I'm sure you will not want to."

Same old mother, Laura thought, they really had enjoyed the last few months together, and now she seem as offhand and distant as ever.

Laura stepped forward to hug her mother and felt her stiffen up cold and hard. It made her think of poor Papa, what a life he must have endured. She hoped in that brief moment that he had found some comfort during his marriage to her mother in some other woman's arms.

"I will phone you and pop in sometime," Laura replied. "Bye."

On reflection some years later Laura came to understand that was her mother's final discharge of her responsibilities to her previous life.

It was a super early September morning for Laura, her first day at university. She had arrived with butterflies in her tummy but brimming with enthusiasm for the years ahead.

She soon made many friends and settled in easily. She was one of the few that had their own pad so they often congregated there for coffee and a chat. She was never short of dates, all the boys were eager for her attention; she found the studying easy and loved the social life.

Time went so quickly that first year she used to go and see the Yatleys quite often, taking Jakey for a walk and then staying for something to eat. Several times she had stopped to see if her mother was at home but she never managed to catch her. She had tried to ring her from time to time but without success, although she did send her a note from time to time to thank her for the money that was in her bank each month. When she was on holiday from uni and the Yatleys were away she used to have Jakey to stay with her, they took long walks together and he loved to sit in the front seat of the car and bark at other dogs that they passed. Laura would have loved to have a dog of her own but she realised it would not be good for it when she was away all day, sometimes getting home late.

Then one Saturday morning she had a phone call from Edna Yatley. She could hear Edna was not her usual cheerful self.

"What's the matter?" she asked.

"Well it's Jakey, he's not too well, he has been poorly all the week and the vet said there is nothing wrong with him, he is just getting old. I think he would like to see you my darling if you have the time."

"I'll come right now," Laura said. She grabbed her car keys and ran from the house. She knew Jakey was getting old because their walks were not so long and sometimes they sat down and had little rests when they were out together. Yet she was sure the vet was wrong, she would soon cheer him up.

She drove as fast as she could, she just wanted to be with him. She almost screamed to a halt in the Yatley's drive. The front door was open she ran into the lounge where Jakey was lying on his beanbag on a sheepskin rug, the Yatleys were sat beside him. Edna put her finger to her lips to slow Laura down.

"I think he's been waiting for you," she said.

Laura got down on her knees and gently stroked him, he lifted his head and almost seemed to smile.

"There you are you can get better now," she said. He took a deep breath and closed his eyes for ever. "No! No!" she cried. "You can't do this to me I need you." She buried her head into his fur and wept uncontrollably the first time she had really cried since her father had died. After some time she got up and the three of them hugged together.

"Come now," said Jack Yatley. "We must think of the good times he had and the fun and pleasure he gave us all."

"Why don't you stay with us now over the weekend?" said Edna.

"Yes I would like to," said Laura.

Laura still visited Edna and Jack quite regularly, yet she missed seeing Jakey and together they often talked about him. The funny things he did that made them laugh the way he looked at them out of the top of his eyes when he knew he was misbehaving.

Laura obviously had to drive by her old home on these occasions. Sometimes she would stop to see if her mother was there, but she never seemed to catch her. It was just the same if she rang her. But then, she never heard from her mother. She did drop her a line from time to time thanking her always for her allowance, which always appeared in her bank every month.

She sometimes asked the Yatleys if they saw anything of her, but it said they saw the car go in and out but that was all.

Edna and Jack had become very fond of Laura over the years and found it hard to understand her mother's attitude. One day Edna said to her husband, "You know when Jakey died Laura uttered the same words as she did when her father went. I think they have been the two most loved things in her short life. I do so hope she finds a husband one day to love as she deserves."

Then one day towards the end of her time at uni Laura went home, put the key in the lock as normal, opened the door and picked up the mail, putting it down on the table as normal while she put the kettle on. Turning back to the table she noticed there was a large brown envelope to be opened. She picked it up almost excited, what could it be? With eager fingers she tore it open, a small bundle of papers fell out together with a letter, she quickly saw it was from her mother.

*Dear Laura,*

*I am writing to tell you that I have sold the house and am going to live in Argentina with a man who I am going to marry. He owns a large estate there where we will live. You are of course welcome to come to visit but I am sure you are so involved with your friends and life at University.*

*I will continue to give you the allowance each month until my death, you of course will receive nothing from my estate as your father's wish that the house was mine to use as I wished.*

*From your ever loving Mother.*

Laura wasn't particularly upset. Perhaps a little shocked, and she hoped this new man knew what he was letting himself in for; but then perhaps her mother would be different with him. She smiled to herself. Do come to visit but no address. She turned to the papers: nothing of any real interest, but there was her birth certificate which, of course, would save a lot of hassle if she ever needed it.

# Chapter Three

Laura finished university and continued to work at Dill's, patiently waiting for her results. She need not have worried – she got her Master's Degree with Honours. She invited Uncle Jerry and Jack and Edna to her graduation, and Mr and Mrs Dill invited them all back to the office to celebrate. When they arrived the whole office staff were gathered to greet her they clapped and hugged her and Mr Dill started opening champagne.

"Let's raise our glasses to our bright young star with our best wishes for a wonderful career in law," said Mr Dill.

"Here, here!" said Uncle Jerry.

"Three cheers!" said Jack Yatley. "Hip hip hip hooray!"

And then it was time to go. Mr Dill came over to Laura and said, "Laura I would like to see you in my office for a few moments, alone." He pointed to the door and she obediently followed his gesture.

"Now, my dear," he said with a smile. "I know the world's your oyster now Laura but I would like to offer you a position here with Dill & Dill for one year, just to let that oyster mature a little. The world of law is hard and cruel and once you have a little experience you will find it easier to get a position in another firm, be it very junior at first. It will also give you chance to take stock in a world outside university."

She had enjoyed working at Dill's but now she wanted something a bit more challenging to get her teeth into. Did she even want to do law? She realised she needed new contacts, interests, something to get her out of this rut she was in and, finally to get that 'PIG' Tom out of her mind. Now she felt sick at the very thought she wouldn't see him. She began to weep again, and just then her phone rang. It was Caroline from Canada. When she and Pauline had graduated, Caroline had gone to Canada to visit relatives with her parents, and they'd loved it so much she got a high-flying job and they all stayed. Whereas Pauline had married her schoolboy sweetheart and was producing babies like a rabbit, three in three years. Was it really three years? Three years since they were all together. Three years she had stayed at Dill's.

"What are you up to?" said Caroline.

"Nothing actually," Laura replied.

"What's up? You sound a bit pissed off. Not got a date with the 'Pig' yet?"

"No, and never likely to. He even said he would like to get into my knickers last night."

"And did he?"

"No."

"Christ what's wrong with the bloke?"

"He just jokes he just doesn't fancy me. So what about you?" Laura asked.

"Well, you know the wonder boy I've been dating? Well I've just given him the elbow."

"Why?"

"It was just not going anywhere, even the sex was boring. I tell you what, why don't you come out here for a holiday? I've got a month's vacation to come. I'm sure you must have some to come to you, you never seen to take time off. It would be great. I'll ring you tomorrow and we will sort it out. OK? Cheers for now."

Laura thought about it for a while. Yes it probably would do her good. She got up but before she could get in to the shower, the phone rang again. It was Caroline.

"Look Laura, I've got a better idea. Come for a year I've got a three-bed apartment here so we can share. We'll take a holiday first so I can show you the country, then when we get back you can get some work. There's plenty of work to find here."

"Oh, I don't know. I would have to let my house and what about my car?"

"Don't put things like that in the way. And at least you would get that stupid arsehole out of mind and sight. Sort it out tomorrow. I'll ring you with the holiday plan. I'm so excited."

By that evening Laura had decided. Yes, she would go. The next morning she asked Mr Dill if she could have a word with him.

"Of course Laura, come on into my office. Pipa's here to take some notes for later, is that all right or is a private matter?"

"Oh no not at all," Laura replied.

"Have a seat then. What's on your mind?"

"Well I have decided to go to Canada."

"Good God girl, whatever for?"

"Well at first a holiday, and then for a year."

"Have you really thought about this? Where will you stay, what about a job? Oh Laura, I do think you are jumping in at the deep end."

"Well not really, Mr Dill. I appreciate your concern but I will be staying with an old friend from uni days. She has a large apartment and tells me it is easy to get a job and I do have enough savings to take a year off, plus if I let my house and possibly sell my car, which will break my heart, I will be able to manage. I have put a lot of thought into this." She didn't dare tell him it was only twenty-four hours.

"Well my dear, I wish you well and I am sure we can find a slot back here if it doesn't work out. When are you thinking of going?"

"Well I thought it would take me a month to tidy up the ends here, plus I'm not sure how long it will take to let my house, et cetera."

"OK then, off you go."

The news went round the office like wildfire and to Laura's shock and delight Pipa said to her at coffee break that she may be interested in renting her house. She loved where she lived, it was right out in the country, but she got fed up with the hour's drive each day especially in the winter time. So perhaps they could have a chat about it after work.

"Of course," said Laura, "how about if you come home with me and take a look around?"

"Good idea," said Pipa.

She loved the house and said, since her old car was clapped, she thought she might like to buy the Mini as well.

They sat and chatted for ages. Laura made lots of tea and brought out some nibbles. They discussed the rent and agreed the price for the car.

Laura said she was happy to leave everything as it was. The two knew each other very well through working together so both sides were happy. They decided to get one of the solicitors to do a simple lease for Pipa to sign, and to cap the deal, Laura opened a bottle of champagne.

It just seemed everything fell into place and Laura thought it was meant to be.

After tearful goodbyes to the Yatleys, and fond farewells to all at Dills' and dear old Uncle Jerry, who declared she could still phone him day or night, Laura was at Heathrow Airport saying a fond farewell to Pipa who had driven her there in what was now her Mini.

"Go now," said Laura after she had checked in, "or else I might change my mind." So they had a final hug and parted.

Laura went through hand luggage check-in and on into the departure lounge with feelings of excitement, fear and she didn't know what else.

Soon it was time to board and, once on the plane, she found she was sitting next to a rather good-looking guy perhaps a little older than herself.

As the plane started to taxi out, he leant forward a little to look out of the window. Laura turned slightly towards him and smiled.

"Sorry," he said. "I'm always nosy at this part of the journey, don't ask me why," he went on with a smile. "I'm Michael," he said offering his hand to shake hers.

"I'm Laura," she replied. She felt his handshake firm and strong, something she liked in a man. She hated it when some men shook hands like a limp lettuce leaf.

"Are you travelling on business or pleasure?" he asked.

"Pleasure and work I hope, I'm planning to stay for a year, I have a good friend in Calgary and we are going to take a month's holiday together and then I will look for some work."

"What do you do?" he asked.

"I'm a lawyer," she replied.

"Well I'm sure you will find something easily in the area in connection with that line."

"And you?" she asked.

"I work for an oil company so I travel quite a lot, mostly to Canada. I live in Surrey in England where I have my own pad but out there the company provide me with a small apartment, not fantastic but it's better than staying in a hotel and it means I can travel light."

With that the hostess arrived with the drinks trolley.

"Can I buy you a coffee or something stronger?" he asked.

"A coffee would be super, thank you."

Michael made the journey so much more enjoyable. They chatted a lot, dozed a little later, had a glass of wine together with their food and found out that Caroline's apartment and his were about a couple of miles apart.

Soon it seemed the pilot announced their descent into Calgary.

Michael leant a little towards her and said, "That's a shame Laura we seem to have made such a hit together. I was sort of thinking we might have joined the Mile High Club. Oh I'm sorry, I hope I haven't offended you?"

"No you haven't," she said with a smile. She knew she had slightly coloured only because she wasn't sure about the Mile High but, she certainly fancied him rotten.

"Well in that case I'll give you my phone number. Here's my card, you never know perhaps we can meet one day for dinner when you are a working girl again."

The plane landed and then they were at immigration. Michael had passed through quickly and it crossed Laura's mind she may never see him again. She handed her passport and all the relevant paperwork to the officer behind the desk. It seemed that he took ages to look at it all.

"Welcome to Canada," he said with a big smile.

She walked on through to the baggage collection and to her surprise Michael appeared beside her.

"Just help you load your trolley, Miss," he said. "And don't forget my number," with that he pecked her on the cheek. The baggage came through and he was gone.

Laura walked through into the arrivals lounge. There was no mistaking Caroline, she was holding up a card which said 'Welcome Laura' but she looked absolutely fantastic in a bright yellow trouser suit and when she caught sight of Laura , she ran forward with arms outstretched.

They greeted one another with hoots of delight and hugs of joy.

"Come on," said Caroline, "let's get going and get you settled in."

They walked to the car park and found the car, a bright red Mini, the same as Laura had been so sorry to sell. It somehow made her feel at home immediately.

"I can't believe it!" she said laughing. "We both had the same car."

"Well just goes to show we have the same good taste. So how was the flight?"

"Well very good and interesting. I had this guy called Michael sat next to me, real dishy says he lives quite near to you, gave me his phone number. I must say I certainly fancied him."

"Well that's good, got the 'Pig' out of your head already."

Laura felt a little pang. "Not exactly."

Caroline's apartment was super, it had three lovely big double bedrooms, two en suite, a large spacious lounge with dining area and a state-of-the-art kitchen and a large terrace area all furnished tastefully. Laura was so pleased for her friend and said so. As she knew, Caroline must have worked hard to achieve so much.

After a good night's sleep the two enjoyed a morning of catching up on things. Then Caroline explained her ideas for the holiday. So the next morning they set off for the Calgary Stampede. Caroline said they could walk there as it would take about ten minutes, not worth taking the car.

It truly was a spectacular experience. On the ground leading up to the entrance there were lots of Indian tepees pitched and, a little further on coming towards them, was a group of Indians in full regalia on horseback, about forty of them riding four abreast. It seemed almost surreal especially when they raised their hands and said good morning. They walked on and arrived at the entrance. Caroline just held up what looked like a pass and they walked straight through.

"What's all that about?" asked Laura.

"Oh, just somebody I do a little work for from time to time, you will meet him later."

And they did. He took them to a sort of private area overlooking the main events arena where they watched the rodeo which included some fun events like Wild and Woolie, where juvenile aspiring stars of the future, some as young as six, attempted to stay aboard reluctant sheep. They were served a beautiful lunch with wine. Laura was to discover on this holiday that who Caroline didn't know wasn't worth knowing. The whole day was a great experience.

That evening as they sat chatting over a snack and discussing the day and what fun it had been. Laura said, "so what sort of work do you do to get this service we had today, Caroline?"

"Oh a bit of legal advice and a bit of this and that."

Laura gave her friend a knowing look.

Caroline laughed and changed the subject.

"Now we need to be away early tomorrow morning. Mum and Dad have invited us for breakfast, it's only about thirty kilometres away, but after we are going to drive on to Banff. You will love it Laura, it's so beautiful, you just wait and see."

Laura was happy they were going to see Caroline's parents. She had spent so much time in their house when she, Caroline and Pauline had been growing up.

The morning broke with a lovely sunrise and they were soon on their way for breakfast.

Caroline's parents were delighted to see them both with lots of hugs and kisses all round.

"We're so glad you are here Laura, it's made this crazy daughter of ours take a well deserved holiday. Now come on in. I expect you are both starving."

It seemed in no time it was time to leave. They piled back into the Mini and with lots of waving goodbye, they were on the road to Banff. They stopped a couple of times for a cold drink and once for fuel, they chatted and laughed all the way and Caroline said how happy she was that they were together again. She felt sure it would be for more than a year once Laura had got a taste of the country and people.

After about five hours they approached the Banff National Park. With its huge gates and toll area to pay your entrance Caroline leant over to the glovebox and took out a card which she held up to the park ranger, who waved her through.

"Another bit of this and that?" enquired Laura.

"You've got it," came the reply.

It was about another fifteen minutes to the centre of town. It truly was a most beautiful area.

"We are going to stay at the Banff Spring Hotel for a couple of nights. That will give us chance to look round and sample the luxury the hotel has to offer," said Caroline.

"Do we have a reservation?"

"Oh yes, I've booked two double en suite, just in case you feel like entertaining."

"Who? I don't know anybody."

With that they were at the front entrance. The porter unloaded their cases and took the car keys from Caroline.

"I will leave them at reception for you, madam."

They checked in and went to their rooms. Everything was just so luxurious Laura began to wonder what it would cost.

"Right now," said Caroline, "I think we should maybe take ten minutes to relax then get ready for this evening. Wear something glamorous, we are going to be treated to dinner here tonight."

This time Laura didn't ask any questions other than, "What time?"

"At the bar at seven o'clock."

She decided to wear her white silk dress with a halter neck and full skirt very similar to the Marilyn Monroe dress lined with a complete all in one body, she knew she looked good in it and hoped it would fit the bill.

She found the bar and Caroline already perched on a stool talking to the barman. "Gee, you look fantastic!" she said. "I've got a gin and tonic and ordered you one as well, you happy with that?"

"Yes great." After a sip at her drink she said, "Now, Caroline, just what are you getting us up to, may I ask? Are we here as call girls, prostitutes or what?"

Caroline shrieked with laughter. "Don't be ridiculous girl, we are being treated by and dining with the owner of the place, he's an old friend and he's bringing along a friend of his to make up the four." With that she raised her eyes slightly and lowered her voice and said, "Here they come now."

Laure turned her head to see the two men walking towards them. One tall, elegant, good-looking and tanned, the other short fat round and nearly bald, all in a flash of a moment she assumed the shorter one of the two must be the owner of the hotel. How wrong could she have been?

Caroline slipped down off her stool. "Hello Marco, let me introduce you, this is my very great friend Laura."

He shook her warmly by the hand. "And let me introduce you to Raymond. He is here on business, he comes from Quebec."

There was much shaking of hands and then Marco suggested they should go through to the dining room. By this time he had slipped his arm round Caroline and was kissing her on the ear.

Two waiters immediately escorted them to a table looking out onto a beautiful lake, they pulled back the chairs for the ladies.

"I think we will have a bottle of Bollinger spec Cuvee as aperitif please, Carl."

"Certainly, sir."

"I trust you like champagne Laura?"

She nodded with a smile. Then Raymond turned to her. "Do you speak French mademoiselle?"

"*Un peu*, but I am very rusty," she replied.

"Then we shall speak in English."

While they sipped the champagne Marco said he had already arranged with the chef what they should eat tonight. He hoped they would enjoy it, he knew Caroline would.

The meal was fantastic and there was lots of easy joking and laughing, and as the evening wore on it was obvious from the body language between Marco and Caroline that they were more than friends. They slowly moved closer together and to Laura's horror Raymond was doing the same to her, in fact at one point he put his hand on her thigh explaining that he was a true Frenchman. She was hoping he could read body language as he certainly didn't turn her on, in fact as nice as he was as a person she thought all he needed was a black beret, a bicycle and a string of onions to create the true image of a Frenchman.

Laura was sure Marco had spent the night with Caroline but didn't comment the next morning over breakfast. After all it was none of her business and if they were going to spend the next year together, she thought they should respect each other's privacy.

They had a good look round in Banff that day and found a nice little restaurant for the evening they booked a table for seven o'clock which gave them time to go back to the hotel have a swim and a sauna before they ate.

Again it was a great evening totally different from the night before. They dressed casually in jeans and T-shirts and flirted outrageously with the waiters and a table of four guys sat near them.

On the way back to the hotel Laura said, "That really was good fun and the guys were so friendly."

"And naughty, but I think this holiday will make you throw away the torch you are holding to that Pig. Good grief it's nearly eleven o'clock! I'm expecting Marco in thirty minutes."

"Oh really," said Laura with a knowing look.

"Well you know what they say Laura, you must make hay when the sun shines, but I think I'm making mine in the dark."

The next day they took off heading for Jasper taking four days to get there. They stopped at Brewster Ice Fields where they rode to the top of the glacier in the vehicle especially designed for this, and who was driving this? A friend of Caroline's. Laura teased her later.

"Didn't think you had done a little work for the driver," she had said. "Not your type I think."

Caroline laughed saying, "No you are right, but did you notice we didn't pay so I think he could be hoping."

"You are absolutely outrageous," Laura said.

Caroline had been there in Canada some years now and had picked up their ways, some of the things she said made Laura cringe at times, she found it a bit coarse, like *shit*, *arsehole*, and *that chap's got a good prick*.

That night they stayed at the Num-Ja-Te Hotel built like an enormous log cabin and privately owned by the Simpson family, the descendants of Jimmy Simpson who together with Bill Peytoe were the two main guides for the railroad through the Rocky Mountains to the west coast.

They had a truly memorable night there. At first they ate in the restaurant which overlooked a magnificent lake that appeared like a mirror, reflecting a glacier that was slowly melting into the lake, framed by two mountains, it was breathtaking. Afterwards they went into the lounge for coffee where there was a small group playing nice music to dance to. Within a short time a young man came and asked Caroline to dance. Laura sat sipping her coffee totally relaxed just daydreaming when she felt a tap on her shoulder.

"Excuse me, I see you are on your own, would you like to dance?"

"Thank you, yes I would."

He danced well with super rhythm, chatted pleasantly and was good looking. When the music stopped he said, "I see your friend is not back, may I sit with you? Perhaps we can have a drink together."

Laura nodded her approval. They sat and chatted for some time when he told her he was the duty manager for the hotel this week.

"Well this must be my luck," she said.

"No mine I think," he replied.

Caroline had not returned at this point. In fact Laura didn't see her again until breakfast the next morning, before they set off for Jasper.

"Look," he said. "I get a suite here with my position, shall we go there?"

"OK that would be nice," she said shocking herself at what she was saying.

The suite was on the same level as the restaurant but more to the side, he opened the door and walked straight through to the terrace.

"I think it would be nice to sit here and find out more about each other. Is dry white wine all right for you?"

"Yes," she replied, thinking, be on your guard Laura how much more does he want to know?

He was back in a few moments with two expensive-looking cut classes which he filled. He was now standing looking out over the balcony.

"Quite romantic, isn't it?" he said.

"Very I would say."

He came up behind her and kissed her on the neck, which sent a tingle through her body –she realised it was quite a long time since she had felt like this. Slowly he undid the zip on her dress waiting for any anti-reaction from her. He gently ran his hands under her breasts which immediately made Laura realise she had lost control, he leaned against her and she knew there was no going back now. Her dress dropped to the ground. He turned her round to face him. He cast his eyes over her body and closed his eyes, slowly undoing his shirt and removing the rest. They were naked together.

"Do you like making love in the open air?" he whispered in her ear.

"I don't know, but I think I will."

He picked her up and carried her to the pale blue double-sized sun lounger.

It was passionate and explosive, exciting, wonderful and long lasting. Laura had never experienced anything like it before. They lay there in utter silence for some time. Then he leant over her and kissed her first on her breasts, then on her neck and then on her lips.

"That was the most wonderful experience of my life," he said. Laura just nodded. "Now it's twelve fifty a.m. and I am on duty till eight o'clock. I must leave you. I hope you can find your way to your room, you beautiful thing."

And he was gone.

Laura didn't quite know what she felt but she jumped up, put her dress on and found her bag and room key and left.

Once back in her room she began to feel a little ashamed of herself, but she had to admit it would take a long time and a certain man to make her feel so satisfied and fulfilled.

As they drove on towards Jasper the next morning, Caroline enquired, "So what happened to you last night or should I not ask?"

"I had wonderful sex with the under manager of the hotel. I don't even know what his name is."

"You bitch!" screeched Caroline. "I've been after him for ages, nobody but nobody gets to have him. What've you got that I haven't? And anyway he's no under manager, his real title is only son of the owners. So go on, what you got..?"

"Just class my dear friend," Laura said with a smile.

Sitting quietly looking at the beautiful surroundings she was going over in her mind last night. Yes, it truly was a time to remember but she couldn't stop letting her thoughts go back to Tom – would it be like that with him? How could she know because they had never got that far? She may dream of wild romantic nights with him but she had to be honest with herself, she suspected that she had never even crossed his mind and he probably hadn't even noticed she wasn't around. Possibly by the time she was back in England he would be long gone, perhaps even married. So she said to herself forget him from here on put him out of your mind forever, but she knew deep down in her heart there would be that yearning that he had been the one making love to her that night, and so she knew he would always be hard to forget.

They arrived in Jasper later that day and again Caroline had the hotel booked. She truly had worked out a great journey – where to stop, how long and when to move on.

"Here we are then. Don't know anybody of importance here so I guess we just have to look up the local talent and see what's out there."

Laura laughed. "What do you mean we have to look for some good-looking, high-flying wealthy men?"

"You are getting the hang of things at last. You never know when you might pass this way again and a few good contacts are always useful."

The next stop was Kamloops, again another interesting drive stopping for snacks and drinks and Laura drove quite a lot of the way. Caroline said she thought it would be a good idea to begin to get used to driving on the right-hand side of the road as she was presuming she would be getting a car as soon as they got back.

It seemed time was running away with them. The next stop was Vancouver where they shopped till they dropped and then turning back down the Weston Sea Board to Calgary. Their trip had taken just a day short of a month. They had enjoyed every moment of it, not only the sights the hotels and the people they had met, but most of all being together again as friends, just like old times.

Caroline had a couple more days off before going back to work so she was able to show Laura around the immediate area together with the workings of the apartment, such as the stopcock for the water, the fuse box for the electric, as they would not always be there together. She also introduced her to the neighbours, one of which Laura told her she thought was very dishy.

"You're man made," said Caroline.

"Hark who's talking, friend."

"Yes I know, but I should forget it. He's a bit undecided what side of the fence he likes most, I think."

# Chapter Four

Now the holiday was over Laura needed to set about getting herself a job. She was open to anything, she didn't particularly want it to be as a lawyer. It wasn't vital that she earned big money or even any money for a year, but that was not her way.

Caroline had insisted that she pay no rent, but Laura had insisted that at the very least she should pay half of the overheads.

Off she went one lovely sunny morning with a spring in her step. First stop the newsagents to get a local paper to start to weigh up what work was out there. She didn't particularly want to go to an agency at this point. She walked on just looking around and then she passed a garage-cum-car sales, and there in the window was a notice 'Staff Required'. She paused for a moment and then deciding she had nothing to lose, she went inside. A pleasant-looking elderly man came towards her.

"Good morning my dear. How can I help you?"

"I see you are advertising for staff, may I ask what sort of work this is?"

"Yes of course, it's for servicing and cleaning cars."

"Oh, I could clean them, but I don't think you would rate my servicing abilities."

"I'm sorry, I didn't think it was for you," the man replied with a smile.

With that she noticed a very smart-looking Mini in the corner, she started to walk over to it. In fact it was a Mini Cooper. No! she said to herself, get the job first, then think about the car.

The next few weeks' job hunting were a little frustrating until, one day after work Caroline, came busting in full of enthusiasm. She had heard of a job that she thought would suit Laura. It was a new legal practice setting up and looking for ambitious people to carry the firm forward.

"Here's the number to ring," she said handing Laura a piece of paper. "It's only a few blocks away from my office so it's not too far to travel."

Laura was on the phone first thing in the morning. After answering a few questions, she was offered an interview that day at eleven o'clock.

She arrived a little before time and was greeted by a very pleasant woman in her forties. She asked Laura to tell her a little bit about herself and her background and her qualifications.

Laura in turn explained that she was only here for a year and was not particularly looking to practice law but maybe something to do with law.

The woman took notes and said they did have an opening that might suit Laura, but the decision would rest with Mr Chatsworth the managing director. If he was interested in her, they would be in contact.

As Laura walked home she reflected on how different Canada was to England; they didn't ask for proof of qualifications, a portfolio or anything but then this seemed to be the Canadian way. She wasn't very hopeful and then to her surprise there was a phone call to say could she come back tomorrow at ten to see Mr Chatsworth?

She arrived again just a little before time, ushered in by the woman she had seen yesterday and introduced to the young man sitting behind the desk. She did think he looked incredibly young, but perhaps he was old but could afford a good plastic surgeon.

"Hi there," he said offering Laura his hand.

Laura noticed how strong his handshake was, which impressed her.

He explained that the position he thought she may be suitable for was office manager. It would mean she had to control the workload of the two main partners deal with their secretaries and all other staff. Because of her legal qualifications she would at times be asked to sit in on certain meetings and because of her knowledge of law she may be asked to help with some cases even attending court. Of course there was one big disadvantage with her.

Here we go, thought Laura, typical. All that glitters isn't gold, there had to be a but.

"And that would that be?" she asked.

"I believe you are only here for a year. Would we be able to alter your mind on that if we find things are working well?"

"I'm afraid I wouldn't like to make any promises on that and I believe there would be a little matter of a work permit."

"And I'm sure we could sort that out." He took a deep breath. "Shall we say 5,000 Canadian dollars a month?"

Laura tried not to let her mouth drop. Collecting herself together she paused and said, "Yes, that will be fine to start."

He gave her a wry smile. Standing up with hand outstretched, he said, "No flies on you I see. Shall we say start tomorrow? Tammy here will get all the relevant details from you, of course the first few weeks will be just getting set up so there may be a few dogsbody jobs for us all to get stuck into. I expect you understand what I mean: no smart clothes, just jeans and T-shirt, and here's to a successful time for all of us. Goodbye till tomorrow."

Tammy opened the door and they left the office, the two of them chatted for a while and then she took the details needed and Laura left.

Out on the street she pinched herself. She couldn't believe her luck, all so casual! But even if it didn't work out she had little to lose. She decided it was such a beautiful day she decided to walk back to the apartment. She knew she would have to go past the garage where she had seen the Mini; at that point she had no intention of going in, but when she got there she just had to go in.

"Hi," said the man she had seen a few weeks before. "Had a quick course in car servicing? The job is still vacant."

It crossed her mind that if she had said yes the way these Canadian's had such an easy attitude she might have got the job, if possibly followed by the sack. "No, actually I've come to look at that Mini."

He looked a little surprised. "Right this way, madam."

One hour later, she drove away in it after much bargaining and lots of coffee. She had got a two-year guarantee, parts and service, a tank full of gas and a new set of tyres when the existing ones wore out.

Some six months later she had popped out of the office to get some teabags when walking down the street towards her was Michael. Michael on the plane, they both seemed to see one another at the same time, they sort of ran together and he picked her off her feet and spun her round, much to other passers'-by surprise.

"Where have you been?" he said.

"Right here in Calgary."

"Well that's wonderful. Now we could have that dinner date, no time to lose, how about tonight?"

"That's a super idea."

"Shall I pick you up?"

"No. Tell me where and I can meet you there."

He thought for a few moments. "How about the Golden Fork, just out on the highway, do you know it?"

"Yes. What time? Seven o'clock, is that OK?"

"Yes. Can't wait."

As she got ready that evening she had butterflies inside her. She decided to wear skirt and a white top that she knew she looked good in.

He was waiting in the car park when she arrived. He walked over to her car, opened the door and planted a kiss on each cheek. "I was afraid you might not come," he said.

"Don't be silly. I'm so happy to be with you again."

He gave her a little squeeze and smiled down at her. "Come on, let's go in, I'm starving."

They had a wonderful evening together and at the end when they left and went to her car, he kissed her gently on each cheek again and said, "Can we have a date next week, same time same place?"

"Of course I would love that."

As she drove home she couldn't help wishing more had come of tonight because he had just the same effect on her tonight as he had on the plane. Perhaps she should live in hope.

A whole seven days before she would be with Michael again. Laura could hardly wait. She had a date one Friday and another on Sunday, but Wednesday was the one she hoped she would enjoy the most.

She was telling Caroline what she was feeling and Caroline teased her unmercifully.

"You sure do get carried away," she said. "You wanna be like me, love 'em and leave 'em. Good God woman you've only just go over the 'Pig', and now here you go again and you've not tried either of them for size."

"Oh shut up," she replied. "You are so bad the things you say and who says I'm over the 'Pig' anyway?"

"Well aren't you?"

"Don't know."

"Well I might be bad but you're hopeless. Come on let's have a glass of wine and forget the men."

"Good idea."

Eventually Wednesday did come. She met Michael at the restaurant and he greeted her with a big hug and a peck on the cheek. Not much improvement there, she thought, I don't think I have much effect on him. All that talk about the Mile High Club! Now he's got his feet on the ground, I don't think he fancies me at all.

They went to the bar for a drink sitting on stools. Michael ordered a bottle of wine saying, "Oh sorry, are you happy with that?"

"Yes of course."

As they waited for the barman to serve them Michael slipped his hand over hers. "So happy to see you again. I wanted to ring you and see you sooner but I didn't have your number so we must rectify that, please."

She smiled back at him, thinking give him a bit of the Caroline touch by saying, "Yes anything you wish."

The barman arrived with the wine and poured them both a glass which they hardly noticed.

Michael leant forward at the same time running his foot up the inside of her leg. "Do you really mean that?" he asked, kissing the end of her nose.

"Well almost anything."

"Like, anything where we might be close together but in a nicer place than in the loos on the plane?"

"Yes," she said. The next thing he said took her totally by surprise.

"Are you hungry?"

"For what?" she asked.

"For food."

"No Michael, I'm not." She wanted to scream at him: I'm just hungry for you!

"Then shall we skip the food and go back to my place?"

"Yes I would like that."

He paid the barman who gave him a knowing look. "Played your cards right there, mate. Would you like to take the bottle with you, or perhaps you've got better things on your mind?"

Michael just raised his eyes and smiled.

"Do you want to come in my car?" Michael asked.

"No, I'll take mine and follow." She would liked to have gone with him but was unsure of the evening's outcome and thought she was better to have her car with her.

He opened the door for her to his apartment and they went inside. Her first impression was that it was small, but then it was only provided by the company he worked for. It was furnished quite simply and she noticed it didn't have a lot of personal touches.

"Make yourself comfortable," he said pointing to a very large sofa. "I'll get us some wine as we didn't get round to drinking the bottle in the restaurant."

Laura was embarrassed by what she had done before she got out of her car at Michael's. She had removed her pants. What sort of slut was she turning into? But she told herself it was all Michael's fault and now, as she sat on his big sofa, she was glad she was wearing a skirt.

Michael came in with the wine, put it down on the table and sat down very close to her on the sofa. He started to cover her face and neck with lots of kisses, then he held her away from him and said, "You are just so beautiful you scare me."

"Oh Michael don't be so silly."

With that he pushed her backwards and slipped his hand under her skirt. "Oh my God!" he said. And without a word he was inside her. His tenderness at first turned to amazing passion and before he lifted himself away from her, he said, "That was absolutely bloody fantastic, just bloody fantastic, you deserve to be fucked!"

For Laura, yes it had been good but not quite as satisfying as she had expected.

He walked her out to her car when she left. "Can I see you at the weekend, perhaps you would like to stay over?"

"Yes that would be nice, I think."

"Shall we say get here about seven o'clock, and I'll cook us a meal."

Time went by and they spent lots of time together, sometimes they made love sometimes they didn't. Michael had to go back to England quite often sometimes for just a few days, often maybe for a month. She was always glad to see him back, and on his return they always had good sex, but never quite as Laura thought it should be for two young people together, or was it just she needed more than Michael?

When he was away she often had dates with other guys. It never seemed to cross his mind she might be asked. And she would never tell him, not because she wanted to deceive him but she just couldn't hurt him. Sometimes she thought it was almost a platonic relationship between them; there was absolutely no doubt she was very fond of him but not in love with him, although he obviously adored her and was always saying how much he loved her and loved making love to her.

# Chapter Five

*Two Years Later*

Laura loved Canada and its people, it was easy to make the decision to stay longer than a year. She and Caroline had had some wonderful trips around, meeting new people and making new friends, and their friendship was just as strong as when they were at school together. The arrangements in the apartment worked out well, they enjoyed being at home together or just did their own thing if they were alone; or if they had a date they brought back they didn't encroach, each one of them made sure the fridge was never left empty and if they used the last of anything they made sure they replaced it.

They often phoned Pauline in England who was always happy to hear what they had been up to, and it was obvious that she was still blissfully happy with motherhood. Her only complaint was Terry: her husband wouldn't let her have another baby YET.

Laura kept in touch with Pipa who, when she had decided to stay in Canada for longer, wanted to buy the house instead of renting as she now had a man in her life with a serious relationship going on. Laura was a bit reluctant to get rid of her dear little mews house but, after careful consideration, thought it was easy to sell to Pipa than to anybody else, or to have to find a new tenant if she bought something else. So after a few phone calls they agreed a price and the deal was done. Pipa said Laura was always welcome to come and stay if she was back home for a visit.

Laura also was still seeing Michael. He was just so nice, kind and gentle but if she was truthful he just didn't light her fire. She often stayed with him and even stayed at his apartment when he was away; he always greeted her with great enthusiasm on his return, but disappointed her by not wanting to make love sometimes for a few days. She sometimes thought their relationship seemed more like an old married couple, but perhaps she was lucky to have him at all.

She loved her job as office controller. The firm had grown in size with not only the two main lawyers but other solicitors for conveyance, divorce and injury compensation to name but a few. In all there was about sixty staff to organise and they were a great team. She worked more closely with Ian Chatsworth than the other partner Klaus Kramer as he dealt with the French-speaking clients and, although her French was good, she didn't always understand the legal implications of French law, but she still organised his appointments and checked things with his secretary.

Ian Chatsworth often asked her to accompany him on some more complicated cases as her knowledge as a lawyer was helpful. This she enjoyed, he was an extremely clever barrister and much sought after with a high fee to go with it. He was also very flirtatious and suggestive, often saying to the younger members of staff things that Laura thought were a bit out of order for a man in his position.

Whenever Laura had accompanied him on any of these cases they always stayed in a top five-star hotel with every sort of restaurant you could imagine. He always tried to persuade her to sleep with him on these occasions saying, "Laura, let's have a bit of fun tonight. Let's have coffee on the terrace in my room and have a little intermit time together, you must know how much I want you."

"No way," she replied. "You're married with a family."

"Yes I know," he said, "but come on, who will know?"

"I will, and besides, you're my boss."

"Not after hours."

She didn't know his wife. In fact nobody at the office seemed to know anything about her, but whatever Laura was not going to be the one to let him cheat on her.

"You are just very naughty," she said.

"Yes I know and I want you to be naughty with me," he replied, touching her knee. "Oh come on Laura, you must know what I feel for you?"

"Yes, only as a quick bonk."

"No that's not true, it could go further. I'm a very wealthy man as I'm sure you're aware of and I could give you a very good life."

"Yes and I have no doubt Ian, but not as the other woman."

"I'm a good lover," he said. "I have a hydraulic arse."

"Oh really, and what oil do you put in that, Castrol?" With that she reduced him to laughter which eased the situation.

"You have such a cruel mind Laura, you are so witty and oh so beautiful and lovely, you make me want you so much."

"Yes and every other female you have wined and dined I think. It's not that I don't approve, in fact I would be only too happy to spend the night with you. I think you have many of the qualities I would find attractive in a man, but not under these circumstances." With that she stood up, bent down and kissed him lightly on the lips and said, "Good night and thank you yet again for a lovely evening and dinner."

The next morning it was work as usual in the court room and as the case finished that day around two p.m. he suggested they stopped for a bite to eat on the way back.

"Fine," said Laura, she had no commitments that evening and Caroline and Michael were both away so it would mean she didn't have to bother about food later. "But no flirting," she said.

"Oh no, just straight to a room, I guess."

She just looked at him and shook her head.

And then there was Carl. Caroline had been to a music festival and returned to the apartment with him. Introducing him to Laura, she said, "I hope you don't mind he's going to stay for a while. I'm just crazy about him and I just couldn't bear to let go and leave him. He's a musician, he played at the festival wonderful, wonderful music, he's a fitness fanatic – great body and you should see it."

I don't think so, thought Laura. He may be fit but he looks like he was the model for the original Toby Jug.

"So is that all right?"

"Of course it's all right, it's your place you know."

"Yes I do know, but I want you to like him as well. In fact I think I'm in love with him so he could be around all the time, and as his work is at night a lot of the time he will be around when I'm at work and perhaps you are here with him."

"That will be fine Caroline, I won't attack him. I'll leave him for you."

She hugged Laura. "I'm so happy."

Laura had to admit she had never seen her friend so excited. Perhaps she was in love.

Carl more or less did move in which was not a problem in itself. As a person Laura liked him a lot, he really was a true hillbilly from Tennessee with an accent to go with it, but in her eyes he had one big problem. He wouldn't keep his clothes on. He would get up in the morning walk around stark naked, it didn't seem to matter to him if they were all there or just Laura and him. She had to admit he did have a super body and tackle to go with it. The other thing she found slightly disturbing was when Caroline came home or even just walked into the room every bit came to life, and he would say to her, "Wan a sit on my stick doll?" in his deep Southern drawl.

Caroline would melt and giggle and Laura wanted to melt with embarrassment, often grabbing her toast, her tea or anything else she may have in her hand at the time leaving quickly before action took place.

It was true Laura spent more time at Michael's now, and sometimes wondered what was best – a cool customer like him or a raving sex maniac like Carl?

Then Caroline said to Laura that Carl needed a rest so she was taking him on holiday to the Caribbean for a month.

"Oh that's great," said Laura with a laugh. "Tell me is the rest from work or sex?"

"I know Laura we are a bit like rabbits, but no, he works hard you know."

Laura quite enjoyed being on her own again. Michael complained he didn't see why she didn't still stay with him most of the time.

Then two weeks after they had departed for their holiday Laura had a phone call from Caroline.

"You'll never guess what?" she screamed down the phone.
"You've left him."
"No Laura, we got married this morning."
She was so shocked she was speechless.
"Are you still there?"
"Yes."
"OK, speak to you when we get back."

Laura sat down trying to collect her thoughts. It was obvious she couldn't stay on at the apartment if they were married. She didn't intend to play gooseberry. Perhaps she would get an apartment of her own. Perhaps this, perhaps that, all sorts of ideas were running through her head at the moment, and Michael was away too, or she was sure he would tell her what was best. Yes, good steady Michael.

# Chapter Six

One week later when Michael had returned Laura had decided what to do. She thought she would return to England, but of course she had no place of her own to go to now she had sold her house to Pipa.

She had spoken to Pauline to tell her about Caroline's marriage and mentioned that she may come back.

"Great," said Pauline. "Come and stay with us, the kids would love it, so would Terry and stay as long as you like."

"Thanks I'll bear it in mind."

Also Pipa had phoned her that week to say she had got engaged to her man and to tell Laura how blissfully happy she was. They had chatted on and before hanging up Laura said she may be thinking of coming back, and was there much for sale there?

"Don't know, but I'll have a look and let you know."

What with all my friends married or going to be married, there's got to be something wrong with me, I'm still on the shelf, she thought.

She was so happy to have Michael back and couldn't wait to tell him about Caroline and Carl's marriage and ask him what he thought of her going home.

"Well they sure worked quick," Michael said, "and I can understand that you feel you can't stay there. But of course you do have here."

Laura looked at him for a moment she hadn't even thought of that.

"Anyway my darling Laura what difference does it make, here or there? I have a pad in both places so we can work something out."

Somehow she felt relieved she knew when she could talk to him about it he would sort it out. Having discussed things with him she felt more at ease but still undecided.

"Now come on I'm home we have the weekend in front of us you can sort it all out on Monday and now I'm going to open a bottle of fizzy to celebrate," he said, heading for the kitchen.

"Yes," she replied, "and then on Monday I will give my notice in and then, when I'm back in England, I can contact Mr Dill my old boss and…"

With that he was stood in front of her, handing her a glass, he said, "Here's to the future." Kissing her on the lips just lightly, and of course, "I love you Laura."

She smiled at him knowing he had not heard a word she had said.

Monday morning when she arrived at work she went straight to Ian's office as was normal.

"Good weekend?" he enquired.

"Yes very, thank you."

"Good sex then, I gather?" he said in his normal suggestive way.

"Well that's for me to know and you to guess," she replied.

"Just wish it had been with me."

"Now down to business Ian, I want to tell you that I am going back to England so I need to give you my notice."

He pushed his chair back. "You can't be serious, you can't possibly leave me!"

"Ian, I'm not leaving you, I'm leaving the practice, I'm not married to you." As soon as she had said that she wished she hadn't, but she was not prepared for what happened next.

"No you are not but you could be if you just wait, and anyway you can't just leave. I must have at least three months' notice from you."

"I don't think so, I have never had a contract with the firm so you could have sacked me at any time so I think that works both ways, but I am going to give you two weeks' notice and if it takes me a little longer to get my flight arranged I could stay until what that date is, if that pleases you."

"No it doesn't please me. And who will take your place?"

"Well Joanna my secretary I think will be able to do a good job and if I showed her more over the next two weeks I'm sure it will work out all right."

"Oh so you do? Well I don't!" With that he banged the desk and stood up, cuffing everything off his desk.

Laura stood back in horror. He walked over to the water dispenser and kicked it violently, sending it crashing to the floor water spilling everywhere. He went on to the long wall unit with his family pictures and trophies he had won at sport when he was younger and knocked them all to the ground, all but one quite heavy bronze which he picked up and hurled at the mirror that was just to the side of where Laura was standing. The noise was tremendous. Instinctively she ducked.

"Stop! Stop!" she screamed.

With that the door came open and Jonathan, a young up and coming member of staff, came in. Surveying the chaos he said rather stupidly, "Is something wrong, sir?"

"Of course something's wrong, you idiot! It's that cow there!" he said pointing to Laura. "Get out and take the bloody bitch with you!"

She could see there were tears running down his face, she was in shock. He had then sunk to his desk with his head in his hands.

Most of the staff were gathered outside the door as Jonathan ushered her out. The look of shock on their face's was obvious. Laura quickly gathered her thoughts about her, looking at her watch: it was nine fifteen a.m.. Appointments never started until ten a.m. and she knew Ian didn't have his first one until two p.m. that day.

Looking at them, she said, "If you could all be in reception at nine thirty I will explain to you what is going on." With that she went into her office to check her make-up and try to absorb what had just happened.

Everybody was stood waiting for her when she arrived. She smiled bravely.

"I expect you are all wondering what all that was about just now. I think I took Mr Chatsworth by surprise this morning by telling him I am returning to England shortly and so will be leaving you all. I have enjoyed my time here in Canada. Originally I came only for one year and now it is over, two and a half years. You have all helped to make my time enjoyable and I will leave with fond memories. My last day here will be Friday week although I don't have a flight date yet. So really I just want to say thank you to you all, and good luck for your futures."

To her surprise everyone clapped.

A few moments later she called Ian's secretary into her office. "Would you phone Mr Chatsworth's clients for today and say owning to unforeseen circumstances he will not be in the office today and could you arrange another appointment for them?"

"Yes certainly. Will he not be here?"

"I'm not absolutely sure but I think that is best for today."

"Who will tell him?" she asked nervously.

"I'll put that on his screen. He checks that constantly particularly before seeing a client." Next she called the office cleaners and explained there had been a slight accident and they might need to take more time tonight.

She was glad she didn't have to face them with a more detailed explanation. Then she called Joanne in and told her how, over the next two weeks, she would be giving her more detailed instructions on the office running as she thought Joanne might be asked to fill the vacancy. She then dealt with all the other things needing her attention. It was now twelve o'clock and she felt she needed to get out of the office for a break. So telling Joanna what she was doing, she went out into the midday sunshine and took a walk.

When she got back to her desk there was an envelope on it. She of course recognised Ian's handwriting. She cautiously opened it, not knowing what to expect. It read:

*I'm sorry.*

*Ian*

She left the office a little earlier than usual. She'd decided to stay at Michael's, she didn't want to be on her own tonight but first she went back to pick up a few things from the apartment. When she arrived there sitting on the doorstep was a most beautiful bouquet of red roses. Funny, she thought, probably for Caroline from one of her admirers. She picked them up and read the card:

*To Laura*

She opened it up and read:

*My dearest Laura, please forgive me!*

*Ian*

Michael was already home when she arrived there.
"Oh this is a nice surprise," he said, greeting her with a hug. "So what do I owe this sheer delight to?" he asked.
She said, "Just get us a cup of coffee and I'll tell you."
After relating the story, Michael just laughed. "Stupid man! Anyway Laura, I have some news for you; the company want me to fly home in three weeks' time, there's some sort of talk about a base in Alaska. So I said I would be arriving in two weeks' time with my girlfriend. That's you in case you don't know. And that I wanted to take a week's holiday to be with you. They said that's OK we will pay for her ticket as well and here, my dear Laura, are the tickets. First class can you believe, leaving in two weeks today."
Laura didn't know what to say except, "Oh!"
Before she knew it, Caroline and Carl were home, she explained that she had decided to go back to England. She had said her goodbyes to her friends and she and Michael were on the plane to England.
Michael squeezed her hand tightly as they took off.
"Don't tell me you're nervous?" she joked.
"No, I'm not nervous, I'm just so happy, I hope you are too?"

They landed mid-morning at Heathrow. Once they had got their luggage they were soon outside and Michael had grabbed a taxi. "Henley," he requested the driver.

They pulled up at a lovely old timbered house.

"Here we are," said Michael. There was a short path up to the front of the house. Michael had never told her much about his home in England, so already she was a bit surprised.

"All yours?" she asked.

"No, just half."

He opened the front door and they stood in a magnificent hall with small black and white tiles on the floor. There were two pieces of antique furniture and a lovely Louis the Fifteenth cream and gold sofa.

"This is our bedroom and bathroom in here," he said opening the door. "And over there are two more bedrooms, here is the lounge with the dining room leading off of it. I like it to be separate, and now the kitchen."

Laura just stood in absolute amazement. "Michael, it's wonderful, typical of you, most people would give their ears for this. Was it inherited?"

"No, I bought it."

"But how? It must have cost the earth!"

"Laura, I'm thirty-three years old and I have an excellent job, no wife, no children."

She realised for the first time how little she knew of this man.

"Come on now, shall we have a quick coffee then a sleep? That's what I normally do. Then when we wake up it will be time for a shower and you can have yours while I get us something to eat."

Laura woke about six o'clock to the smell of something cooking. Getting up, she went to the kitchen. There was Michael cooking spaghetti.

"Hello, sleepyhead. Go and have a shower and a walk round, then when you are ready we can eat."

She found her white Marilyn Monroe dress which she had purposely put on the top of one suitcase. Yes it was nearly three years old, but timeless and she knew she always looked good in it. She also knew Michael had never seen her in it before, and she so wanted to look good for him tonight. She slipped off her clothes turned on the shower and stepped in, the water tumbled down over her body. She felt good. Yes, she was glad to be back.

When she was dressed she did take a look round the other bedrooms. They were all so tastefully decorated, the curtains were to die for, beautifully draped. She went on into the lounge where Michael was sitting reading, he looked up.

"God, you look fantastic! I can see that dress is going to cause me some trouble later."

"Is that getting it off?" she enquired.

"Amongst other things. So are we ready to eat then?"

She just nodded. Off he went to the kitchen to bring back the food.

"Gosh Michael this is very impressive, you always said in Canada you couldn't cook."

"No I can't. Here I have Ruby, she looks after the house when I'm away, cleans when I'm here and preps food for me when I want her to and then I just finish it off." He disappeared back to the kitchen again. "And tonight we are going to celebrate with real champagne," he said popping the cork. He filled the glasses and then sat down placing his hands over hers. He said, "Laura, marry me."

She looked at him unable to say anything.

"I've waited so patiently and long to ask you, but until you could see what I had to offer you here I couldn't ask you." A silence fell between them. Then he said, "Let's drink to us to a long and happy life together."

He didn't seem to notice she hadn't actually answered him. he went on to say whatever he had was hers. If she wanted to change anything in the house she could, and over the next week he would take her out to show her around. As sometimes he would have to be away as she knew, although if she wanted to she could go with him as they still had the small apartment in Canada to use, if they wished.

They had a wonderful meal together. Michael from time to time touched her hand, saying, "I'm so happy Laura."

Then they went into the lounge. Michael carried the glasses and the rest of the champagne, she sat on the couch and Michael beside her, he pecked her on the nose.

"I hope you are as happy as I am."

"Oh yes," she replied but in her heart she knew her happiness was being back in England.

After a while she got up and walked to one of the big arched windows looking out on to the garden. It was all very softly lit. She could see some beautiful weeping willow trees, and a pretty summer house.

"What's beyond the trees?" she asked.

"The river. This is Henley on Thames you know." With that he got up and walked behind her, kissing her on the back of the neck. "You smell so delicious," he said. He ran his finger down her back and the zip on her dress.

For God's sake, undo it, Michael! she thought, but no such luck.

"We will explore it all in the morning, but at the moment I think we will explore the bedroom."

They put their glasses down and he led the way. When she was in there earlier taking her shower she hadn't noticed that in the middle of the panelled wall was a handle. Michael pulled it open and immediately a light came on, to reveal a large dressing room.

"This is my side and this, my darling, is yours."

Laura looked in surprise everything she liked, such as shower gel, hair shampoo, deodorant, soap, body cream even down to perfume, it was all there.

"Michael you are incredible."

"Now bed I think."

He was already in bed when she came out of the bathroom. She unzipped her dress and slipped in beside him. Within seconds he was inside her much the same as normal and within ten minutes it was all over and he was asleep.

## Chapter Seven

Laura found it hard to sleep. She lay on her back eyes wide open her body had been aching for Michael's. Was she unreasonable? Perhaps he was tired; it had been a long day, but then he did the journey from Canada so often. So now the proposal, was this what she wanted? Her idea was to come home, buy herself a house, get a job. Now here she was in this beautiful house with a man perhaps she didn't understand.

Eventually she must have fallen asleep, only to be woken by Michael stood at the end of the bed saying, "Come on sleepyhead, wake up. We have lots to do today and Ruby is here waiting to meet you, and she has the breakfast ready."

She jumped out of bed and she was naked. She went up to Michael and put her arms around him. He ran his hands over her body. "You are so super, you make me want to do nice things to you."

"Then do them."

"No we don't have time, you naughty girl, but God! After last night I can't believe I am so lucky to be able to look forward to that for the rest of our lives."

She obediently got dressed, all the while thinking, I must have missed something. Perhaps I fell asleep, perhaps it wasn't as quick as I thought.

Going into the kitchen she met Ruby. She instantly thought what a nice person, she appeared almost motherly.

"Hello it's nice to meet you," she said with hand outstretched.

"Yes, it's so nice to meet you. You can't imagine how happy I am to hear you are to marry Mr Michael so soon. Shall I call you Mrs Michael now?"

"Oh no, just Laura will be fine," she replied, feeling almost sick at the thought that she almost seemed trapped when she wasn't sure if this was what she wanted: to be Mrs Michael, and besides it all seemed so formal. Was this truly Michael's wish, or just the way Ruby saw it?

Breakfast was great. Ruby ran round making sure they had everything they needed, though there was nothing more they could have needed. Only me wanting to be stuffed stupid by my husband-to-be, thought Laura.

"Right then let's get on, first of all I'll show you round the garage. Come on, wife-to-be."

Once again she followed obediently. Michael opened the door and there inside was a Porsche 911 and a Range Rover.

"Wow!" said Laura.

He held up a bunch of keys. "These are yours for our cars, and these are mine," he said producing another set from his pocket. "I expect you want to use the Porsche when your busying around and when I am away. But the other one is good if we have friends with us and of course when we have the children, although we will have to change it for a people mover as the family grows."

Laura looked shocked.

"Don't look so shocked. I don't intend to make you pregnant just yet," he said, smacking her bottom.

The rate we are going it could take a long time and I could possibly miss the act if I'm not careful, Laura thought.

"Now here are our bicycles so as we can ride along the river together sometimes. We will do that later today, and we will pop in and meet my friends so as you are not lonely when I'm away. I must introduce you to Cedric, he has some sort of boat arrangement with a small engine cleverly concealed. Mounted on top of the boat is a chair with a set of peddles so he sits in the chair and it looks like he is pedalling this small rowing boat down or up the river. Of course lots of people stop and look, which he loves. He normally wears a cream and maroon blazer and a straw boater.

"And no trousers?" she asked with her head on one side.

They both fell about laughing and she thought, yes, this is more like it. Maybe Michael is just a bit uptight with all that he is trying to do for me.

By the Wednesday of the week they had not made love so on the Thursday morning when Laura woke up, Michael was still asleep on his back. Bit of luck, Laura thought: she peeped under the covers and liked what she saw. She moved over close to him and gently ran her hand on the inside of his knee, slowly running it up to his stomach. Opening his eyes he looked at her and said, "What a wonderful way to be woken up in the morning."

She leant over him and kissed him with all the passion that was bottled up inside of her. She slipped her hand back down to him and said, "And what a magnificent things this is, shall we use it?"

She couldn't believe what he said.

"Oh no, this is just early morningish. I always like it to be special, like it was in Canada."

For the first time since she had known him she blew her top. "Michael we are young! We are supposed to be getting married. Since we have been home you hardly kiss me, we have made love once, if that's what you call it. Is this normal, is this the way our life will be? You talk about having children, it's not a mechanical exercise, you know."

He looked at her in disbelief. "But Laura I want to make sure you have everything, that's why we don't have time for sex."

"Don't be ridiculous, you make time if you love one another. It should be like Caroline and Carl, they couldn't keep their hands off one another."

"Oh, and I suppose you want me without my clothes on."

"No. Now you're just being stupid, but at least we should find time for one another sometime in the day."

"What, do you mean every day?" he exclaimed in horror.

"Yes, if needs be twice a day!" she screamed back at him.

"Please don't shout like that, Ruby can hear you."

"Good, 'cause that's another thing I can't live with." She got out of bed and ran into the bathroom wanting to slam the door, but her foot caught in it by mistake.

When she was showered and dressed she went rather sheepishly out into the kitchen, wondering what reception she would get.

"Good morning, breakfast is ready," Ruby said with a smile.

Michael never commented on her outburst. He acted as though it had never happened. In fact, she wondered if he ever did take on board things he didn't want to hear.

The next morning was Sunday. Laura woke feeling a little cold. Opening her eyes she realised Michael had pulled all the covers off her and was just staring at her naked body.

"You have a fantastic body," he said running his hand over her stomach and down in between her legs.

She stretched and moaned appreciatively. "Are you morningish?" she asked hopefully.

"Yes, but we don't have time."

"Why?"

"Because I am going to get dressed and make us tea and toast as I have given Ruby the day off. Then we are off to church so, as you can see, where our big day will be and speak to the vicar. Then Cedric's having a drinks party after which we will have a little ride out on our bikes. Then we are going to have a picnic dinner down on the river bank or, if it's too chilly, we can pop into the sun house."

"Seems like it's all sorted then."

"Yes."

"So what do you think I should wear?"

"Whatever you think, you always look the part. But I would like you to wear that soft blue crochet dress for the picnic. Just the dress, nothing under."

She looked at him in surprise. "So I'm going to be with the Michael I know from Canada tonight?"

"Just be down at the river by six and I will be there with all the necessary."

"Is that body or food?" she enquired.

He just laughed and disappeared.

The day went so quickly. She had particularly enjoyed Cedric's party – not so much the church as Michael got quite annoyed when the vicar said they needed to make an appointment to see him. When they got back to the house after the bike ride, it was about five thirty.

"Go get changed," said Michael.

So off she went obediently. When she got down the garden to the river he was already there with the big rug on the ground, lovely big cushions, champagne in the ice bucket and laying back waiting; she sat down beside him.

"Oh Laura, I can't wait to be married," he said brushing her nipples with his lips through her dress, which immediately responded to his touch. "I'll pour some drink or I'll want to make love to you right now."

"Well do then."

"No later. I want to talk about the wedding plans when I go back to work tomorrow. I want you to go and see about the reception, invitations, colour scheme, honeymoon et cetera so as I can decide what is best." With that he handed her a red rose and kissed her passionately. "Now let's eat," he said opening the picnic basket.

Laura was amazed at its contents. There were quails' eggs, caviar, smoked salmon, cheeses, strawberries, chocolates, so much she couldn't take it all in and, of course, red and white wine.

"What do you think?" he asked.

"Just fantastic." Thinking all the time, Sod the food and get morningish!

Pointing back to the house, he said, "I would like to buy the rest of this place if it comes on the market. Then it would be big enough to bring up the children and, when we are old, you can tell the grandchildren how we made love on the riverbank under the willow trees."

"But Michael, we haven't."

"No but we will."

Laura knew she was drinking too much but she had got to the point of not caring. It was obvious in a little while Michael would say it was time for bed and highly unlikely that they would do anything than go to sleep in the bed.

"I hope you have enjoyed these last few days and especially this evening as much as I have, although you haven't had the pleasure I've had of just feasting on your beautiful body in that dress. I will have to be up and away early in the morning so if you are not awake I won't disturb you, my darling."

True to his word he did leave early next morning. Laura was aware of it but pretended to be asleep. She knew by now that she had no intentions of doing wedding planning as he had instructed and now she knew she had no plan to have a wedding. She liked Michael a lot, perhaps even loved him a little, but there was no way she could spend the rest of her life with him: he was a nice, good person but a complete control freak. If when he came home he wanted to know what she had found out for the wedding she would say something to fob him off, she wasn't quite sure what; but more to the point was how was she going to tell him she didn't want to get married? After all he wanted to give her and share with her, how could she be so unkind?

Getting up she showered and dressed and went into the kitchen to make herself some tea. She was taken by surprise to see Ruby there.

"Oh hello Ruby, I didn't expect to see you this morning."

"Good morning Mrs Michael."

"Please call me Laura."

"Yes whatever you say, Mr Michael said I am to do whatever you think, and what would you like now?"

"I would like for us to sit here together and have a cup of tea and I will make it."

Michael arrived home about four o'clock. He burst into the door picking Laura up and spinning her around. "You will never guess what!" he said, "We are to open a new depot in Alaska and I am to be the sole manager, double the salary which means we can buy the rest of this house. We will have a house up there and still keep the love nest in Canada, they will pay for your travel, they will pay for the children's education.

Oh Laura, this for me is a dream come true. Just one problem: I have to fly out first thing tomorrow morning."

She couldn't believe her ears. He was so excited about the new post he didn't even ask what she had been doing all day.

"I must go and pack a few things more than usual, though as I won't have anything there like I do when I'm going to Canada." Suddenly he stopped. "You don't mind not coming up straight away, do you?" he said. "At least it will give you time to get on with the wedding plans."

"I don't think so Michael."

"Oh don't be silly, you are absolutely clever enough to do it alone my darling."

"No Michael, there is not going to be a wedding." But he had already left the room and she didn't think he heard what she had said.

When he came out case in hand he said, "Now off to bed. I think we need to get some shuteye as my flight is four a.m. so we will leave here at one o'clock. You will come with me, please?"

"Yes of course."

On the drive to the airport he took her hand and squeezed it.

"We are lucky to be so in love. Oh and before I forget, I left in our dressing room a paper with the address and phone number of the office here. You can ring them if you need me to make a decision about anything, or if you want me to look at invitations or guest lists for the wedding post it to the office and the next guy coming out will bring it with him. There won't be any phone as such for three to four weeks, so I have made arrangements for the flight for you to come out for Christmas. I hope I may have some decent accommodation sorted out by then, but if not we can go down to Canada."

But this time they were pulling into the airport car park. If she had commented she didn't think he would have heard her he never asked her what she thought, he just told her what they were going to do.

Once inside the airport he quickly charged up to the check-in desk. Putting his arm around her they walked to the entrance of the departure lounge where he turned to her and kissed her goodbye. It was probably the first decent kiss he had given her since being back in England and she was sick of all this pecking he did, on her nose, forehead and body.

"Now on your way and get planning."

"I'm sorry Michael. I don't think I can."

"What?" he said smiling at her. "That's just premarital nerves." With that he picked up his hand luggage and was gone.

She stood there looking after him with an enormous sense of relief. Walking to the car park as though a great weight had been lifted from her, she got to the car and, sitting inside, she put her head back and thought: Now for the great escape.

# Chapter Eight

Arriving back at the house she put the Porsche into the garage, let herself in and went through to the lounge. She placed the car keys on the desk, took out a piece of writing paper and wrote:

*Dear Michael,*

*By the time you get this letter I will be out of your beautiful house. I have decided I cannot marry you. I have tried to tell you, but I couldn't make you hear. I know you would have given me everything I wanted, but I think in time we would have made each other unhappy. I think you are a wonderful person and will always remember the great times we had together, especially in Canada where I felt you let me be a free spirit. I'm sure you will find someone who will make you happy and give you the family you crave. Please don't try to contact me. I hope you will find it in your heart to forgive me.*

*With my best wishes,*
*Laura*

She took out an envelope folded the letter and went to the dressing room and wrote the address of the office on it, she felt sadness in her heart but had no regrets. Going back into the lounge she put it in her handbag ready to post when she left in the morning.

She looked at her watch. It was two thirty in the morning. She went into the kitchen and made herself a strong cup of tea, sitting at the breakfast bar she decided what to do. First she needed to buy a car then she needed a house and a job, she knew her bank balance could suffer all this, but she also knew she wanted to get her life back on track.

She knew Ruby would be in by eight o'clock and she decided to tell her she was going away while Michael was away, so perhaps she would carry on as before as he wished.

She then went to the bedroom and packed the one case she had managed to unpack since her arrival. She clipped it shut and put it in the hall and then went to get the other four that were still in the spare bedroom from the day they had arrived back. Back in the lounge she sank into the sofa and decided as early as she dared she would ring Pauline to see if she could bunk down there just for a few nights until she found a flat to tide her over. She must have nodded off as she woke with a start: it was nearly seven a.m. Going to the phone she dialled Pauline's number. To her surprise Terry answered.

"Hi Laura, we wondered when you got back and when we might see you. What you up to?"

"Well Terry I'm after a favour. Can I beg a bed for a few nights?"

"Of course, when you arriving? Actually I'm on holiday for a week. Going to do some DIY so that means you and Pauline can perhaps do a couple of things together she will love that."

"If I get there about nine thirty will that be OK? Just go and ask Pauline, perhaps."

"No, it will be a great surprise for her."

Next she phoned the taxi firm and booked the cab for eight fifteen. She wanted to see Ruby but she didn't want to get into much conversation with her. Just an explanation albeit not the true one, and a friendly goodbye.

She was glad the taxi driver had opened the rear door of the car. It wasn't that she didn't want to talk to him but she just wanted time to think and also to take a look at the countryside and calm down from her whirlwind time she had experienced with Michael. Poor dear Michael, her thoughts went back to him, but she had no regrets. Well, perhaps a tiny one when thinking of that Porsche. She sort of smiled to herself.

"Going on holiday?" asked the driver.

"No. Just come back from Canada."

"Great place, went there once."

During the journey he made an odd comment but was certainly not intrusive in her thoughts.

The journey took just over an hour and they pulled up outside Pauline and Terry's about nine thirty. She paid the fare and got out.

"I'll bring the cases, miss."

"Thank you," she said with a smile.

She knocked on the door and Terry opened it with a grin from ear to ear. "God you look great!" he said. "Come on in, Pauline's not back yet from taking the kids to playschool. She walks 'cause she thinks it keeps her fit just as if looking after us lot is not enough. I haven't told her you're coming yet but as you're a bit earlier than you thought, that's great. I'll go and get the cases in and make us a coffee and then if we sit in the kitchen she will come bursting in with Poppy in the buggy. I can't wait to see her face."

They had hardly sipped the coffee when the door flew open and Pauline was calling, "Hi sex bomb, Poppy's fast asleep, I'm all yours."

Terry looked a little embarrassed. "She doesn't mean it like you think. It's just that she's supposed to be helping me with the DIY today," he whispered.

Pauline had left Poppy in the conservatory in the autumn sun. She walked into the kitchen and stopped dead. "I don't believe it, oh my goodness this is wonderful isn't it Terry? How long can you stay, are you going to stay with us, please!"

"If you can put up with me for a couple of days?"

"Of course we can, you must have so much to tell us."

They were now hugging one another like two teenagers.

"Well," said Terry, "I can see I'm not going to get much work out of you wife, so why don't you two take yourselves off to the pub and have a bit of lunch and chat after Laura's unpacked? I can look after Poppy until you get back but if you could get the kids on the way home, that would save me from stopping all my hard work."

"Oh you're a darling," she said giving him a kiss.

He smacked her on the bottom and they all laughed together.

Laura immediately felt at home. It was just the sheer relaxed atmosphere and she could see the love between them.

Over lunch Laura filled her friend in with all the details from Canada, Caroline and her Toby jug look alike hunk, to the luxury of what could have been her life with Michael.

The next day she borrowed Pauline's little car and went to see about getting her own wheels. She had noticed about halfway through her journey yesterday in the taxi a board that said, 'Show House For Sale'. So she took herself off in that direction to see if she could find it again – not thinking of buying, just to look and get an idea of cost as in three years or so things had changed in England.

By the end of ten days she owned a new Mini. What a sucker she was for them, and to top it all, a three-bedroom house fully carpeted, curtained and furnished with every appliance you could think of, at a knock-down price she couldn't believe. After all, she had come back with only clothes and a few keepsakes, she had no furniture and that alone would have taken ages to shop for and sort out. OK, some of the things were not exactly her choice but she could live with them until she got time to change them and if she had rented she felt that was throwaway cash.

She had enjoyed staying with Pauline, Terry and the kids and although they said stay as long as she liked, she felt she was intruding. Settling in was easy but, having spent a lot of her bank balance, she needed to find work.

# Chapter Nine

It was now six weeks since arriving back home. What a lot had happened, Laura reflected. She had bought her new house which had been luck. The builder wanted to get rid of it to move on and as she was a cash buyer and not in a chain, it suited them both to complete quickly. She also had a new Mini in the garage so she had wheels; she intended to have a change of make but just couldn't resist having one of her favourite friends, perhaps when she was a little older she would have a change. Now all she needed was a job to top up the bank balance which had been hit a bit hard. Yes, tomorrow she would start looking. Standing at the lounge window looking out into the garden, which had been landscaped, she realised she would need a mower of some sort; the grass had already grown an enormous amount, and this was something she knew nothing about. Buying a house and a car was one thing but a mower was a different matter. She was going to need a lot of help, if only she had thought about it she should have got the builder to supply one, whatever was he thinking of leaving her without a mower, and a man to use it?

Thinking of a man she realised she hadn't had one of those for what seemed like a very long time. Not to go to bed with, but just as a date, something else she must start looking for, and then she thought of Michael, dear sweet caring Michael; she hoped he had been able to understand why she had left, and then for the first time in maybe a year or more she thought of Tom, wondering where he was and if he was married. She quickly put that thought out of her mind. Silly as it might seem, she didn't want to think of any other female having the luxury of him all to herself. Not that she was every likely to know any of the answers to her questions but she didn't think she would ever truly forget the heartache he had caused her. She shook her head, trying to rid herself of those days.

Next thing mower shopping. Off she drove to the village which was quite nearby. After a while she saw a sign saying: 'All Types of Mowers Repaired'. This must be the place, she thought, she parked the car and walked in.

"Hello love," said a voice from far in the back. "Mower broken?"

"Well actually no," she replied as the voice was walking towards her. "It's that I need one and I don't know where to start."

"Soon put that right then, what yer got? Ten acres or pocket hanky?"

She looked at him and laughed. "Well I suppose outsize man's pocket hankie you would call it."

"And no man to do it?"

"You got it in one."

"Good looking gal like you and no man? Well, you've come to the right place."

For a moment Laura wondered what was coming next. He wasn't quite her type, even if he could cut grass.

"You need to go down the road about a quarter mile, that's where our sales room is. Hang on a minute, I'll give 'em a ring and tell 'em you're coming."

She did as she was told and watched while he picked up the phone and dialled the number. She stifled a giggle as his hands were so covered in grease she was imagining what the next person to use the phone would think or even look like if they rubbed their face without realising a member of the black hand gang had been there before them.

"Hi Dick, some good-looking bird here wanting to get a mower. Sure you can sort her out. Knowing you possibly in more ways than one, would do it meself but she's not my type, a bit too posh, I thinks. Cheers then."

Thank God for that, thought Laura. She smiled at him nicely and thanked him and left. She found the shop easily if not a little hesitant as to what Dick would be like.

"Good morning madam, can I help? Have you just come from our workshop?"

"Yes I have, and it's just a mower I'm looking for."

"Come this way and I will try to help you. I do hope Fred didn't embarrass you too much, he is a good man just a little outspoken."

"No not at all, he was most kind."

It occurred to her how well spoken Dick was, dressed in a well cut pair of trousers, white shirt and tie, about thirty years old, not particularly good looking but he had a certain presence about him. Within half an hour she had left the shop with the mower in a box in the back of the car. There was a bit of assembling to do with the handle but Dick assured her that it was simple and, if she had any difficulties with it, someone would go along to sort it out. Not Fred, she hoped.

First job on getting home was to get the mower out of the box then fit the handle. Then to get jeans on and all she had to do was cut the grass. Much to her surprise it all went well. She was just standing back admiring her work and thinking how good it looked, when over the fence to her right appeared two hands and a face.

"Made a right mess of that you have, got a lot of work to do to get that looking good."

Laura immediately felt he hackles go up, and, most unlike her, she said, "I'm so sorry it doesn't please you but as I didn't ask for your opinion I don't care what you think." She then thought, of gosh I suppose he's my neighbour that's got us off on a good foot. With that she could hear what sounded like a younger woman's voice.

"Who are you talking to Dad?" she heard her say.

"Some girl next door made a right cock up of cutting her grass and I told her so."

"You are so rude? You do make me so cross at times. That's our new neighbour, not exactly the politest thing to say to her."

"Well it's true. You know I say what I think, she will have to get used to me if I decide to move down here with you two although I don't think I will. I don't like your cooking and the way you two are always fooling about, absolutely stupid if you ask me, no don't think I'll stay. Rather be with people who act normal."

Laura knew she shouldn't be listening but then it was in the garden and the old man did have a loud voice.

"I think that would be a very sensible thing to do for you, to go back. In fact I'm happy to help you pack your things right now and take you back we can be there by about eight o'clock you're always welcome to come for a holiday and I think that way we can still stay friends."

"Friends? I don't want to be a friend of yours you horrible bitch. I don't know what my son could ever see in you, I never liked you and I know he will not be happy when he comes home and finds me gone."

"Well I think you might be wrong on assuming that Dad, but I guess I'll just have to live with it. But perhaps I just happen to know his thoughts better than you. Now, come on in and let's get going."

Although Laura didn't know anything about the situation she was overhearing it was making her laugh. He obviously was quite a difficult person but the daughter-in-law had made a good job of handling the situation, and as they must have headed for the house she heard the woman say: "Now before we leave I'll just phone Patrick." Presumably her husband and the old man's son. "To see if he is happy with the idea."

"Don't bother. I'm sick to death of you, him, this horrible area, this toff house and I want to go home."

"Come on then, let's just part as friends," she said.

Their voices trailed away and even Laura thought she was glad he was leaving, but she did feel a bit guilty it was her terrific grass-cutting job that had set the ball rolling, but perhaps one day she would get a chance to apologise.

She woke early the next morning ready for a trip into Oxford, have a look round and pop into the old office.

Walking into Dills' later she was greeted with great enthusiasm. To all the old faces it seemed as though she had never been away. Pipa gave her a great hug, and Laura couldn't help thinking how great she looked, ten years younger, new hairstyle well made up, it must be the man in her life.

"Is Mr Dill in?" she asked. "It would be good to see him if he has a moment."

"For you, I'm sure he will, he often asked about you as you know you were the apple of his eye," said Pipa.

"Oh I don't know about that," said Laura feeling a little pinkish.

With that the door of Mr Dill's office opened.

"Why, Laura! How wonderful to see you. I knew you were back but it's great to see you, no need to ask if you're well," he said stepping forward to give her a hug. "Come on in and tell me what you have been up to."

She told him a little of her time in Canada and that she had bought a house near High Wycombe with which she was delighted.

"So now you are looking for a job? I would suppose this this the reason for your visit to us?"

"Oh no! I just thought it would be nice to see you all again but actually, as you mentioned it, I would like to have the recent lawyers' magazine for us lot, if you can spare it as I do need to find something, obviously."

He pulled open his drawer and handed one to her. "Came last week I think, best of luck." He stood up and walked to the door with her. "Ever hear from your mother?"

"No, she's remarried. I hope they're happy, he is Argentinian and that's where they live, I think."

He just shook his head. "Well if you're stuck come and see me, I expect we would find something for you." He kissed her affectionately on the cheek and went back into his office.

On the way out Pipa stopped her and said she was having a few people to supper on Friday and would she like to join them?

"Thanks that would be nice, what time?"

"About seven, OK?"

"Yes great, bye for now."

She left the office and decided to take a walk up and down the street just for old times' sake. As she walked she began to think of her uni days, all the fun she had with friends and then all the heartache she had suffered over Tom, that gorgeous hunk of man. She wondered where he was not for the second time in the last few days. Would he still have that same effect on her? Would he be as fantastic now as she thought he was, three years ago? Well, she would never know.

On Friday she was looking forward to Pipa's supper party and quite eager to see her man and of course the house which once was hers. She arrived about six forty-five, unusually early for her. She knocked on the door and was greeted by this tall blond, good-looking guy; she sort of did a double take, if this was Pipa's man she could see why she looked to good, what a find.

"Hello, I'm Hans. You must be Laura. Come on in, it's truly great to meet you although I've heard so much about you I feel I know you.

"Oh dear, I hope it's all good.

"Yes, and the naughty bits as well."

"That must be something I don't know about," she said with a smile.

"I'm only teasing you."

With that Pipa came down the stairs looking absolutely fantastic in a superb green dress. Hans put his hand out to her, nothing was said but Laura could just see the love between them. Pipa stepped towards her and the two girls embraced.

"Hey I didn't get one of those," Hans said and they all laughed." She nodded in reply. As he disappeared she turned to her friend.

"Where did you find him, has he a brother? I can see why you look so great, you're like the cat that's got the cream, you lucky woman."

With that Hans was back, handing them both a glass. Raising his hand he said, "Here's to a great evening. Have you told Laura whose coming?"

"No but just about to, we have three friends of Hans and two of mine you might know. Ross, he works at Dills but I think he came just after you left. He's very nice I think you will like him, I hope so you are sitting next to him."

With that there was a tap at the door and everybody seemed to arrive together. It was a great evening, super food, wine and company and, as Pipa had predicted, Ross was a very nice guy and having a bit in common they got on like a house on fire. Soon the evening was over and after the goodbyes Ross turned to her and said, "Where's your car parked?"

"Right here," she said.

"Oh that's a pity, I was hoping it was a bit further away so I could walk with you because I was also hoping to ask you out for a drink tomorrow evening, if you haven't got a better offer."

"No I couldn't possibly have a better offer, I'd love to come."

"Good. Do you know Jesters here in town? If so shall we say eight o'clockish?"

"Yes that will be great, so cheers till tomorrow," Laura said, getting into her car.

As she drove home she felt quite excited. At least she had managed to get a date, not that she was desperate to get into bed with a man but it was obvious she didn't appeal to Fred. She wondered if she was looking a bit over the hill.

As it turned out they had a super evening together. So much so she invited him back to her place.

"I've got some cheese and crackers and a few bits and pieces we could eat if you're interested, the only thing is I live just outside High Wycombe. Does that bother you? If it's too far to come I quite understand."

She opened the front door and let them in.

"What a great place you have. Did you have it before you went to Canada?"

"Oh no, I owned Pipa's place and then when I decided to stay on longer than intended she bought it from me, so when I got back I got this one. It was the show house so it was perfect for me, with everything included and of course it was a quick deal which suited me and the builder. All I need now is a job to top up the bank balance."

All the time she was explaining things she was getting the foodey bits out. She went to open the wine and he took it from her and did the honours. She picked up a tray, he picked up the glasses and followed her to the lounge. It was all such an easy time it seemed as though they had been friends for ages, and to top it all he told her of a firm of lawyers who a few weeks ago had been advertising for staff. He wasn't sure what the situation was now but if she had a pen he could jot down the name of the firm and she could at least give them a ring on Monday.

"That would be great," she said.

They chatted away and nibbled the food and drank the wine and before they realised it was one o'clock gone when Ross looked at his watch.

"I'm really sorry Laura, I hope I've not outstayed my welcome, but we just seem to have so much in common you're so easy to be with."

"You don't have to apologise. I have had a most enjoyable time."

"So does that mean I can see you again?"

"If you ask me the answer will be yes."

He stood up and they walked to the front door where he turned to her and took both her hands for a moment. She thought he was going to kiss her which she wouldn't have minded, but instead he said, "Thank you. I will ring you."

She watched him walk away and closing the door she thought yes, she had enjoyed being with him. Somehow it was comfortable in a rather nice way. She walked back into the lounge and picked up the glasses and bits and took them to the dishwasher and wandered off to bed, feeling relaxed and sleepy.

Monday morning dawned bright and early. This was the week to get a job even as a road sweeper if needs be, she thought. She went downstairs and found the piece of paper Ross has left with her on Saturday. Dialling directory enquiries she got their number. Now all she had to do was wait until nine o'clock to speak to someone there. After showering she got dressed and fiddled about trying to kill time. At five to nine she couldn't wait any longer, she dialled the number not hoping to get a reply.

"Good morning may I help you?" was the reply she got.

"Well I hope so, I believe you were looking for staff a little while ago, and I am enquiring if you still have any vacancies."

"Not all positions have been filled, may I ask what are your qualification?"

Laura briefly explained she was a qualified homicide lawyer but had been in Canada for the last three years where she had held the position of office manager in a large solicitors' practice but had recently returned home to England.

"If you could hold the line one moment I will speak to Mr Casey our managing director."

"Of course," replied Laura holding her breath hoping for a positive answer. Back came the woman.

"Could you come and see us at ten thirty this morning for a short interview?"

"I will be there, and thank you."

She rushed upstairs, flung open the wardrobe and grabbed her best red suit – she had no time to lose. She checked her make-up and hair, picked up her shoes to match her handbag which she would change into when she got there and, hurrying to the garage, she was in the car and away.

She found the place with no problem and a parking place. This must be my lucky day, she thought. She was earlier than she had expected so she sat for a while to relax and gather her thoughts.

As she walked into the office she realised she hadn't given her name on the phone.

"Good morning, may I help you?" said the woman behind the desk. Who Laura recognised from the voice to be the person she had spoken to earlier.

"Yes I'm here for an interview, I think it was you I spoke to about it?"

"Oh yes I'm sorry, I didn't catch your name."

"It's Laura, Laura Parks."

"Good, do have a seat and I'll tell Mr Casey you're here."

Laura did as she was asked and realised she was a little nervous. Within a few moments the woman returned.

"Please come through," she said holding the door open.

Laura got up and went in. Her instant impression was of a man probably in his mid-forties, quite a lived-in face with a very nice smile. She instantly liked him. He stood up and shook hands with her.

"Do have a seat," he said sitting down himself. "So you're looking for a full-time job I take it, and you're a lawyer?"

"Yes I am, I gained my degree at Oxford."

"Well I have to tell you we don't have any vacancies for a lawyer but I must say I am rather interested in your knowledge as office manager. Can you give me a brief idea of what that would entail and what I could expect from you as we sure are in need of someone to bring some sort of organisation here."

Laura briefly outlined how she would control appointments for every solicitor, brief their secretaries see to the mail, in fact make the day-to-day running of the practice run smoothly.

She didn't exactly feel over hopeful of the outcome of the interview, he didn't seem to really ask her the right questions. He sat back in his chair gave her that nice smile and said, "Uhm, let me think about it. I would like to discuss it with a couple of other members of my staff, ultimately any decisions are mine but I do strive to keep harmony on my side. Could you give me the name of your previous employer in Canada?"

"Yes of course. In fact, I can do better than that, here is their address and phone number on my old business card."

"Nothing to hide there then?"

She shook her head. A thought was going through her head, How would Ian react if they asked for a reference? As quick as she thought of it she put it out of her mind, what will be will be.

He stood up held out his hand saying, "I'll let you know."

"Thank you for your time," she said and left.

Back in the car she thought, Go on looking girl. She decided, as the rest of the day was hers, she would drive up to see Pauline. She stopped on the way and picked up some goodies for the kids to scream over, a few beers for Terry and some flowers for Pauline.

There was lots of hugs and laughter when she arrived and she enjoyed being with them. She stayed for about three hours and then returned to sanity in her own place; she loved seeing them all, but the noise was tremendous.

Back in the luxury of her own pad sitting with a quiet cup of tea she noticed a red light flashing on the telephone. What's that all about, she thought, crossing over to look.

She picked up the receiver and replaced it thinking perhaps it was a warning light that it had not been replaced properly from the last call, but no. So she left it and went back to her tea. Sitting contemplating the next job hunt her eye fell on the red light again. This is stupid, she said to herself, get the instruction book out and try to solve the problem. Book in hand she read through: no, no, no and then red. Red light On, press and hold then, press twice to hear message on answering machine.

"Oh interesting," she said out loud, so doing as the instructions said she heard:

"This is Casey Solicitors here, unable to speak to you earlier. An appointment had been made for you to see Mr Casey at two p.m. tomorrow, Tuesday re vacancies." She stared at the phone in disbelief. If she hadn't solved the problem she might have missed the appointment completely, what a disaster that could have been. After all, they must surely have something to say to her or they wouldn't have phoned her.

Leaving home at one o'clock the next day not wanting to be late for what might be a job prospect she was full of enthusiasm. She found a parking place and almost bounced down the street to the office, she realised she was twenty minutes early but was quite happy to sit and wait. She observed complete chaos while she sat there, everybody rushing around as though they had a bus to catch. Not one of them stopped to ask her if they could help her. OK she didn't need it, but she could have been a new client.

Dead on two p.m. Mr Casey came through the front door. Seeing her sitting there he said, "Hi hello Laura, come in, take a seat, right now I've decided we would like to offer you the position of Office Manager, something that will be new to us all here but I am hoping it will bring an end to the disorganisation that at times drives me mad. I'm not saying that they don't all do a good job but there never seems to be the right communication between offices so they are always rushing about with folders and frankly wasting time because they stop and chat. Not that I mind that, but I just hope you may be able to sort us out."

Laura smiled at him. "Yes, please excuse me but I did notice a bit of chaos when I was sat waiting."

"Well that's good, perhaps you will be our salvation, I think it will be a bit of an uphill struggle to start so you must treat them gently, but as I had such a glowing report by email from your old boss waiting for me when I got in this morning, I'm sure you will cope. I'm saying all this but you haven't said you will accept my offer." He paused. "I think take home pay to start two hundred a week."

"Thank you, I accept."

"Good start now," he said with a laugh. "No, I realised I can't expect that but I do think it would be a good idea for you to meet everybody today, for me to introduce you and explain your position while you are here. I'll get everybody in here as soon as possible, it may be four o'clock as some of them will be with clients but that will give us a bit of time to discuss your ideas. What do you say?"

"Sounds great to me."

"Shall we say Thursday to start, just to get the hang of us all? Good, now there is a young girl left school this year been with us a couple of months, Natalie, she's a bit of a dogsbody for everybody, makes tea, tidies up, does a bit of filing but according to her end-of-school report she is good with the computer, but of course never gets a chance to use it because nobody has any time to show her anything. I think if you had her as your assistant that might be a good idea. I think what we need is to get every client's details on file, still having the confidential matters in the paper files for when they come to see whoever is dealing with them."

"Yes I agree to a certain extent, but I assume each solicitor has a computer in his office so I would set up an internal link system which would bring up the client's details but all confidential matters could only be accessed by a password which they would install. Obviously someone, possibly yourself, would have to know all the passwords which could be kept on your computer with a password in case of sickness or some other reason for absenteeism."

"Laura we are on the same track, I like it. Now I'll get Natalie in and introduce you."

After meeting Natalie, a bright-eyed pretty little thing, and all the rest of the staff the afternoon was soon gone. Before leaving it was decided Laura's desk would be in reception which caused a cheer from all the main players. Mr Casey also explained to them that Laura would start on Thursday just to get her and Natalie sorted out and installed in reception so as to greet each client properly, and generally find her feet.

She said goodbye to many of them as she left and headed for her car, feeling very happy with herself.

# Chapter Ten

After putting her car into the garage she noticed a very smart E Type Jaguar turning into the estate, driving very slowly. It was obvious they must be looking for someone. As it got to her it stopped so she bent down to look in.

"Hello just the person I'm looking for, do you remember me?" It was the well spoken voice that she recognised first.

"Of course. The mower man Dick."

"That's me, I thought I would like to make sure you got it together all right."

"Yes it's fine thank you."

"And using it?"

"Well that could be a matter of expert opinion, I think it looks great but my neighbour had a recent visitor who told me what a mess I'd made of it."

"May I take a look at it because it's pretty impossible to do that with a mower of that quality, unless of course it has a fault."

"Yes come on in."

She went to open the front door as he got out of the car. He didn't just walk straight in, he tapped the door first, which impressed Laura. A perfect gentleman, she thought. She took him out to the garden awaiting his advice.

"Nothing wrong with that a little wobbly on the lines but if I remember this mowing is new to you so you will get better with a bit more practice."

Laura giggled. She wasn't quite sure if it was the relief of the state of her grass cutting or the relief of having got a job today. "Would you like a coffee or a beer or glass of wine?" she found herself saying, after all she did have something to celebrate and it would be nice to have someone to have a drink with.

"Well yes, if I'm not intruding I would love a beer."

She led the way into the lounge. "Do sit down please."

When she returned with his beer and her glass of wine she was pleased he was sitting in one of the chairs and not on the sofa. Not that she minded but it made it easier for her to sit in the other chair because, after all, she didn't know this man and she thought it was better not to be on the sofa together in case he thought she was too forward.

"So what brought you to this part of the woods then?" she enquired.

"Well you and the mower of course, but I wasn't quite sure which house I was looking for."

"But how did you know where I lived anyway?"

"Well perhaps I shouldn't say, but I asked Fred if he knew and he suggested I try them new houses what old Potter's son built. So I came to look and my luck was obviously in."

She smiled at him warmly. "So is that what you do to all new customers?" she asked.

He looked at her a moment and said, "No, only the pretty ones." She got him another beer and herself a glass of wine and then he said, "There's a little bistro just a bit further along the road to our garage, would you like to come with me and have a bite to eat? It's sixish now so by the time we get there, have a drink at the bar and have a look at the menu it would be time to eat, what do you think?"

"Yes I'd like that I'm starving, I haven't eaten all day. I managed to get a job today so I've sort of got something to celebrate."

"And so have I," he said, "I've found you. Will you come in my car?"

"Yes that would be nice as long as you don't leave me to walk home."

They sat at the bar on stools and sipped their drinks. They chatted away about nothing and suddenly a complete silence fell between them, and then he leant forward and kissed her, not just a peck but the real thing. It lasted for ages, she thought, but I loved every moment of it.

He drew back from her saying, "I'm so sorry but I've wanted to do that from the moment you walked in the show room and looking into those beautiful eyes I couldn't help myself."

"That all right, I liked it. You can do it any time if you wish you're very good at it."

The food was very nice but soon it seemed it was time to go. They arrived back at her house, she didn't ask him in and she felt he didn't expect her to. She thanked him for the super evening adding she was happy she knew where to go with her grass and mower problems now, they laughed together.

He said, "You don't need that sort of trouble to see me again, I was hoping maybe we could make a date for Saturday. Could we say pick you up here eight o'clock?" She nodded. He leant over and kissed her again. "Goodnight lovely Laura, until Saturday."

She got out of the car and he drove away.

The new job was going well for Laura. The other members of staff were very friendly and seemed to like her new ideas. Her little assistant was a real dream, she was eager to learn, very good with the computer, quick to put Laura's ideas into action, never moody, a trait some young girls were often guilty of and she had a good sense of humour for one so young. In fact, she was totally bright-eyed and bushy-tailed and Laura found working with her a joy.

The social life was pretty good also for Laura. Most weeks she had a date with Ross, he would take her to a pub for a drink and sometimes she invited him to her place for a bite to eat, they always had a pleasant time together, but it seemed just as good friends; he never seemed to want anything more from her. She also spent quite a lot of time with Dick, that was very different and he always wined and dined her in the best places and, she had to admit, he was the best man she had ever been kissed by, he was always a perfect gentleman, kind and gentle, but he did make her laugh one evening by telling her he liked to be called Richard and not Dick. She also had a new friend Jerry, he lived opposite her in the close. She met him when the neighbours had a housewarming party, they invited everybody from the other four houses together with some other friends of theirs. It was nice to meet them all.

There was the older couple who lived at the far end, Peggy and Charlie, another couple in their late twenties he was very down to earth but she was a bit posh making sure that she told everybody how they had furnished their house with antiques, and all the soft furnishings had come from Harrods. And then there was Jerry. She got on with him like a house on fire. She was unsure about his sexual preferences but she certainly warmed to him. They chatted away with ease, talking about the area that was new to both of them, agreeing how happy they were to have found the close. The party went well, everybody mixed easily and when it was time to leave she and Jerry left together for their own places and then, to her surprise, he asked her if she would join him for a meal that he would cook for them the next evening, and she readily accepted. She didn't have another offer and as she liked to go out on a Saturday evening and was a free agent, there was no reason not to accept.

"That will be great, what time would you like me to come?" she asked.

"About seven o'clock, OK?"

"Sounds good to me, goodnight, thank you."

On getting indoors she noticed the red light flashing on her phone. She pressed the button only to hear Richard's voice.

"Laura where are you? I need to speak to you urgently, I have a favour to ask, if it's OK by you I wondered if I could come to your place tomorrow evening, if I pick up a Chinese takeaway we would have it with a bottle of wine and we could have a chat, please ring me as soon as possible."

Funny she thought, well it's too late to ring him now, I'll do it in the morning. It seemed as though she had only just got into bed when she was woken by the phone ringing, she picked up the received and before she had time to say anything she head Richard's voice.

"Good morning my beautiful Laura, did you get my message last night and is it OK to come round this evening?"

"Well actually, no I'm sorry but I'm out tomorrow."

"But Laura I thought it went without saying we do spend Saturday evenings together, what are you doing? Please excuse me for asking, have you found someone else?"

"No I haven't Richard, but I am going to have a meal with a friend, but we could do it on Sunday evening, if you like."

"Yes all right then can we say early evening because I'm very eager to see you. It seems ages ago we last were together, bye for now I'll try not to think of where you are this evening, bye."

She felt really bad about letting him down and not telling him exactly where she was going, maybe this would be a wake up call for him to go a little further which she wouldn't object to, but she wondered what was the favour he was wanting to speak to her about. Well, she would just have to wait until tomorrow, but he did sound a bit upset; but then he didn't own her and he had never said they would always see one another on a Saturday evening.

Jerry opened the door to her with a grin from ear to ear. "Come in," he said kissing the back of her hand.

He had prepared a beautiful three-course meal for them both, and during the time they were eating he explained why he had moved to the close which confirmed Laura's thoughts about his sexuality. Apparently he and his long time partner had split up over Jason's jealously of Jerry having some female friends, which he liked to entertain when Jason was away on the cruise liners where he worked as a steward and entertainer.

"I do miss him," Jerry told Laura. "Silly boy but we couldn't go on like that never having trust, but it's over now and I will move on."

She had a most enjoyable evening. The food was super and he was very interesting to listen to. He told her a little about his family and background and explained that sometimes it was difficult for relatives to understand gay people and it can be difficult to make friends with non-gay people. It was quite late when she said goodnight and thanked him for everything.

The next day being Sunday she had a lie-in, turning over in her mind what could Richard want to ask her. She must have dozed off again and woke with a start: it was twelve o'clock, but she still had time before Richard came to tidy up. At three o'clock there was a knock at the door, she went to open it and there stood Richard. Very early evening, she thought to herself.

"Is it all right Laura? I'm sorry I'm so early but I couldn't wait, can I come in? I haven't got the Chinese yet, I thought it was a bit early, but I just wanted to see you, do you mind?"

"Of course I don't mind," she said stepping forward and stretching on tiptoes to kiss him. He just put his arms around her and held her tight.

"I must know Laura, was your friend a man last night? I'm sorry but I'd like to know, if you prefer my company rather than some other man's."

"Well yes I have to tell you it was a man but not a man like you Richard, he is a friend but a gay friend," she said laughing, "so stop worrying you crazy man. Now come in it's too early to eat so let's be very naughty and open the wine, before I get too concerned about this favour you need from me. You get the glasses out and I'll get the wine for you to open," she said, heading for the kitchen.

Sitting closely together on the sofa he said, "Well I have to go to Paris on Friday to a lawn mower exhibition and I would like you to come with me, please."

She looked at him in surprise and said, "Richard I don't think that's quite my scene. As you will know I'm no expert in that department." She could hardly stop giggling.

"No, no, Laura I don't mean you to come to the exhibition. I just would like you to spend the weekend with me, we would need to leave here on the flight about lunchtime on Friday and return late on Sunday evening. What do you think?" Please say yes. We would stay at a five-star hotel, we would have dinner at a good restaurant that night, Saturday I would have to go to the exhibition and I thought you might like to do a little shopping. I would arrange a driver for you so as when you had had enough, you could go back to the hotel take a swim or jacuzzi or maybe just relax. I should be back by six o'clock and then we could dine on a glass roof boat on the river, then on Sunday we would walk, talk have a little lunch in a bistro. I know, perhaps go back to the hotel and relax together before flying hone, please please say yes!"

She looked at him with surprise and said, "I would love to come but I have only been in my job a few weeks and so I don't know if I can get the time off, but I will ask Mr Casey tomorrow as soon as I get in."

He leant towards her squeezing her hand. "Please try very hard," he said.

"I will do my best to get it sorted tomorrow, but how is it you seem to know Paris so well? You already have a game plan by the sound of things."

"Oh yes, I thought I had told you that I worked for Peugeot for two years, I really enjoyed it and probably would still be there now but, when my father had the opportunity to buy what is now our showroom, he asked me to come home and run it for our company. I must admit it was a hard decision for me as lawnmowers were not my wildest dreams. But now Laura, I can show you around and that will make me very happy, I think we would need to be at the airport about eleven o'clock, the flight's only just over one hour so we will be there by two o'clock, we can check. I can show you around the hotel where the health spa and beauty room is in case you want to use them on Saturday when I am at the show, and then we can go for a walk, or just talk, or drink coffee, or wine or champagne." By this time they were giggling together like children.

"Just a minute," she said, "we don't even know if I can come with you yet, perhaps we should stop making plans until I speak to Mr Casey tomorrow. But I must say it sounds as if you know the hotel well, is it where you take all your lady friends?"

"No, only the special ones just like you. No, I am teasing you, but I have stayed there a few times on business, paid for by my old company, I think you'll like it."

They drank the wine and then Laura suggested they should have a cup of tea and a piece of cake. She went to see to it in the kitchen and after a few minutes he followed her, leaning on the worktop beside her.

"You do make me feel so happy and relaxed with you. I'm just so glad you needed a mower." And this statement sent them into fits of laughter. She picked up the tray and they took it into the lounge. As she put it on the table he turned her around and kissed her.

"Shall we scrap the Chinese and go out to eat?"

She really wanted to say, 'no let's make love', but she was not sure how he would react to this statement, so she decided to keep quiet and behave.

At the restaurant they looked at the menus and before they could think they were back on the subject of Paris, and then Richard said something that had been crossing Laura's mind, as to what rooms they would be having at the hotel.

He leant forward and looked very deeply into her eyes saying, "I have booked a double suite, is that going to be all right? It has two en suite bathrooms as I know you ladies like to take your time to get ready. I didn't think you would go for the typical French way of basin and loo with just a curtain across. And that's if you're lucky!"

They were not late leaving the restaurant and back at her house she didn't ask him in as she thought she would keep what she hoped for until Paris.

The next morning she arrived at work as normal, Natalie was already there bright as a button. She had already collected the mail which they sorted as normal. Natalie took the piles to the different offices, and Laura took the appropriate ones into Mr Casey's office for his secretary's attention. She looked through the door to his private office where he was sitting at his desk.

"Good morning Laura, what can I do for you today?"

"I have the offer to go to Paris for a few days, but I would need to be at the airport by eleven a.m. on Friday, I know I have not been here long enough to request time off but if I was to come in early on Friday and make sure everything is in order would you consider that possible?"

He pursued his lips for a few moments. "How well is Natalie coping, in your opinion? Can she see to the mail on her own, answer the phone and deal with the clients in reception in your opinion?"

"Oh yes Mr Casey, she has done so well and I know she would like the opportunity to show us all how capable she is."

"Well in that case I think as long as you have sorted everything within reason by Thursday at the end of business and primed Natalie, I will be happy to let you have the whole day off assuming you will be back on time on Monday morning, and by the way I am pleased with the way you are getting us all knocked into shape, thank you," he said with a broad smile.

"I was not expecting you to say that, but I am very grateful, and thank you for your time." She left his office full of excitement.

As soon as she arrived home that evening she phoned Richard. "Guess what," she said, "I've got the whole day off isn't it fantastic? I really am so excited Richard."

"Oh Laura, that's wonderful, I'll get to you about nine thirty a.m. so as it gives us plenty of time to get to the airport, park the car, perhaps have a coffee before we fly out. I might not see you until then as I've a few things to sort out before I go. Take care you precious thing, see you Friday. Bye for now."

# Chapter Eleven

She spent the next few days deciding what to take. She decided to treat herself to some pretty new underwear and while shopping for that, she saw a very glamorous cream lace negligee; it was ridiculously overpriced but she decided to have it. She only hoped Richard would appreciate it.

She was up, showered and ready to go by eight o'clock. She had decided to wear her dark blue suit with a white frilly necked blouse that she knew flattered her neck and face. She did have butterflies in her tummy. She didn't really know why and then for the umpteenth time she must have looked for Richard to arrive he was finally there. She opened the front door and he was out of the car up the path and hugging her. Picking up her case, they left for the airport.

During the flight which had left absolutely on time he ordered some champagne, raising his glass to hers he said, "I can't think of anybody more desirable to spend the weekend with, I could do without the exhibition but then perhaps without that I wouldn't have had an excuse to get you to come away with me."

Arriving at the hotel he was greeted by the doorman, who spoke to him in English. "How nice to see you, sir, it's quite some time since you have stayed with us."

By the time they had checked in and arrived at their suite their cases had arrived and been unpacked, which slightly amused Laura: she was thinking thank goodness I had the new undies. This really was five-star treatment, perhaps not surprising though as the whole air of the place was total luxury.

"What would you like to do now?" he asked her.

"Could we go to the Eiffel Tower?"

"Your wish is my command," he said walking towards her holding her close and running his finger from under her chin down, in between her breasts.

Laura felt he did it almost as a test of her reaction, she smiled at him saying, "Do be careful. You don't know how demanding I might become."

They went to reception where Richard ordered a taxi together with one to take them to the restaurant where they were eating in the evening. He spoke to the receptionist in French and, as Laura's French wasn't that good, she didn't take much notice; but it did remind her of the night she and Caroline had spent on holiday in Canada with Marco and Raymond, the amorous little Frenchman who she didn't fancy. The taxi arrived in minutes and Richard explained to her he had asked for the taxi to do a short trip of the sites. First stop was the Eiffel Tower.

"Would you like to go up it?" he asked her.

"No, but I'd like to get out and just walk around it, if that's OK. I can see there is a big queue so just looking is good, thank you," she said turning to him and planting a kiss on his cheek. He put his arm round her as they walked, it was a beautiful sunny winter's day and she was happy to be with him. Getting back into the taxi the driver took them along the Champs Élyseé, under the Arc de Triomphe and all the other typical touristy sites.

Back at the hotel, Richard said, "Oh do forgive me Laura I'd quite forgotten, we haven't eaten anything. Are you hungry?" he said looking at his watch. "Actually it's nearly half past six, and the taxi's coming at seven thirty to take us to the restaurant for dinner, can you wait that long?"

"Oh yes that's fine, because we do need to get ready. What shall I wear? Or more important, what would you like me to wear?"

"Nothing really, but it might cause a bit of a stir," he said with an impish grin.

They sat and chatted for a while and then Laura said, "I think I ought to be getting ready now, as a typical woman it takes me a little while." She stood up and pointing to the door each side of the bed she said, "Which one is mine?"

"I will sleep on the right-hand side of the bed so I can hold you in my left arm, so you take the left door, and I will be sitting here waiting for you all ready to go just before the taxi comes."

She heard the telephone ring just before she was ready to step out. She had decided to wear a simple black halter neck dress, together with her silver fox fur jacket, she opened the door and walked towards him.

He stood up and just stared at her. "My God Laura, you look fantastic."

She smiled at him and said, "I'm glad you approve." She noticed he had put his hands in his pockets. "Have you lost something?" she asked with a mischievous grin.

"No, I'm just trying to control something. It's the effect you have on me, if only that bloody taxi wasn't here, I expect you heard the phone, it was reception to say it was already here, so I suppose we had better go."

"Will it keep for a little later?" she inquired. He looked at her and they both started giggling.

The evening was wonderful, the food was wonderful together with the wine, and he was wonderful. They had planned to walk back to the hotel but when he asked for the bill he also asked for a taxi. He knew he couldn't wait to get her back there and he was pretty confident that she felt the same.

He felt the key would never go into the lock. He seemed to be fumbling like a guilty teenager, he thought, but then they were inside. He pulled her close and slipped off her jacket.

"I'm out of control now," he said.

"I'll just slip to the bathroom," she replied. Once inside she undressed, sprayed herself with perfume and slipped into her negligee. Richard was already sitting up in bed he had his hand on the top of the covers next to him.

"Something I need to tell you Laura, I always sleep in the nude."

"So do I," she said letting he negligee fall to the floor and slipping under the covers and into his arms. Their lovemaking was long and satisfying. The next thing she remembered was to be woken by Richard getting out of bed.

She noticed as he headed for the bathroom that he was naked with a very sexy bottom, but he had on his feet a pair of fluffy white socks. He reappeared with his bathrobe wrapped round him but with a pair of black socks on. He came and sat on the bed beside her and pulling back the covers he buried his face into her breasts, to which she immediately responded.

"I don't really want to leave you now Laura, but I know you understand I must go to the exhibition, I promise I will be back as early as possible hopefully by six o'clock. Just phone reception when you need the car. I have arranged he will be available all day for you. Remember, we are going on the river tonight we have to board at seven thirty." He then kissed her, exploring every part of her mouth.

She took the advantage of the car and did a little shopping just buying a few bits and pieces. She then decided to go back to the hotel and have a sauna, massage and facial all of which she enjoyed. Back in the suite there was a knock at the door. She went to open it and, to her surprise, there stood Richard.

"Wonderful!" she screamed. "Have you played hookey, you're nice and early."

"Yes I couldn't concentrate with the thought of you here and me not with you, I just collected enough info to convey to my father and then I deserted. I just hoped you would be back from your shopping, my luck must be in because here you are." With that he scooped her up and took her to the bedroom where he slowly undressed her, caressing every bit of her body as he revealed it. She shuddered with anticipation as he literally ripped off his clothes and slipped inside her. She didn't think it came much better than last night, but she was wrong.

All too soon it was time to fly home, the lovemaking was wonderful and so was their sightseeing. On Sunday they planned to walk and see the pavement artists and then on to the bistro that Richard knew, but first they nipped back to the hotel to indulge themselves in each other before lunch, and after lunch they couldn't wait to get back there again before flying out.

One thing had intrigued Laura, and she couldn't help wondering why on earth he always had his socks on; so feeling adventurous she thought she must find out why. At the most convenient opportunity she whispered in his ear trying not to giggle, "Tell me Richard, why do you always wear your socks?"

"Oh shut up!" he said. "I thought I had better things for you to look at rather than my socks, but it is because I have no toenails, don't laugh I know it's funny and when I tell you how it happened you'll probably laugh."

"No I won't, please tell me," she said.

"Well not so long ago I ran over them with a mower."

"Oh dear how terrible for you." She found she did want to laugh and was having a job to suppress it.

"There you are, I told you it's funny but I can assure you it was painful at the time." But with that they both started to giggle which became a little uncontrollable.

"And you said I wasn't very good at cutting my grass," she said. This set them off giggling again.

The flight landed on time. They collected their baggage and the car and drove off back to Laura's house. Richard carried her cases inside for her, thanked her for a wonderful unforgettable weekend, kissed her goodbye and, looking at her very intensely, said, "You are just so beautiful. I'll give you a ring in a few days."

She took her case upstairs, unpacked, took the dirty washing downstairs and put it in the washing machine, made herself a big mug of hot chocolate and together with two Digestive biscuits she decided to go to bed. She intended to be at the office by eight o'clock in the morning to just check that everything was in order and that Natalie had seen to everything as Laura wanted. The cleaners were always there from about six a.m. so she would have no difficulty in getting in. Sitting up in bed sipping her chocolate she reflected on the sightseeing which was interesting, the hotel was superb, the boat trip was romantic, and the sex had been worth waiting for and she felt very pleased with life. She smiled to herself on reflecting on the men in her life since being back in England they didn't exactly list as the greatest lovers. Michael, yes dear Michael the control freak, Ross no lover to date, don't hold your breath, Jerry the gay, and finally Richard the furry sock man; but she had to admit he was the best to date, and he certainly was a gentleman and knew how to treat a lady.

She was at the office just before eight next morning, she checked that everything was ready for the start of work at nine just as she had requested of Natalie. She noticed there was a few new appointments that Natalie had made and they were all in order. Laura was feeling rather pleased with how she was coming along and she intended to make sure Mr Casey knew this as well, about eight thirty the man himself arrived.

"Good morning Laura, good weekend?"

"Excellent, thank you for letting me go, and I must say Natalie did everything I asked of her. Do you have any comment to make?"

"No, not at all. I think everything ran very smoothly in your absence, you are obviously teaching her well, nice little thing could go far."

Laura wondered if his early arrival was just to check on her, but she didn't mind. After all she was still a very new member of staff and he hadn't had time to test her reliability yet. The next person to fly through the door was Natalie.

"Did you have a good time? Did I do OK, did I?"

"Stop, stop," said Laura, "have you forgotten something like good morning?"

"Oh I'm sorry. Good morning, but I just wanted to know if I'd pleased you and got everything correct, and did you have a good time?"

"Yes, you did, yes I did, and I'm very proud of you." With that she put her arms round the little thing and gave her a big hug.

By Wednesday Laura had heard nothing from Richard, Ross had asked her to go to the pictures to see a Barbara Streisand film on Thursday, so it was Friday before she really thought perhaps she ought to give Richard a ring; but it was just the answerphone when she did, so on reflection she decided not to say anything. Saturday she still heard nothing and then began to wonder if perhaps she had offended him by commenting on his sock problem.

Well if that was the case he just had to get over it. She decided to tidy the front garden, sweeping up the leaves when she saw Jerry doing the same thing. She went over to him and decided to ask him for supper.

"I'm going to cook some pasta of some sort or other tonight, however it turns out it won't be in the same league as your cooking. How to you feel about joining me? I might even ask my neighbours if I get brave."

"Yeah it will be great I'd like that, I'm expecting a couple of phone calls early evening so would eight o'clock be OK?"

"Absolutely fine I'll pop in and ask the others now, see you later."

They had a great evening together and Jerry kept them highly amused with his stories. They probably drank a bit too much wine but they sure did enjoy themselves. Laura had taken Richard into consideration in case he just turned up, as he seemed to take Saturday evenings as theirs; she had to admit she was a little disappointed when he didn't show up. Everybody finally left and she was surprised to realise it was nearly four a.m. She decided just to walk away from it all, she was tired and ready for bed. She'd have a good clear up in the morning.

It was mid afternoon when she finally got straight and hoovered round. Just about to sit down she glanced out of the window only to see Richard getting out of his car, she was pleased but decided to let him knock the door before opening it, and certainly didn't intend to comment on his lack of contact. Once inside she felt he was a little uneasy, and then suddenly he almost burst out saying, "Laura, I don't want to get married. No I mean, I can't get married. No, I mean I do want to get married but –"

"What are you talking about Richard? How have your got yourself into this situation? You just have to tell her the wedding's off."

"Laura it's you I'm talking about. Yes you, after last weekend in Paris I thought you would expect it."

She walked over to him and put her arms around his waist. "Richard, we had wonderful sex and a wonderful time in Paris but surely we are adult enough to be able to have a great relationship without that sort of commitment? Let's just be good lovers." She looked at him and realised his eyes were brim full.

"You just don't know what I've been through this week, you are the best thing that's happened to me in ages and what you have just said makes everything even better, and do you really mean it that we can carry on just like this?"

"Yes, I certainly do not want a committed relationship and definitely not marriage; but I do like a little close contact from time to time."

## Chapter Twelve

Christmas was so close Laura was reminded by a phone call from Caroline in Canada.

"You coming back for Christmas? We'd love to see you, what do you say?"

"Thank you for the invite but I think I will spend it here this year. Besides, I'm not sure if Michael will be back at his old apartment there if he hasn't managed to get a house sorted out in Alaska yet, and I really don't feel I want to stir up any emotions for either of us, now. Is Carl still prone to walking round in the nude?"

Caroline started to giggle. "Well to tell you the truth Laura he's got me doing it as well now. We like it, there's no delay for action."

"My God, that's definitely made up my mind not to come, I'll pay you a visit when you've changed your ways, I don't think I could cope with you both floating around like that."

Putting the phone down she started to think seriously about Christmas. She was sure Richard and she would not be spending it together although they had a very good relationship going, but at times his duties seem to lie with his family, which was fine by her and kept things just how she liked it. Ross she knew was going home to his parents in Scotland so that ruled him out. Pauline had inquired some weeks ago as to what Laura would be doing and invited her to their house with her family, Terry's family and all the kids, and as much as she loved them all a whole day was just too much. She thought at the most she could deliver the gifts Christmas morning, stay for a bit and then make an excuse to leave.

Christmas Day actually fell on a Tuesday, and Mr Casey to everybody's delight had decided they would close the office from the Friday lunchtime before until the Wednesday of the New Year. The ten days leading up to Christmas had been good. Richard had taken her to a show in London on the Friday and stayed at her place overnight, she was a little ashamed to admit they had spent a long time in bed the next morning just enjoying themselves, without Richard thinking he had to marry her; she knew she liked him but she didn't think she loved him. On the last Friday at the office Mark, one of the young solicitors, invited her to a party he and his wife were having on the Saturday.

"Be delighted if you come Laura, there will be quite a mixed bunch there, a couple of spare single men, another guy going through a divorce, in fact I'm dealing with the poor sod (a dirty one) but all pretty informal, mostly couples, about twenty of us in all.

"Sounds great, yes, I'd like to come, but where to you live?"

"Clagdon House a bit out in the country but here are the directions," he said, handing her a so-called map.

Taking it Laura said, "What sort of time and what's the dress code?"

"About eight to eight thirty p.m. and typical woman what shall I wear, I think the ladies will probably wear the long casual things you're all wearing at the moment, does that suit you?"

"Yeah sounds great, look forward to it," Laura said with a smile.

There were many happy Christmas wishes as they all left the office. Laura was still not sure how she would spend Christmas Day; if Jerry was at a loose end she might even ask him over. Wait and see, she thought.

She was busy most of the day on Saturday. Richard popped in just for a coffee, nothing more, and said he probably would not see her until a good week to ten days into the New Year. She didn't question why. He stayed for about half an hour, wished her Happy Christmas, gave her a hug and was gone. She realised that she had forgotten to give him the small gift she had bought him, it was just aftershave, but then she thought he didn't come bearing a gift for her. Not that he should, and she felt guilty for even thinking so, but sometimes she didn't really think she understood him. Yes, their physical relationship was reasonably satisfying she thought, for both of them; but not the mind-blowing experience she would want to spend the rest of her life having. She briefly compared it to the night she had spent on the edge of the lake in Canada.

In her mind she had decided to wear a cream knitted dress to the party. It had a high neck, cutaway shoulders, very simple and well fitting. She thought as she hadn't worn it for a while perhaps she should go up and try it on. Looking in the mirror she was quite pleased with the reflection and with her dark red hair, the colour looked good: yes, that's what she would wear. She wasn't really sure she wanted to go when it was time to leave, but not having a better offer and not wanting to spend the evening alone, she picked up her car keys and left.

She arrived about eight thirty having found the house quite easily. Mark welcomed her warmly, taking her coat he said, "Wow, you look stunning."

He introduced her to Sally his wife. Laura had spoken to her on the phone but hadn't met her before, she seemed very pleasant and friendly. Mark then took her into the lounge and introduced her to about a dozen or so other people, he slipped a glass of wine into her hand and said, "I'm not going to make you shake hands with everybody here, but here is Kate and David and this is Jenny with her new husband Rod, I'm sure you'll get to know the rest, they're all quite normal, I think. There's a few more though, there. In the kitchen, and in case you lot are wondering who this lovely thing is, she's our office Rottweiler: keeps us all in order, but we all love her."

Everybody chuckled and smiled, one of the girls put her hand out to welcome Laura into the group which Laura thought was very friendly and nice. As she sipped her drink she noticed a few chaps coming in from what she assumed was the kitchen.

"I've come to see the Rottweiler." She heard one of them say, as she turned round she then heard him say, "Oh my God, I don't believe it, it's my beautiful frog!"

It seemed to Laura as if an electric shock went through her body, the whole room went silent and she realised it was Tom, Tom the Pig who had caused her so much heartache all those years before. She felt sick. She didn't want this, after all she'd left England to forget him, not that she ever really did. For a second that seemed like ages he held her eyes and then he was there with is arms gently around her and gently kissed her on the forehead; she realised everybody was just looking at them.

"Trust you Tomas," said someone which made everybody laugh and returned the conversation to normal.

"Where have you been?" he asked looking intensely at her.

"In Canada for nearly three years. I returned to England about four months ago, but where have you been?"

"Well I spent a while working in Dubai but I'm back here now, working for Shell. I do a bit of travelling for them, but that's not interesting or important. What is, is that I've never forgotten the last time I saw you. I've obviously had my relationships along the way but it was always you and your face that I couldn't forget, and then I realised I was in love with you."

Laura narrowed her eyes and gave him a penetrating look.

"Please don't do that, I do mean it," he said.

She smiled at him but in her heart she knew she loved him too but was too scared to think about it. She really wanted to walk away, but couldn't.

Sally then called everybody to have a bite to eat, but neither of them wanted to eat. Right at the bottom of the staircase was a large round step, they sat down on it and chatted about old friends and old places; their glasses were now empty, so Tom went to fill them.

"Whatever you do, don't go," he said.

When he came back some other chap was sitting on the step busily chatting to Laura. He immediately felt insanely jealous; noticing the chap's glass of red wine was nearly empty, he went back to the kitchen, grabbed a bottle of red wine he didn't care which, came back to the pair of them held out the bottle to the guy thinking he would stand up and let his glass be filled. But he just sat chatting lifted up his glass, saying, "Thanks mate, jolly decent of you."

Tom did no more than put the bottle down out of the chap's reach so he would have to get up if he wanted more, then he picked up Laura's and his glasses. With that, saying "Excuse me," he stepped over them and sat down on the step behind. This all amused Laura, she thought to herself what has happened to this confident self-opinionated Pig? Surely this cannot be that he just wants to be with me? People had finished eating and Mark turned the music up and, as luck would happen for Tom, a pretty young girl came and asked the chap talking to Laura to dance. Still sitting on the step behind her he opened his legs and pulled her back gently against himself, he bent down and kissed the top of her head, she smelt so good he wanted to eat her. After a while he asked her to dance he held her so close, and she remembered those oh-so-many times they had been together with all their mutual friends and he had asked her to dance, just as one of the crowd, teasing and joking with her all the time, never knowing what she felt. She enjoyed the party and meeting new people; several other chaps asked her to dance and she was very aware that Tom never took his eyes off her, even when he was dancing with someone else.

About two a.m. he said, "I think I've had enough, how about you?"

"Yes," Laura agreed.

"Can I take you home?" he asked.

"No, I have my own car here."

"Then can I follow you home in my car and come in?"

"No you can't," she said with a giggle.

"Why? You know you want me to."

"No I don't, and anyway I have only just moved in, and it's not straight yet," she said lying through her teeth.

"But I bet you have a bed?"

"Yes I do, but not for you to get into, all those years ago you may not remember you said you didn't want to get into my knickers, and now you think I'm going to let you get into my bed?"

"Well perhaps tomorrow? It's Sunday. Can I take you out for late lunch, say I pick you up about two o'clock? I know a nice little place right out in the country, I'll book a table there."

Laura nodded approval.

They went to find Mark and Sally, to say their goodbyes and thanks then wishing everybody a Happy Christmas and a great New Year they left. It was strange that their cars were parked opposite each other.

"I'll follow you home anyway," Tom said. "Then I'll know where to pick you up tomorrow, and if you haven't relented tonight perhaps I can have a tour of the new pad tomorrow."

They both got into their cars and drove off, taking about twenty minutes to get to Laura's place. She parked her car in the drive and went back to Tom, who was leant on the bonnet of his car. He took her hands and pulled her close to kiss her: it was the most wonderful moment of her life, she didn't want to stop, but eventually they parted he got into his car and left.

She went inside her house and felt as though she was walking on air. She got into bed just lying there unable to sleep from sheer expectancy and excitement so many things and thoughts going through her head, she must have eventually fallen asleep, but suddenly she was wide awake with the most horrifying thought: Mark had told her when he invited her to the party that one of the men was going through a divorce. Was it Tom? She couldn't bear to think about it. Yes, it could be, he said he had a few relationships. Why didn't she ask him if he was married? She started to cry. She felt sick, very hot but shaking as if she was cold. Say he had children, say he went back to his wife? Sometimes Christmas made people see things differently. She tried to see sense; if he was Mark's client who was having a divorce, surely she would've seen him at the office? But did he come on the Friday she went to Paris with Richard? By this time she was out of bed pacing the room. It was over three years since she had last seen him and the thought of not being able to have him was as bad now as it was then. Last night he said he was in love with her but that could've been a heat of the moment thing for him. Yet she knew it was love. She recalled how an old lady once said to her 'You're not in love till it makes you sick'. Why didn't she let him come in tonight? At least she would have known what it was like to be made love to by him, she felt she would die if she never had that experience. She went downstairs made herself a cup of hot chocolate – always her comforter – went back upstairs and got back into bed. Pulling herself together she tried to reason: yes, she knew what she would do, in the morning she would telephone Mark and ask him. At that point she couldn't even force her chocolate past her throat, and exhausted she nodded off.

When she woke at first she felt excited about her lunch date with Tom but then her fears returned. Getting up she went to the bathroom, looked in the mirror and was horrified at what she saw; her eyes were swollen and red, mascara was running in streaks down her face, what a mess! She went back into the bedroom only to see Jerry walking up to her front door; she went downstairs to let him in thinking, he was possibly the only man she didn't have to worry about how she looked.

Opening the front door to him he said, "Hello Laura, I've just popped over to..." he stopped. "Shit, you look terrible, are you ill, or what? Let me come in." With that she started to cry again. He put his arms round her saying, "There, there my darling, tell Jerry all about it."

"Oh Jerry, I've had such a terrible night in bed."

"With or without a man?" he said trying to lighten things up a bit.

"Without. Last night I went to a party and met the man there who made me run away to Canada, because he wasn't interested in me. Now he says he knows he loves me, I think he might be married, or having a divorce! I can't go through all that heartache again and now I'm going out to lunch with him at two o'clock, and last night I wouldn't let him come in. Now I wished I had, it's such a mess."

"How do you feel about him? Do you want to go to lunch with him, do you love him?"

"Yes Jerry I do, I always have done and always will."

"Right then we have to get you looking good for two o'clock, time is running out. It's just like Cinderella. Have you got any cucumber?"

"Cucumber? What's the use of that?" That's no substitute."

"Come now my darling, no need to be vulgar. We need two slices to lay on your eyes. Go upstairs, get rid of all that smudged make-up, put your face cream on, get the cucumber slices, lay on the sofa here with them on your eyes while I pop home and get some cream to take the swelling down. When I come back I'll make us a nice cup of tea and we will try to get you presentable for when he arrives."

She did as she was told, feeling quite stupid with the cucumber on her eyes. Soon Jerry was back clutching what he called his miracle cream; he made the tea and propped another cushion behind her head so she could drink more easily with the cucumber still in place. She had to admit she felt better already. After about twenty minutes he removed the cucumber, declaring the redness nearly gone.

"That's looking a good deal better, now for the miracle cream," he said.

"What is it?" she asked.

"Haemorrhoid cream, all the stars and we gays use it."

She started to laugh. "Don't give me any more information please, I'll just take your word for it, and if it works be eternally grateful. Nobody I know would have such good inside information, darling."

They sat sipping tea for a while longer then Jerry said, "I actually was coming to tell you I'm going away for Christmas, but I think you'll possibly be otherwise engaged. Its twelve o'clock now, I think it's about time you went and relaxed in a bath with some nice smellies and then get ready for your man. I'm going home now. You have a great Christmas, and I'll catch up on the progress when I get back."

"Oh thank you Jerry. I do feel a lot better now, you are such a good friend."

Laura was ready and waiting by two o'clock, but by a quarter past two there was no sight of Tom. She was trying to stay calm but was beginning to become anxious that perhaps he had better thoughts and was not coming. She checked again for the tenth time to make sure she looked OK, and then he arrived. After about half an hour's drive he pulled over and stopped the car at a place with a magnificent view.

"Let's get out and look," he said.

The air was fresh and exhilarating. The sun was shining in a cloudless bright blue sky, he wrapped her coat around her and kissed her with passion that she couldn't help but return; he held her at arm's length and pulled the soft fur collar of her coat up around her face, saying, "We can't lose each other ever again, Laura."

They walked back to the car and continued on their way to lunch. They went up the drive to a lovely old country hotel with beautiful gardens. Inside Tom was greeted like an old friend.

Does he bring all his acquaintances here, she thought?

"This is Laura," he said introducing her to the owner, the manager, she didn't quite know.

"Very nice to meet you," he said shaking hands with her.

"Will you go straight to your table or would you like a drink at the bar first? We have some warm Glogg there which I think has a festive smell."

"We will go into the bar then, will you bring us some menus to look at please?"

The lunch and service was exceptional, not intrusive but attentive. Laura and Tom chose to have coffee in one of the lounges, just the two of them in front of a glorious log fire sitting on a sofa that you just sank into, filling in lots of little details about each other. Before they knew it it was gone six o'clock.

"I think we had better get the bill," Tom said.

They said their goodbyes to the staff and stepped out into the cold air.

# Chapter Thirteen

As they walked to the car Tom put his arm around Laura; he opened the door for her to get in and, looking at her, he said:

"I'm so happy Laura, I hope you feel the same."

Once inside the car he sat very quietly for a few moments then turning to her he said, "I've got something to say but I'm afraid to say it."

Laura felt sick. "Then perhaps don't say it."

They hadn't touched on previous relationships during their lunch and she knew now what was coming, he was going to tell her he was married. He put his arms round her and tried to hold her. She pushed him away.

"Stop it, I don't want to hear it." Tears were starting to stream down her face she had her thumbs in her ears and the rest of her hands over her face. She started screaming at him between sobs. "Tom, I can't stand going through this over you again, I wish I'd never gone to that party at Mark and Sally's, I wish I'd never met you again! I know exactly what you're going to say, that you're married, and as it's Christmas you feel for the children's sake you must go back to them all, and her. I hate you, I hate you! Pig is a good word for you. I never want to see you again, you made me sick four years ago when all you did was tease me and poke fun at me. I managed to piece myself together by going to Canada and now what? You've come back to destroy me again!"

At this point she was sobbing so much and could hardly breathe. She opened the car door hoping to run away as far as possible from him.

He leant over and grabbed her hand, almost shouting at her, "Shut the door Laura and listen." He tried to turn her towards him. "You have it all wrong. I love you!"

She wouldn't let him speak she thumped his chest with her fists, almost in a hysterical state unable to control her emotions, she had gone from the euphoria of meeting him again to the empty feeling that she now had, she wanted to die.

He was quite shocked at the state she was in he just had to make her listen, he put his hand over her mouth and shouted, "I'm not married! I never have been married. And I don't have kids. Or a dog!"

She drew her breath in with a silent sob. "You're not?"

"No, no I'm not, what made you think I was?"

"Mark," she managed to squeak. "He said he was dealing with a divorce for one of the chaps who would be at his party and when I got home that night I couldn't stop thinking it must be you. Tom I love you, I'm so happy."

"Well I must say you don't look it right at this moment, but to get back to my original question I wanted to ask you to come back to my place and spend the night with me, you beautiful bedraggled frog. All I want is for you to say yes."

"Yes I will, but I don't have any other bits and clothes with me."

"For what I have in mind you don't need clothes, so we'll worry about that tomorrow. I only have a little country cottage, thatched and cosy, one bedroom, and no immediate neighbours, only the sheep and cows in the fields."

Pulling up in front of the cottage she thought it looked like a chocolate box, it was absolutely beautiful even in the dark.

"Come on, it's cold out here and I can't wait to get you inside." He opened the door and flicked on the light, taking her coat he said, "Would you like coffee or something else?"

"I think the something else would be nice," she replied.

He picked her up and carried her to the sofa. Pulling her to him he kissed her, then pushing her back he stood up and removed all his clothes apart from his briefs. He then slowly removed everything she was wearing, caressing every bit of her body as he revealed it.

"You're hardly wearing your briefs now," she said.

"And what would you expect?" he said. With that he was inside her, the ecstasy for both of them was explosive and quick. Looking at her he said, "I'm sorry, but I think we have waited so long for this, but as far as I'm concerned we have the rest of our lives to enjoy one another, quick, slow, long, upstairs, downstairs, in the sun, under the stars, just never to be parted again." He eased himself from her and they sat entwined together until he said, "Now I am going to make real love to you," picking her up and carrying to the bedroom.

This time it was long, passionate, exploring each other in every way possible, until they fell asleep exhausted. When they woke the sun was shining through the windows. They laid there in silence for a while until Tom leant up on one elbow looking down at her, saying, "I know I wasn't the first, I wish I had been. But the fit is so perfect, I'm sure we are made for each other."

She smiled and said, "If you have been the first it may not have been so good, but I can tell you for me you found that G-spot that up until now I only though existed in books."

He smiled at her, kissing her breasts. They made love again.

After some coffee Laura said, "I really must go home. I have things to see to."

Tom put his finger on his lips. "I have a good idea. Let's spend Christmas and New Year together. From what you were talking about you don't have any family commitments and, as you know, I don't either. It will be our first one together. Yes, we'll spend it here together."

"I can't," she said.

"Why?"

"Well, well... I don't know," she replied.

"Look, I'll take you back to your place, you can collect everything you need and some clothes, I've got shopping to do. You can do whatever you have to do, and let's be really childish and hang up our stockings tonight and see what Father Christmas brings. I'll pick you up about two o'clock then together we can get all our Christmas goodies to eat and bring back here." He wagged his finger at her. "Then no more lovemaking until after dark," he said, smacking her bottom.

"You seem to have it all worked out," she said giggling at him. "But I don't need much persuasion, it sounds wonderful."

Tom dropped her off at the door and disappeared. She hadn't felt so happy before in her whole life. She jumped into the bath, packed everything she thought she might need – two suitcases full in fact – together with all the personal bits and pieces, toothbrush, tooth paste, deodorant and make-up. Oh God, Laura thought, the stocking! What am I going to get to fill Tom's? She hastily dressed and jumped into her car to go shopping for him. What did he like? She'd basically known him all these years but didn't know much about what he would like.

She decided to drive a little bit further and go to one of the department stores. The first thing she set her eyes on to buy was a Christmas Stocking. After nearly an hour she had some aftershave, the type she had seen in his bathroom, two miniature picture frames, some chocolates, a tie, a bottle of port and a torch. She then remembered when she picked up the stocking she had seen a little furry frog and decided she would put it on the top of his stocking, just for a laugh. Back at her house she tried it all in the stocking. It went great. She took it all out again and put it in a small holdall so Tom wouldn't see it. She was rarely excited about Christmas, something she hadn't felt since her father died.

She was ready and waiting by one forty-five p.m. At two fifteen Tom hadn't arrived. She began to get a little anxious, perhaps he had regretted asking her to spend the time with him? After all everything had happened so quickly, even their first lovemaking together. She thought about it and relived the moment with great pleasure. And the second time, the third and the fourth time, embarrassed by her own longing and feelings. She was sure he had enjoyed it too, but as the minutes ticked by depression began to set in.

She sat on the cases not daring to think. Just after two thirty he screamed to a halt outside her house. She opened the door and ran to meet him, giving him a hug.

"I thought you weren't coming," she said.

"Don't be daft," he said. "You're so insecure, we have to cure that. Come on I'll get your cases, good grief are you coming for good? Don't worry, I don't mind if you are. I'm so happy," said Tom, giving her a quick cuddle. "All this shopping this morning I'm quite exhausted, it's not my scene at all; but I wouldn't mind a quick love-in before we go and get the goodies."

"Not too exhausted for that then? But perhaps we had better save it for later, you can make it up to me then," said Laura.

They quickly dumped the cases at his house as time seemed to be running out to get the shopping. The plan had been to go into Croydon but there was so much traffic he suggested they should go to a little village he knew, a few miles away. He remembered they boasted of their late-night shopping on Christmas Eve just as used to happen many years ago. They parked the car not knowing what they would find, they could already hear the Christmas carols and, as they turned the corner into the square, they could see an enormous Christmas tree in the middle of the road beautifully lit with the brass band and the carol singers who were all dressed in red cloaks with hoods, edged with white fur. Mesmerised they just stood and listened, it was such a lovely atmosphere. Everybody seemed in such good spirits it was such a change from the big city. They decided to walk up one side and back down the other, shopping as they went.

Their first stop was in a typical old-fashioned looking country store. Tom picked up a large basket at the door and they went to the meat and poultry counter.

"What can I get you, sir?" a middle-aged rotund man asked them with a beaming smile. Each looked at the other: they hadn't even thought about what they needed. "Looks like you have other things on your mind," he said with a twinkle in his eye. "My name's Mr Nice. I own the shop, shall I make some suggestions? Is it just for the two of you for the festive season? I suppose you can cook, young lady?"

"Oh yes," said Laura.

"Right then, I'll put something together. You go over to the vegetable counter, get what you like, then come back here in about fifteen minutes and take what you fancy. How's that?"

"Sounds good," said Tom.

Like children off they went as told, chose their vegetables, and then moved to the wine area.

"Let's get some champagne," said Tom.

That took a little choosing, and then Laura said, "I think we ought to get some pickles and cheese, what do you like?" she asked with a giggle. "And perhaps we need some gravy mix, bread sauce and stuffing."

"Laura, I know you like it but I can't stuff you here." His comment made them both laugh out loud, but it didn't seem to matter; it just seemed to fit in with the atmosphere of the store. Having put everything they needed in the basket they went back to Mr Nice who, as promised, had an array of things ready for them.

"Just say what you want," he said pointing first to a small turkey, then a piece of ham, a couple of steaks and a pheasant. "You could pop the pheasant in the freezer for New Year or later if you wish, and I think you'll need this bacon perhaps for breakfast, what do you think?"

"Yes we'll take it all," said Tom.

"What about eggs?" Mr Nice inquired. Laura nodded her head. "Nigel? Bring a dozen eggs over please."

They paid the bill and left the shop loaded and happy. Only to hear Mr Nice calling, "Stop a minute," and walking towards the door towards them, he added, "Don't forget you'll need some bread. Look, over there is the bakers, Purse there will have just taken a lot out of the oven, go in and see him he'll look after you, and a Merry Christmas to you both," he said patting Tom on the shoulder.

There was quite a queue outside the shop but they decided they would join it anyway. They could browse the window while they waited, only to discover that they both liked Yule log. Once inside they were soon served with the bread and they had some rolls as well, and of course a Yule log together with some yummy-looking mince pies. The young girl serving them was very happy and smiley.

"Yah wan cream wid ya Yule Log?" she asked.

"Yes please," said Tom, "but please tell me how does that work?"

"Well, you tells I wat you wants and I gets it from the Frigidaire you see. Pint or 'alf, single or double?"

But this time Tom was finding it difficult to speak without laughing so Laura stepped in with, "Double please, and I think four pints of milk, though perhaps two pints of double cream, thank you."

Tom looked at her saying, "All that cream, what will we do with it? Rub it all over each other and lick it off?"

"Shush!" said Laura. "What will people think if they hear you saying that?"

"Don't know, and don't care, just like the idea, maybe we'll try it later."

"Anyway it makes nice Irish coffee and sorry I don't like milk powder."

The young girl put everything into a big brown paper bag and handed it to Laura, and Tom paid wishing her a happy Christmas they left the shop.

"Well I think that's about it my lovely pig, let's cross the road and go back to the car."

Halfway along the road and outside the flower shop people were drinking hot toddys. Before they knew it a young man was standing in front of them with a tray.

"Way likes un," he said.

"Yes, why not, now much?" Tom asked putting his hand in his pocket before taking a glass for each of them.

"Nutin, we just gis it away, weer not like that bloody grabbing lot in the town, we be noice people," he said.

Sipping the drink, Laura said to Tom, "Funny accent both the girl in the bakers and this boy have, they can't be local surely but perhaps they're related."

"Yes, that's right," said a man over Laura's shoulders. "Brother and sister, came up here from the West Country for a holiday with their grandma liked it both got jobs here in the village and stayed. Nice kids, everybody likes them. You new around here? Haven't seen you before," he asked.

"Yes," said Tom, "we live about ten miles away, couldn't face the parking in town and I remembered this place from some time ago and so we came here, I was very glad we did."

"Nice to chat to you," said the man, "got to get my cloak back on now we are going to sing again for about an hour." He put his hand out and shook both of theirs warmly, saying, "I'm the landlord of the Goat and Garter pub about a mile on in the other direction, drop in and see us sometime. Merry Christmas and Happy New Year to you guys."

With that people seemed to move on and there in another shop window was the prettiest Christmas tree you could wish to see, artificial but complete with decorations and lights. They looked at one another.

"Yes, let's get it."

"I'm just so glad we made the decision not to go into town, I think we will remember this for ever," said Tom.

Back at the house Tom packed away the booze, put up the Christmas tree and put the meat in the fridge while Laura found some bowls to put the fruit in. She pulled the curtains and put a match to the fire.

"What shall we eat tonight?" she asked him.

"I'd quite like frog," he said.

"Funny you should say that, I'd quite like pig, shall we have it as an appetiser?"

"Good idea, let's have it in front of the fire, and then steak and salad in the dining room with a bottle of wine for the main."

"And I will make us an Irish coffee afterwards. And you can decide what to do with the spare cream."

## Chapter Fourteen

They had their appetiser in front of the fire and the next thing Laura knew she was waking up feeling a little chilly, the fire had died down, she was naked, and Tom had disappeared but she could hear him in the kitchen, she realised she must have nodded off. She hopped up and went to the door leading into the kitchen popping her head round it she said, "Hello my darling, I'm sorry I just fell asleep."

"I know, and God you looked so gorgeous doing it with the firelight flickering on your body. Come here," he said putting his arms out to her.

"I can't I haven't got anything on."

"So? Why do you think I want you close to me, it's only us here and nakedness between two lovers is a pleasure and joy, come."

Almost reluctantly she came out from behind the door walking into his arms, he held her back from him, she sort of frowned with embarrassment.

"Don't be silly Laura, I don't understand you, we slept in the nude, we made love in the nude, so what's the difference?"

"I don't know, it just seems strange to have no clothes on in the kitchen," she said with a giggle.

"That's crazy," he said, "I'm not saying you should open the door to the postman without your clothes on but for just the two of us it should be the most natural thing," saying that he gently stroked her breasts. "Look how you are responding to my touch, your breast and nipples have become so hard and it's normal for that to happen between two people in love and you shouldn't be ashamed or embarrassed by your response, we should always be able to touch each other's bodies like this, not just before lovemaking but just because we want to, arousal Laura is so rewarding in love, we will practice it always I hope. Now I suggest you go and indulge yourself in a nice hot bath, and I will get a meal ready to eat a little later."

He kissed her on the top of her head and said, "Go before I change my mind."

As she laid back in the bath she couldn't believe how happy she was things had moved so fast yet she felt so relaxed and contented although perhaps a little ashamed at the amount of enjoyment she was having from Tom making love to her. Her mind went to Caroline and Carl remembering how she had found it difficult to understand their need for each other's bodies, although it could be said Carl was not exactly embarrassed to exhibit his nudity in front of anybody, seemingly.

Together they had the most wonderful Christmas Eve and then before going to bed they hung up their stockings. Laura woke she knew it wasn't time to get up yet but she wanted to get downstairs to fill Tom's stocking, she slipped quietly out of bed, found the bag she had strategically hidden with his gifts and groped her way down the stairs to the fireplace she didn't want to put the light on as she didn't want to wake Tom up. She hung the stocking nearest to the door with the help of the torch which she had bought to put in it, then on the top she put the frog, quickly going back to bed. Tom was still fast asleep but she folded her body around him which he responded to with a satisfied sleepy grunt.

"Wake up it's Christmas Day," he said in her ear. "Let's go and see what Father Christmas has left us. Come on, I can't wait," he said slapping her tummy and pulling the covers off her. "Out of bed, out of bed!"

"What just like this?" she said.

"Yes just like that, you know what we talked about yesterday and anyway Father Christmas is far too busy finishing his rounds to be still in the lounge looking at us."

Out of bed she got grabbing her perfume from the bedside table spraying herself all over. "We are just like two naughty teenagers instead of two responsible adults," she said.

"You're right I know, but it's just so wonderful."

Hand in hand they went down the stairs into the lounge there was Tom's stocking with the frog sat on top of it and Laura's with a pink pig.

Tom put his arm around her, pointing to the stocking he said, "Look, just another to show we are made for each other we even have the same daft sense of humour. Wait a minute I'm just going to get the champagne and some glasses."

"Bit early for that isn't it?" replied Laura.

"No, not at all."

They sat on the rug and took the gifts out of the stockings one by one in turn, sipping champagne and giggling as they went. Tom had bought for her bath oil, a little make-up bag, some perfume, some blue earrings and some pretty undies. She bent forward and stroked his face.

"Thank you so much you wonderful man."

"I think that may be something in the bottom of the stockings still," he said.

She picked it up and pushed her hand right down into the toe. Her fingers clutched on a round object, she looked at Tom with a frown.

"Go on," he said.

She pulled it out and gasped it was the most gorgeous solitaire diamond ring she had ever seen. "Oh Tom!" she gasped.

He passed her glass to her and said, "Here's to us my darling, please have it as your engagement ring."

"But, we have only known each other for a few days," she said.

"No, four years and a few days, get it right, and that's long enough for anybody," Tom said. He took the ring from her and put it on her finger. Much to the surprise of both of them it fitted perfectly. "Is it a yes?" he asked.

"Yes, it's a yes!" she replied.

"And now I am going to put the clip on the rest of the champagne while we go and have a shower together for the first of many hundreds of time I hope, and then we will get ready to enjoy this wonderful Christmas."

Together they had the most wonderful Christmas. They walked across the fields from Tom's house and into the woods where they walked through the leaves kicking them in the air, just like children, they held hands as they walked, giggled and just enjoyed being alone together, they talked a lot, just finding out how similar they were liking many of the same things. They would return to the cottage with rosy cheeks, and sometimes Tom would chase her saying, "Wait till I get you home woman, I'm going to beat you."

Once inside they would take off their coats, and sometimes a lot more. Making love was just so wonderful, sometimes fast and furious as though it was the last time ever, other times long, luxurious, indulgent for each other but always passionate.

On the Saturday after Christmas Laura was in the kitchen and heard Tom answering the phone. He came out to her saying, "I'd completely forgotten it was going to be New Year's Eve in a couple of days and that was one of my friends, Eric, on the phone reminding me that I had said I would join them to celebrate, there will be about ten of them, plus us if you like, it's black tie and a rather nice Italian restaurant about half an hour from here. So what do you think?"

"Yes I think that would be nice. Don't you?"

"Well yeah, after all we've not seen anybody else for five days, not that I'm complaining my darling, just to have been alone with you has been the most wonderful time of my life. So shall I ring him back and say we'll go?"

"Yes."

The New Year Eve's party was super. Laura enjoyed meeting Tom's friends and their wives and girlfriends.

The next day, New Year's Day was to be their last together and was something they were both aware of but didn't mention to each other, tomorrow they both must return to work and step back into the real world. Without discussing it much they decided Tom would drive her back to her place about seven o'clock. He told her he had to fly to Zurich on a ten a.m. flight on Wednesday morning, returning Friday night.

It was a business meeting, so there was no getting out of it, he had to attend and this would happen from time to time, he explained to her.

They spoke very little on the way to her house. She touched his arm and thigh from time to time and he returned it with a smile.

"Chin up," he said, "I'll be back on Friday." He carried the cases just inside her front door. He squeezed her hand saying, "If I do any more I'll never leave, just go inside shut the door and don't look at me driving away."

And so he was gone. She had to work very hard not to cry, everything had been so wonderful, meeting him again, being engaged, loving him so much it hurt, it has been like a whirlwind. She felt very lonely and realised, perhaps for the first time in her life since her father had died, that she felt wanted and loved. Now she must get her act together. There were two things she must do, one she must phone Ross and explain about meeting Tom. Not that that would be too difficult as really he had only ever been a friend. And then there was Richard. Of course he had told her wouldn't be around until ten days into the New Year but she felt it might be difficult to explain things to him, so she felt in all fairness she must try to see him as soon as possible. Yes she would go to the showroom, she didn't think they closed until five thirty p.m. and so, if she could get away promptly from the office either tomorrow or Thursday that would be the best idea. She didn't really want to leave it until Richard maybe visited her, not that he wouldn't be welcome, but it could prove to be more difficult. She decided to phone Ross straightaway, she thought he would be home from Scotland by now ready for work in the morning.

She realised dialling his number she was a little nervous. But hearing his voice she found it quite easy to talk to him. Dear Ross was so kind and understanding and wished her all the best for the future.

She said to him, "You are always welcome to come and see us, I am sure you and Tom would like each other." She wished him Happy New Year and said goodbye. Having got that over she took the cases upstairs and unpacked them, got things ready for work in the morning and decided to have an early night.

Larry was the first to notice. "Hey Laura, is that an engagement ring, have you been keeping secrets from us? Who's the lucky guy, do I know him?"

"Yes, it's Tom. Tom Blakeslee."

"You're joking! I don't believe it, I know he's quite a guy but you and Tom, you could have only known each other for less than two weeks or so."

"Four years and nearly two weeks roughly," she replied.

The news soon went around the office, followed by congratulations hugs and handshakes all around. Mr Casey returned from his lunchbreak about two-ish as he walked through reception and he looked at her saying, "I hear congratulations are in order Laura, would you please come into my office for a few moments?"

"Of course, I'll be right with you."

"Well I'm pleased to hear your news. I gather the writing will be on the wall for us, so may I ask you what are your plans for the future? You must know what an asset you have been to my company and if you have wedding plans, perhaps I could have some warning so as we can together find a suitable replacement."

"Oh there are absolutely no plans for a wedding Mr Casey, you would realise neither of us are teenagers and I think we need time to adjust to things after all we have both had up to now very independent lives. I promise to keep you informed. Did you have a good Christmas and a New Year?"

"Sit down Laura, as you ask I will tell you. Jackie my wife invited her parents to stay, they are very nice, I like them but when they're with us Jackie puts the shutters up, we have a big old house with thick walls but we can't have sex in case they hear us, good God she has two brothers and a sister, does she think the stork delivered them to her mother and father? Then there's our two kids. Our daughter arrived Christmas Eve with boyfriend Emmanuel, one of the great unwashed, long-haired, creeping Jesus sandal-wearing, out-of-work artist types. She promptly announces that she hopes she is pregnant by Emmanuel, because Emmanuel would like that, but they do not plan to marry because Emmanuel wouldn't like that. Then shortly after that bombshell our son arrives with a friend who we knew was coming, seemed quite a nice guy until we are told they only need one bedroom as they are lovers. Jackie as usual produced a wonderful Christmas spread for us all showing absolutely no disapproval of the kids even though underneath she wanted to kill the pair of them. Anyway late Boxing Day the kids departed. Emmanuel driving our daughter's car. What's he do? Runs over our cat and costs me £1,000 for the operation for three broken legs plus £100 a day for convalescence plus food, I ask you plus food, I think I'm in the wrong business. Anyway by New Year's Day morning Jackie's parents had gone and we had decided to have a few local people in for drinks. One couple living about a quarter of a mile away admittedly just across the field as the crow flies told us that our Labrador had buggered their pedigree dachshund and would we pay for the operation to terminate the pregnancy? Jackie said apologetically, of course we will, and then got really cross with me for saying no, which resulted in them leaving early and consequently Jackie not speaking to me for the next day. I wouldn't have minded but our poor dog is seventeen years old, so arthritic his daily walk is from the front door to the car. We have to lift him in, take him for a ride with the window down so as he can get some nice smells, yes we must be bonkers, and then lift him out when we get back. If we take him down the garden for a pee we have to go with him in case he falls over. So how the bloody hell did he get to their dog? By taxi? No way, no way, I think. Then before getting here this morning I had to go for just a normal check-up at the doctor's and then his nurse phoned a little later to say my blood pressure was high and not too surprising and they wanted to see me tomorrow for another test and to top it all some uninsured bastard ran up the back of my car on the way here. So with all that and no chance of getting my leg over at home, I may as well have stayed here with a TV, a bottle or two of whiskey and a takeaway."

"So I gather that's a no." Said Laura

With that Mr Casey smiled and they both fell about in helpless laughter.

The next day she was able to leave a little bit earlier than usual, so just before five o'clock she was at Richard's showrooms. She walked in to be greeted by someone who was almost a clone of Richard. She quickly assumed it must be his brother but he was not so tall, and she instantly noticed his hard eyes whereas Richard had a very pleasant smile and air of charm about him. This man gave her the feeling that he had a smell under his nose as though, if she was a customer, she was definitely a person beneath him; in fact he slightly unnerved her. Why was he here, had something happened to Richard?

"Good afternoon, madam, and what do you want?" he asked.

Laura wanted to say certainly nothing of yours, but instead replied, "I've come to see Richard."

"Why and what for? There is nothing he can do for you that I can't," was his reply.

Laura didn't know what was going on but immediately her hackles were rising, how rude and arrogant this man was. "Well that's just where you're wrong, and why I wish to see him is none of your business. Is he here?"

With that Richard appeared. "Laura, how delightful to see you, I'm sorry I've been so busy I haven't managed to speak to you. I do want to talk to you, could we have dinner together tonight?"

This was the last thing she wanted to do. She felt it may make what she had to say more difficult. "I'm really sorry Richard, but I can't tonight."

All the time they were speaking this objectionable character was stood listening and watching. She would've found it so easy to tell him not to be so rude and ignorant, but she held her tongue.

"Well could we just manage a coffee just along at our little bistro, please?" he said with almost pleading eyes.

She didn't have the heart to say no. Without a word Richard got his jacket, caught hold of her arm, opened the door for her and they stepped out onto the pavement.

"Who was the horrible person Richard?"

"My brother unfortunately, take no notice of him, wait till we get inside and I'll explain everything."

They were greeted as normal by the very friendly owner who they now knew quite well. Richard looked at him and then at Laura.

"Let's make it a bottle of wine, that will take us longer to drink than coffee. Yes, bring us a bottle of the dry white we normally have and just a few nibbles to go with it please, Jacko."

He led her over to a table in the corner, took her jacket and held out the chair for her. Sitting down himself, he leant across the table saying, "Dear sweet Laura such a lot has happened since I last saw you. My father for my Christmas present said he was extending the business and bringing in my brother Perry as another partner. What an impossible situation, my brother and I just don't get on and as I tried to explain to my father in a village like this you need to be courteous and friendly, not my brother's best points. This has been brewing for about six weeks now and I could see there would be no changing father so I applied back to Peugeot where I worked before and, to my amazement, they gave me a good position with a good salary and I start there in Paris in two weeks' time. I'm actually leaving on Monday. I would've been so see you before then, but I need to find an apartment and get myself sorted out. I'm so sorry Laura," he said taking hold of her hands and looked very closely at her. "Will you forgive me? And I suggest that if you need anything done to your mower you go to the workshop. Please say something."

"Richard I came here today feeling sick and sad to tell you my news, but now you have told me yours I don't feel so bad. Tell me, you do have many friends in Paris so do you feel you will make a new life there and perhaps find someone you would feel you could love enough to marry?"

"Oh I just don't know Laura, I have to admit and perhaps only to you that I'm a bit gutted at the situation here with the business. We also have had such a good relationship and sex you must admit and I know I will always have a place in my heart just for you; but I think we also understood that it wasn't a love story, we just enjoyed the pleasures we gave each other and the time we spent together, and now I think you are going to tell me that you have found that person."

"Yes, I am Richard. And I'm also going to tell you that I lied to you about tonight and that if you still want to take me out to dinner I am free."

"Fantastic, I cannot think of anything better. Shall we just stay here or would you rather go somewhere more glamorous?"

"Here will do fine, if you remember this is the first place we'd ever had a coffee together so as we can part friends, it seems the perfect place to do it."

# Part 2

# The Manley Brothers

# Chapter Fifteen

*Four years later*

Tom and Laura had now been married for two years, Tom's contract with Shell had almost finished but as well as paying him a fantastic bonus they had asked him if he would stay on and do some consultancy work when needed. This meant he had to become self-employed, some days working at home and some days on site, he was beginning also to pick up work from other companies. In the last six months with Shell he had been working on the Solent, right down on the south coast. He liked the area very much and had often said to Laura that he would like them to settle down there one day. On his daily drive to and from work he had noticed a large detached house being constructed and would often go home and speak about it to Laura and on occasions when Laura had gone down with him he had always pointed it out to her. It was six weeks before he was due to officially leave that he noticed the gardens had been landscaped and curtains were at the windows. Feeling almost obligated to look he stopped the car got out, seeing there was nobody about he walked round, being nosy enough to look in the windows.

    The carpets had been laid and he could see some very nice pieces of antique furniture. Yes, this was certainly something that he could imagine he and Laura would be very comfortable living in. He walked back to the car and continued on his way home, eager to tell Laura about it.

    Four weeks later driving home he couldn't believe his eyes, there at his dream house was a For Sale board. He passed it almost before he could stop, he knew he had to back up and take another look. Yes, there it was for sale; he grabbed a piece of paper from the seat beside him and scribbled down the agent's telephone number. He didn't know why, he knew the price would be way out of their league, but he just felt compelled to find out all about it. Why was it on the market now? Why had there been no board up during construction? Why were the curtains up and the carpets laid? Why? Why? Why?

Tom's mind was working overtime. He couldn't wait to get home to tell Laura about the house being for sale. He was mentally doing the sums in his head as to whether they could afford the house, after all their assets were quite good with his bonus money together with the money they could raise if they sold both their houses. He had a very small mortgage on his house and Laura had nothing outstanding on hers so perhaps, if the new house was not too much money, maybe they could get a bridging loan or a small mortgage?

Stop surmising, he said to himself, wait until you get home and discuss it logically with Laura. The traffic seemed particularly heavy this evening, or was he just imagining it?

Arriving at the cottage he jumped out of the car grabbing the piece of paper with the agent's number on it. Key in the lock he was shouting, "Laura! Laura! Come quickly." She came rushing down the stairs.

"Whatever is the matter?" she asked searching his face for an answer. "What's gone wrong? Have you had an accident?"

"No, nothing like that, it's our house, it's for sale. I can't believe it Laura, when I drove by on the way home there's a For Sale board outside. I've got the name of the agent here, I'll just give then a quick ring in case they are still open." He grabbed the phone and dialled the number.

"I'm just inquiring about the house for sale in Chester Street. Can you tell me what is the asking price?" Laura heard him ask followed by, "Oh really, could we make arrangements to view it tomorrow? Yes, ten thirty a.m. will be fine." There was a pause. "My name is Tom Blakeslee, my wife and I look forward to meeting you tomorrow."

As he put the phone down they looked at one another in disbelief.

"I know we will not be able to afford it, but what did he say the price was?" she asked, not really wanting to hear the answer.

"It's £400,000," he replied.

"Can we please. I would just like it without even seeing inside."

"Well I think we just have to do the sums. You make some tea, I'll get some paper and pen, and we will see what we can raise."

The tenants who were renting Laura's house were happy to buy it, which was a quick sell; they put the cottage on the market and miraculously a buyer came along quickly, offering a bit less than they wanted but they decided to take the offer as a bird in the hand is better than none. And so together with Tom's bonus and a bit from Laura's trust they scraped the money together. Within three months they had moved south.

It was Monday and Tom was off to meet a new client, leaving some mail for Laura to see to in the local post office. After saying goodbye to Tom she tidied round and decided to walk down into the village which was some ten minutes away. They both loved their new surroundings and found the village people very friendly. Always ready with a hello and a smile, so different from living in London.

Arriving at the post office there was the normal queue which was never a problem as people chatted together while they waited. As Laura stood there she was reading the notice board only to see a card saying WANTED GIRL FRIDAY, SOME LEGAL KNOWLEDGE HELPFUL. PHONE MR HENRI ON 730730. Soon the queue had gone and she found herself at the window being greeted by Rita, the postmistress. A cheery happy lady that seemed to know everything about everybody. Laura asked her for the stamps she required and realising there was nobody waiting behind her she inquired about the girl Friday advert.

Rita was delighted to give her information, but prefixed it with, "Are you looking for job then Mrs Blakeslee?"

The fact the she knew Laura's name quite surprised her. "Well, I don't know. Not really, but it sounds interesting, do you know anything about it?"

"Oh yes, it's the Manley boys, very nice, very respected, just suit you down to the ground." With that she slipped a piece of paper under the window saying, "That's the number, save you writing it down. It's the big house just three doors inside Chester Street, opposite side of the road to you up there on the top of the hill. So you could walk down and back, quite easy for you, just bring the car when it rains."

Laura took the piece of paper thinking Rita was speaking as though Laura had got the job already. With a smile and a cherry goodbye she left the post office. On the way home she made a point of looking at the house just three doors up as Rita had explained. She quickly realised it was a solicitor's office, reading on a rather black brass plaque: Manley, Manley and Manley. She walked on up the hill feeling slightly curious, perhaps she should find some work after all, the house was in perfect order, and the garden, and although they were not on the breadline a little extra cash would be useful, she still had some money in her trust but they had decided to keep it in case a rainy day ever came She got indoors, made herself coffee and decided to ring Mr Henri. Dialling the number she heard a very pleasant, well-spoken voice answering, "730730."

"I'd like to speak to Mr Henri if that's possible please."

"That's me, can I help?"

"Well, I noticed your advert in the post office today and wondered if you could give me a little more information please."

"I think the best idea would be if you came to see us. Shall we say ten thirty a.m. tomorrow? Will that suit you?"

"Yes. That would be fine, my name is Laura Blakeslee."

"Fine Laura, I will meet you in the front hall, just push the front door open and walk in and I will be there to greet you, thank you for calling, goodbye."

Laura put the phone down wondering what she had let herself into, but it was only an interview. Her thoughts went to this Mr Henri, he sounded middle-aged with a delightful tone of voice, well-spoken but not with a plum, and who was the us? She really should have asked a bit more. Perhaps they were looking for a cleaning lady that could answer the phone, she giggled to herself.

When Tom came home she explained to him what she was doing tomorrow. He laughed saying, "Better look out, might be some old man wanting a bunny girl type secretary, better have your best and sexiest undies on."

As it got to ten thirty the next day Laura was feeling a bit apprehensive, especially with Tom's teasing. She arrived at Mr Henri's door a few minutes before time. Pushing open the door she stepped into a large reception room to be greeted by a well-dressed gentleman in a dark pinstriped suit holding his hand out to shake hers saying, "Laura, I presume? I'm Mr Henri."

"That's correct, good morning," she replied. His handshake was firm and strong, something Laura liked in a man.

"Well come this way," he said pointing to the door on his left, "come and meet my brothers." He held the door open for her and there stood two more well-dressed men. "Let me introduce you to Mr William and Mr Robert." They all shook hands and Mr Robert held out a seat for her.

She noticed both the men were very well dressed, Mr William in a dark blue suit with immaculate shirt and tie and somehow she didn't know why but she warmed to him. Mr Robert also very well dressed in a pale grey suit with lilac shirt and tie, topped with a shock of bright red hair.

"Well now let us explain what we are looking for. I gather you have some legal experience or perhaps you wouldn't have answered our advert?" said Mr Henri.

"Yes," said Laura. "I'm a qualified homicide barrister, but for the last few years I have done organisation in legal offices dealing with appointments for clients organising staff and general running of the practice. I can supply references if you so wish."

"Sounds just the thing we are looking for, what we need is someone to update us. We have computers but don't use them with efficiency, somebody to organise our appointments and the whole set-up in general. We are not a busy office but just need sorting out. Now if Mr Robert shows you around, you can see the task you would be confronted with."

Mr Robert stood up. "What a good idea," he said pointing to the door.

Laura found she was obediently following him. There was four large rooms off the main entrance each brother having one as his office and Mr Robert pointed out that the fourth could be Laura's. Beyond these four rooms were two smaller rooms, one as a kitchen with a lot to be desired for and the other a bathroom and toilet, clean but very antiquated: the end wall was oak panelled. Going up from the entrance was a beautiful wide curved staircase, across the entrance to this was a rope from which a *Strictly Private* sign hung. They returned to the office where the other two brothers were; the three brothers in turn shook Laura's hand saying, "Please write your phone number here and we will let you know."

Laura left the office thinking What a waste of time, but couldn't help but giggle to herself all the way home.

That evening she and Tom were off to a barbeque at some friends that Tom had made while working at Shell. They were an easy couple to be with and they all got on very well together. They had to be there around six o'clock and Laura knew Tom may well be late getting home, so she decided about four o'clock to go and have a bath and get ready, so if he was late she could help him get ready. From time to time through the day she had chuckled to herself about the Manley boys, as Rita had called them; they were charming she had to say, all three seeming so different, they intrigued her she had to admit but as for working for them she couldn't begin to guess what that would be like, but then that wasn't her problem as she probably would never see them again.

As she lay in the bath she was surprised to hear Tom's keys in the lock. "I'm up here," she called out to him. "Come on up I'm in the bath."

"OK, two minutes I'll be with you." He appeared with two cups of coffee, handing her one and pecking her on the nose he sat down on the bath surround.

He looked tired, she thought. "Was it a good day?" she asked.

"Yes it was, I'd really like to get the contract. It would be good for us financially and I think could lead to more work."

She nodded and smiled at him, he put his cup down and took hers away from her and leant down to kiss her properly.

The look of her naked never ceased to arouse him. He explored her mouth with his tongue and she responded. He passed his hand over her breasts and then down between her thighs, she wriggled appreciatively, she stayed there for some minutes, as he sat back she splashed some water over him.

"Look you've made me all wet," he said laughing.

"Then come on in with me, because you've made me all wet," she said with a grin.

"No, I would rather come in you if you get out of the bath." He picked up her bathrobe from the floor and held it up for her, she stood up waiting to be wrapped in it but he dropped it down and picked her up and carried her to the bed.

After their lovemaking they both lay back exhausted and Tom dozed. Laura just revelled in the delight of it all. She looked at the clock not sure if Tom had anything to do before they went out, so looking at him lying there naked she decided to wake him by running her hand over his body.

He opened his eyes and looking at her he said, "You are so bad, you're not going to have it again. Well not until later tonight if you're good, you little tramp."

"I was only trying to wake you up in the way I know you like best because we will have to get ready soon for the barbecue."

He sat up and swung his legs off the bed. "Yes I know but I have just a couple of things to jot down about the work today, I will have to be there all day tomorrow as well, but I think it will be worth the input."

They were up early the next morning and, over a little breakfast, Tom remembered about Laura's job interview. "So how did that go yesterday for that job?" he asked.

"Well, nothing really," she replied starting to giggle. "It was really weird. Three well-dressed, well-spoken charming men who never did really give much information about the job, showed me around, said they wanted to be updated, asked me to leave my phone number and that was it. I must say the house itself was super, in need of TLC and a good muck out so I don't really know what to say. Shouldn't think I fitted the bill."

With that he got up, picked up his briefcase, gave her a squeeze and hug and a kiss and was on his way.

Laura decided she'd do some gardening that morning so after doing a few jobs indoors she was just putting her boots on when the phone rang.

"Good morning Laura," said the voice on the other end.

She recognised it immediately at Mr Henri from yesterday. "Good morning to you Mr Henri," she replied slightly surprised at his call.

"We would like you to come down to the office this morning at nine thirty, if that's possible?"

She paused for a moment intrigued. "Yes, that will be fine." Putting the phone down she looked at her watch: just thirty minutes to get ready and get down there, what a surprise. Somehow she didn't think they would be asking to see her to say she hadn't got the job, so what was this?

She was down outside the office with five minutes to spare. Standing back she took time to look at the house, it really was a fine example of a Georgian property although right on the road it occurred to her that possibly, when it was built, the road was much narrower. She opened the door and stepped inside. There stood the three brothers, all smiling.

They each shook hands with her warmly and she was ushered into Mr William's office once again. What took place in the next hour Laura was to remember for the rest of her life.

It was Mr William who began to speak.

"Now, what we would like you to do is to take on the job of running the office for all three of us bringing us up-to-date computer wise, organising the redecorating of the place, only downstairs nothing to be done upstairs or in the rooms upstairs at all. There may at times be a small amount of legal work but very minimal, as after all the practice is very small now. Robert here deals with conveyance. I deal with wills, and Henri here deals with divorce. So once the computer system is up and running we would do our own paperwork, but we would want you to check it and mail it. So as you will probably realise we don't deal with much homicide," he added with a smile. He continued, "Over the next few days we would like you to put together a plan of how you think we could improve the place décor wise together with costing also the cost of new equipment that you think we might need, we do like to use as much local business as possible. Now over to you, Henri."

Mr Henri cleared this throat. "We would each pay you 100 pounds per week in three separate cheques, we will place into a separate bank account £30,000 for equipment, décor, to be topped up as and when needed. Every Friday by eleven o'clock you would give us a breakdown of expenditure and the remaining balance of the account. On the whole we work Monday to Thursday nine a.m. to one o'clock. On Fridays we work nine a.m. to eleven o'clock. You will sign all cheques together with one of us and sometimes we extend the bank holiday weekends to a longer period. We will of course need your signature on some forms we have here for the bank. And as a postscript we would all like hot chocolate at eleven o'clock except Fridays. Now Robert will walk round with you again, you'll need pad and pen to make some notes."

Mr Robert, today looking very dashing in a blue suit, stood up saying, "Come on Laura let us look, this is so exciting I can't tell you how I'm feeling, especially about the new idea of hot chocolate."

Laura thought, I don't know about you but I'm in a complete whirl. Pen and pad in hand off they went, she made a few notes particularly about the kitchen and bathroom but much of it she just visualised. Each office had a computer, not particularly old but she guessed needing new software. There was no fax machine or copier, and the telephones looked like antiques. As they came back into the main reception area where the beautiful staircase was roped off, she inquired if this was living accommodation.

"Good grief," said Mr Robert with a wave of his hand, "just for storage darling, but it is a no-go area most definitely. But I must say you cannot possibly know how grateful I am to have a female around." And then looking at her with head slightly on one side he said, "Oh, I didn't mean to offend you. I just think we could be two of a kind on the fashion front."

Laura could hardly contain herself at this statement but she returned his look with a smile, feeling just a little more sure that Mr Robert was perhaps AC/DC. They went back into Mr Williams' room where the forms for the bank were ready to sign. Laura at this point was not quite sure if this was an indication that she had the job or did it all hang on her plan and costing? Trying to think clearly, which was becoming increasingly difficult by the minute, she said, "Would it be better for me to sign the form when I bring back my suggestions as they may not suit your ideas, you may dislike them."

"We won't," said Mr Robert. "And anyway we need to get it to the bank to set things up."

"Am I to understand I have a job?" Laura asked feeling rather pushy.

"Oh yes," Mr Henri replied, who appeared to be the slightly more business like of the three.

She became a little bolder saying, "May I ask if there is a trial period?"

"No, that's all right. You'll like us, we are quite easy," said Mr Henri.

"So when would I be expected to start?" she cagily asked.

"Well if you can get things going, come in Friday nine thirty and we will take it from there. Does that suit you?"

"Yes," said Laura, thinking what have I got myself into?

"Good then. Robert, perhaps you will see Laura out."

She stood on the pavement outside thinking was this a dream? It was really quite crazy, could it be for real?"

# Chapter Sixteen

Laura walked on up the hill to her home, amused, confused, but also with the feeling of excitement and anticipation. If she really was to be given a free hand in reorganising the redecorating this set-up it was a challenge that she knew she would enjoy. She put the key in the lock and let herself in, she didn't know if she wanted a coffee, a brandy or paracetamol. She looked at her watch and was surprised to see it was just before eleven o'clock, it seemed as though a whole day had passed. She decided a glass of red wine was in order.

Tom wouldn't be home until late afternoon at the earliest she thought, so she set about getting her ideas onto paper and looking in the telephone directory for local builders, decorators and cleaning people who she could get estimates from for her ideas. She knew she had to get the office equipment sorted out but she was hoping to twist Tom's arm to go with her to help make decisions. In her opinion the kitchen and the bathroom were the biggest jobs to be done, whereas the offices and reception area needed no real structural alterations, just redecoration and some new furniture. Before she realised it the time had gone and she had done nothing towards their evening meal. She was busily peeling the potatoes when Tom arrived home.

He came up behind her at the worktop in the kitchen putting his arms around her and kissing her gently on the back of the neck, something he knew she loved. She could feel his body hard against her, something she could normally never resist.

"Yes, I think we've got the work, I'll know on Friday when I go back. But now, it's been a long two days and I just want to relax with you in the way we like best," he said pushing his body now even harder against her.

She slipped out of his grasp and to his utter amazement said, "No, I haven't the time. I have so much to say to you so best to put that thing under control and listen to me."

Tom was stood with his mouth open and perhaps a little afraid of what she would say to him. Never since they had become lovers had she ever refused him, just what was going on? He sort of stomped off into the lounge, followed by her.

"So what's so important to come between us like this?" he questioned, looking very straight at her.

She giggled and planted a little peck on his cheek. "Don't be such a sulky baby, it's just that so much has happened today that I'm bursting to tell you, I haven't stopped loving you so don't worry. Let's just cuddle up on the sofa and I'll tell you. But no hanky-panky until I've finished."

"You my girl will not get any so-called hanky-panky after refusing me," said Tom.

"Don't be silly, you know you couldn't stand it. Anyway you now have a working wife. I've got that job at the solicitors."

"You don't say so? But do you really want it Laura? You don't have to work, you know."

"No I know I don't, but I think this could be quite easy once I get it sorted out and it's close to home, quite a challenge but interesting and different I think. It's really only part time, so I'm happy to give it a go if that's OK by you?"

"Yes that's fine, when do you start?"

"Well I would think next Monday, but I have to draw up some ideas and costing for Friday. So I was thinking perhaps you might be able to give me a hand."

"Hey, I'm not on the payroll. Incidentally, how much are you going to get?"

"Well it's an odd system. I'll get three separate cheques one from each partner of £100 each."

"So what are you expected to do for this, take your clothes off et cetera?" Tom laughed.

"Don't be silly, this is just what makes it interesting, they want me to organise and run the office, but best of all they want me to update the ground floor area, with a working capital of £30,000 with one of the partners and myself able to sign the cheques, and all. Yes Tom, working Mondays to Thursdays nine to one and Fridays nine to eleven o'clock, not bad eh?"

"Got to be a catch somewhere, seems too good to be true, but from what you said from the first interview they were a little odd. Still give it a go."

"Yes, that's what I think. I also thought that if you had a little time tomorrow and are going to be working from home, perhaps you would come and help me chose and get some prices for the office equipment, they want me to use as many local people as possible and there is a shop in the village where I think we could get or they could order most of the equipment."

Tom looked at her, wagging his finger saying, "Yes I'll come, but only on the understanding that this new adventure of yours doesn't get in the way of me getting my leg over with you, like it did just now."

She snuggled up close to him put her hand on his crotch saying, "I promise, cross my heart hope to die."

By Thursday evening Laura had all the details ready for Friday morning. Tom had given her a lot of help and they had found what they thought would be a suitable computer, printer, photocopy machine and shredder. They had contacted two local builders with a view to giving estimates for work to be done. Also a cleaning firm. She had produced three copies of her ideas, one for each brother. She had packed into a bag a kettle, half a dozen bone china mugs which she had left unused in the cupboard, some sugar in a container, a large jar of drinking chocolate, some teabags and a spoon, some antibacterial spray, a cloth, rubber gloves and some loo cleaner. Tom was leaving home at eight in the morning and she planned to be at the office just after nine o'clock.

Opening the door and walking in she could see Mr Henri at his desk on the left and on the right Mr William at his. They both looked up as Mr Robert appeared out of his office, walking towards her with a welcome smile by which time the other two brothers were in the reception room.

"Come now," said Mr William, "let's all go into my office and see what you have to deliver, Laura."

Sitting down in front of the three of them she felt a little nervous, but she swallowed hard and, taking the paperwork out of her briefcase, she began by saying, "I have prepared my ideas in triplicate making to easier for us all. I am concerned that you may think me rather impertinent and even rude, which I apologise for in advance."

"Not at all," replied Mr William. "That is exactly what we have asked for." Already he was looking at the notes.

"Well," began Laura, "As far as the office equipment is concerned I have listed that on the front page, I think if I have a computer in my office which will link to all of yours I would be able to give each one of you details of your daily appointments. Always assuming you are familiar with the general workings of the computer."

"Yes we are," replied Mr Henri.

"Particularly when we have a difficult case that we pass on to the London office," chuckled Mr Robert.

This was something Laura didn't know about, a London office, but decided she would question that later.

"As far as the office itself is concerned, if I may be so bold to suggest I take the empty office on the left-hand side adjacent to Mr Henri's where it will be easy for me to come to reception as soon as somebody enters through the front door. I would like to place the Queen Anne table across the staircase replacing the strictly private sign with a large silk flower arrangement on a large pedestal." She noticed this seemed not to go down too well so followed it with, "I had thought perhaps this was living accommodation but Mr Robert did explain on our tour that it was just storage, presumably the doors into each room would be locked." There was no comment from the three men so she moved on swiftly. "I have spoken to two local builders as I feel both kitchen and bathroom need to be refurbished, I suggest the bathroom which is very large could be made into a separate washbasin and loo for clients. Leaving enough room for a private loo, washbasin and even a shower for yourselves if you need perhaps to go on somewhere after work, saving the problem of going home first."

"Now that is a truly brilliant idea," said Mr William.

"Now as far as the kitchen is concerned I think the basic needs there are a sink, perhaps a microwave, a small fridge, a few basic units, you could spoil yourself with the dishwasher but I think me and a pair of rubber gloves would fit the bill."

At this point they all laughed, which really relaxed Laura and made her bolder.

"I think the dishwasher would be a good idea," said Mr Henri. "Yes, put that on the list Laura."

"Now for your offices I think they should all be recarpeted and because the windows are so elegant, it would be nice to have some curtains. I think they should all be the same. I could get some samples and you could come to an agreement on what you like, all the rooms need redecorating. I would suggest something like a magnolia emulsion or, considering the age of the house, wallpaper would possibly be more in keeping." She was now looking from one to the other of them seeing if the reaction was good or if she going far too fast.

They were all smiling, so she continued.

"There will of course be lots of little touches we can add as we go along. I would like to say though I find it strange that the only door out from the ground floor, apart from the front door, is in the kitchen."

"There is a door in the panelling that takes you through that room with the doors leading onto the patio and garden. I'm sorry, did I not point that you when we were looking around?" said Mr Robert.

"No, you didn't but that sounds interesting, perhaps we could look at that room some time? With regards to the reception area I think some extra lighting would be good, the Chesterfield is perfect, a small table suitable for a magazine and ashtray together with a couple of antique or repro chairs would make it more acceptable to the eye. You will see when you look at the details I have given you I have tried to set out my ideas with bullet points, which I thought you could tick or cross through as you wish." Then leaning slightly back she smiled at them all saying, "And so gentlemen, I rest my case."

To her absolute amazement they all stood up and clapped and she felt herself blush. She looked at her watch. It was just before ten o'clock, which surprised her; it seemed to have taken much longer. "And now may I suggest I make you all a cup of hot chocolate?"

"Wonderful," said Mr William, "but I don't know how."

"Trust me," she replied.

She went out into the reception and picked up the bag with the things she had brought with her. Going to the kitchen to put the kettle on, she returned not too many minutes later with the drinks.

"Only three cups and very nice ones too may I say, but where is yours?" asked Mr Robert.

"I didn't think it right for me to bring mine in and assume to drink it with you."

"Nonsense, go and get it," he said.

Returning with her cup she was thinking, I think I'm going to like this job.

"Now," said Mr Henri, "we have a few questions for you. Are you Mrs Blakeslee? Do you have a young family? Where exactly do you live? Do you drive here and if so, where to you park your car?"

Laura smiled. "Yes I'm married to Tom, we don't have a family, and we live in the new house here at the top of the hill. I will normally walk to work, but this morning as I had a bag to carry I drove down, I parked my car in the pub car park just a little further down the road on the opposite side, they were not around so I will go in on my way home and apologise."

"No need for that, we own the land there but we let the pub use it and it's good for the village so you have no problems there."

There was more chat about her ideas so she said, "I'm sure you'll want to look at my suggestions over the weekend so I'll wash the mugs up and be on my way. See you on Monday nine o'clock, I believe that's correct?"

"Yes, come back into here before you leave."

"Of course," she replied.

She wiped out one of cupboards and put all she had brought in that morning away. She put her coat on and went to say goodbye, when she remembered the comment about the London office.

"Excuse me," she said, "but may I ask will I be dealing with the London office?"

"No, no," said Mr Robert, "it is the old family practice but we just send work there that we don't particularly want to deal with, hence our comment to you that we don't have much homicide to deal with here. I think our two biggest cases, not homicide, of late are Mrs Daily, sixty-five years old used to putting everything on account, but the problem was she never paid the bill. She would go into the ironmongers here, pick up all sorts of things – drinking bowls for the dogs that she breeds, have to say she smells like one too – rolls of wire, netting the odd rake, couple of trays of dog food et cetera."

By this time they were all giggling, Laura included, even though she didn't know what she was giggling at.

"Mr Cook the shop owner was getting very fed up with this and arranged with Jack, the local bobby that he would phone him when Mrs Daily came into his shop and if she didn't pay he would apprehend her at the door as she left with the goods. Anyway Jack did as planned, but being a slight man and Mrs Daily being a large lady she brushed him aside, sending him to the floor, saying 'Speak to my solicitor Robert Manley, he will sort you out'. So after Mr Cook had dusted Jack off they arrived here at the office. After explaining everything to me I just paid Mr Cook a cheque for the whole outstanding amount avoiding a possible court case and prosecution for Mrs Daily, or even an assault of a police officer, and suggested that in future when she was in Mr Cook's shop he got one of his staff to walk round with her making a note of what she had, and sending the bill to us to pay. This of course meant I had to go and see her. I made arrangements to go early one morning on the way here. I rang the bell and she opened the door in her dressing gown, not a pretty sight I can assure you."

By this time there was a bit of a lull in the story as Mr Robert was laughing so much at what he was to tell next.

"'Hello dear boy you've just come in time I've dropped my corsets over the back of the boiler. Will you get them out for me?' What else could I do but say yes, not only was I covered in dogs' hairs, grease and dirt but so were the corsets and when I held them up they were holey with rusty metal pieces sticking out. I handed them to say saying, 'I think this is my good deed for the day so if you would just be kind enough to settle this bill I have paid for you at the ironmongers by writing a cheque, I will be on my way'."

Needless to say they were all laughing together at the story.

"And the other case if you care to hear it?"

"Yes, I would like to hear it if you have the time please," said Laura.

"It's not quite so pleasant," said Mr Henri, "but go ahead anyway," he indicated to his brother.

"So," began Mr Robert, "this was the story of Mr Cheeksman, OBE, decorated for First World War bravery, but sadly as the years passed he fell into decline, drank a bit and then a bit more with other good drinkers of the village, spending his pension on booze rather than food he eventually became an alcoholic. When he came out of the pub after drinking with his chums he would go onto the convenience store and buy a couple of bottles of vodka on the basis that it didn't smell on his breath. The fact that he couldn't walk straight gave the game away but of course he didn't realise that. Things went from bad to worse, his wife left him, and his daughter disowned him."

"Yes," chipped in Mr Henri, "and do you remember how he always wanted to shake your hand if he was able to see you, he was so filthy and the stink was indescribable!"

"Yes," continued Mr Robert, "by this time he was buying his two bottles of vodka as early as six in the morning he would go into the pub until two p.m. When they closed he'd come out intending to go home to sleep but often didn't make it and would fall into the hedge or someone's front garden so you could imagine how everybody talked about that. He would eventually wake at sometime late afternoon-early evening when he would drag himself up either to go home or straight back to the pub and at some point he would go to the convenience store again and pick up a sandwich or a pie but didn't pay. He didn't really even know where he was. But the manager was a kindly young man, he knew what was going on but chose not to take any action. Unfortunately he was off sick one evening when Cheeky went in nearly paralytic, the temporary manager, a woman, an absolute dragon to put it mildly, was not so kindly. Cheeky wandered around for quite some time, it was a very cold night and he probably was cold too, anyway he got to the vegetable display and decided to pee on the cabbages. To be honest it would've been better if he'd done the usual thing and peed in his trousers. Anyway to cut a long story short the dragon phoned the police and poor old Cheeky got carted off to the nick. And I don't know how but we were asked to take the case on and so we became involved. Asked in court what his defence was, he said he was very sorry but he had left his glasses at home and thought he was on the grass outside the shop. All of this of course was not a good enough excuse. Henri here was dealing with the case and fortunately knew the judge well so it was decided, if he could make some arrangements for Cheeky to go to a home for retired naval officers, there would be no further action. Henri did a brilliant job and for Cheeky it was the best thing that could've happened. He now has a beer at lunchtime and perhaps a couple of whiskies in the evening. In fact they say he has become an asset to the home."

"That's a lovely story," said Laura.

"And now young lady I think it's time for you to leave," said Mr William. "But first here is the bank statement showing the money we have deposited. We haven't got the cheque book yet but that will come in a few days no doubt. Here are your three cheques and we look forward to having you on the staff."

Laura looked at him in surprise. "I really don't think you should be paying me for this week, I've hardly done a thing."

"You have," he replied. "You've made us feel very happy about the prospects of the practice. And thank you."

As she left and walked to her car she felt a very warm feeling about these men, though she hardly knew them. Were they married? Did they have families? Where did they actually live? But somehow they seemed to have such a good relationship together she guessed as children they must've been brought up very close with lots of fun and love in their life. Perhaps in time she would learn more. If she had been speaking out loud that would've proved to be an understatement.

When Laura arrived home she decided to telephone the building firms she had spoken to about estimates for the kitchen and bathroom alterations. She felt the Manleys were quite eager to have these two rooms seen to even if they had reservations about some of the other ideas. Curiously she thought the least area they may not want to change was the reception, particularly removing the private sign at the bottom of the stairs. Perhaps she would just have to be a little patient with some things. After all they hardly knew her, but seemed to be putting a lot of trust in her.

Tom arrived home very early afternoon, she could tell as soon as she saw his face that he'd got the contract from this new company. Picking her up and squeezing her tight he said, "That was quite a lot of work and effort but now for the rest of the weekend I'm going to do the work and put the effort in on my lovely wife. But I suppose you will want to tell me how you morning has gone with Bill and Ben and the Flower Pot Men and the little Weed," he said laughing.

"Don't be so unkind, they really are very nice, and liked most of the new ideas. But you'll never believe they paid me for a whole week's work."

"You're kidding! You didn't do any, I did most of it. They couldn't have given you a whole £300 surely?"

"Oh, now you're interested."

"Yes maybe, they may want more from you than you think, and that's what I'm interested in. Don't forget I'm the one that sees to all the servicing of you."

"Tom, don't be so crude that's a horrible thought, they are probably all married with beautiful wives and families." She stopped for a minute to think: well, not too sure about Mr Robert, she giggled.

"Well enough about all that," he said heading for the kitchen. "Get your clothes off and get upstairs woman. I'm going to find a bottle of bubbly in the fridge for us to drink while you persuade me to make love to you. Go before I change my mind."

"You mean before it's too late by the look of you," she said pointing at him.

The weekend seemed to go so quickly but Laura did persuade Tom to go with her to make the final decision on the office equipment, especially the new computer. As the shop was in the village and they knew the Manleys they said they would order it which would take a couple of days. Normally they would want payment before ordering but would be happy to deliver to the office when it arrived and collect the cheque then.

# Chapter Seventeen

Laura opened the door to the office. Stepping into the reception area she could see to her left Mr Henri sat at his desk.

"Good morning," she said.

"Good morning to you," he replied.

Mr Williams' door was open to her right and she could see he was on the phone she raised her hand to him, he smiled and raised his. She realised at that point they would need to reorganise the telephone system, something she hadn't thought about on her brief tour last week. First on the notebook: get phone system.

With that Mr Robert appeared from his office all smiles, saying, "Hello Laura, can't wait to get started."

All three men were now standing with Laura in reception, and Mr Henri began by saying, "We have about an hour before William has his first client so let's get firing out of the blocks, we are very happy with all your ideas with a couple of exceptions William is not too sure that he wants to redecorate his room and we think we need to have further discussion about the private area upstairs. So if we come into my office , we can discuss where you intend to start."

Laura took off her jacket and got her pen and pad out of her briefcase, scribbling on the top 'BT' and then she began by saying, "Over the weekend I have ordered all the new office equipment which will be delivered within the next couple of days, to be paid for on delivery. I have arranged for two different local builders to come and give estimates for the kitchen and bathroom, one tomorrow morning and the other on Wednesday morning. Depending on what your redecoration ideas are we may ask them for estimates for this. I have contacted a cleaning firm who with your consent will completely clean the reception area, the panelling, the staircase, chandelier, the black-and-white tiled floor which I think should not be carpeted. They will clean and polish the furniture and wipe down the walls which I think do not need redecorating. I think this is where we should start and I suggest this should be done on a Saturday so as to cause least disruption. And if you are willing I would be happy to be here with them while they are working, but of course this means I would have to have the key as I assume none of you would wish to be here."

"That's perfectly OK," said Mr William.

"As far as the offices are concerned I think we should start with yours Mr Henri, then Mr William's and finally Mr Robert's. I estimate perhaps a maximum time for each as long as we are completely organised upon whether paper or paint et cetera, if we put a little thought into arranging appointments for each of you so as you could double up on the office so as not to be out of action. You must tell me what you feel," she said looking at them.

"I think we all agreed to go ahead," said Mr William. "One thing we all want you to do is to become familiar with all our existing and past clients this of course will entail quite a lot of reading for you, but as you have legal knowledge we think this would be a good thing. How do you feel about that?"

"Yes that's fine," replied Laura. "And in time I can get basic details on the computers so as when you come in the office first thing you can pull up the screen to see what clients are coming to you that day, and I will have the respective folders on their more intricate details on your desk. And until we get this set up I would like each day before I leave to look at your diaries for the next day. And I think that should start this morning as it should be my job to arrange all appointments for you of course to begin with. Until I get to know the clients and the way you as individuals like to work, I may need a little input from you as to your clients. It's now nine thirty-four a.m. and without seeming too bossy, I think I need to start my day," she said standing up.

"I would like to see you in my office at some point," said Mr Robert. "Perhaps when you come to check my diary."

Laura picked up her briefcase and handbag and headed towards her office. It was worse than she had realised the other day, but in time she had no doubt she would be allowed to improve it. She took herself off to Mr William's room just to get the name of his first client who should be arriving within half an hour, so as she could greet him appropriately and show him in. On she went to Mr Henri's took his diary, finally to Mr Robert's.

"Come in, come in," he said excitedly. "I've had the most wonderful weekend, darling. After you being here last Friday I went with one of my dear friends" – no name Laura noticed – "and found the most wonderful fabrics and things for my office and I would like your approval." As he walked towards the window picking up two large carrier bags, the first thing she thought was his hair was even brighter than before. Was that a friend's handiwork or had he been to the hairdresser? She had to admit he was wearing another beautifully cut suit, perhaps just a little too pale for the office, all of which fuelled her imagination of his sexuality. He floated around the office draping pieces of fabric here and there and everywhere from heavy brocades, too delicate laces. Together with pictures of pink Dralon-covered furniture. "As I told you the other day I'm so happy to have another girl around, I know we shall be great friends."

Laura wanted to say, where's the other girl? And she was finding it hard to be serious and keep a straight face. Some of the ideas he was suggesting she felt were more in keeping with the boudoir than an office, but she hoped in time she could steer him in the right direction, perhaps a cream leather suite or chairs rather than a pink chaise longue, after all his office was last to be seen to. So with this in mind she suggested they should talk more in detail about it later, which seemed to please him.

As she went across the hall to her office the front door opened. A tall middle-aged grey-haired man stepped inside dressed like a gentleman farmer. Knowing Mr William's first client was about to arrive and having made a mental note of his name, she ventured to say, "Good morning, you have an appointment with Mr William, I believe. Please take a seat and I will see if he's ready for you."

The man smiled in reply and sat down.

Laura tapped on Mr William's door which was a little open saying, "Mr Collins is here, shall I show him in?"

Mr William smiled at her in a rather bemused way. "Yes, please do."

And so the first week of working for the Manley boys took off. It had its chaotic, hilarious, disorganised moments. During that first morning she realised the thing she needed the most was just a telephone at hand. She had already moved the table that stood against the wall, across to the bottom of the stairs so at least she could stand behind it when a client came in to give the appearance of being part of the set-up. And when she left to go home that day she explained to Mr Henri that she was taking some of the files home, particularly the ones of the clients that had been in that morning, so as to make a start on understanding their needs. She also asked if she could arrange for an extension to the reception area, just for now. But perhaps they could give this some thought as to a new system, which she was happy to deal with when she got home.

"Absolutely fine," Mr Henri said, handing her a front door key. "Goodbye, see you tomorrow."

Tuesday and Wednesday had been taken up with the builders, BT for the telephone which she was delighted to have sorted and of course some clients. Each day she was taking some work home being very careful not to put Tom's nose out of joint although he always wanted to chat with her about the day's events with Bill and Ben and Little Weed. Thursday Tom left early to work away from home that day. So being able to let herself into the office she arrived there about eight a.m. She managed to get quite a few things sorted out without too many interruptions. Eventually all the brothers arrived though nobody had an appointment with clients until ten thirty. After greeting them all she made them all hot chocolate, something she had in mind to do most mornings instead of eleven a.m. once she was settled in and things were more organised. About some thirty minutes later the front door opened and in stepped a very attractive lady in her sixties, Laura estimated. She was wearing what could be described as a flasher's mac, beige in colour, having seen better days together with a large-brimmed black felt hat.

"Good morning," said Laura stepping out from behind the desk. "Can I help you?"

The woman pushed straight by her saying, "Don't be ridiculous girl, I'm here to see Williams," and with that walked straight into his office almost slamming the door behind her.

Laura stood back a little bemused. Don't know what that is all about, she thought to herself.

Some half an hour later the lady reappeared walking up to the desk, she said, "I knew it was a ridiculous idea to get some flibbertigibbet of a girl in. I suppose you come from the council houses at the back of the village. I suggest you go off and get some training in manners if you intend to stay here although I don't suppose you'll be here long My name is Mrs Longwait, ending in *th*, and don't you forget it. And furthermore..." then she was stopped in her tracks by Mr William.

"Effey," he said looking straight at her. She turned tossed her head and was gone.

He looked at Laura raised his eyebrows and laughed, he could see she had a look of what is that. "That was Ethel Longwait, really a dear old friend, but can be a bit of a dragon, I love her to bits, a bigger snob you never will find bless her heart. Sometimes she visits me three times a week but when she's very cross with me she stays away to punish me, sometimes for two weeks. I'm sure she will consider you to be one of her friends given time." With that he went back into his office.

All the new office equipment arrived on Friday and Mr Robert came out and gave them a cheque. When they had left Laura took the opportunity to ask him about the door in the panelled wall.

"Yes come," he said, "here look," as he slipped his hand under one of the horizontal panels about waist high, the door came open.

"What a beautiful room," said Laura as they stepped inside. It was the width of the house and about fifty foot deep with four eight-foot high arch-shaped French windows, it was filled with beautiful antique furniture all dusty and pushed up together. The curtains and carpet were very shabby and the windows very dirty, but she could vaguely see through them into what looked like a beautiful garden.

Mr Robert walked over to one of the sets of windows and opened them. He stepped outside and Laura followed him: the garden was truly magnificent, beautiful rhododendrons, high firs and scotch pines obviously lovingly cared for, flower borders and lawns like billiard tables perfectly edged, against the gold pea-gravelled paths. She could hardly believe her eyes, but could see he was looking at it with great pleasure.

"Who does all this?" she asked. "Is it you?"

"No, no I do like to put a little effort in but two of my boys do all the hard work and make it look magnificent. You probably haven't seen them because they come at weekends or on the lighter evenings after five. Make a good job don't you think?"

"Without a doubt," she replied. "I didn't realise you were married and had sons, you must be very proud of their work."

"Yes I am dear Laura. But I must tell you they are not my sons and I am not married. I feel you do understand."

They turned and walked back into the house.

Later that morning when it was time for the office to close she asked if she could confirm with the cleaners that they could start on the reception the next morning, Saturday, and if Tom her husband was free would it be OK if he came along with her to start the set-up of the new office equipment?

"That's fine," they said handing her her pay cheques.

Tom arrived home to find Laura making a bite to eat for lunch. He gave her a quick hug saying, "It is such a lovely day let's eat out on the patio, and you can tell me all about the day's happenings and if you've had another dressing down from Effey, or any other eccentric carryings on."

Laura laughed turning to say, "Perhaps we should talk about your day Mr Perfect."

"I'm going to open a bottle of wine to go with the lunch, is it nearly ready?"

"Just on," she replied.

After they'd finished eating they took the wine and their glasses over to the sun loungers.

"I think it would be nice to go out and eat tonight," said Tom, "but right now I think I'd like to do bad things to you."

Laura giggled. She always teased him about lying in the sun as it always made him randy. "Well I might let you do bad things to me if you would do good things with me tomorrow."

"Such as?"

"Will you come down to the office with me tomorrow and help me set up the new equipment? Because you're far more used to doing that sort of thing than I am, and I could show you around, none of the Manleys will be there only the cleaning people, please."

"It depends how quickly you get upstairs, or are you going to take your clothes off here? On second thoughts, perhaps that's not a good idea. Two on a sun lounger is possibly more uncomfortable than in the back of a car."

The lovemaking that followed was so passionate, exhausting and quick. Afterwards she just lay in his arms contented and at ease with the world. After some fifteen minutes he leant over her saying, "I'm sorry that was so quick, but sometimes I just can't contain my passion for you," he then kissed her on the forehead and then on the lips, exploring every part of her open mouth and she, in turn, explored his. With his free hand he cupped her left breast, which was so hard he knew she was ready to make love again; he gently moved down over her stomach to which she responded by opening her legs: she was warm and wet, something that always made him desire her even more. She wriggled in anticipation looking deep into his eyes and their lovemaking this time was long, luxurious and gentle; as he thrust into her she squeezed him with her pelvic muscles, making him groan with satisfaction. This time they came to the brink several times before climaxing exactly together.

He lifted himself away from her saying, "Darling Laura, I love you so much."

They must've laid there some half an hour, Tom just vaguely dozing, Laura relaxing but wide awake. After a while he woke. Putting his hands over hers, he said, "What are you deep in thought about? Did I not satisfy you or are you thinking of work again?"

"None of those things actually. I was just thinking how wonderful my life is with you, how happy you make me. To think if I hadn't come back from Canada and gone to that party that night, we may never have met up again."

He noticed a tear trickle down her face. "Please don't cry, that's all in the past, what happened to us before that time has made us the people we are."

"Yes I know, but it scares me to be so lucky. I don't deserve it, or you," she replied.

"No, you certainly don't deserve me, now dry your eyes, get out of bed you lazy bitch, go get showered and decide where you would like to go tonight to eat. And by the way, I will come with you tomorrow."

They were up bright and early the next morning and at the office by seven thirty. Laura showed Tom around explaining what was going to happen. She went to the panelled wall and, to her surprise, found the door opener quite easily.

"Don't you think this is a lovely room?" she asked him as they stepped inside.

"Yes, what's going to happen here? What plans do you have for this," he said looking around with interest.

"Well I haven't even discussed this with them, it's only a couple of days since I first looked in here as you know. But I'm fast thinking it would be a lovely room to sort out, it needs nothing structurally, just decorating, updating, perhaps I'll get the builder to take a look when he starts work. But just look out into the garden before we go back, look how beautiful it is. I don't know if Robert's boys will be here today, it will be quite interesting to see them. Perhaps we'll take a look later."

As they went to leave the room she noticed amongst the furniture stored at the end of the room two chairs which she thought would be ideal for the reception. Pointing them out to Tom they went over to them and lifted them out, all in perfect order no broken bits, just very dusty.

"Let's take them out and get the cleaners to see to them together with the rest of the furniture in reception, I think they'll do well instead of buying some more. Just think, I might have saved some Manley money."

Later in the morning, going back in the long room, they did see the boys in the garden. Laura went out and asked them if they would like a coffee and, after speaking to them, it only seemed to confirm the feelings she had about Mr Robert's sexuality.

By three months further on all the decorations and alterations including the long room had been completed, all furniture had been cleaned and polished new carpets laid and new curtains hung, even Mr William decided he would have his office refurbished after all. Laura had been given a complete free hand. Even down to removing the old strictly private sign at the bottom of the stairs where now stood a large pedestal basket of top quality silk blooms. She managed to persuade Mr Robert to have soft white leather furniture and modern pictures on the walls, which they chose together.

She duly produced an individual balance sheet each Friday as had been requested and was given her pay cheque in return. She always made sure she paid approximately the same amount from each brother's balance, sheet keeping things equal. To her this was definitely a different way of running things but they all seemed happy with the situation. She also had to check the balance in the account but it barely went below the stated amount as it had an automatic top up supplied to it. From where that came from, she was never sure.

She was slowly piecing together their lives as she was asked to deal with small incidental matters, rates, bits of maintenance, a cheque for plumber or gardener. It would seem they each had a house of their own. Mr Robert she grew to know most about as he always liked to have what he called girly chats with her. His home was an exclusive penthouse suite in an exclusive area overlooking the sea towards

Bournemouth, while Mr Henri's was a thatched cottage in the New Forest, very old and requiring a lot of upkeep. Whereas Mr William, who Laura had to admit was her favourite brother, had a house in Sandbanks in Poole in Dorset, a very exclusive area.

During this three-month period Mrs Longwait pronounced Longwaith made at least two visits a week to Mr William and now often stopped to have chats with Laura on her way out. How right Mr William was in describing her as a snob! She always spoke about her deliveries from Fortnum & Mason, normally in a hamper she would say. Laura remembered with a smile after her first few weeks there how she had said how glad she was that the Manleys had Laura to help them and of course she could see they had chosen her for her intelligence, smartness and knowledge of the law. Laura wanted to say that's a change of heart, on our first meeting you told me I needed some education, but she bit her tongue and smiled. She also talked a lot about Conrad and how he always liked to have an appetiser with the evening meal and he was particularly keen on quail's eggs and pumpkin seeds, of course the best from Fortnum & Mason and of course Mr William often dined with them, and so Laura assumed Conrad to be her husband. She then went on to say of course she always laid the table for dinner with linen, starched napkins folded correctly which of course looked best with her Royal Dolton bone china and best cut crystal glasses. And of course her male guests always wore black ties.

Laura always just nodded at all this information, just trying to keep her composure. She had a vision of the men sitting at Mrs Longwait's dinner party table nude apart from their black ties eating their Fortnum & Mason goodies, and this made her want to giggle.

Slipping into the office before the others on the first Monday after everything was finished, she placed a little note on each desk saying:

*In view of the fact I have so enjoyed refurbishing your offices and spending your money I think it's only right that you should inspect it all. How about 10 am in the front reception?*

*Hope to see you there, Laura.*

When Laura had told Tom what she had planned to do he said, "You're getting as barmy as they are. I can't believe they haven't looked round, and what about Mr Robert's room? How's that going to go down?"

"That will be all right as long as he's not wearing his new dusky pink suit."

He looked at her not knowing if she was kidding or not. But they both fell into fits of laughter.

"Laura," Tom said, "you wonder why I love you so much, it's because you're crazy."

Laura walked out into reception at exactly ten a.m. The three boys were there. She started the tour in the new bathroom as she knew they had been using the clients' one until then. She thought Mr Henri and Mr William seemed almost embarrassed by its luxury. But Mr Robert's swooned over it saying he thought it was quite divine. The kitchen was the next room and then a grand tour of one another's rooms.

"Bet you're glad you relented and had yours done William," said Mr Henri.

"Yes I am. And personally I think the new curtains look just super from the outside and of course the brightly shining nameplate, which Laura had to get the cleaners to polish up."

Finally she took them to the long room as she called it. She actually had a feeling that they truly hadn't bothered to look at it before. She could see they were all visibly delighted. With Mr Robert commenting how nice it was to see the garden through the windows now they were clean. They stood for what seemed quite some time without comment, and she wondered what was going through their minds. Did this room have any memories for them? Perhaps she would never know.

Then Mr William said, "I think we should have an office warming party. What do you think?"

Much to her surprise they seemed to like the idea – yes they would have a sort of cocktail party. Quickly the ideas came from all of them and just as quickly it was decided they would invite about twenty-five guests each. They would have caterers, waitresses and wine waiters. Perhaps Laura would arrange it? They all looked at her hopefully. She could bring her husband and perhaps half a dozen or so friends along. They would make a list of their guests and Laura would get the invites sent out. They set the date for six weeks ahead last Saturday, which gave a couple of weeks to get the invites out and about a month for people to reply.

"Is that OK by you Laura?" Mr William asked.

"Yes that's fine," she replied thinking this could be interesting. What friends did they have or would it be clients they invited? Just wait and see. "Do we have a budget for all this?" she inquired.

"No, we haven't had a party for years. No expense spared," said Mr Robert.

When Laura left the office and went home her head was full of thoughts of the party and serve her right, she had been landed with organising it. For starter she knew Tom wouldn't want to go to it let alone invite some of their friends, she would have to do some persuasion on this point. She knew Tom found it hard to take the Manley set-up seriously, but felt perhaps her related stories hadn't helped the impression he had of them.

Tom had been working at home this day, continuing on until about eight in the evening. Laura had prepared the sort of dinner that she could serve just when he felt ready for it. They finally ate about nine and watched a bit of television before going to bed. Tom went on ahead she made some coffee and took it upstairs for both of them.

Laying there drinking it Tom suddenly said, "Oh, how did the review of their own premises go for the boys?"

What a marvellous lead in, she thought. "Well as you ask it was good, but the biggest surprise of all was the long room. I really don't think they had even realised it had been done, so now they are going to have an office warming party to celebrate, inviting about twenty-five people or so each."

Tom began to laugh. "From what you tell me they haven't got twenty-five able-bodied clients between them. They are probably going to have to get them out of the old peoples' home, but I suppose they might come with the young nurses and if they are male nurses that will suit Mr Robert down to the ground, from what you've told me, he could take them into his nice little office."

Laura was smiling a bit as by this time she knew Tom was going to elaborate more, he was laughing so much at his own thoughts.

"It's not quite that easy," she said.

"Why? What's your involvement?"

"They want me or organise it and I have invited you," she had spoken without hardly drawing breath. "So I thought we could act as hosts, not friends. And I can't do it on my own without you." She didn't say about inviting friends she knew that would be the last straw.

"No, no, no, no, no," said Tom still laughing.

"Yes, yes, yes, yes," said Laura running her hand over his thigh and groin which had the desired effect she wanted.

"Now look what you've done?" said Tom. "I shall have to use this now."

"No, no, no, no, no," said Laura, but by now she was holding on firmly to his penis at the same time kissing his neck. "No using it unless you agree to host with me at a party and if you break your promise I will never have sex with you again."

"Well that's a pretty stupid and empty threat," said Tom. "You'd never last more than two days, but just in case you mean it, I agree to your terms."

"OK," she said climbing astride him.

# Chapter Eighteen

Laura woke with the sun streaming through the windows, she looked at the clock and was surprised to see it was eight o'clock. Tom was still fast asleep, it was the day of the Manleys' party and half of her was quite looking forward to it, while the other half was rather anxious. The numbers had risen from the original overall total of seventy-five to 102 each day in the last week one of the brothers had added just a few more and her worry was how many more that she didn't know of? She had told the caterers to provide for 125 but they seemed very at ease with it, all in a professional manner telling her not to worry there would be enough food and champagne for all.

She slipped out of bed quietly deciding to make breakfast for her and Tom and take it back to the bedroom. She put the coffee machine on and went into the downstairs bathroom to freshen up and brush her hair. Returning to the kitchen she made some toast and got the tray ready to take back upstairs.

Tom was awake and sitting up in bed when she walked in the room. "Stop!" he said. "Sometimes Laura you make me sick."

She looked at him in absolute horror. "What do you mean?" she asked.

"Just stand still," he said, "I just want to look at you with the sun coming through the window behind you and silhouetting your naked body and lovely hair, just to think that I couldn't have this pleasure if you had married Michael, that's what makes me sick my darling. I love you so much the thought of not being able to have you and love you makes my heart ache."

She smiled at him with relief saying, "You gave me a bit of a shock there. But can we have breakfast now as my arms are aching stood here holding this tray?"

She put the tray down on the table beside him, leaning forward to kiss him he slipped his hand between her thighs – she was warm and wonderful and slightly responsive.

"I love you," she said, climbing onto the bed and sitting cross-legged in front of him the way she knew he liked, remembering how he had taught her that first Christmas they had spent together that being naked with the person you truly loved was the most natural thing in the world.

He picked the tray up and placed it between them.

"I'm going down to the office about two o'clock Tom, just to let the caterers and the florist in. I wondered if you would like to come down with me and take a quick look round before this evening, or have you lots of things to do today?"

"Well I'm going to be busy until about twelve o'clock I guess, but I will come down with you."

"What have you got to do?" she asked.

"When we have finished this breakfast, Mrs Blakeslee," he said, "I am going to shag the arse off you." Putting the tray down on the bedside table he grabbed hold of her, caressing her from head to toe and then making the most wonderful passionate love to her. He eased himself off her, rolling her over onto her stomach. "Now," he said, "I'm going to do that again and if you don't agree you can call it rape."

"I could, but I think I'm going to like it. That's if you can make it."

"Don't worry about that, I can make it," he said, straddling across her, kissing the back of her neck and gently stroking her back.

She moaned appreciatively as he gently parted her legs just a little and then a little more. She could feel he was aroused again and she couldn't think of anything better than the wonderful feeling of his pressing against her. She wasn't sure if she could fully climax again so soon but just to have him inside of her was her greatest desire. He continued to stroke her body becoming more and more aroused himself all the time. She eased herself up on her elbows and he slipped his hands round to cup her breasts, whispering in her ear, "I think my darling, my wonderful darling you are ready."

She said nothing, just brought her knees up.

As promised Tom did go to the office and was quite impressed by the new look. The guests were invited for seven so they returned there about six thirty. After a few minutes Mr Robert arrived Laura introduced him to Tom, the two men shook hands and Mr Robert suggested it would be nice for them to have a glass together. He then took Tom off to show him around.

By seven fifteen Laura estimated most of the guests had arrived and then in came Mrs Longwait. Laura had to admit she really did look very smart, she was wearing a pale lilac outfit with dark mauve shoes and handbag. At least she hadn't arrived in the usual flasher's mac and black felt hat. She smiled at Laura and went on through into the long room, walking up to Mr William making an exhibition of greeting him.

It was a beautiful midsummer's evening and people spilled out onto the terrace, the atmosphere was very good and everybody seemed to be enjoying the champagne and the canapés. Being one of the world's greatest people watchers it was hard for Laura to decide which guests had been invited by which of the Manley brothers, she estimated there were no obvious gays. Of course there was the obvious couples but she noticed there was at least ten women that seemed to be unaccompanied, all extremely chic and well-dressed, possibly ranging from forty-five to sixty-five years old. Were they mother and daughter, or perhaps daughters accompanying parents who were clients that Laura didn't know? She was greatly impressed with the way the brothers were moving amongst everybody chatting, laughing and so obviously enjoying themselves, she realised they were experts at this and was once again reminded of how little she knew about them.

With that Tom was at her side. "Going well," he said, "and I must say that Mr Robert is a nice chap, I enjoyed talking to him just now."

Laura looked at him and smiled. "Didn't believe me, did you?"

"Come on, think we should circulate girl, and anyway looks as though there's a few tasty birds here."

"All too old for you," she replied.

After a while they became separated and Laura noticed Tom was being chatted up by Mrs Longwait. That will be interesting, she thought; still, knowing him so well she knew it wouldn't be a problem. She was so glad that he was there with her and she noticed how people just seemed to want to speak to him although he had the ability to charm and move on, just like the old days when she was so in love with him and felt she was just one of many of the girls to him. How times have changed nowadays, she felt so loved and safe with him. As the evening wore on she noticed Mrs Longwait was always hovering around Tom, speaking a few words whenever she could. She did a mental headcount and estimated there must be about 150 people there, but the champagne and canapés were still flowing, meriting a pat on the back for the caterers. Looking to the left she realised she was being beckoned by Rita from the post office who was stood with a group of other local people including, to her amazement, Mrs Daily and Mr Cook from the ironmongers. So no hard feelings there, nowadays. Jack the local bobby was there with his wife and several others from the village. On getting over to them she shook hands with them all, saying how nice it was to see them at the party.

"Yes," said Rita, "I was just telling them all how I got this job for you."

"Oh," said Laura smiling politely and trying not to giggle.

"Bloody good show," boomed Mrs Daily. "Bloody good thing for the Manleys, always a bit chaotic, and Robert's a bit limp you know."

"Not too limp to save your bacon," chipped in Mr Cook.

Laura quickly jumped in to change the subject saying, "What a lovely evening it is. Have you stepped outside and looked at the garden?" The last thing she wanted was any controversy in this little group.

Although the invites had stated from seven p.m. to nine p.m. at ten o'clock there was still quite a few people left. Laura went over to the caterers and suggested that the champagne should stop flowing and also stop the canapés. They were grateful to be able to clear glasses. By ten thirty everybody had gone except Mrs Longwait.

"Come along Effey, I'll see you home," said Mr William.

She said her farewells to Robert, Henri and Tom, whose hand she held very tightly, saying, "Good night dear boy such a pleasure."

"Well," said Mr Henri, "jolly good evening Laura. If we go now perhaps Tom and you will lock up and be on your way."

"What about Mr William?" Laura inquired.

"Oh, he's got a key if he wants to come back in, but I expect he'll stay at Effey's tonight."

Back home Laura and Tom sat on the couch together with a coffee chewing over the evening.

"What do you think of Mrs Longwait?" she asked. "I saw she couldn't leave you alone."

"Oh yes I had a job to get rid of her, hearing all about her antiques, her silver and her family heirlooms, shopping at Harrods and Fortnum & Masons, and of course designer clothes. Had a job to avoid her at the end."

"Yes I know exactly what you mean, Mr William says she's an old friend, a bit of a dragon and an absolute snob, but he loves her to bits. I think they may have or did have a bit of something going at one time. Take tonight for instance, he took her home."

"I think you're imagining things, anyway two hours was enough for me," said Tom.

"I reckon a good one hundred and fifty were there tonight Tom, still we didn't run out of anything thank God."

"No, well done my love and I must admit, I quite enjoyed it all, the people were very nice but I think there was more friends rather than clients there, and from the little I spoke to the three brothers they seemed extremely nice men, well-educated and perfect gentlemen, yes. I think I feel quite safe with you working for them."

"Well that's a bit of luck that's how I feel about them," Laura replied. "And do you now Rita from the post office informed a few of the locals that she got the job for me."

Laura arrived at the office by eight thirty on Monday morning to check round before the brothers got there, the cleaners had been in on Sunday so all should have been seen to. Looking around everything was in perfect order. Then just on nine o'clock as if by arrangement all three men arrived together.

"Good morning to you all," said Laura with a smile.

"Bloody marvellous night," said Mr Robert.

"Yes," sanctioned the other two.

"You certainly did a magnificent job," said Mr Henri.

"Thank you so much my dear," said Mr William. "Please give our thanks to Tom, a very nice chap I really enjoyed chatting to him before the guests arrived, just wasn't enough time, like to catch up with him again. Let him know he's always welcome here."

"That's nice, I'll tell him later."

With that the phone rang it was somebody for Mr Henri wanting to say thank you for the invitation to the party and expressing how much they had enjoyed the evening. And that was how the day progressed, the phone never stopped before they knew it it was time to go home.

The next day Tuesday there was lots of mail, mostly thank you letters, some addressed to all three brothers, and some to the individuals. It seemed Mr William had the most and Laura hazarded a guess that quite a few of those were from the single ladies, judging by the envelopes. Normally she would open all the mail but she had declined to do that this day, surmising that most were of a personal nature.

She didn't particularly want to see Mr Robert's in case any of his thank yous were from his gentlemen friends, likewise from Mr William's lady friends. It seemed to have pleased all three men to have had such a response to the party. She didn't know if there had been one from Mrs Longwait, but then perhaps she had thanked Mr William when he took her home;

but she had to admit she was surprised that she hadn't been to the office.

Mail and phone calls were still arriving on Wednesday. And then on Thursday in came Mrs Longwait, bursting in to see Mr William's office just as normal. Something Laura had been accustomed to now, although this morning she did wave to Laura on her way in. There seemed to be lots of laughter coming from the office so Laura assumed all was well, she was in her office when she heard Mrs Longwait calling her; she went out into reception to see what she wanted.

"Wonderful party my dear, and what a delightful husband you have obviously well-read, -bred and -educated. But then I knew with your taste and elegance you would be married to someone like that."

Laura smiled nicely and really had to bite her tongue wanting to say, What me? From the council houses who needs to learn how to greet clients? Instead she just said, "Why thank you."

"Now my dear I have just been talking to William, he is coming to dinner with Conrad and I on Saturday week and I've told him I'm going to invite you and Tom. Shall we say seven o'clock for canapés? Fortnum & Masons of course. Conrad prefers theirs. Black tie of course. Goodbye," she said and was gone.

Not giving Laura any time to comment, the possibility that they might not be free that evening didn't seem to occur to the woman.

Laura knew Tom wouldn't want to go and she would have to make up some plausible excuse as to why they couldn't be there. Yet a little bit of her was curious to meet Conrad and see inside the perfect house.

Tom was working at home this day so as soon as she got in she spilled the beans. "Guess what, we've been invited to dinner together with Mr William to Mrs Longwait and Conrad."

"That's nice," he said.

"You can't be serious," she replied.

"Why not, don't you want to go?"

"Well half of me does and half of me doesn't. She's such an old cow, so insincere telling me how good I am and how wonderful you are, well-bred, well-read and -educated. I expect she will be fawning all over you like she was at the party, she's such a hypocrite, if truth be told I expect she would just like to invite you without me."

Tom threw his head back laughing. "Obviously she can tell class when she sees it! Charming woman, I do believe you're jealous Laura."

"Don't be ridiculous," she said. "Anyway what makes you say yes? Its black tie," she threw in just as an afterthought.

"Well I'd quite like to meet Mr William again and who knows, Conrad could be quite interesting. At least she doesn't boss him around, he didn't come to the Manley's party," said Tom.

"She said he had another engagement, so there."

Laura's last two words made Tom laugh even more.

"What are you laughing at?" she asked.

"Just you my darling, just like a little schoolgirl saying 'so there'."

"Oh shut up!" she said, beginning to laugh with him. "So I take it it's a yes then?"

"If that's what you wish, you get us into these things so I can't help you."

"See you tomorrow evening then," said Mr William when it was time to leave the office on Friday. "Dear Effey she means well," he said with a chuckle. "Always a little over the top but I guess you have sussed her out Laura."

"Bloody black tie, don't you think this is a bit ridiculous Laura?"

"Yes darling I do, but just do it and shut up." She gave him a look of *You were warned*. She had decided to wear her red taffeta which fitted really well, and she knew Tom liked her in it.

Looking up he said to her, "I don't think you should put that on," coming up behind her.

"Why?"

"Well you know what that does to me and I'm likely to rip it off and have a stay home night with you on the sofa," he said.

They parked the car in the pub-cum-village car park only to see Mr William getting out of his car. "Perfect timing," he said.

They crossed the road together and then to Laura's surprise Mr William produced a key to open the front door of Effey's house. "Come on in," he said. "We are here Effey," he called.

With that a vision in blue appeared in what Laura could only describe as the perfect Charleston dress, heavily beaded and fringed complete with Charleston headcap with the fringed edge just lying on her forehead and the exact same coloured pointed-toed shoes. Mrs Longwait greeted them with a kiss on each cheek saying, "Do come through into the lounge, William will you please pour the champagne darling? Moet Chandon, of course." Turning to Tom and Laura she said, "Please call me Effey socially," casting her eye at Laura as if to remind her of her position in the office.

They nibbled the canapés and sipped champagne and the chat just flowered, mainly because Mr William and Tom seemed to have a lot in common and the same sense of humour. Sitting in the window was a large grey parrot.

"Good evening, good evening," it kept saying.

It seems to be totally free just sat on a perch, there was a lot of shucks on the floor together with a lot of droppings. Effey then excused herself to go to the kitchen. Laura then had a chance to look around; it was a pleasant room with some good antique furniture and nice pieces of china, but lots of bloody bird shit everywhere, which was quite a shock to her.

Coming back Effey announced that dinner was about to be served and the menu was foie gras with Melba toast. Fortnum & Mason's special steak pie with puréed potatoes. Mashed thought Laura ungracefully, while Effey continued. Dessert was chocolate truffle pudding with double cream. "Just especially for William," she smiled at him and pursed her lips, and he nodded back appreciatively.

There's more to this old friendship than meets the eye, suspected Laura.

"Is this all right for you both Tom and Laura?"

"Oh yes of course," they both replied.

"And of course we will have cheese with vintage port afterwards, and then fine Viennese coffee and a good French brandy back in the lounge again. Now let's go through to the dining room, William will show you the way and I'll get Conrad."

Laura had almost forgotten Conrad, her only real reason for wanting to come tonight. Going into the dining room the table looked magnificent with so much attention to detail, they were followed by Effey carrying the parrot.

"Do sit down," she said placing the parrot on the back of one of the two empty chairs, sitting down in the other she turned to the parrot saying, "Now Conrad be a gentleman and behave nicely to our guests."

"Of course, of course, thank you, thank you," it said.

Laura didn't dare to look at Tom she could hardly contain herself. Conrad was a parrot, not a husband, and to cap it all on the table in front of the seat where Conrad sat was a bowl which Effey explained was pumpkin seeds.

"Please," said the parrot and she fed him a seed saying, "he doesn't like foie gras so these are his starter, he will have a couple of our canapés for main course and he's happy with the dessert."

"Well that's a bit of luck," said Tom.

"Yes I'm glad you understand him but then you are such an intelligent person, I can see Conrad likes you. For some people especially men who come to dinner with us I have to give them the big Panama hat to wear to protect their ears, as if he doesn't like them he is inclined to show his feelings by attacking them, naughty boy."

Mr William looked at her saying, "I've told you before get a cage."

"What? What?" screeched Conrad. Everybody laughed and the parrot squawked, which was an absolute relief for Laura who was finding it difficult not to burst into fits of giggles.

The evening was pleasant enough although the cheese, brought in still in the special hamper, could've been delivered five years ago, a little mould on cheese that shouldn't have mould and some rather suspicious-looking holes in the blue cheese. Possibly made by a sharp beak. Also around the Camembert which rather resembled a CD, if somewhat small.

It certainly had been an interesting evening and fun they left about eleven p.m., much later than they had intended, leaving Mr William still there and wondering, as there was no Mr Longwait, whether he would leave before morning.

They drove in silence to their own house which only took a few minutes. Once inside they just looked at one another and creased up.

"I don't know about you my darling, is she stark raving bonkers? I can't believe what we've just been through, let's have a nightcap."Said Tom

"Yes, that's a great idea. You get the brandy, and I'll make the coffee."

They sat down on the couch together.

"What an absolute hoot! And as for the bloody parrot screeching and shitting everywhere, I just don't know. But one interesting thing I found out is that Mr William is an avid sports fan and said when he gets a couple of tickets for a good rugby or football match, he'll let me know."

Mr Robert had requested that fresh flowers should always be kept in the party room. The local florist replaced them every ten days but sometimes they needed a little topping up with water. Going in to check one morning, Laura heard a noise behind her and there was Mr Robert.

"Oh great," he said, "I do love the flowers don't you?"

"Yes I do and the garden looks fantastic through the windows. You haven't asked me to pay any bills for the two men. And I never see anybody out there, are you doing it yourself at weekends?"

"Good grief, none of my handiwork. I think I told you before about my two boys? I'm sure you know what sort of arrangement I have with them. I try to keep my private life to myself. I pay them in kind dear boys, Sammy and Georgie; they do such a good job all for the love of it, and I think for the love of me. I feel you understand what I'm trying to tell you."

Laura found it difficult to find any words so she just smiled knowingly.

"Yes they come along Saturday and Sunday mornings and do what is needed. I normally come about midday, we have a drink together here in my office – incidentally they love what you have helped me do to – then sometimes we go out for lunch or back the their place. They have a small apartment together. Or mine just to relax and be nice to one another. I know my brothers don't approve but they never comment or challenge me. I think I should have been the daughter my darling mother longed for. I know my lifestyle will be my downfall in the end as when I'm on holiday here or abroad I just ring for a call boy. I would just like to say thank you for your understanding. Well better go and do a little work. See you in a mo."

She stayed in the room for a little longer than necessary, she always had suspicions but now they were confirmed by Mr Robert himself. Just a little bit more of the Manley jigsaw puzzle...

# Chapter Nineteen

It was a beautiful summer. Tom and Laura decided not to go abroad for their holidays but just to take short breaks away, fairly close to home, they had made lots of new friends so they entertained more with barbecues so guests could enjoy the pool and everything was quite relaxed. They also took time to explore the local area and find new restaurants. One such day they took off in the direction of the New Forest stopping at Bucklers Hard on the river Beaulie, and to their amazement saw Mr Robert on the back of a thirty-six-foot Sunseeker boat; he noticed them and invited them on board.

"Come and have some champagne and lobster with me and my friends!" he called.

Tom looked at Laura. "Not too sure about this," he said under his breath.

"Oh come on, let's go. I like a bit of lobster," said Laura.

There was rather too much bare flesh for Tom's liking especially as it was all male. After about an hour they could see things were getting a bit raunchy and made their excuses to leave. He made her laugh when he told her he was not afraid for her safety, but scared to death for his own, and particularly concerned of one young man who kept winking at him.

"What a bloody waste of life, I'm sure a lot of these young men get whipped up into these situations by the obvious wealth of the older men, although I must say your Mr Robert certainly had a good-looking body for his age."

"Oh so you weren't too scared to look then?" laughed Laura.

"Don't be ridiculous. With a G-string no bigger than a piece of ribbon front and back it was hard not to see the lot."

When Laura saw Mr Robert the next day at work she made no comment of their meeting, and neither did he; of that she was pleased about.

Tom and Mr William became quite friendly and often chatted if Tom popped into the office. One such day he told Tom he had some tickets for a special rugby match at Twickenham and asked if he would like to go with him.

"Be delighted," said Tom.

The only problem was he nearly drove Laura up the wall by the way he kept talking about it in anticipation. The day turned out to be a great success and they discovered that they had many sporting loves in common which resulted in them going to cricket matches, motor racing and football matches together, always with the best seats and, despite the age difference, they seemed to have a lot in common with the same sense of humour. Laura often felt that Mr William liked to think of himself as a father figure to Tom.

Before leaving the office one Friday lunchtime Laura happened to say to Mr William that she and Tom were going to Bude in Cornwall for the weekend. To her surprise he said so was he.

"Perhaps you both would like to come and have dinner with me? I'm staying at the Saunton Sands Hotel. What do you think?"

She was surprised at this invite but accepted it knowing Tom, wouldn't mind even though he always said these short break weekends were just to make love to her.

"That would be nice, thank you."

"Great. I'll book a table for eight p.m. on Saturday. If you come about seven thirty we can have a drink first."

It was a wonderful balmy summer's evening when they arrived at the hotel.

"Good evening," said the receptionist at the desk. "Mr and Mrs Blakeslee?" Tom nodded. "Your friends are out on the balcony, please come this way."

Seeing them Mr William stood up. "Ah great, you've found us." Shaking hands with Tom and kissing Laura on each cheek. "Let me introduce you to Petra," pointing to the lady with him.

She stood up to shake hands. She was elegant and expensively dressed, possibly no more than forty-five years old and very beautiful. She had a lovely smile which somehow made you instantly like her.

The evening was a great success they laughed a lot and before they knew it, it was one a.m.

"I really think we should be leaving now before we get thrown out," said Tom.

"Yes I suppose so," said Mr William. "It's all right for us we only have to go upstairs, but you have the drive back, the evening's gone so quickly we must do it again sometime."

They all walked out to the front entrance shook hands and parted.

"Well, what about that the dirty old bastard," laughed Tom. "It just shows you never can tell. But I must say she was charming and rather beautiful, don't you think?"

"Yes I must agree, I noticed you were charmed. What a surprise and shock really, he didn't mention her when he invited us. Actually I'm really quite pleased for him perhaps he's not as lonely as I think."

"I don't think he's lonely when I've been to anything with him he always seems to have lots of friends which he speaks to. It's strange we chat a lot when we are out together but when I think about it, he never talks about himself and really I know very little of him, but I'm pleased for him like you. God knows what Effey would have to say if she ever found out. But just think Laura, what different women they are."

Time was to show a very different life of Mr William and one time after he and Tom had been to rugby at Twickenham he suggested, if they drove up in his car, then Laura could drive to Hindhead to meet them for dinner as he had a friend who lived nearby where he would stay the night and Laura and Tom could drive home together; and so they met Joanna. Another lady, possibly fifty-five years old, but again very charming and good looking and obviously more than just a friend.

The next time Tom and he went to cricket Tom ventured to mention his lady friends, jokingly teasing him about Petra, Joanna and Effey. He wondered if he was being a bit too inquisitive but was really surprised at the reply he got.

"You know, my boy, there's nothing nicer than a beautiful woman, especially in your bed. After all you have one in Laura, and it may shock you to know I have many, I love then all. And then of course there is Effey, dear Effey, she has a special place in my heart. Forty years ago we had a brief affair but she married someone else which didn't break my heart, five years ago when her husband died she thought we could pick up where we left off, but time had not been kind to Effey and she had turned from a beautiful fun-loving girl into a dominating snob. Don't get me wrong, I'm very fond of her and take her away for the occasional weekend. I think she likes people to think we have raucous sex on these occasions, in fact I dare say she might even have implied this to Laura, but I always make sure we have separate beds as my appetite for lovemaking seems to disappear when she puts her nightie on. I think you know what I mean."

Tom was a little speechless at this confession yet said he totally understood. That night after he and Laura made love and she lay in his arms, he said, "Laura, promise me that as we grow old together you will never wear a nightdress."

She pulled away from him and sat up looking at him saying, "Whatever makes you say that? You taught me how wonderful it is to feel each other's bodies naked. I hope we'll always feel the same, even if we are wrinkly together."

Mr William had the ability to make Tom and Laura laugh with some of his stories. One day he said, "I think it is time to take Effey on one of her upper crust living visits to London." Explaining what it meant he went on, "I drive us up to Harrods, buy her everything she wants including several new outfits. She always insists on bringing these things back with us so as she has a supply of Harrods bags so as she can use them when she goes into the village. Then we go into the food hall and she chooses enough to fill at least one hamper with Harrods on the side to be delivered to her house." At this point he starts to chuckle a bit. "Poor Effey, however distasteful she might find the driver she always insists he comes inside for a cup of tea, only to the kitchen though. This gives time for any passers-by the chance to see the Harrods van parked outside her house. We then go on to the Ritz for tea. It's better than having a night at the Carlton, which we used to do, but as you know Tom I don't care for her night attire nowadays. Poor Effey I love her dearly, but only on my terms. It's a bit like grabbing a granny."

Then sometimes he would ask if he could bring someone for dinner adding, "I'll bring the wine and champers but if we enjoy ourselves too much I don't want to drive her back to her place and get done for drink and drive, so is it all right to stay?"

Laura always teased him saying, "Of course you naughty rascal."

Summer seemed to be slipping by – it was August and still wonderfully warm. Tom and Laura were so enjoying life, lots of love laughter and fun sometimes with friends sometimes just alone, when even a silence is not the problem. Laura suggested to Tom one lazy Saturday afternoon when they were relaxing in the garden that perhaps they should invite Effey and Mr William to a barbecue, or perhaps dinner.

"Oh no," said Tom, "Not Effey, yes Mr William fine, but I don't know if I could stand her."

"Oh you like a bit of bird shit." Laura started to giggle. "Yes, I know, but she loves you and tolerates me and after all it would be just polite, don't you think?"

"No, I don't think, can't you just hear the criticism? What are you a masochist?"

"No, I'm not. But after all Mr William has been good enough to take us out and we can't really ask him on his own."

"We could ask him with one of his other bits of stuff, that would be better, don't you think?"

"Yes I do, but I think first it's got to be Effey."

"OK, I'll get delayed at work that evening."

"Let's just do it and get it over with, if it's too bad we never have to do it again."

"Bloody right we don't."

"I'll just speak to Mr William and sort something out then."

It was all arranged for the following Saturday early evening and they had decided on a barbecue. Tom couldn't wait for it to be over and Laura felt much the same.

Mr William had picked Effey up and even Tom had to admit that, dressed in a sort of safari suit, she did look quite classy. They had a glass of champagne to start with and then Tom fired up the barbecue. Mr William walked over to him and they were chatting away happily.

"Would you like to show me around your little house?" Effey asked Laura.

No I wouldn't, thought Laura, what a cheek and it will give her plenty of ammunition to criticise our lack of valuable silver and antiques. Nevertheless with tongue-in-cheek she replied, "If you wish but it's no show piece." It actually was not as painful as Laura had imagined it might be, although she was very pleased she had the whole place spick and span.

Having finished the tour without too many criticisms they went back to the garden where the barbecue was just about ready for the steak.

"Ah, here you are, just in time for a glass of wine. Mr William and I are into the white, would you like that Effey or would you prefer something else?" Tom asked.

Looking at him like a puppy dog she took his hand saying, "I would like red please, perhaps a good Merlot or Cabernet Sauvignon darling, I can't stand these cheap reds around nowadays, I'm sure you understand what I mean."

Tom threw a quick eye contact to Laura. "Of course, I have just the thing for you will a Chateau neuf de Pape do?

"Yes I knew with your class you would understand."

"Well I suppose you would know about the cheap ones as you must've tasted them to know you don't like them, or have you become a label connoisseur my dear?" chipped in Mr William.

They all laughed together and Laura noticed Effey's black look she gave him.

"I'll just pop in and get a bottle," said Tom.

"Bring the tray of nibbles back with you," said Laura.

Returning in a few moments handing the tray to Laura he proceeded to open the wine, sniffing the cork with a flurry of delight, which made Laura want to giggle. She stepped up quickly towards Mr William, offering him a nibble.

"Here we are especially for you Effey, you shall have the whole bottle to indulge in," said Tom. "Now I must get cooking."

The evening actually went quite well with Effey complementing Laura on the aperitif as she called it, adding she could tell the smoke salmon was of high quality nearly as good as she bought herself. By the time they had eaten the main course Effey was two thirds into the bottle of red. Laura produced the sweet which was just fresh strawberries and cream, and the Tom suggested they should go in for a coffee and brandy.

"But only the best *brandy*, I'm sure you know what I mean," he said looking at Effey, who was beginning to be a little squiffy.

She nodded appreciatively and blew him a kiss. Once inside Mr William took a wander round the downstairs rooms without asking, which pleased Laura to think he felt at ease in their home. She served the coffee and Tom poured the brandies.

"Nice house you have here, I can see quite a few things have been done to make it just a little more special, did you have it done by a professional or did you do it yourself?"

"Yes, we did most of it ourselves. You know the thing, Laura made the bullets and I had to fire them."

"Well done, it's great."

"I agree," butted in Effey. "Far better nowadays to have married a man who can do things, than a man from a titled background such as my husband was."

"Yes I agree with you," said Laura. "The old saying where there's muck there's money is to true, like us we can afford nice food and wine and lifestyles, and we are not afraid to get down and clean our home and do our garden chores ourselves, a bit peasant-like, don't you think, Effey?"

"Um," came the reply from a rather pissed Effey.

Laura felt quite good at her comment to the biggest snob she had ever come across, being on her own ground it was easy whereas when she was at work it would have been considered rude for her to say such things. She had said it with good humour and made the men laugh. After a couple more brandies, Mr William said he thought it was time they departed. "We've had a super evening," he said.

"Yes, and now I must get you into bed," said Effey, leaning heavily on him.

They made their way to the front door with the normal thanks and pecks on the cheek.

Tom bent forward out of earshot of her, saying in Mr William's ear, "This does not mean the nightdress nightmare?"

Both men roared with laughter and the pair were gone.

Closing the front door behind them, Laura and Tom collapsed in helpless laughter.

"What did you say to him?" she asked.

"I just said was he about to have the nightdress nightmare. You know Laura, I really do like that man, his sense of humour. I'd really like to know more about him as I've said before"

Tom had been to a football match with Mr William. Laura was in the kitchen preparing the evening meal. She heard him come in the front door and within a few minutes he was standing behind her, kissing the back of her neck and cupping her breasts.

"Behave!" she said, flicking some water at him.

"Since when did you want me to that?" he laughed, slipping his hands inside her sweater and flipping the hook on her bra undone, he could feel her immediate response as her breasts became hard. "I love you so much," he whispered against her neck. Still holding her close he said, "Mr William asked me today if we would have a dinner party for him and a friend, and I did not think you would mind."

"So what did you say, who's the friend?"

"Well female as you might've guessed, her name's Zoe and she Swedish, that's all I really know, and I said I'm sure you wouldn't mind."

"Yes that's fine, but don't you think it's funny that he didn't ask me at the office?"

"No, not really I think he likes to keep business and pleasure separate which is fair enough."

Zoe turned out to be absolutely charming, possibly at the most in her early forties. It was as if they had all known one another for years, the chat flowed easily with much laughter; it was late when they left.

Turning to Laura after wishing them goodbye and closing the front door Tom said, "I reckon he's going to get his leg over, and that's exactly what I'm going to do, just leave everything we will clear up in the morning as it's Sunday. Now, get up those stairs."

Soon it was December and the Manleys announced the office would be closed for three weeks from 18$^{th}$ December so would Laura let the relevant clients know and make a notice for the window? Mr William told her later that he would be going to Bermuda for the whole time to get some sun.

"Do you need me to arrange flights or anything?" she asked him.

"No, I'll let the London office do that for me," he said.

It seemed strange to Laura that they trusted her so much with things, but there was always some thing's that she didn't do for them, particularly for Mr William. She realised there must be a great deal she didn't know that was perhaps always dealt with at the London office. Still, she felt it wasn't her place to delve but even more it made her think what secrets could be upstairs.

It was the Friday before Christmas so as usual she put the detail sheets on each man's desk and received her cheques, wishing each one of them separately a Merry Christmas. She went back into her office to make sure everything was closed down for the holidays and, picking up her coat and handbag, she walked out into reception and there to her surprise stood the three men together.

Robert stepped forward and handed her a little blue velvet box saying, "A small gift from us just to say thank you for looking after us so well during your first year here. You truly have made a great difference not only to our business, but to our lives."

She was quite shocked and didn't really know what to say, she stupidly felt herself blushing. "Thank you so much. I must tell you I've so enjoyed being here."

"Well Happy Christmas and New Year," said Mr Henri holding out his hand to shake hers. "It truly was a good day when we found you."

"Too true," said Mr Robert also shaking hands with her.

"Look after that Tom while I'm away," said Mr William putting his arm on her shoulder.

She laughed and left.

As she walked home that day she wondered what sort of holiday period they would have. She was sure no doubt Mr Robert would have some naughty things lined up with his boys and friends. She truly hoped Mr William would be with friends, she had no idea if he would be in a hotel alone or was he taking a lady friend with him. She smiled to herself, yes, he probably wouldn't be lonely. But Mr Henri she really didn't know. He was such a nice man, but always seemed to have such sad eyes; she was sure they hid a secret.

She was home by now and letting herself in she realised Tom was home too. How lucky she was to have such happiness with him, and for a brief moment she thought of her mother whom she hadn't heard from for some years now, she didn't even know where she was. She remembered those difficult Christmas times before her father had died. He was always trying to please her but never really succeeded, she was such a cold woman.

Tom came out to greet her. "What's the matter? You look a little sad and tearful."

"Oh nothing, just thinking about my parents and their sad relationship together and how lucky I am to have you."

"Of course you are, after all I'm the greatest and don't you forget it. I wine you, dine you and fuck you, how could you wish for more?"

"A cup of coffee would be nice and then I'll show you my Christmas present."

"Shall be done. What have you got then?"

"Don't know, it's a little blue box, I'll open it while we drink the coffee."

Sitting closely together on the couch she picked up the little blue box. She opened it to find the most beautiful three corded gold bracelet with several diamonds in it.

"Jesus!" said Tom. "If they are real they must have cost a fortune, you can see it is not brand new so I would assume it is probably antique. You sure you only do the office work down there?"

Laura just gave him the look of death.

# Chapter Twenty

It was a cold and frosty bright Thursday morning in February. Laura was almost ready to leave for the office, and looking out of the window she decided to walk. Tom had been working at home since Monday on a new project which was almost completed. He had suggested that when she finished work they should go out for some lunch. So if she left her car at home he could pick her up from the office. Finding an extra scarf and her warm gloves, she kissed him goodbye and left. She knew that both Mr Robert and Mr William would be late getting in this morning as they were going to see a client over a boundary dispute.

Arriving at the door with key in hand she realised it was already open. Concluding that Mr Henri was already there, she walked in and could see him at his desk in his swivel chair looking out of the bay window, which was quite normal when he was considering a client's case. She said a quick good morning and hurried on to the kitchen to put the kettle on to make him a hot chocolate, as was normal. As she took off her coat the telephone rang, then in came Mrs Longwait. She dealt with the phone call, and then explained to Effey that Mr William would not be in until later, with that the phone rang again and Effey waved goodbye and left.

It was not half an hour since she had arrived, she hurriedly went back to the kitchen to make hot chocolate. Picking up the mug she went to Mr Henri's office. He was still sitting looking out of the window, so she placed the mug on the desk saying, "Sorry it's a little late this morning." She stood there for a few seconds expecting him to spin round but he didn't. "Are you all right?" she asked.

As there was no reply, she walked around the desk to face him. He had a lovely smile on his face quite unusual she thought for this normally sad-eyed man. "Are you all right Mr Henri?" she asked again.

And then she put her hand out to touch his, it was barely warm and to her horror she realised he was dead. She grabbed his phone and dialled 999, giving the details. She then phoned Tom. Hearing his voice she almost screamed at him, "Get down here as quick as possible please, I need your help quickly!"

Tom in his usual calm way said, "What is it Laura?"

"He's dead!" she said.

"Who's dead?" he asked, thinking in a selfish moment, God don't let it be Mr William, I like that old boy. "OK I'm on my way." He jumped in the car, not stopping to lock any doors, and was at the office in minutes.

Running through the front door he found a very shocked and white-looking Laura. Putting his arms around her and holding her tight, he said, "Have you phoned the ambulance? Who is it?"

"Mr Henri. Well, I think he's dead. Oh Tom, I've never seen a dead person before, it's so sad he looks so happy."

Tom smiled inwardly at Laura's comment. "Come on, let's go and find him, is he in his office?"

"Yes, and the worst thing is the other two are not here yet they're out seeing a client. Oh Tom, I don't know what to do."

"OK darling, it'll all get sorted. I think you're just a little in shock at the moment."

Tom could see instantly that he was dead but he had to admit that he didn't know the man very well, but he did look happy. Thankfully with that the ambulance men arrived, they quickly took charge of the scene obviously checking for any signs of life before lifting Mr Henri gently onto the stretcher and putting him in the ambulance.

"Are you relatives, would you like to come with him?"

"No, my wife just works here and I came because she telephoned me to come, we only live at the top of the hill, she arrived for work as normal and found him. His two brothers, who'd normally be here, are seeing a client this morning before coming into the office."

With that the police arrived, obviously needing to take a statement from Laura. One of the ambulance men gave the police some basic details and left. As the ambulance pulled away Mr William and Mr Robert arrived.

"Good God what's going on? What's the ambulance doing here?"

Tom stepped in explaining in the kindest possible way by saying that Laura had found Mr Henri not feeling too well, and taking control of the situation had phoned for the ambulance, he ushered the two men into Mr William's office. Closing the door behind him he said, "Come sit down, I expect you are shocked."

"So do we need to go straight to the hospital? Was he in pain? Had he fallen, or what?" asked Mr William.

"No, I think a little more serious than that, I think it was a massive heart attack."

"Are you saying he's dead?" asked Mr Robert looking at Tom intensely.

"Yes, I think you must accept the truth, I am no expert but I think if it's any comfort it was quick, and Laura and I can both assure you that he looked so peaceful and so happy."

The brothers looked at one another and it was hard for Tom to read their thoughts. "Can I get you both a drink of whisky or something?"

"No, if you could manage it, I think two hot chocolates would be marvellous."

Tom went off to the kitchen and within a few minutes he heard Laura letting the policeman out of the front door. She quickly joined him in the kitchen.

"What are you doing?" she asked.

"I asked the two of them if they would like a drink and the request was for hot chocolate, so here I am. It's a little opportunity for them to be together for a few minutes but I think now you are free we should make it four hot chocolates. I'm sure you could do with one, and although we may be a bit presumptuous I think it's an opportunity to go and ask them what they would like us to do for them as far as funeral arrangements are concerned."

"Yes I suppose you are right, Tom. What would I do without you, you're so level headed?" She leant closely against him and he kissed her on the forehead.

Carrying the four mugs of hot chocolate they went back to Mr William's office. The two men were sat there perfectly composed looking up at Tom and Laura as they walked in.

"Ah good, you're going to join us," said Mr Robert.

"Well yes, we thought it might be a moment for you to tell us what we can to do help with the procedures, if you wish."

"Very kind and thoughtful you dear things, but the London office will deal with everything, the funeral will be in Lymington where he lives, they will sort it. But if you, Laura, would telephone Henri's clients and if they wish to proceed with Manley, Manley & Manley perhaps you will rearrange the appointments. Robert and I need a few days off to collect ourselves so if you could rearrange our appointments as well, shall we say until next Wednesday? And I'll ask the London office to let you know immediately when the funeral is so as those appointments on that day can be rearranged as well," said Mr William.

With that the two men stood up and finished off their mugs of chocolate with Mr Robert saying, "We will be off now. Can we just leave you to run things in our absence, hold the fort so to speak?"

"Yes of course."

Tom shook both the brothers by the hand as they left.

"If you would like us to attend the funeral we would be happy to do so but we also understand that for Laura as staff, this could be considered improper."

"Not at all dear boy, be assured you are both very much more than staff, but it won't be necessary."

The two of them stood looking at one another for a few minutes only to be interrupted by Effey. She stormed straight into Mr William's office.

"What are you two doing in here? What was the ambulance doing?"

Laura shot a glance at Tom.

"I think I had better get on with things, perhaps you can explain the morning's happenings to Mrs Longwait darling."

It was a very silent and shocked Effey that left that day, declaring, "Thank God it wasn't my William."

Laura set about telephoning clients with appointments in the next few days. Not that there were that many, but it took quite a time as everybody was eager to hear what happened. Tom stayed on and sorted Mr Henri's office out, just generally rearranging everything. By one o'clock Laura had spoken to the clients who happened to be in that day.

"What about this going out to lunch today?" asked Tom.

"Oh, I'd almost forgotten, but I don't feel very hungry, I'm sorry do you mind if we just go home?"

"No, of course not, I think it's a good idea, we've got plenty more days we can go."

Once home she admitted to Tom that she felt absolutely drained.

"That's normal darling. Come, sit down and I'll go make us a cup of tea and find something for us to nibble at."

Sitting together on the sofa a little while later sipping the tea Laura said, "You know Tom, I seem to know so much about the Manleys and yet so little, the upstairs of the office, why have none of them ever married? OK we know about Mr Robert, what and why?"

"Yes I understand what you mean. We probably know a little more about Mr William's private life. I assume there is quite a bit of wealth there but when I go to football or whatever he never brags about anything, he's just so normal and a thoroughly nice chap. And I must admit to my disgrace this morning when you phone I thought like Effey, I hope it's not Mr William. I know that's really selfish but the truth."

"I didn't have the time to think that but I do feel the same. But I also am so sorry for Mr Henri," she replied.

That night Laura didn't sleep well and at three o'clock she got up and walked to the window. Tom woke up to hear her quietly sobbing, he hopped out of bed and went to her putting his arms around her, she snuggled into him saying, "I'm sorry I woke you."

"Don't be silly I was expecting this, it's been a hard day, it's good for you to cry. You had a big shock."

"But it's made me think Tom, I said I'd never seen a dead person before but now I know my father was already dead when my mother called me to go to the neighbours. Why didn't she call me earlier? She must've known he was dying or at least quite ill, all I would've wanted to do was hug him and kiss him goodbye. His hand was so cold when I held it, whereas Mr Henri's was still warm."

"Well maybe that's your answer my darling, perhaps he died in his sleep some time before she found him." Tom felt a silent sob go through her body.

"Yes, but she knew how much I loved him. Did she hate that relationship so much was this her revenge?"

"No, I'm sure it wasn't. After all you were young. She probably just wanted to protect you. It's in the past now Laura, there is no point in dwelling on it, just remember all the lovely times you shared with him." They stood quietly still in front of the window he holding her tightly.

"Now I'm going to tuck you back in bed go and get us a nice, warm drink."

Down in the kitchen he made two cups of coffee deciding to put a good dash of Tia Maria in Laura's. He found her sat up in bed and looking at her: his heart ached for her, she looked so beautiful with her hair tumbling onto her shoulders despite her tear-stained face and puffy eyes, he just wanted to make love to her, knowing full well this was not appropriate. He slipped into bed beside her, handing her a coffee, they sat quietly for a few minutes.

Laura said, "This is lovely coffee you make it so much better than me," then taking another mouthful she looked at him, "you bad man you laced it."

"Yes I know but only yours, I hope it will help you go to sleep."

Eventually they lay down she in his arms and slept.

In the morning Tom said that he would go to the office with Laura. She had dealt with any clients that should have been coming in but he thought she may be a little apprehensive of being there alone. He said he would take his laptop and finish off the work that he should've done the day before. He could quietly sit unseen in her office while she rearranged appointments with other clients of Mr Henri's. How wrong he was: they arrived at the office just before nine. Within ten minutes Effey was there and it seemed as though the news had gone round the village like wildfire.

Rita arrived from the post office followed by Mr Cook from the hardware shop, all wanting to know exactly what happened yesterday. Effey was holding court telling them what had happened, but making it up off the top of her head into a drama that she held a leading part in. Then came in two other people who Laura recognised as being locals but not clients, which enabled Effey to repeat her story embroidered a little more.

Tom walked out to reception to see what all the chat was about. He and Laura exchanged glances as Effey caught sight of him.

"Oh darling boy, please make us all some coffee."

As Laura commented later, he was so shocked he just did as he was told.

Next in boomed Mrs Daily just as Tom arrived with the coffee.

"No coffee for me," she said, "I'll have a glass of red wine, I think there was some left over from that party, jolly good stuff too."

Laura followed Tom back to the kitchen saying, "Bloody cheeky cow, what do they think this is, a wake?"

"Looks like it's going that way," Tom replied. And they both fell about laughing.

With no exaggeration by ten o'clock the reception area was full, the noise was tremendous.

"We will have to open the long room if this carries on," said Tom.

Effey was calling to both of them as though they were her personal staff. "I think some people would like some white wine, William always kept a few bottles in the fridge just get those open darling."

Tom looked at Laura. "I think you could say we have lost control," but they were quietly obeying the commands.

In total Tom counted about thirty heads at one time but with some coming and some going it was hard to know exact numbers. All he knew was that he kept giving Laura glasses to wash up as the supply was limited, but sadly not the wine. By eleven forty-five they were all gone, Effey drifting out the door like a prima donna.

Suddenly it was quiet. Everybody had gone, they looked at one another in sheer disbelief with Tom saying, "Did you hear Effey?"

"I thought at one point that she was going to say she gave Mr Henri mouth-to-mouth resuscitation, but I think she saw me look at her and decided against it. What a carry on! Incidentally I think I'll ring Mr William to explain what happened this morning. I would hate him to think it was our doing. I'll do that now, perhaps while you're washing up."

"Yes I think that's very wise."

Tom dialled Mr William's number half not expecting to get a reply.

"Hello William Manley, who's there?"

"Hi it's Tom here, sorry to disturb you how are you today?"

"Yes, not too bad, what can I do for you?"

"Well I thought it was only right you should know I came to work with Laura this morning, just as a little comfort discreetly hidden in her office to finish some work on my laptop when we experienced the most extraordinary morning. Effey arrived within ten minutes of us only to be followed by half the village who wanted to know what had happened yesterday, she held court giving her orders for coffee. OK that didn't matter, then Mrs Daily arrived, didn't want coffee, would have a glass of your red wine left from the party, then Effey said you always kept a few bottles of white wine in the fridge so we were to get that out as well, which Laura had a few choice words under her breath to comment on to me, and they've only just gone, and I didn't want you to hear this from the jungle telegraph."

By this time Mr William was laughing. "Don't worry Tom, you obviously coped very well under your new boss, typical of Effey. I expect she could have received an Oscar for her appearance. It's OK, but thanks for letting me know."

"How are you?" Tom asked.

"I'm OK. Tell Laura I shall come in on Monday there's nothing I can do here at home and I'll sort her wages then. I'll tell Robert about today so as to stop any gossip. And thanks to you both."

# Chapter Twenty-One

Spring came quite late that year and Easter as late as it can be. The office had adjusted to the loss of Mr Henri and very much to Laura's surprise she still received the same wages but now just in two cheques for £150.00 each. The two men had decided they would close the office for a week from the Wednesday before Easter until the Wednesday after. It was on the Good Friday morning about eight o'clock when the phone rang. Tom answered it and Laura could hear him.

"Oh my goodness, when? Can we help?"

Laura stopped what she was doing realising that whoever it was and whatever the conversation was about by the look on Tom's face, it was serious. She looked at him with a questioning eye and he whispered back, "Mr William," and then as an afterthought, "he's OK."

"Would you like us to take you to Brighton? OK then, I know Ocean Village in Southampton quite well. Give me the name of the road and I'll find you." There was then a silence as Tom listened to what was being said. "I'll be with you in fifteen minutes or so," he said, putting the phone down.

"What's going on?" asked Laura.

"Well you'll never believe it – now steady – but Mr Robert's been found dead. I don't know all the ins and outs, but I'm going down to meet Mr William at Robert's apartment in Ocean Village. He says not for you to come as the police are there and it's all a bit messy."

"What, has he been murdered?"

"No, I would guess it's something to do with his lifestyle."

"Oh no, he always said it would be the end of him, but how Tom?"

"I don't know darling, and until I get there and find out I can't tell you, but when I know something I'll ring you."

Hurriedly he grabbed a sweater, kissed her goodbye and went. Laura found it hard to settle all sorts of thoughts going through her head. Poor Mr William, two brothers dead in less than three months. Surely this would be the end of Manley, Manley & Manley?

It was gone eleven thirty a.m. when Tom phoned to say he was on his way home.

"What's actually happened?" she asked.

"I'll tell you when I get there, pretty messy."

"How is Mr William?"

"Yes, he's OK he's a tough old nut, I'll see you in a while."

Laura found it difficult to concentrate or do anything sensible, her mind was going in circles. Poor Mr Robert, was it the end he had predicted for himself? She looked hard at Tom when he got in. "Are you all right?"

"Yes, I'm fine," he said lifting his eyes and shaking his head, "what a bloody mess!"

"Do you want to tell me?"

"Well for starters I met Mr William at the address he gave me, that's a penthouse suite believe you me, Laura, fabulously furnished, beautiful place. He explained to me that he was woken by a phone call from the police to say an accident had occurred at Mr Robert Manley's apartment and as next of kin would he be able to be there. Apparently he knew possibly what the situation would be, told them he would be about half an hour, and telephoned us because he didn't want to go there alone. He apologised profusely but said he was sure we knew Robert's lifestyle and wouldn't be surprised at what we might find. So I said where do we have to go to? Apparently he lived in another penthouse suite in walking distance from Mr William, so off we went. Police swarming everywhere. We knocked on the door, they let us in and then wanted to know who we were, and took our details. Then I said, has he been taken to hospital? What exactly happened, is he here? The police said, no sir, I'm afraid the gentleman is deceased. Forensics are in the bedroom with the body right now. I said, who found him or reported the incident, are you suspecting foul play? The policeman said, I cannot comment on that at the moment sir, but the person who informed us is a well known call boy in the area, we have interviewed him at the police station with all the details. I'm sure you can understand what possibly may have occurred. Actually Laura I was a bit irritated by his last comment I thought I hope he's not looking at Mr William and me, thinking and here's another couple of 'friends'."

"Oh surely not Tom."

"Well, you don't know, there we are two men, one the brother of the bloke in the bedroom whose obvious sexual needs were satisfied by a call boy. Anyway eventually the forensic guys left and I heard him say under his breath, normal thing. And then another officer asked us if we would like to go in, Mr William said, I don't really want to Tom, but just to satisfy myself I would like you to look please."

"Oh darling, how awful!"

"I couldn't refuse him, anyway I felt so sorry for him, but Jesus there was just a white sheet thrown over the body and there was an awful smell of chocolate which I could see was covering the lower half of his body and he was tied in bondage to the bed. The whole room was filled with the most weird contraptions plus whips, black leather underclothes and all sorts, in a few minutes I had seen enough. I should imagine he just had a heart attack and I suspect that is what will go on the death certificate."

"So what did you say to Mr William?"

"I just said he's peaceful enough. Possibly a heart attack. What else could I say? After all he's an old man, a second brother dead in a few months. That's quite a lot to cope with in anybody's book, but he did comment after a longish pause, uhm, over-exertion I expect, so I think he had a good idea of the situation. Then he said, come on boy, we'll walk back to my place. I went inside with him asked him if he was OK. He assured me he was but walking over to a glass cabinet and taking out two glasses he said, I think I'd like a little brandy, will you join me? I nodded yes, and then he said, I think I might ring Robert's two garden boys to go and tidy the place up. I know they have a key, they often used to spend time there with him and they would understand the situation with no idle gossip, would it be too bad for them to see and deal with?"

"And you said?" Laura asked.

"I said I thought that would be a good idea. After all Laura, I expect they had many a gay time there. What a pun," he said, and they both started to laugh.

"Not exactly the best choice of words."

Later on in the afternoon Tom asked what they were going to have for dinner and, if there was enough, did she think it might be a good idea to ask Mr William to come and eat with them if he didn't have a better offer and was feeling a bit lonely?

"It's roast lamb, that's fine by me I've got plenty."

On telephoning him Tom was surprised how pleased he seemed to be asked.

"That would be really nice, about seven shall we say?"

Under the circumstances they had a very pleasant evening Mr William repeatedly apologising for their interrupted day. They chatted a lot with him explaining how he loved Bermuda. It was quite late when he left he thanked them profusely for their kindness.

Once in bed they began to chat about the Manleys again. There was so much they didn't know and probably would never know, but they certainly found it very intriguing.

# Chapter Twenty-Two

Late evening on the Tuesday after Easter the phone rang. Laura picked it up and was surprised to hear Mr William on the line.

"Sorry to disturb you, but I have been doing some thinking over the weekend about the situation now both my brothers are dead. I know we are closed until Thursday but I would like you and Tom to come down to the office tomorrow morning I need to talk to you, can we say nine o'clock?"

She was a little surprised but said, "Yes that's fine, normal time nine o'clock, see you then."

Of course this set both Tom and Laura wondering what would the outcome of this meeting be, but they were both pretty sure it was to be the end of the firm of the Manleys. After all why would Mr William want to continue? He obviously had no need to keep it going for the money, he liked to travel, and he liked to socialise with his various lady friends.

After about half an hour Tom said, "I think we've chewed this over enough Laura, so now I'm going to start chewing you."

On arriving at the office the next morning Mr William apologised for asking them to come in but, having messed up their whole Easter, he hoped they would forgive him.

And so the most extraordinary story unfolded, he said, "Laura you must have realised my dear brothers and I trusted you implicitly. There is nothing within the business that we had to hide from you. You have taken us into the twenty-first century not only with new technology but with rearranging the office and house in general. We now have two empty offices and I thought Henri's old office we could perhaps get local societies to have it for their meetings, charging just a small sum which we could put towards a fund for anybody in need, and now as we are reduced to just the two of us in the office, I thought we could do with an extra pair of hands which might also introduce additional business. There is a young man called Paul Irons, he's twenty-eight years old now, he was an extremely bright and intelligent lad who wanted to do law. Unfortunately his father died unexpectedly and his mother became an alcoholic and blew all the money, he was brought to our notice by the local school so we decided to support him through college and university until he was able to earn a salary. We had and still have very little contact with him but he now practices at Wares Solicitors in Southampton. I believe he's a good all-round solicitor and extremely nice guy to boot, and I think you and I Laura should ask him to come and see us with a view to him joining us. Of course, it needs to be thought through and only with the consent of Wares, we don't want to be accused of stealing him so we need to look at the best way to go about it.

"The next thing I'd like you both to know a little of the Manley history, my brothers and I were all brought up in the most wonderful loving way by our parents, they taught us good manners, kindness and to share, and to love just as they had loved us and one another until their dying day. We spent many holidays in Bermuda when we were young, our father bought a house there and that is why I still love to go back there from time to time. We had a caring family that looked after us all those years ago and now continue to live in and run the place for us, although now I think I have to say me.

"In time Father set up a practice out there, Manleys solicitors of course and now the two youngest boys of the family, Tito and Rio, about the same age as yourselves run the office under the umbrella of the London office.

"As far as we boys were concerned we were educated at Eton and on leaving went straight into the London office to work. Our training was good but we had nothing on paper and Father could see that with litigation going the way it was, it would be better for us to be established in a small friendly community. So he brought the house here and set us up in practice under the eye of the London office if we should need any extra advice, he also bought us an apartment each here in the south and put a substantial amount of money into our bank accounts. He gave us absolutely no pressure, he wished us well saying work hard, be honest and make a good go of it. Luckily we did, I must say as young men we worked hard, we had a wonderful time, wine, women and song, but all in moderation. I think I feel I have the same today," he said with a smile.

"None of you ever married though," said Laura.

"Henri married. Did you not know?"

"No, I just assumed as I never heard of a wife that there wasn't one."

"Terrible, terrible business. He had the most lovely wife and daughter."

It was obvious to both Tom and Laura that Mr William was somewhat distressed by this conversation, he stopped talking for a moment and bowed his head.

Mr William continued, "Jenny, of course our parents' only grandchild was getting married to a Frenchman and Henri and Mattie his wife had a lovely house in the South of France. The reception was to be held in the gardens and we were all going down as a family for four days, but Jenny and Mattie were going down two weeks before to make sure that everything was correct with the preparations." He paused again, obviously reliving the time.

"Mother and Father held a little party at their house in Richmond for close friends who were unable to be at the wedding. Jenny and Mattie left the next day. We were so excited and looking forward to everything. In the early hours of the next night Henri had a message from the French police to say there had been an accident and both occupants in the car were dead and would he go for identification purposes? Father went with him but there was nothing to identify, both were burnt to death. As you can imagine we were absolutely distraught and dear Henri never really quite got over it, he brought back what he thought were the ashes and that is what the two gold pyramids on his desk were, the larger one for Mattie and the smaller one for darling Jenny."

"What a terrible sad story, I had no idea and I thought the gold pyramids were paperweights. Now I can understand those sad eyes," said Laura. "That's why he looked so happy when he died, maybe he's with them now."

"Perhaps, perhaps," replied Mr William, he inclined his head. "We can only hope so, you know he never went to France again. He made a gift of everything to Jenny's husband to be and returned to England with Father, a broken man.

"So sorry I digress, let's move on. Now let's come to the matter of the rooms upstairs, where you have never been, but always pestered us about, it's full of old files and boxes. Many of the files up there go back to our great-grandfather's time, they come from the London office. When father bought this place for us he realised the upstairs would be ideal for storing old papers of clients' past details. The London office was very respected with many affluent and influential clients needing to be sure of complete confidentiality, such as Edward and Mrs Simpson, and later the Profumo case that nearly brought the government down. Most of it I think could be burnt now, I was wondering if you Tom could take on the task to sort the pages out? Anything you thought needed to be kept could be put to one side and we would get a second opinion on, for history's sake."

"I don't see a problem with that but it may take some time to do as I do have my own client's work to see to, but yes I'm happy to help," said Tom.

"Many of the boxes in the other rooms are full of memorabilia of my mother and father. I think there are things from our childhood, unwanted wedding gifts and some things from Mother's old family home. I know for a fact her wedding dress, our christening robes and first teeth of all things and the gifts they gave each other and all manner of things. I would like to make some sort of display in their memory, I envisage perhaps a long glass showcase at the top of the stairs and some niches with bits and pieces in, you get my idea?"

"Yes I think I do, I'll put some thought into it and with Tom's help I'm sure we could come up with something," said Laura.

"I want it to be a beautiful, tranquil area – perhaps we could even make a library up there? I think you both understand what I'm getting at. And now for the last and most important thing the story of my parents' lives, their great love for each other and some of the precious things they held most dear, because I am the only living member of the Manley family I want somebody to know their history. Someone I can have trust in with an intelligent brain and a good knowledge of the law, and you two fit the bill."

Laura was looking at him in disbelief. Never before had they ever discussed their parents or their past.

"Two days before my father died he told us he had written the story of their love and life together. And he made me promise that when my mother died we as brothers would have the story written in their memory. He said I am sure it will hold surprises for you all but do not be embarrassed or ashamed of what you read you boys were conceived with passion and undying love."

"Are you going to write it?" Laura butted in excitedly.

"No I'm not."

Tom gave Laura a look of *shut up*, which she did.

"So to continue," said Mr William, "I took his hand in a reassuring way, then Mother came back into the room took him in her arms he closed his eyes with a smile and never regained consciousness, she didn't leave his side until his last breath three days later when we were all together."

Laura was finding it hard to disguise her sadness. Mr William leant forward and put his hand on hers.

"I know my dear. We three boys were obviously distressed, Father was nearly ninety and had just died of old age, not illness, he was just tired and went to sleep. Mother seemed to have such a calmness about her, she got us all together in the lounge and told us our father's wish was to be buried on the small island opposite the shore of our house in Bermuda. We knew it was there and looked just like a sand dune in the ocean, but that was all. Please explain more, said Robert. Mother looked out of the window looking more at ease than she had done for the past week, she said, well your father bought it for me and we called it our Love Island and when we were in Bermuda as a family and you would be safely tucked up in bed with Nanny Biddy to keep an eye on you together with the staff to protect you, your father and I would take the little boat across to the island and return early in the morning before you three were awake. We wanted to ask so much but we were so shocked. And Mother went on, now we will have the funeral in a few days. I have sorted most things out with the vicar, dear Edward, he has been so helpful and understanding. I suppose we will have to put the details in *The Times*. I don't know how many or who will come, but there will be no 'after party', you know how your father disapproved of that, he always said the true friends went to a funeral because they genuinely wanted to, all the others went just to be seen and for the free booze afterwards. It was a bit like as he always said to you boys, we give you as much as possible when we were alive which gives us all pleasure, which we couldn't see when we are dead. Now the coffin will remain in the church until the next morning and then the funeral directors will take it to the airport, to travel with me.

"We seemed to just sit there with our mouths open. She stood up and so did we in a sort of daze she hugged us all. Don't be sad my darling, she said.

"When all the arrangements were made although she had most of it arranged we pleaded with her to let us go with her, how would she manage when she got there? Don't worry, she said, there's a little stone hut on the island and in preparation for this time the old staff know exactly what to do to take care of everything and they will row the boat across to the island. Please just let one of us go with you, we can't bear to think of you alone, Mother, you who always needed such love and care, Robert said. Mother replied, I'll be fine I will have my love with me.

"There was just nothing we could do to persuade her," said Mr William. He paused. "Sorry," he apologised, "but it's still such a dreadful memory, even now it makes me emotional. Anyway we all went with her to the airport. It was possibly the most traumatic day of our lives, once again she hugged us to her. She said, not to be sad, Papa and I will always be with you. And she walked away from us into the departure lounge, with hindsight she never said a word about her return or when we would see her. Five days later we received a call from the local doctor in Bermuda, who we knew well as a friend. He said the two men who had rowed them to the island had gone back three days later as Mother had requested, only to find her dead beside Father's coffin with a note requesting them to place her in the coffin beside Father, also saying, *my love is gone, my heart is broken, please carry out our wishes so as we can be together for ever. We love our sons, asked them not to grieve but to be happy for us.*

"Ten days later we had to go to the London office to hear the reading of the will. It was read by some, excuse my language, bloody arrogant jerk who seemed to forget we could have had him sacked on the spot. Apparently there was a multimillion pound bank account, shares, property all to be shared between us equally, with two provisions, one that we would continue to work the country office of Manley, Manley & Manley. And that the book would be published. With that the obnoxious jerk folded the paperwork and then with his arms resting on his folded fingers, he said, I assume you'll carry out his wishes, as far as the book is concerned, do you have knowledge of this?

"My brain quickly jumped into action. I had not discussed this with Robert and Henri, no no, I lied, not because I was afraid of the task, but I didn't want to open a can of worms until we had a chance to see and read it. Then the jerk continued, it is possible this is a figure of your father's imagination at death. He stood up ending the meeting, shook our hands with something resembling a wet lettuce leaf, and said with an air of sarcasm, it would be difficult to imagine that you cannot do well and carry out your father's wishes with this fortune.

"We came back to the office here with the paperwork, found the book amongst the papers. There was three copies, one for each of us."

"So now we are going to write it?" said Laura.

"No, no," said Mr William, "you know it's a strange thing when you read about your parents' past, you have no idea about. You think when you are young you invented sex, it doesn't occur to you to think about your parents' passion, they are just a mother and father, wonderful gentle loving understanding parents who gave us all the love and protection and everything else they could give. We always knew they loved one another but to read about the intimate details is quite embarrassing. So we decided the book copies would go into the safe with the rest of the papers to be kept in mothballs until such time we felt differently, but of course that time has never come, and now there is only me, the least I can do is to put it into someone else's hands that I can trust for safekeeping."

Both Laura and Tom were looking at him with wide eyes, thinking they discovered later the same thing, what the hell is coming now, is he going to ask us to write it? But no he didn't, what he did say was:

"So while I'm alive I'm giving it to you both so you can read it, all I ask is that you do not destroy it and that you will make sure it doesn't die with you. It's such a long time since I looked at it in any detail, by today's standards I don't think it would be classed as particularly shocking. But with two Manleys dropping like flies I needed to get this off my plate, although I'm not planning to follow them for some years yet. Now I'm going home to Sandbanks, collect a few things and spend a few days with Madeleine, just don't fancy Southampton at the moment."

"Not Effey?" inquired Tom with a cheeky grin.

Mr William waved his hand. "No, not Effey, I want to be with somebody that makes me feel young, wanted, well and alive at this moment with perhaps a little hanky-panky to boot. I'll come back on Friday week Laura. I'm sure you can sort everything out, the funeral will be over, and we will put all our new ideas in place and begin the rest of our lives." With that he stood up and handed them the copies of the book in a grey folder, saying, "Good reading." He winked and was gone.

Popping his head back in the door to say "You can call me Bill if you like, it's easier."

And read they did.

# Part 3

# John and Arabella

# Chapter Twenty-Three

## *Preface*

My name is John Manley born in 1894 into a very loving, wealthy family, whose wealth came from our industrial ancestors.

I'm thirty-five years old and a barrister. I work in the family solicitor's office Manley & Son in London. Most of our work is for the government which means that I have been fortunate enough to do my part for the war effort here, although many of our staff were not so lucky.

I'm not married and am considered to be one of the most eligible bachelors of the time. I adore women and have loved many but have not found one I truly want to spend the rest of my life with. That is until I met Arabella, we married when I was thirty-five and she was just seventeen, and this is the story of our love and life together.

> Of the desolation I felt when I thought she might die.
> Of the joy she gave me with the birth of our three sons.
> Of the passion she loved me with, and
> Of the uncontrollable fear when I thought I may lose her.

I'm a very fortunate person. I am conscientious and work hard for my clients, I have a large circle of good friends and I suppose you would say I'm a socialite. I love partying and people and I have to admit I have probably lost count of had many beautiful women I have made love to. I like them to be glamorous, well-dressed and with a good figure but never another man's wife.

I hope I am perceived as a gentleman, considerate and gentle in lovemaking. I have had many relationships in my life but never one that made me think it would be perfect for both of us. I love the feel of a woman's skin, perfume and the curves of the female body. I have very few that I would class as real close male friends, maybe some half a dozen. Amongst those are Charles and Tim, we were all at Eton together. On leaving we all went into different walks of life, I law, Tim medicine, and Charles went into the army. He is the only one of us three who is married, possibly the best looking of us all with the opportunity to have married one of the most beautiful girls we all knew, but to our amazement he met and married Mabel who just seemed to sweep him off his feet; a rather plain, plump, not so exciting girl, but she obviously had what it took to please him. He has been very successful in his career in the army and is now attached to the War Office, it would not surprise me if in time he is made a Sir, of which I would be really proud for him. He and Mabel produced a daughter, and believe it or not they asked me to be the godfather.

At the time I did point out how unsuitable I thought I would be for this role, but there was no changing their minds. I of course was there for the christening and I always marked birthdays with a little piece of suitable jewellery together with something at Christmas. I haven't seen the child since a month after her christening as Charles was sent away on duty and was able to take the family with him. We write from time to time, but I think it is now some twelve years or more since we were face-to-face. One day we would have a lot of catching up to do.

This morning in my mail I received an invitation for Jocelyn Tate's annual weekend bash saying you can arrive Friday or Saturday, but definitely be here by Sunday for the party, she's a rather wild bohemian type of woman she lives in a beautiful old mansion with her extremely rich husband. Every year he takes a week off to go shooting in Scotland, and she always has her annual party, perhaps rave would be a slightly more suitable description.

I think I shall decline this year as the week after the event I have a particularly involved and difficult case to defend, and although I have already done most of the groundwork I feel I need to keep a clear head prior to it. I see on the invite this year it is called the 'Western Knight' and she prefers everybody to wear fancy dress but it's not at all compulsory. I think I'm slightly put off going to the last year's party called 'Just Be Naughty'. I did telephone beforehand and asked exactly what that meant, to which her reply was that or anything. I went but didn't enjoy it, even for me it was a bit too way out. She had hired a lot of male waiters which wore nothing but bowties, it's not that I'm a prude but I don't particularly find male tackle attractive, especially in varying states of arousal.

As the evening went on most of the guests seemed to get whipped up into the excitement. By the time I left most of them were in different stages of undress up to nudity, and although I wasn't in the least bit interested in watching couples having sex, just lying around on the couches and on the floor here and there, too many of the guests were highly excited by the activity.

So with hindsight my next best thing to do is to phone straightaway to thank her but decline this year. Unfortunately at the end of my conversation with her I found I had accepted. She had talked me into going for just the Sunday, leaving Monday morning with the promise that I could have my own room and bathroom in the mansion so that I could slip away when necessary. Although, she giggled, that the goings-on last year had got to her husband's ears and he was none too pleased, so it's going to be a little more sedate this year.

On arrival there I realised when the door was opened by the butler that most of the normal staff were around and there was already quite a few guests there. He showed me up to my room and all seemed well. I returned downstairs where they were serving champagne and nibbles to realise there was quite a lot of people there that I knew. I stood chatting to somebody I hadn't seen for some while when, at the top of the magnificent sweeping staircase, appeared what I could only describe as the most beautiful woman I had ever seen, she glided down the stairs and it appeared that every man's eyes were on her and I have to say sadly a lot of the ladies' eyes were green with envy. As she stepped off the bottom step she seemed to be enveloped into the crowd.

The champagne flowed, the canapés kept coming and I was quite enjoying the evening, but all the time my eyes kept drifting to this woman who was wearing an off-the-shoulder full-length turquoise dress which draped across her body as if that was all she was wearing. Against her red hair and slightly tanned skin the whole effect was exquisite. I made my way over to Jocelyn to inquire who this beautiful thing was. Turning her head and looking in the direction of my gaze she told me she was one of her daughter's friends from school, and she was staying with them for a few days. "Don't know what her name is though you'll have to find one of my girls and ask them." I didn't find out her name, but two hours later I was making love to her. We had gone to my room and just stripped our clothes off. She sat astride me and I didn't know how to control myself, she had the figure of an angel with breasts large for her size, so firm, with the most gorgeous large dark brown nipples I had ever seen. She took me in hand and somehow brought me three times almost to a climax and twice more she brought me to near explosion only to reduce me each time with the most wonderful fingers any man could imagine, I was in absolute blissful agony, unable to wait any longer I tipped her over onto her back and we made the most wonderful passionate love I had ever experienced. She lay beside me for a few minutes and then said "We have a party to go back to, see you later." She whispered it in my ear. I have to say I was quite ready to fall asleep with the memory of what I could only describe as mind-blowing sex. I was unable to get her out of my mind and so I returned to the party. I didn't see her again that evening and I was almost consumed with jealousy in case she was with another man. At three a.m. I thanked Jocelyn for a wonderful evening and went to my room, sleep just evaded me. I had been told that breakfast would be served at eight onwards for any of the houseguests. I didn't want to eat anything but I just could not miss seeing this woman again, although I knew I was being ridiculous and that the likelihood of her being up early morning would be remote. One hour later on my fifth cup of coffee, only as an excuse to wait longer, she walked into the room beautifully made up, wearing what looked to me like a town suit. I smiled at her wondering what her reaction would be. She smiled back, came close to me and whispered in my ear, "Marvellous." I didn't comment but I hoped she meant last night. I questioned that she was up early. She told me she had to catch the train to London that day to do some shopping. I couldn't believe my ears and, looking at her, I said I was going back to London would she like a lift? But I am going very soon , I told her. She squealed with delight, "I'll just dash and get my bag," she said.

We chatted about nothing really on the journey, my mind was whirling trying to think how I could perhaps get her to stay with me tonight. I asked her when she had to go back to the mansion and she said she was leaving on Wednesday but it didn't matter if she didn't go back until then. And silence fell between us. Then she said, "I wouldn't mind to stay with you until then." We drove straight to my apartment which was in Sloane Square, I carried her bags up and I carried them out again to the taxi I had ordered for her on Wednesday morning, to take her back to the mansion.

On that Monday morning I opened the door to my apartment, we stepped inside and I showed her around. I had three bedrooms and said she could have whichever she would like. She said, "Yours will be the best." I looked into her eyes and had to put my hand in my pocket and hold tight. I then did something I had never done in my life before. I went to the telephone and spoke to my secretary at the office and lied to her that I was unwell and would not be in today.

By the time I had put the telephone down and walked back to my bedroom she was lying there absolutely naked, propped up on one pillow. "Ready?" she asked, opening her legs just enough to be inviting in the most elegant way you could imagine. Within minutes I was inside her, she was just so wonderful – so tight, so warm. I lost count of how many times we made love, she was insatiable – but so was I. The fact that we climaxed together every time to me was just so perfect, fulfilling and rewarding for both of us. I always thought that I was the best lovemaker, but this woman was a match for me.

We stopped only to make some coffee and occasionally grab a snack which fortunately I had in my cupboard. I made sure she was not hungry or thirsty and asked if she would like to go out and eat. "No," the reply came, "we are living on love juice."

And so I lied again to my secretary on Tuesday but said I would crawl in on Wednesday. When we parted I think we both understood this was just the most wonderful time that we would never forget, whatever path our lives took. I called her Jane.

I went back to the office on Wednesday morning. I knocked myself into shape but not without some thoughts of the last few days. By the following Monday when I had to fight my client's case I was beginning to settle back to normality. The case lasted three weeks and I know that was very good for me, I had to concentrate in the day and in the evening I worked late at my apartment, knowing that to win this case would make my name at Manleys pseudonymous amongst top lawyers.

It was six months later I had a phone call from Charles to say that he was coming back to London and had been promoted with a new job at the British Embassy. He was obviously very pleased about it and said of course the family would be moving back as soon as he found a suitable house for them all, and they were twisting his arm to have a big party at the Ritz. "Sounds good," I said, "let me know. It will be good to see you all especially my goddaughter I think she's fifteen the end of this year."

"That's correct," Charles said. The invite arrived for me mid-October, sure enough it was at the Ritz. I was really looking forward to it and it would be good to have Charles back in circulation again. The invite had said bring a lady if you wish. But knowing that I would know so many people there, I decided to go alone.

On the night there was much greeting, hugging and shaking for Mabel and Charles and by the time I actually got time to speak to them, the party was well underway. People were dancing and generally having a good time. "Tell me," I said to Charles "where's my goddaughter? I haven't seen her yet."

"I suspect surrounded by men young and old. She's going to be trouble. John, you as guardian and me as father are going to have to keep a strict eye on her. There she is," he said, pointing to the figure of a young girl, hair piled high, chatting and laughing surrounded by several young men. "Come on, I'll introduce you to her because she's not the baby you last saw."

Walking up to her Charles tapped her on the shoulder saying, "Here my darling, meet your godfather." As she turned around I nearly died, she was the woman I had taken to my bed at Jocelyn Tate's party. She held out her hand to shake mine giving absolutely no sign of recognition of me. Did she not recognise me? Did she not want to recognise me? What would Charles say if he knew?

Twenty minutes later I discreetly left not having said goodbye to Charles and Mabel. As there were so many guests there my hope was that they wouldn't notice my absence and I didn't want to have to make some lame excuse to them. Arriving back home I pulled myself large whiskey, something I very rarely drank. I think I was just searching for a comfort, I felt physically sick, my mind was in a whirl: here I was a thirty-five–year-old man having made love to or been made love to by a girl not yet fifteen years old, my godchild, and my best friend's daughter. What a bloody mess! If only Jocelyn had told me she was a friend of her younger daughter I would've known roughly her age. If only I'd spoken to her more about herself, but then with hindsight that would've been difficult when she almost raped me. I realised I was just looking for excuses and there were none, but how the hell did Mabel produce such a beautiful thing? Yes Charles was good-looking, but, but, but... And how could someone so young understand men, surely she hadn't been around long enough to have gained such experience? I closed my eyes at such a thought and that body, she was fifteen going on twenty-five, I tried to make an excuse for myself. What would Charles say if he knew? One thing I knew for certain it had to stop, although I knew my whole being didn't want to. I just would have no contact with her, and would continue dating as before. Pouring myself another large whiskey I then tried to console myself that it was possible that she would not want to have any more to do with me, having found out who I was.

I decided I would try to sleep. Going to my bedroom all I could see was Jane and so decided to go and sleep in one of the other bedrooms. With the help of the whiskey I must have eventually fallen asleep. I was awakened by my doorbell ringing: it was ten a.m. Sunday morning, I got out of bed and slipped my towelling robe on. Opening the door, there stood Jane, I didn't know whether to close the door or drag her in as quickly as possible, in case somebody saw her. I decided to let her in was the best idea.

"What are you doing here?" I asked. "You can't come here, you must never come here again," I said.

She smiled saying, "Don't be silly, why not?"

"Why not?" I replied. "If your parents ever found out they would kill me. Now come into the lounge," I said, leading the way, pointing to the armchair. I said, "Sit down there and we'll sort this out now, once and for all."

She obediently did as I asked, slipping her coat off as she did so but leaving it so it sort of framed her body. I sat opposite her about ten feet away on the sofa. "Did you come in a taxi?" I asked not waiting for the answer I'll telephone and get one to take you home now."

"Wait just one minute," she pleaded, she got up and walked over to me sitting on the floor at my feet, which I quickly picked up and tucked under me so as not to touch. She was wearing a white silk blouse with no bra and I could clearly see her beautiful dark brown nipples showing through it. I tried to take no notice. Then she delivered the next bombshell by saying, "Did Daddy tell you on Saturday that he's been offered the position of the chargé d'affaires in the British Embassy in India. We've just got here and Mummy and I am so enjoying the social life, we've got lots of invites to parties and dances and glamorous functions which we like and now this, anyway I'm not going."

While she was telling me this, she slipped her hand on my robe which obligingly fell open. I knew the only decent thing to do was to remove her hand, which I did. "Why are doing that?" she asked.

"Because it's not correct," I said.

"Don't be silly John, look at you." And with one almost gazelle-like move she had taken me inside of her, there on the sofa. When we had reached a climax, I don't know what came over me, but I picked her up and took her to my bed.

When we laid there exhausted, I said to her, "As much as this is just so wonderful, it is the last time." She cried. But I stood firm and said most cruelly, "Now go home and come back when you've grown up. I have many beautiful women to take to my bed and you, my dear, spell trouble."

She looked at me, got up, picked up her clothes and went to the bathroom. I telephoned for a taxi to arrive as quickly as possible. When she came out I helped her on with her coat and walked her to the front door where, thankfully, the taxi was waiting. I closed the door feeling totally drained and the biggest bastard in the world.

Three days later I was in my office when my secretary buzzed me to say Charles and his wife were in reception and would like to see me if possible. Just ask them to take a seat for a few minutes I said. I knew what this meant and I tried hastily to put my thoughts together, ready for the shit to hit the fan.

I stood up and went out to find them, shaking Charles' hand and pecking Mabel's cheek. Lyingly I said nice to see you both, come on in, here have a seat. To what do I owe this honour? Thinking to myself, you fool what a stupid question under the circumstances.

"Well, I haven't seen you since our party," said Charles. "We've been rather busy and I don't know if you've heard that I've been offered a position in the British Embassy in India."

"Oh no, well done." I lied. "Congratulations."

"The problem is Arabella [my Jane]," chipped in Mabel.

"Yes," said Charles, "she is refusing to come with us, refusing to stay at school and in general being a perfect brat, having floods of tears day and night. She thinks she's twenty and can do as she pleases when she's not fifteen yet, so we thought we would come and see you because she thinks, as her godfather, she could stay here with you."

Something seemed to grab my throat and I was rendered speechless.

"Yes," said Mabel. "I can see you realise that it is quite ridiculous just as we do, so we thought we'd come and tell you, knowing how strong-willed she is and what she's like. [Not as well as I know what she's like, I thought], in case she approached you with her idea and put you in a difficult position. So if this should happen please make it a definite no and quite impossible."

Suddenly I felt unimaginable relief.

"Yes yes, I quite understand," I replied. "No worries." We chatted for some half an hour or more and they left. A little bit of me thought, give it a few years. When they return she would've grown up, then perhaps... I quickly tried to put the idea out of my mind.


Laura and Tom seemed to have been reading for ages. They were certainly finding Mr John Manley's so-called book interesting but it was very hard to read as there was almost no punctuation.

"Where have you got to?" asked Laura as each had a copy to read. "Do you want something to eat? I know we have both been picking at snacks but would you like something more now?"

"Yes I would," Tom replied. "Reading this is making me randy, get your clothes off and get upstairs and be prepared for a shagging."

"Tom! That's disgusting," came her reply. But Tom noticed she was already halfway up the stairs.

## BACK TO READING JOHN'S BOOK THE NEXT DAY

I threw myself into work and there was plenty of it, there was a scandal running through the government and we at Manleys seem to be getting a lot of work from it. Some clients were in trouble and some clients thought they might be in trouble and might be needing our services. The whole office was manic and there were many late nights and early mornings. My father was well pleased that we had been asked to deal with matters.

Charles and Mabel together with Arabella – despite her protests she never came to me about them, thank God – had left for India. I had a few lines from Charles saying they had sailed on the *Kaisar-i-Hind* ship first class from Tilbury. Arabella seems to have got over her stress, and is enjoying life on board, being the centre of attention with crew and passengers alike, I don't know why when she walks in a room everybody looks. Quite a handful. We have taken Bindey Wales, you may remember her, John, a local girl when we were young, now a trained nurse, with us as chaperone cum companion for Arabella. She is thirty-five years old, will possibly always be a spinster, very nice to have around and thank goodness she and Arabella seem to get on well.

I managed to make time to take a few of my regular female acquaintances to wine and dine and take back to my apartment. The pressure was still on at the office and I was finding it difficult to sleep or eat. The Whitsuntide holiday weekend was approaching and it had been decided at the office we would take a break. I telephoned Georgina – somebody who, if I was to marry, probably would be the perfect person. She was beautiful, intelligent, gentle and understanding, we seem to know one another so well that even a silence was not difficult between us. I asked her if she would like to spend the long weekend with me in Brighton. She eagerly agreed. I picked her up on Saturday morning, she was her usual bubbly self but I knew I was less enthusiastic about being with her. She knew the pressure that we were under at the office, so when I just failed to be able to make love to her she just took it all in her stride saying, "Let's not try that any more this weekend. We'll catch up in that department later, let's just enjoy being together."

I was disappointed that I had failed to rise to the occasion for Georgina, and to be honest surprised. Work continued at a hectic pace. And most nights when we finished I just go and have a couple of drinks in the pub, go home and fall into bed. At least I was finding I could sleep now. My father commented how thin I was looking. Eventually our workload subsided then, getting out of the bath one morning, I caught a glimpse of myself in the mirror: Was that really me? What a mess. I could see my ribcage, and my penis looked about two inches long with balls like tennis balls, perhaps there was something wrong with me. Was this the beginning of old age? If it was I didn't want to join in. I'd heard about prostrate problems, was this it? Perhaps it was time for me to get a check-up. I didn't want to go to my old family doctor so I rang Tim who was a GP. I got dressed and went to work about ten a.m. I tried Tim's number, a very nice voice answered. I didn't want to tell her anything, so I said I was a friend of Tim's, John Manley and could I have a private word with him? Two seconds later Tim was on the phone. "Hi John, great to hear from you. What's it all about? Party coming up or something?"

"No, I'd like to come and see you, got a bit of a problem. Don't want to advertise it so wondered if you could give me a bit of a once over?"

"Yes of course," Tim replied. "Today about four o'clock OK? Look forward to it, perhaps we could have a drink together afterwards."

"Thanks," I said not knowing if I was relieved or scared, but I knew I had to do something.

Tim greeted me warmly on arrival at his practice. I explained my concerns.

"OK," he said, "get on the couch."

We chatted away during the examination. He asked a few questions about my sex life or lack of it, did I know the women that I slept with? How much did I drink, eat, sleep? He then took a couple of X-rays. And then tested for prostrate.

"I need to take a blood sample," he said, "and then I'll test for diabetes if you can pee in this pot. Get dressed, then we'll have a chat."

"So as you can tell me I've got some venereal disease and condemn me to the scrap heap?" I said.

"No, not at all!" he replied.

I got dressed just as he finished the diabetes test

"No, nothing to worry about there, you have absolutely no signs of prostrate, and the X-rays show no sign of disease. Of course the blood test will take a while to come back. But I don't think that's going to be anything to worry about, either. But you are extremely thin. I have a few more ideas of your problem – come, sit down. Shall we have a whiskey together?"

"That would be nice," I said. "So as you can give me the really bad news? I must admit I'm not surprised on the last three dates, couldn't even begin to get an erection. I tell you I'm scared how long have I got?"

"At least another fifty years I should think. Your problem's in a different place: it's in your head, not in your dick." I sipped my glass and he said, "I hear old Charles has got a pretty impressive job in the embassy in India, took Mabel and Arabella with him, bit of a shock to you? I hear you were getting your leg over his daughter."

I looked at him in disbelief.

"How did you know that?" I asked.

"Charles told me," he replied I couldn't believe my ears.

"Charles didn't know, Tim. I'm positive he didn't know."

"Believe you me John, they knew."

"I didn't know her as Arabella, I had no idea who she was, I knew her as Jane," I told him.

"Yes, they knew the whole story, they didn't blame you but therein lies your problem. You're in love. It's Arabella John."

"Do you really think so?" I said. "I was once told by an old lady that you weren't in love until it makes you sick. Perhaps you are right."

"No doubt I'm right, John."

"But what can I do now she's gone? She's too young, she may not feel that way about me, and she's my goddaughter."

"Well, you've got to get her out of the system somehow. Write to her, tell her what you feel. Not only will it help to ease your mind, she may put you out of your misery one way or the other. Not just one letter, I think. You must give it at least four to six months, this could be a courtship by love letters."

Suddenly I felt a little better.

"Do you know Tim, I think you could be right. In everything I do I think of her, in every woman I have dated since her I can only see her beautiful face. I just would not admit it to myself. I do so hope you are right. Thanks."

"Well keep in touch. I'll phone you in a few weeks with the blood test results. Go home, and get writing."

That evening I decided to put pen to paper. Should I go the whole hog as Tim had advised, and tell her my feelings? Or should I just write a simple letter asking if all was well and how was she liking her new home, and then follow it later with more explanation of my feelings? If I was to take some three months or so to declare my love, perhaps a cautious start would be a good thing. Anyway, I was forgetting I would be able to tell from her replies what her feelings were.

I awoke the next morning feeling good. I went to the post office on my way to work and, having got the correct postage for the destination, I posted it into the box and headed to my office with a spring in my step. I had not considered the length of time my letter would take to get to her or even for her to reply. After ten days I was searching the mail fervently every day. Nothing. I then thought perhaps it never got there, so I decided to write again, much the same letter. I didn't want to contemplate whether she just wasn't interested.

That week Tim rang me to say the blood test was clear.

"How's your writing?" he asked. I told him the situation, but said I was feeling a lot better, his advice seemed to be working. Three months passed. Sometimes I wrote twice a week, each letter explaining more about my feelings for her. I then began to question myself: was there no reply because our brief relationship had meant nothing to her? More letters and two weeks later I found myself making inquiries as to the best way to get to India. I have to see her even if it meant being shunned. I could of course contact Charles to announce my arrival, but it was possible he would refuse to let me see her as he and Mabel apparently knew of our relationship. I had made the arrangements not to be in the office for three weeks on the excuse that I was going to visit Charles and family. Everything sorted including visa, money, gifts to take, seasick pills. I was off to the travel agent to get my passage. When my secretary put my mail on my desk that morning I could see a foreign stamp sticking out of the pile, my heart began to beat wildly, I grabbed it with enthusiasm, realising at the same time it wouldn't be from Arabella because I always wrote to her with my home address. Fingers trembling I knew it was from Charles, possibly telling me to back off and get lost, and Arabella was marrying some high-flying horrible arrogant twit from the Embassy. Pulling the contents of the envelope out I went to the last page only to have my fears confirmed. There was Charles' signature. Not that of my wonderful beautiful gorgeous darling Arabella. And so I read with heart in mouth:

*My Dear John,*

*I'm not quite sure when you will receive my letter but I'm putting it in the embassy bag to hasten delivery. It is with great sadness I have to tell you Mabel passed away yesterday. She contracted salmonella which the doctors were unable to treat. Although I am much stronger than she the doctors have confirmed I too have the bug, they believe we picked up from the dinner party we went to. Thank God Arabella was not with us.*

*So my dearest friend I am asking you to do the only thing I know to protect our darling daughter. I'm sending her home with Binney, you may remember we brought her with us as a companion for Arabella, and they have become very close thank God, Binney understands Ari very well although not to overbearing, and Ari loves and trusts her.*

*They will board the boat from here in two days' time, the sixth of June, arriving in London 26th June, please meet them.*

I looked at my calendar on my desk knowing exactly what the date was but suddenly my mind had gone blank. It was now June 20th.

Five days to go. I read on, hands shaking:

*I have made arrangements for them to go to Little Heads. You no doubt will remember our home back there in England which we have kept running by Mr. and Mrs. Potts who hopefully will be expecting them, from the detailed letter I have sent to them concerning money. I have discussed with both Binney and Ari everything and explained I will follow when I am better. But I know in my heart this will never be, but only Binney realises this. I am asking you to marry Arabella.(Which she doesn't know.) And take care of her. I know she has never stopped loving you and I only hope you can find space in your life to take care of her. I must tell you I am ashamed to say she never received any of your letters as I destroyed them. If only I hadn't been so full of my career ambitions, I would never have brought them all to this godforsaken hole. And so my dear John, I entrust our beautiful daughter to you. I say farewell and please forgive me.*

*Yours,*

*Charles.*

I reread the letter in case I had misunderstood its contents. I stood up and walked to the window, feeling numb. I walked back to my desk and sat down, placed my head in my hands and wept uncontrollably, in sadness for my friends

But in happiness for myself. I tried to collect my thoughts together; in five days they would be arriving home. What to do next? I stood up again. I sat down again. My heart was pounding. Oh, Just to see her, to touch! Again I knew with every nerve and bone in my body I loved her beyond belief. And then in another horrendous moment I thought OK Charles said he knew she loved me, but say she didn't? Say when she got off that boat she couldn't stand me? Well I would just take care of her just to be able to see her every day, yes that is what I would do. I looked at my diary: with a little manipulation I realised that, with the time I had planned to have off to go to India, I could now use to be with Ari and sort things out.

I decided to go to Little Heads that evening to see the Potts and find out if they had received Charles' letter, and if so what they would feel about the news. I need not have worried, they seemed to know me and greeted me warmly, shaking my hand and inviting me in for coffee. What I hadn't realised was they had been with Mabel's family for many years and had known Ari from the day she was born, as well as Binney who had helped with the new baby.

They were where very upset to hear of Mabel's death but very excited about, as they put it, having the two girls home. I explained I was a little dazed by it all and had been asked to pick them up from the boat. What I didn't know and the Potts didn't say was did they knew that Charles had asked me to marry Ari, and would they think me too old, or was I kidding myself that they thought I was at least fifteen years younger than I looked?

After quite a lot of chat about the past and their relationship with the family I begged my leave of them, saying I had quite a lot to see to before the girls arrived. I stood up and thanked them for the coffee, they walked with me to the door shaking hands again and bidding me farewell. Mrs Potts followed me to the car, touching my hand she said:

"You know she was so broken-hearted when they took her away, I hope you can mend it."

I looked at her and could see her eyes were full of tears. I leant forward and kissed her on the forehead, and got into the car and left.

As I drove away I felt relieved that I had met the Potts, they seemed good people.

The next few days flew by, I tidied all my paperwork at my desk and told my secretary that I would probably now be away for three weeks. But I wanted no telephone calls or messages until I appeared back in the office. I woke early on the 26th. This was the day I had been waiting for. At nine o'clock I telephoned the docks to see what time would the boat would be arriving. Five p.m. I was told, disembarking would start after five fifteen. I decided I would do some shopping to fill the fridge with goodies in case Ari and I needed anything to eat if at any time she was here with me. I would also get some champagne, in hope that we had something to celebrate. The time dragged so long that morning. I decided I would leave for the docks at four but at three o'clock bathed, dressed and ready to go I could wait no longer, so I decided a slow drive was better than a long sit. I had bought a red rose to give her on arrival, so carefully laying it on the front seat I took off. I actually never did give her the rose, as I decided an old man giving a young girl a rose at the docks might embarrass her.

I thought my heart was going to stop as the first passengers came through to leave the ship. Then suddenly she was there, my darling Ari, running towards me, she looked more beautiful than I'd ever remembered, dressed in a beige silk dress which fell over her breasts, tumbled to her hips and finished in a pleated skirt, with slightly darker shoes with pointed toes and high heels. Without thinking I threw up my arms to greet her and within seconds I was holding her close. I knew at that moment I could never live without her. Soon Binney was stood beside us. I let go of Ari and shook hands with her. We waited for the porter to bring the luggage and made our way to the car nearby. I opened the boot for him, while Ari opened the passenger door, picking up the rose.

"For me?" she asked.

We held each other's eyes for what seemed an age, no words needed.

We all three chatted away on the journey back to Little Heads, Ari sat so close to me I could feel the warmth of her body. After a little while she slipped her hand on my inner thigh, it was like an electric shock going through my body, I tried hard to concentrate on driving. She slowly moved her hand upwards until it was in my crotch, I was out of control. I just hoped Binney couldn't see what was going on. When we had nearly reached our destination Ari suddenly kneeled up in the seat to face Binney, saying:

"I was thinking Binney I will go with John to his house for a few days so we will drop you off at Little Heads, it will give you a few days to adjust and sort yourself out and perhaps relax a little with the Potts. I know you love them dearly, and will have lots of catching up to do telling them about our travels, and before Father gets back John and I have lots of things to sort out. Is that OK?"

"Well," said Binney. "Perhaps you should ask John first it may not be convenient for him."

I couldn't believe what I was hearing, "That will be fine." I mumbled. Mind in turmoil, heart racing, was I really hearing this? As we pulled up to our destination, the door opened and there stood the Potts. Ari jumped out of the car and ran to greet them, followed quickly by Binney. They quickly explained what was going to happen, and it seemed to me Binney was quite pleased with the situation.

"Now," said Ari, "all we need to do is to get Binney's luggage, and then I think we should be going. I'm rather tired and would like to rest, but it's just so wonderful to be back, and when Father arrives everything will be great."

"We quite understand my dear, perhaps you will come and have some tea with us in a few days? It's been a long journey and you have had a traumatic time with poor mummy dying," said Mrs. Potts. She hugged Ari to her.

"Go and have a nice rest, I'm sure John will look after you."

"I hope so," she said, looking at me.

"Of course," I replied.

With goodbyes said we were in the car and on our way, some forty-five minutes' drive. She sat very quietly on her side of the car and neither of us spoke. Me, too afraid to in case I had read the signs wrong earlier. Pulling up outside my apartment I switched off the engine, hopped out, opened the boot to pick up the cases and walked to the door. Unlocking the door I stepped inside, switched on the lights and Ari was right beside me: we were in each other's arms kissing and hugging. I kicked the front door shut and we were ripping each other's clothes off like savages, and the love we made was the most beautiful passionate enjoyable sex. When we had finished we just lay there enjoying each other's bodies only to repeat our lovemaking again, we had hardly spoken during this time only to moan in ecstasy. When Ari pleaded for a third experience I reminded her she had professed tiredness, and needing rest to the Potts. She just laughed in that wonderful delightful way, putting her fingers on my lips.

"Aren't you glad," she said.

That week I realised that all I wanted was an Ari to be mine for the rest of my life, my whole being was happy, my body satisfied and I knew she felt the same. I didn't know what we did that week,, we ate a little, drank some champagne, and made love in every possible way. The only thing I stopped for on that first day, thank goodness, was to ring Mrs Keith my cleaning lady to say take a week off with pay as I'm away. Putting the receiver down I pulled the cable out of the wall: I didn't want to hear or see anything other than Ari. We even ignored my doorbell when it rang one day.

Arabella has grown from a girl into a woman in the time she was away. I didn't know if she had read about satisfying a lover, or if she had gained personal experience. I didn't care. We fitted to perfection. She teased me, she caressed me and stroked me and her body responded to my every touch – this, for me, was true and perfect love. On waking on the Friday morning of our first week together I rolled over onto her. She immediately responded.

"I love you," she said. "You may well realise my darling when I was away I looked for the satisfaction I had with you before I went. I cannot lie and say I didn't enjoy it, but nothing ever came up to you. I am not ashamed to tell you this because I feel it has made me what I am now, able to satisfy you in every way which is what I want to do for the rest of my life. Please hold me safe."

"I will I will always, you gorgeous thing, but now we must talk," I replied. She raised her body up off of the pillow, saying:

"Before or after lovemaking?"

She pushed her breasts up to my lips.

"After, maybe," I said.

"Perhaps." She giggled, running her hands down over my backside. "I can feel you mean before."

"No I don't," I said.

"But John, I can feel you don't mean no, and look at me," she said, pointing to her nipples.

"I know," I said, caressing and kissing her breasts, knowing I had never seen any so beautiful as hers: lovely, soft, slightly tanned with large dark nipples just as though they had been painted. Just asking for attention as I had remembered them on our first encounter.

"No I am in charge," I said, knowing what I was about to say to her. To either make or break my heart.

She looked at me intently with head on one side eyes wide open.

"Marry me Arabella," I said.

She took a deep breath, looking straight through me. I thought for a terrifying moment she was going to say no.

"Oh Ari," I blurted out. "I'm not really that old, I'll do anything you wish as long as we can be together."

A tear ran down from her beautiful eyes.

"Yes," came a whisper. I cradled her in my arms.

"Then why are you crying?"

"I'm just so so happy," she said.


Tom put his 'book' down, looking at Laura who was still engrossed in hers. He said, "I think I'd like to go out tonight Laura and take a break from this sex manual. Jesus, I can't believe this man wrote this so many years ago, it just goes to prove how wrong today's thoughts are about life years ago, it really hasn't changed. Anyway what do you think? After all, this Easter has been rather odd, and as the office isn't open until Monday again then Mr William. not coming in until the following Friday, I could probably come down with you and do a bit and we could have a look around to see what to do with the upstairs, I know you have clients to telephone and see to, so what do you think."

"Good idea, we can read on later it's just that I feel I'd like to have finished it by the time Mr William. returns. Yes let's put them down and be ourselves," said Laura.


## THE BOOK CONTINUED. (READ BY TOM AND LAURA THE NEXT DAY)

On the Saturday of that week I received a wire from the Foreign Office to say that Ari's father, Charles, had died and according to his wishes he was to be buried out there with Mabel his wife. I was uncertain how to tell Ari, I was not sure how she would react, would she want to call off the idea of us being married, would she want to return to India? I had to admit I was afraid of the consequences. It was a lovely early spring morning and we had plans to go and make some arrangements for our wedding. I was in the lounge when Ari came down the stairs fresh from her bath, wearing only her bathrobe which clung to her damp body like a spider's web in the morning dew. Her hair was tumbling down over her shoulders and into the cleavage of her breasts. I held out my arms to her, I wanted to protect her from anything horrid but I knew I must tell her the news right now. I put my lips to her ear and whispered "I love you." Pausing for a moment, I said

"Ari, I have some bad news, your father has passed away." I felt a shudder goes through her body. She was silent for what seemed an eternity. She then held herself away from me, tears running down her face she said:

"I love you."

We decided to go to Little Heads and tell them the news, but before that I felt we had to try to discuss our future. As reluctant as I was to do this I knew I must know what she wanted. Would she want to put things on hold for a while to reassess her feelings and future? So gingerly I asked the question.

"Please tell me, would you like time to think things over before we marry, or does this change your feelings on the marriage?"

There was what seemed to me to be an intolerably long silence between us. Then she took my hands and said:

"John, I have loved you for ever. If I can be with you as your wife, that is my one wish. Yes, I am devastated by Father's death but he's there with my mother, and I have no wish to be anywhere else but here with you. I want the wedding to go ahead and I think under the circumstances my parents would have wanted it to. I don't know if Father has made a will. But I think he would want things to go on as they are, for instance, Mr and Mrs Potts to stay at the house and Binney to be well cared for. You probably will know more about Father's affairs as his solicitor than I do, I will assume apart from a few gifts. I will be the biggest benefactor and therefore able to make these decisions. I am so sad today, but I'm not a child and have already given a lot of thought about this day when it came. I knew in my heart when I left Father it would be our last time together. He was trying to be so brave for my sake but he was so ill, I think his reason for sending me home was that I could be looked after by you. I think he knew I would never get you out of my head and that eventually I would want to come home to England, even if he was still working out there. My biggest fear was that you would have forgotten me and be married to one of those glamorous chic women that have always surrounded you. And I know you have dated, loved and had affairs with many."

I kissed her gently on the forehead, unable to believe the wisdom in her words but understanding there would be some sadness to come in the next few weeks. Ari went off to get dressed and I telephoned the Potts and asked to speak to Binney, knowing that she knew the situation when they had left and of Charles' request of me. Hearing her voice, I told her the news and explained we would go and see them all that afternoon.

"Oh dear, has he gone? How is Ari, have you told her? And how is she?"

"Yes she knows, and I think she expected it. Not quite so soon perhaps, she is obviously sad and has shed a few tears but she's very strong and sensible about it."

"Good," replied Binney. "And the marriage?"

"Yes, it is her wish and mine. We will go ahead, maybe smaller under the circumstances perhaps, just close friends to the ceremony. I think it will be at St Luke's, but listen Binney, could you tell Mr and Mrs Potts before we arrive? I think it would be less stressful for Ari that way, and about her father's wish for us to marry."

"Yes, that is fine John; and may I say I will be here to help in any way possible. As you know, I'm very fond of Ari and we are very close."

Before we left to go and see them I explained to Ari what I had asked Binney to do. On arriving there was much hugging and kissing and tears, but if truth be told I think Ari instilled a sense of calmness amongst all of us. She explained that it was her wish that we would be married at the end of the month, a small affair with lunch there at Little Heads for a few friends and close colleagues of mine, after which we would leave for a few days' honeymoon. Then a memorial service would be arranged for her parents a little later. All this was news to me but, while explaining the details, she was looking at me holding my eyes and left me nodding in approval.

On the way home I pulled up outside a house that was for sale, about fifteen minutes from Little Heads. How would you feel if we move from my apartment to here? I asked. If you think that's a good idea then I am happy, she said.

"We can't go in now, but I have looked. It has five bedrooms and a big walled garden, after all we may need it for children, if we decide to have any."

She giggled. "Well, already we are getting quite good at practicing."

I didn't know and didn't care what people were saying about Ari and I. The wedding was over, the honeymoon was in Devon and we were in heaven. We returned home and arranged the memorial service which was attended by about 300 people. I think I found it more daunting than she did. She looked absolutely beautiful in her neat black dress and hat, just as she had done on our wedding day. I was so proud to be her husband.

I was back to my normal routine at my office. We had moved to the house I had looked at, it was perfectly decorated but Ari took time choosing furniture and soft furnishings, as I didn't have enough from my apartment. She was in her element, like an excited child not able to wait for me to get home to show me what was new and what she had done that day. She had an almost insatiable lust for love, which I rose to on every occasion.

We were invited to lots of functions and private dinner parties. It seemed everybody was just charmed by her beauty, personality and warmth. We in return entertained a lot, she was so good at it; organising menus and drinks, it was as if all I had to do was be there by her side. I loved it. We still had Mrs Keith my cleaning lady from my apartment who Ari got on with like a house on fire, and sometimes the Potts and Binney would lend a helping hand. There always seemed to be lots going on, the house and life was perfect

Then one day when we had been married about four months I was in my office when Binney came to see me, wondering if I had a minute to see her.

"Of course, come on in. I bet you've been shopping got a little tired and need a lift home?"

"No. John I just want to have a private word with you. OK, let's have some coffee together, I'll get some organised and we can have a chat," and so sipping our coffee she began.

"I know how happy you and Ari are and it makes me happy to see you."

"So?" I said.

"I think she's pregnant."

"Pregnant?" I exploded. You have just made me even happier, I think, jumping up and hugging Binney. But why has she not told me herself? Mind you, I'm not surprised the amount of practice we have put in...

"Oh Binney, this is just wonderful! I must be the happiest man alive."

"But John this is why I'm here, I don't think she realises she's pregnant. Her periods stopped before she left India and I think, with all that has happened and the fact that she is so fit and so in love, she hasn't given it a thought."

"So what are you trying to tell me? Does it matter if she doesn't realise?" I asked. There was a short silence and then she said:

"I don't think the baby is yours."

"What?" I exclaimed, sinking into my chair in disbelief. "But why Binney, why?"

"I don't think you can ever understand her desperate plight when her parents took her to India. She tried to forget the love she had for you, the love she thought she could never have, and this is the result."

I was speechless. Putting my head in my hands I felt physically sick. Surely I was not to lose her now? I looked up and said to Binney. "I don't care. I will bring the child up as mine together with the rest of the children we will have."

"I know you will John," Binney said. "But the problem is the baby will be Black."

I found I was crying and Binney was around the desk to comfort me. I buried my head into her embrace.

"Now, now," she said. "I can help."

"Help? How can you help?"

"As you know I'm a qualified midwife and can deal with the birth. But you will need to have her under a doctor's care. Surely you must have a doctor yourself who will become your family doctor, both now and in the future? If you wish I can move in to help, but I would still like to keep my home at Little Heads."

"Oh Binney what a mess!"

"No, no it doesn't need to be. Just calm down and tell me if this is what you would like."

"I don't know, please give me a couple of days to think. At this moment I just don't know. I just want her to tell me and to reassure me that she still wants me and not the father of this child."

"I can assure you that she will. But when you have decided what you want, just tell me and I will suggest to Ari that I think she's pregnant and must make some plans to see your family doctor and make arrangements to have the baby at home with my help. Be brave John, we will get through this. You know how fond I am of both of you, and I think of Ari as my own daughter, and you have made her so happy. I know you will go on and have a wonderful family together. I will go home now and wait to hear from you."

It was about twelve o'clock. I buzzed Jane and said, "Cancel any appointments I have this afternoon. I need to be free."

I walked up and down my office, my mind in a turmoil. Should I confront Ari? Should I go with Binney's ideas? But most of all I wanted to block from my mind any man lying with her. I tried to rationalise: I have had many women, why should it not be that she had other men, but to have a child which wasn't mine could I cope, but what were the alternatives?

We had an invitation to a party that evening which I knew Ari really wanted to go to. I left my office to go home, and she greeted me with her usual loving enthusiasm, asking me about my day and chatting about hers. I looked at her thinking: I don't know anything about pregnant women and babies, but to me you don't seem anything different to usual. We got ready to go to the party and, as she stood up from the bath, I looked at her naked body. No, it couldn't be right. She walked towards me, saying:

"Darling, is something wrong? Are you not feeling well? We don't have to go to the party if you don't want to."

"No I'm fine, we will go.'

I must say my mind was in a whirl at the party. Ari looked absolutely stunning as usual, male and female being enchanted by her charisma, people just loved her, and so did I, my decision was made: I would speak to Binney.

After dealing with the mail the next morning the first thing I did was to telephone Binney, fortunately she answered the phone. Clearing my throat I said.

"I have decided to take your advice."

"I'm glad John, trust me please."

"I know it may raise eyebrows, but I will bring the child up as mine.'

"Yes," she replied, her lack of comment slightly disturbed me.

"Should I wait until Ari tells me she is pregnant?"

"Yes, wait. I will talk to her over the next couple of days suggesting, I think, she's pregnant and say that she must tell you. But she will need to have the care of the doctor, although I will be with her for the delivery. Now, you must sort out who you will have for your family doctor. Explain your wife is expecting her first child and she thinks she's possibly two to three months pregnant. Also explain my relationship with her, companion and chaperone, before you were married and that I am a qualified midwife and will be living with you, and then if he comes to the house we can meet him and discuss Ari's details fitness, and anything he wants to know, and tell us how he will deal with the birth."

"Yes," I said, "thank you."

My next phone call was to Tim, my old friend from Eton, who had sorted me when I thought I was done for. Fortunately he was at his practice. I had forgotten with all that had happened that he didn't come to our wedding and probably didn't know about our mutual friends, Charles and Mabel, being dead as he had taken a year off to travel.

"Hello John! Haven't heard from you for some time, how's life going?"

"Fine. Actually I have to come your way tomorrow and wanted to see if you feel like having a bit of lunch with me?"

"Yes, great idea. Let me just check my diary... how's one o'clock? There's a pub just around the corner from the surgery here, Lord Louis, meet you there.

I walked into the pub the next day, Tim was already there.

"Gosh man, you look fantastic, about fifteen years younger than when I last saw you. Tell me all, did my advice work?"

I nodded and smiled.

"So did you go to her, or did you just get over her?"

"No I didn't go, I wrote to her nearly every day but she didn't get the letters, Charles confiscated them."

"So now you're flying your kite just like the old days, lucky bastard."

"No, I married her."

"Jesus," he replied. "I can't believe that."

"Well Mabel died and Charles knew he was going to, he wrote to me realising the mistake in taking Arabella to India, saying he was sending her home for me to marry her which was what she desperately wanted. And now we are expecting our first baby and now we need a family doctor, and I wondered if you would take us on?"

"Delighted old chap, where's she going to have the baby?"

"At home." And then I explained about Binney and about her suggestion of a meeting.

"Yes good, how far gone is she, two months' maximum?

I felt a bit sick at this question and hoped my hesitation didn't show. "We don't really know, we've been married about three months but we got a bit of practice in before." Tim laughed.

"You old bugger you haven't changed, but I think I should see her sooner rather than later. Perhaps one day next week? Speak to her, give me a ring and we will make a date."

"Thanks a lot," I said, thinking *Ari please tell me soon*. We chatted on about his travels and what he had been doing and enjoyed a really nice lunch. Driving back to the office I felt a bit more at ease. That evening we ate at home and sat by the fire, afterwards nothing was said and we went to bed and made love, and again during the night, she still said nothing.

The next morning I telephoned Binney and told her I'd got the doctor organised and asked if she had mentioned to Ari that she thought she was pregnant. Not yet was her reply.

It was now a week later and still Ari had said nothing to me. Then, as we lay in bed together I gently ran my hand across her tummy, it was as if I'd pulled a plug. She told me the whole story of how she tried to forget me and had got into a relationship with one of the staff at the British Embassy and now she thought she was pregnant and she feared that the baby was not mine. I lied and said I didn't care, it probably was mine anyway and that I was over the moon that we would have a child. The fact that she didn't say the father was Black or anything about her feelings she may still have for him was my salvation.

"We will delight in it whatever, and give it all the love we can," I said kissing her tummy. "It will be precious and I hope one of many." I was absolutely amazed at how I coped with the situation, if I had practiced what to say it wouldn't have been as good. I explained to her that we would get Tim, a friend of mine, to be our family doctor and perhaps it would be a good idea if Binney moved in with us for a while. Ari readily agreed.

Everything moved on quite normally. We wined and dined and went to parties, hosted guests at home, she just became more radiant as the time went by. Then one morning I was in my office when I had a phone call from Binney, she sounded very worried and said would I go home immediately. Ari was not well and was losing a lot of blood and was in great pain, but she didn't want me to be called or worried. I slammed down the phone not able to get to her quickly enough.

I ran into the house and up the stairs: Ari looked terrible. I quickly phoned Tim, who said he would come immediately. I went back upstairs there was so much blood I couldn't believe my eyes. I held her hand tightly feeling so absolutely useless.

Tim did arrive quite quickly. He took one look and said, "Call the ambulance, she's very ill John."

Once in the hospital the surgeon said he must operate but he wasn't hopeful for either of them.

"I can't lose them, they are so precious!" I screamed. He took my hand and said:

"I can assure you we will do everything possible."

Two hours later he appeared very grave-faced, saying:

"I have saved your wife and I hope your baby Mr Manley, your wife is very weak, and will need to be very careful until the end of the pregnancy. Your family doctor here who you are extremely lucky to have, I know him well, he will keep a very close eye on her. You may see her now for just a few minutes, please don't tire her. She needs sleep."

I actually stayed with her then for the next three days and nights, just sitting afraid to leave her in case she left me. Within two weeks she was just her normal self, it was just so difficult to try and keep her calm and quiet but, with the help of Binney and the Potts, we managed.

We had been married just six months. In that time Ari had turned our house into a beautiful home for us; she was there for my needs when I returned from the office, all she wanted to was to wait on me and please me. How could I have wished for more? And although she was pregnant she was just as insatiable in our love life as ever. This worried me a little as she had been so dangerously close to dying. I did speak to Tim about it but his advice was, if she's comfortable and there's no bleeding, to have a happy contented mother will make for a happy contented baby. It was now obvious to all that perhaps she was in early pregnancy, she always looked stunning and even then when she walked in a room she turned heads, and I still doubted that the baby wasn't mine.

After eating our usual evening meal we sat quietly together by the fire. I noticed she seemed a little uncomfortable. I questioned if she was OK, but she assured me she was fine. Then, just before it was time for us to go to bed, she looked at me and said she thought it might be a good idea for Binney to come and stay. Of course this immediately put me into panic mode. Although it was quite late I telephoned Little Heads. Mr Potts answered, I apologised for the lateness and asked him if he would bring Binney to us? As Ari seemed a little uncomfortable and felt safer with her here. Without any hesitation he said of course, immediately.

That night our daughter was born. I had telephoned Tim as Binney suggested and he said he would come at any time if Binney thought he was needed. She came to me explaining Ari is very weak, she'd lost a lot of blood. I think nothing to worry about tonight we will get the doctor in the morning unless the situation alters. She's sitting up holding the baby and wants you with them.

I went to her kissing her head and the baby's, I realised by looking without a doubt she wasn't mine, but so tiny and beautiful.

"Do you love me enough to forgive me? This is Henrietta, will you love her too?"

"Of course my darling. You are the two most precious things in my life."

At that point Binney came in saying:

"Ari you must sleep now, you will need all your strength. I will take the baby, you must both understand she is very small and very weak."

I lay on the bed that night beside her unable to sleep but just wanting to be near Ari who, for the first time I had ever seen, seemed exhausted. She slept deeply. Around six a.m. Binney came in with some tea for us both. Ari woke and looked considerably better for which I was thankful. Binney sat on the bed. Taking both of our hands, she said:

"You must both be very brave, we need to get the doctor here. Henrietta was just too frail and too weak to make it."

The next few weeks were difficult. We buried Henrietta Manley, our firstborn. I will never know the truth of what took place that night and in the morning between Binney and Tim, but to my dying day I know what they did was for us. They were our greatest friends.

I decided we should take a few weeks' holiday away in the sun, and be alone together. Ari was very enthusiastic and so one Monday morning we flew off to Bermuda. We had a small Manley office there which I was interested in just to take a look at. We walked barefoot on the sand, swam in the warm water, talked and relaxed. Ari's recovery from having the baby was good, we made love and were able to put tragedy behind us.

Nine months later our first lovely son was born. Binney was with us, there was no complications and he was fit and healthy, we called him Henry. We were in heaven, Binney was like a mother hen, and the Potts were like grandparents. We were like one big happy family. One year later we produced William and eighteen months later Robert. I was just as fascinated by Ari as the day I first met her and I had my wonderful boys, but I knew she still wanted a daughter.

It was decided in the London office that it would be a good idea to do more business in the Bermuda office; more people were going for holidays, local wealthy people who needed advice on their business activities. For me this was ideal as I could take the family there for all the school holidays but still be working in an advisory and overseeing capacity. I found an old colonial house that was to rent, complete with staff. It was very large but I felt, with our ever extending family, it would be ideal. After all the boys were growing up fast and as a late father I wanted to spend as much time as possible with them. Ari absolutely adored it, her squeals of delight when she first saw it were unimaginable. As a family the first year of our lease was absolutely blissful, we played with the boys, we swam with the boys, their little bodies became so tanned and healthy. We had taken Binney with us which was a great help with the boys, but the staff were unbelievably wonderful and the children adored them all. And then the house became available for sale and so I bought it, and Ari wanted to use her inheritance money to improve it decorate it and make it our home, and what a wonderful job she did. We also demolished the old mud huts with no facilities that the staff lived in and built them little bungalows to the left of the house and to the right we built a workshop for any work that needed to be done on the house and boathouse, it seemed that every member of the staff had a little boat one way or another. They were delighted with all the new activity, but it was small reward for what they did for all of us. The front of the house was typical of the area and quite imposing but the back had lovely verandas leading from the downstairs rooms and pretty verandas with stairs down to the ground from the upstairs rooms. Looking out onto a beautiful sandy beach with a pretty little island just a boat-row away, which meant the boys could wake up, jump out of their beds and run into the water often chased by their mother. Often at night when the boys were tucked up in their beds with Binney and the staff to look after them, we would take one of the little boats and row across to the island; it was our secret, we named it our love island. We would lay in each other's arms naked in the moonlight and act like new young lovers again. Ari still had the ability to arouse me with just a single touch of her hand on my body, the bliss was unbelievable even if we didn't actually make love. I sometimes questioned what had I done to deserve to have this wonderful person to be my wife and to give me my sons.

The boys were eleven, ten, and eight and a half years old, and were so much fun for us whether we were in England or Bermuda. Our houses were always filled with laughter and the way they played with their mother, for me watching is almost like having four children. They play pranks on me, like putting salt in my tea, and tying my shoelaces together, and like their mother they all just want to have fun and please me. They all liked to bring the post to me so Ari had to check to share it out between them, so if there was less than three letters she would have some pretend ones ready. The worst thing was Sunday mornings in England. We always had the papers delivered and it was always a fight between the boys to be up first to bring the papers to us in bed. The problem was two of them would always be disappointed, so Saturday nights I always had to remember to put the ladder up to the bedroom window, then after the first delivery I'd climb out of the bedroom window taking the papers with me, to put them back through the letterbox twice more so as each one of them had delivered them to us.

Ari was wonderful at organising what she called the trivia, leaving me to deal with what she called the big things in life, and that suited me fine. In fact I don't think I ever questioned one of her decisions. For instance she didn't want the boys to go to boarding school while they were still young children and although I had my doubts, I agreed as to be without them, with their noise and their chaos and their pranks, would have been unbearable.

It was to be her birthday. The boys were whispering and beginning to talk about the secret things they were going to do for her, we were going to be at the house in Bermuda at the time, and without them knowing I had secretly made squatters rights on our island, paying quite a small amount to the local councils so as I had it in writing. In a very selfish way I only wanted the two of us to know this, so for the sake of the boys I had bought her the biggest box of chocolates I could find, which sent the boys into dreamland helping her eat them.

Unable to keep total secrecy any longer I told her when we went to the island that evening, I was going to give her real birthday present to her.

She giggled and said, "Does that mean you're going to make love to me until the sun comes up?"

"No, it means I have bought the island for you, now it will always be ours to the end of our days."

I felt so happy to be able to give her something that she loved and was so precious to us both.

It always frightens me when I considered our age difference. Whatever years I had left would never be enough to love her.

Funny how things come about. I often walked to the workshop and boat store, I liked to have a little chat with the boys who worked for us, and two days after Ari's birthday I did just that.

They were all laughing and teasing Cico about his forthcoming marriage and he was saying he was going to sell his little boat to pay for things. My ears pricked up: it would be nice for Ari and I to have our own boat instead of borrowing one of theirs. I said I would like to buy it, name your price. After the business negotiations were over and I realised I had paid more than the going rate, which I didn't mind, I said OK, as part of the deal you must now put the new name on it for me. It's going to be called *U. & .I. R. 1*. And it must be at the water's edge in front of the house by sundown, or no deal.

And so we had our own boat. That evening when the children were tucked up in bed we walked down to the water's edge. She said, "It's a different boat. Why?"

"Because it's our boat. Look at the name, do you think it's correct?" Her joy and excitement made me realise why I loved her so much.

"Yes," she whispered in my ear.

We at Manleys were asked to deal with a particularly high profile fraud case, I knew it would take some months and probably run over the boys' summer holidays. We were excited to be asked to take it on and knew it would be good for the practice. And the obvious income generated from it was not to be dismissed. It began in March and was very high pressure, but I was enjoying it by the middle of July. I estimated it would be another two months before the case was closed. So I was trying to persuade Ari to take the boys and Binney and even the Potts if she wished to Bermuda. Although we both knew in our hearts they wouldn't go, it was so far away for them.

She was very reluctant, saying it would be the only time we had been apart since we had been married. I knew it would be difficult for both of us we had such a tactile relationship, I tried to point out how the boys loved being there and how good it was for them. I said I would go as soon as I could. After much debate and tears she decided our personal sacrifice should come second to the boys well-being; they of course as usual were excited about seeing all their young friends, totally unaware of our feelings. We made love the night before they left as though there was no tomorrow. We both found sleep difficult to come. I told her I was dreading taking them to the airport. She said she had thought a lot about it to, but had decided there would be no tears and for the sake of the boys the parting would be brief, she would make out she was as excited as normal, and I knew this would be the best way, she was just so much stronger than me. Little did I know I was to regret my persuasion of her to go as one of the most hurtful things in my life.

Back home the house was empty. It felt cold but it wasn't cold, I poured myself a large whiskey. Suddenly I thought, What if the plane doesn't make it, what if something goes wrong, how could I live without them? I tried to collect my senses. I was up early the next morning wanting to get to the office to try to hurry this particular case along. Just before I left my secretary came in with a telegram I opened it with trembling fingers, it said:

ALL WELL. COME SOON MY DARLING. BOYS HAPPY. ME DESPERATELY UNHAPPY. CAN'T LIVE WITHOUT YOU. ALL MY LOVE YOUR ARI.

I won the case for Manleys, the case that had kept me and my family apart far too long. But with only two days until they returned it was pointless for me to go out to them. I couldn't wait to have them back and have a house full of fun and laughter again, and to hold my darling wife in my arms. The plane's touch down time was two p.m. I was up at six in the morning, my restlessness reminded me of when I waited for Ari to come home from India and by ten a.m. I couldn't wait any longer and left for the airport trying to kill time in any way possible, my excitement at seeing her although in a different way had not diminished over time.

Suddenly we were all together again, hugging and kissing in a big circle including Binney. The boys were laughing and jumping around, Ari and I could only exchange eyes.

Mr and Mrs Potts were at our house and she had made a big stew for all of us to eat together when we arrived. We pulled up outside the house, the boys jumped out and ran to the door which Mrs Potts had left open, followed by Binney. Ari and I were alone for just a few minutes, I took her in my arms and held her close.

She said, "We will never ever do this again under any circumstances."

I said, "I know it was terrible."

When the boys were tucked up in bed and Binney and the Pottses had left for Little Heads, Ari and I had a chance to catch up. She was sat at my feet, I picked her up and took her to our bedroom. We made love as though it was new. We talked and made love again, until she said:

"John, how I have ached of his moment, whatever you may think in the future."

Putting my finger on her nose I said, "What a silly thing to say." Little did I know what was to come. And so we fell asleep.

The boys went back to school and life returned to normal but, selfishly, I wanted Ari to myself. So it was decided we would go to Bath for a long weekend without the boys. Binney was quite happy to come and look after to the boys and we decided to ask the Pottses to move in as well, to help getting them to school and all their other activities, football practice, coping with the mud afterwards and we knew they would get all their favourite foods and be generally spoilt, so no need to worry.

We took off for Bath on Friday morning after the boys had gone to school. We checked into the hotel, took a long walk in the early autumn sunshine, we ate a snack in the bar in the hotel and drank a little champagne, we were just so happy to be together. That night we explored each other's bodies as though it was the first time, and I still marvelled at her beauty.

Saturday was a day of perfect pleasure. Of course we missed the boys but the thought of the whole weekend together was absolute heaven. We woke about eight a.m. and ordered breakfast in our room, it was super to have the time to ourselves, we just lay in bed chatting until about nine o'clock.

About an hour later I got up to shave and take a bath. I was lying back relaxing in lovely warm water when Ari came in. She just slipped in with me, a sheer delight.

We got dressed and left the hotel heading for the Roman Baths, what an incredible place to visit. Those Romans certainly were clever. Moving on from there we did a little shopping, we bought a few things for the boys, and little thank you gifts for the Pottses and Binney. Walking past a jewellery shop I said, "Come, let's go in. I want to buy you something to remember this weekend by."

Once inside we looked at many things, finally deciding on a bracelet. A three-coloured gold band about two inches wide with a few diamonds in it.

Laura let out a squeal of delight.

"What on earth is the matter?" asked Tom, looking up from reading 'the book'.

"You'll never believe it, have you got to the bit where they're shopping in Bath yet?" she asked excitedly.

"No why?" said Tom.

"I think they've just bought the bracelet that the brothers gave me for Christmas. The description is perfect," she said getting up and walking over to him. "Look read it here."

"Yeah, the description sounds like it. How interesting, we knew it wasn't new but I don't think we had any idea that it actually belonged to Arabella," said Tom.

AND SO THEY READ ON

Ari was so excited the proprietor an Italian asked us if we were celebrating a wedding anniversary and, in true romantic Italian style, he said we looked so in love we must be recently married. Ari giggled in her infectious way and explained, no, we have three boys at home we are just escaping for a naughty weekend.

Walking back to the hotel we saw a tea room. We had skipped lunch and it was about three o'clock, so we went in and had a cream tea.

I noticed when we walked in everybody looked towards Ari. She did look radiant with her fur-collared coat framing her face. We arrived back at the hotel, the room was inviting and warm, the sun was setting and shining through the bay window. I sat on the seat there for a few minutes and Ari suggested we undress and lay on the bed. She held in her hand a little bottle of her favourite body oil.

"Come," she said, "let me give you a massage." The smell of musk-like oil and her naked body made me want to take her, but she took control.

"No," she said. "I don't want you to make love to me until tonight, I want you to be full and bursting for me. After dinner when we get to bed, I want you to fill me up."

"Ari you are so bad."

But as normal she had her way, she brought me to almost fulfilment three times only to control me with her wonderful fingers. And each time she was fulfilled, which only made my desire more as I felt the warm liquid coming from her body. I fell asleep exhausted. I woke to the sound of her having a bath, still naked. I went to the bathroom and leant over, kissing her breasts which were just above the waterline. She put her hands up and cupped my testicles.

"Wonderful," she said.

"And you Arabella Manley are an absolute tart, but I love you. Now leave me alone before I explode."

Just as I wanted she giggled adding.

"But please, whatever you may think of me, you are and always will be in the only man for me."

At the time I didn't realise the implications of her words.

When dressed and ready to go she was wearing a long white Grecian-style dress with her hair piled high. She looked to me like a Greek goddess and when we went into the restaurant, it seemed that waiters appeared from nowhere wanting to escort us to our table. The room was quite full with lots of chatter going on but, as we walked through, I could hear chatter stopping, and the eyes of everybody looking at her. She just had that ability to cast a spell, just as she did it for me.

We enjoyed a perfect meal with nice wine, both understanding that tomorrow night at home we would have to behave like respectable parents. Back in our room I all but ripped her clothes off.

"This may be rape, Mrs Manley, but you deserve it."

"Exactly what I planned," she replied.

I woke to find her sitting in the large bay windows with her knees held up under her chin. I realised she was crying. I got out of bed and went to sit with her taking her hands, I said:

"Why are you so unhappy?" With the early morning sun just coming up I looked into her beautiful green eyes so sad from crying. I held her close.

"Nothing can be this bad," I said.

"It is, I'm pregnant," she said.

"That's wonderful darling. Perhaps we will get the girl you long for."

"But John... it's not yours."

I was speechless and devastated. What could this mean? Was it to rip our lives apart? She was now sobbing uncontrollably, and I was pacing up and down trying to think.

"Well we obviously have to talk and make some choices. I'm glad you've picked this time to tell me," I said sarcastically. "At least we have time without interference to discuss the outcome here and now." I paused, "How do know it's not mine and who's is it?"

She held her arms out to me. I ignored them. I've been through this once before with her. I ran my hands through my hair, our lives shattered. I then looked up at her saying, "So who's?"

"I'm two months' pregnant."

"So it happened in Bermuda?"

"Yes."

"So will it be Black!" I screamed at her.

"Yes."

"Could it be one of many men?" Not really wanting to hear the onset.

"No, no, no!" she sobbed. "I only want you. I only ever want you, what shall we do? Please don't stop loving me, please don't send me away. Please let me tell you how it happened."

"No thank you, I don't want to hear how you prefer Black dick to white and the details of how good it was. You bitch. I suppose as I haven't made you pregnant again for eight and a half years to get this daughter, you thought you'd try another way, letting me think it was mine? And then because it was one of many black and white men you got scared, and now you're trying the sob stuff to make me say it's OK. With Henrietta I forgave you, but not this time."

She closed her eyes. I could see the agony on her face.

"That's just not true. Nothing could ever be better than you."

"So how come you're in this situation then? I suppose the next thing you'll tell me is that he just walked by and it happened? You must think I'm some sort of idiot. What do you take me for?"

"I love you, I just love you."

"What a load of rubbish, we are parted for six weeks and you can't keep your legs shut, what a wonderful mother let alone wife! What do you think our boys are going to think of you when they find out? When I tell them sorry, you've got a black sibling because your mother can't do without sex for a few weeks?"

At this point I grabbed my clothes got dressed and just left the room. I walked and walked I didn't know for how long, I kicked at leaves that were beginning to fall, trying to defuse my anger and hurt. Eventually I went back to the hotel with still no answer for us. She was still sitting in the window but obviously dressed and ready to leave, everything was packed she looked at me.

"I did try to warn you," she said.

"Don't be stupid. How could I have ever have interpreted the words *you're the best I only want you*? As *sorry I'm expecting another bastard child*?"

"But John," she came to me with her arms open again.

I pushed her away. "Don't get near me. You may not know but it's very difficult for a man to come to terms with an unfaithful bitch of a wife." I couldn't believe what I was saying but at that point I was so full of hate for this Black bastard who had touched my wife. I wanted to kill him and I wanted to hurt her for the hurt I was feeling.

I grabbed the cases and told her to be in the car in fifteen minutes. I went downstairs, paid the bill and drove the car to the front door. She was there waiting. The plan had been for us to arrive home late afternoon so as we could have some time with the boys before bedtime and school the next day, although we hadn't arranged an exact time with Binney and the Pottses, so our early arrival wouldn't have rung any alarm bells.

We drove in complete silence until almost home. When I said we will act as normal until I have time to decide what I am going to do, I do not want my boys upset or to know about their mother until I choose to tell them.

"Our boys," she corrected me, "but I do agree nobody will ever know. But if you'd just let me explain it may help."

"Explain, help? Don't make me sick," I muttered.

Everybody was delighted to see us back, the boys had much fun lined up for us and I don't think anybody would ever have known not all was well. On the surface we both acted the scene well but, when the boys were in bed and we were alone, we never spoke. We still lay in the same bed for the sake of the boys and, as hard as it was, I made absolutely no attempt to touch her.

It was Monday morning. I was in my office absolutely fraught with the situation between Ari and I, I could tell she was as upset about everything as I was. I just didn't feel I could give in. I asked myself over and over again how could she do this to me. All I could think of was another man making love to her, all I could visualise was them lying together, him touching her body, she responding in a way that should only be for me to know. She was my wife, it was only for me to possess her. I wanted to punish her but I think I was punishing myself more. I tried to concentrate on the paperwork on my desk when the door into my office opened and there she stood. I wanted to rush to her take her in my arms and never let her go.

"Hello John, may I come in?"

I just looked at her and nodded, she was wearing an emerald-green suit which fitted perfectly just exaggerating the perfect curves of her body, the morning sunshine was streaming through the window settling on her red hair, the very sight of her raised every passion possible in me. It was so easy to see the effect she had on people when she walked into a room. I didn't stand up because I didn't want her to see the effect she was having on me. I wanted to make love to her there and then. She sat down in front of me just far away enough for me to be able to see her beautiful crossed legs. And then she began.

"I've come here this morning my darling, because we just can't go on like this. We could never live apart, you are eaten up with jealousy, and me with remorse. So I'm here to tell you exactly what happened and how and who. I know you may say again you don't want to know but if you don't let me explain it will eat you away for ever, and kill us both, and for the sake of our boys we cannot let this happen."

"Just tell me, just tell me you didn't go to our island."

"No, as disgusting and unfaithful as you think I am, I would never ever go there without you."

I sat there like a lamb to slaughter.

"After the boys were in bed I took a long walk along the shore and on the way back I met a young man who was on loan to your office for six months. The one whose young wife had been tragically killed in a road accident. He recognised me and we started to chat and he said in two days' time he would be returning to his company's office near where he and his wife had lived. He said he didn't think he would ever get over losing her and that he would never find love like they had again. He was very upset. I tried to console him and said time is a great healer. He said he hadn't seen you in the office and was there a reason? I said you were very busy in England with a special case and that it was your wish that I bring the boys out for their normal summer holidays. I told him I hated being without you and it was the first time we have been parted since we were married. When we were back to our shoreline I asked him if he'd like to come and have a coffee with me. We took the coffee and then a brandy and then a brandy and before we knew it we had drunk a bottle. It was about ten thirty p.m. and he said he should be going. I walked with him back to the end of our shoreline, you know, where the little gate is. He thanked me for my understanding and kissed me on the cheek. John, we were both very drunk. And suddenly we were intimate. There was no passion, there was no clothes removed, no touching; it lasted about two seconds, I can hardly remember it and I'm positive he doesn't."

I felt sick at this point. I wanted to get up and run away, but knew this was not the thing to do if we were ever going to get over this, and I think she knew how I felt. I said:

"If only I had not persuaded you to go without me."

"If only I had stood firm and not gone," she said.

We looked deeply into one another's eyes and there was what seemed to be an eternal silence between us.

"Promise me that is the truth?"

"What I've said about that night is the absolute truth, my darling. I swear on our boys' lives."

"Then we must find a solution," I said. "Do you have one?"

"Yes there are two," she said. "I have discussed things with Binney and we will sort it out."

Before she could say more I banged my fist on my desk making her jump and saying with a raised voice. "You will do nothing of the sort this time between you, it is criminal to take a baby's life. And you will both end up in prison for the rest of your days and I will personally see that you do." I thought she had almost ignored what I had said and continued without comment at my outburst.

"Option one, we think the baby should be born out in Bermuda. As you know, I would be able to conceal my pregnancy with the correct clothes from friends and especially from the boys. We could bring it back and say we had adopted it.

"Of course there would be some explaining to the boys why. But most importantly could you accept it."

"Accept it! I accepted Henrietta Manley didn't I? Do you remember her? Not as much as I do the dear little girl you had. Was that part of a plan you had with Binney? A dear little girl born because of your lust?" Immediately I was so full of remorse. What was happening to us? It was as if I had turned a knife in her, I couldn't bear to see the way she looked. But still she went on.

"Option two, there is a lovely young couple distantly related to the house staff who are desperate for a child, but unable to have one. Binney has spoken to them and told them there is a possibility she might know of a baby that could be adopted, not mentioning any names at all. Binney will take the child within minutes of it being born to them, as you know this often happens out there when young girts have an unwanted baby, adoption just happens without formality. This is what I want and favour. It would be brought up in a loving home in its own culture and surroundings and would enable us to carry on with our lives. I plead with you John. For the sake of our boys."

We hadn't rowed since the day we met but here I was, a prominent barrister reduced to a mess by the thought of not having my wife with me or not being able to forgive, not only destroying my world but, more importantly, our whole family.

I collected my thoughts, got up and walked to the window . After a few minutes Ari followed me, putting her arms around me and kissing the back of my neck. I knew at this point we had crossed our hurdle. I turned round to look at her, she held her face up to me; I kissed her, held her close pushing my body into her. She undid the button on her skirt which dropped to the floor, she wore nothing underneath it. I fumbled in my trousers like an inexperienced schoolboy, desperate to release the uncontrollable monster inside them. Within seconds we were one again. Yes, we had crossed our hurdle.

Afterwards I thought what would we have done if somebody had walked in on us? The boss making love to his wife in his office. But normally they knocked. After we'd collected ourselves together, I said:

"When do we go to see Tim?"

"I shan't see him. I don't intend to involve him for your sake."

"But what if something goes radically wrong?"

"Then we may have to call him, but remember I've had the boys fit and strong and I have Binney. Some women less fortunate than me never have a doctor, just the midwife. Trust me, I'm sure it will be fine."

"So how do you see it all coming together or happening?"

"I think it will arrive in March, so if we have Christmas at home and we can go to Bermuda for the rest of the boys' Christmas holidays together as normal. Then while we are there you usually go to the office some days. I thought if you could somehow tie up some money for the family and baby. Binney will have all the details and the contacts with them, so neither of us would ever be named."

"Is she going to be happy to do this, have you discussed it with her?"

"Yes, I have. In fact it was she who suggested this was the best way to deal with it. Then we will all come home. The boys will go back to school, everything will be normal. Easter is early next year, end of March, so if we all go out mid-March it will be just like our normal Easter holidays. When the time comes Binney and I can deal with it, if necessary you can take the boys exploring the island for the day, and if it's at night they will be asleep. Everybody will be happy and at the end of the holidays, we return home."

"Are you absolutely crazy?" I said.

"Just a little." She replied giggling. "But I love you."

And so much against my better judgment this was exactly what happened. We are back in England, we took the holidays in Bermuda, our boys are the delight of our life and growing up so fast. I find my crazy, wonderful, beautiful, exotic, Ari as desirable as the day I first met. And I pray we may have many many more years together.

---

It was early morning on the Sunday after Easter. Tom had woken early, the sun was streaming through the bedroom window where he lay quietly thinking over the events of the last week. The death of Mr. Robert, the meeting with Mr William, on Wednesday culminating in being given the book to read. And then of course there was the business of him being given the job of clearing one of the rooms upstairs and he wasn't even working for them. Not that he minded as Mr. B.(as they now seemed to call him.) and he had become good friends over the short time Laura had worked for the Manleys; it was funny, since they'd finished reading the 'Book', how he and Laura had discussed different little bits in it. Such as did the three brothers ever know about the two daughters that their mother had? And as Laura pointed out, although they never knew John and Ari they felt as though they had been let into the history of the family.

Tom lent over Laura who was still fast asleep. He kissed her on her nose and then on her lips, she opened her eyes and smiled at him.

"Breakfast in bed?" He asked.

"Are you requesting, or providing?"

"I'm providing. Followed by other husbandly duties," he said, pinching her nose again.

He returned shortly afterwards with the breakfast tray saying, "I think we will go down to the office this morning and just take a look."

On Monday morning Laura placed the folder with the 'Book' in on Mr William's desk ready for him on Friday morning. Sunday had been quite successful they had spent longer at the office than they had intended but came away with some quite positive ideas. In the room with all the papers in they discovered two very large antique glass-fronted shelved cabinets. These they thought would look super at the top of the stairs and perhaps they could find or have made something to link the two together with a plain glass front to exhibit the wedding dress in, if they ever found it. By this time they were both very excited about the possibility of bringing it all together so much, they spent most of the day there.

Laura left Tom with the papers and started to lift the lids on the boxes in the other room, squealing with delight as she uncovered crystal, silver-labelled wedding presents, jewellery labelled from *Mummy and Daddy*, then a child's silver bracelet labelled *from my godfather*, a baby's christening gown, three little tiny boxes labelled *first teeth*, and then four little tiny boxes labelled *hair* – two red, two brown. Her mind flashed back to the 'Book': was this fourth box Harriet's hair? She called Tom.

"You've just got to come and see this. It's like relating it to some of the things in the book."

And so they had gone home dirty, dusty and full of enthusiasm.

Thursday morning, Tom was upstairs with black bags trying to sort the rubbish from what possibly should be kept, to the definitely must be kept. Laura was on the phone when the door opened. She looked up and was surprised to see Mr William.

"Couldn't wait to get my teeth into the new ideas, so here I am. Thought I'd get in contact with young Irons and see if you two have got any ideas for upstairs," he said, as he disappeared into his office. Only to come out again two minutes later holding the file.

"Read it then?"

"We certainly did, and Tom's upstairs getting stuck in and looking a little dusty."

"Oh, great I'll go up and see him. No appointments or clients today?"

"No, you weren't supposed to be here."

"Good, get the chocolate ready, three cups, bring it up."

Laura was amazed at this man, his attitude after having experienced a very difficult time, and also at his enthusiasm for his new ideas.

They sat on crates and sipped the chocolate. Mr William. had the folder on his lap.

"So what do you think then?" he asked pointing to it.

"Interesting," said Tom. "It actually reduced your Girl Friday here to tears in places."

Mr William. just nodded.

"Yes it does have its moments, I must admit. I think you're going to find a few more of those moments amongst the boxes, including his diaries. There's a lot in the other room of Father's day to day life before he met Mother.

"Mostly about his social life, who he laid, and who he would like to lay, he was certainly no angel: young, successful, reasonably wealthy and I think a gentleman. Quite good-looking and a perfect catch for a young lady, but I think when you find them the bonfire is the best place, although they probably can clarify things in more detail.

"So does that mean you have read them all?" ask Tom.

"No, not at all, but just enough to want me to stay in ignorant bliss, and that applies to his so-called book. In fact I think you will probably know more about Mr and Mrs John Manley's private and family life than I do. But now I have cleared my conscience, with you I have not let Father's dying wish be lost," he said.

"So would you say you boys were a chip off the old block?" asked Laura.

This made Mr William. throw his head back and roar with laughter.

"Now that would be telling, but I've had my moments, and still do, there's life in the old dog yet you know."

"Another thing. I think the folder should now go back into the safe," said Tom.

"Oh yes, I forgot to give you the combination it's 705-2-705-6," said Mr William.

"I don't think that's a good idea for you to give us that at this time," said Laura.

"I think Laura is right," said Tom.

"Look, you are all I've got to give it to, so I want you to have it, end of subject," said Mr William. "Right now I have some phone calls to make and you two have lots to do, so let's get on. And when you're ready I'll take you out to lunch and you can spill the beans on your ideas for upstairs."

The next few weeks were very interesting for both of them, Tom found about 1000 books all possibilities to start to stock a library, some were obviously law reference books but some were novels, history and travel. At least they'd have something to put on the shelves, which had yet to be thought about and installed. He also found some interesting papers on Edward and Mrs Simpson, and the John Profumo case which nearly brought the government of the time to its knees. He placed these to one side together with other documents which he thought might be of importance, to be looked at by an expert in this field.

Laura eventually found the wedding dress and quite a lot of other clothes as well. Tom and Mr William actually made her try it on for size; it was probably by today's standards about a size 8, just that little bit too small. But as she didn't plan to wear it anywhere it didn't matter. But both the men said it looked perfect. Mr William said they couldn't imagine how much pleasure it had given him to see something of his mother's again. Besides the little things she had found on that first Sunday she came across some lovely chests. Some had obviously come back from India, the sort of thing people were paying a lot of money for in antique shops. Most of these were empty but one in particular was full of lovely silver cutlery and table ornaments, all lying in green baize trays all divided into sections, each section having an ivory tag below it saying what actually fitted into it such as sugar shaker, table vase, serving spoon, coaster, all of a bygone era. There were beautiful cut glasses possibly unwanted gifts as one of the boxes had a note on it. *One of many sets given to John at different times*, it said *I will keep in reserve for when we have smashed or chipped the existing ones!* She thought this was probably in Ari's handwriting, and seemed to show she had a sense of humour. There were also some nice pieces of furniture which she could envisage being part of the room when it was finished. Some of the ornaments she thought would look nice in the downstairs long room, particularly two large crystal candelabras which she took down and placed on either end of the long table together with a large crystal rose bowl. Of course, she needed to have approval from Mr William. She need not have been concerned about it, when he saw it all he said:

"Oh that is just absolutely wonderful, I remember these three pieces when we were children and Mother always had the rose bowl full of the red roses, and now I come to think of it every week Father always gave her red roses and I suppose that was where she put them. As a child you don't understand but I would imagine it was to show his love for her. I think we should do that too, perhaps you could arrange that with the florist? I'm sure she wouldn't mind as she does all the other flowers, and I also think we should leave these doors into this room open at all times, it's a beautiful room and you can see right through into the garden. Yes, that's a good idea."

Soon everything was happening and taking shape. They had interviewed Paul Irons and although Laura had reservations, Mr William. persuaded her that he would fit the bill, and quite frankly she didn't really feel she could object, but he just seemed so wet behind the ears; he had moved into Mr Henri's office with very little fuss but it was just that he would turn up for work wearing a brown suit, top button only done up looking a bit like a schoolboy together with black shoes, or a black suit and brown shoes. Or to cap it all a blue blazer with a green shirt. His wife was quite pleasant but very old-fashioned, they had two little girls that looked like Victorian children, not allowed to step out of line, and she imagined in not too many years to come if not already he would be worried about his haemorrhoids and his egg for breakfast not being on the toast the right way round. Not exactly a Manley man!

Within three months everything was sorted. Mr William. was as enthusiastic as ever and pleased with everything.

He always went off to Bermuda for Christmas and sometimes Easter. He regularly asked Tom and Laura to go with him if only for a week of his normal month's stay. They had always gracefully declined; Tom felt it was good for all of them to have some space, not that he and Laura minded the fact that he often popped in to see them and they very much appreciated his generosity, and apart from the fact that they had both become very fond of him, they didn't want to take advantage of him.

For Laura it was different now at the office. With Paul Irons and his secretary taking on nearly all new clients the office was now open Monday to Friday nine a.m. to five p.m. which gave her more flexibility obviously she was always there when Mr William was in but she had more time to deal with enquiries and bookings for use of the other rooms in the house, see to Mr William's charity work which was quite a thing in itself.

They often took a long weekend away and sometimes it would coincide with Mr William being in the same place at the same time, generally with one of his lady friends, when he would suggest they all had dinner together, which with few exceptions they were happy to do. It was after one of these evenings when Tom and Laura were back in their room at the hotel they were staying at, that Tom said to Laura:

"Have you noticed lately how he introduces us as either. *This is Tom and his wife Laura* or, *this is our Laura and her husband?*"

"So what's so strange about that? He often says in the office when someone wants something, 'Oh see our Laura about it'."

"Yes but that's different, I've noticed for instance when I'm out with him on my own there's always someone he meets and he always introduces me saying *our Tom*, wouldn't you think he would say, *my friend?*"

"I think you are just being silly. Anyway you know what it's like nowadays, people are quick to think two chaps together, one younger, and I expect most of his friends know he's never been married."

"No. I think Laura, he wants people to think we are his family. Do you remember when he took us to the boat show and when we met those people just before we went onto the SunSeeker stand, he introduced us then as 'our Laura and her husband Tom', and what did the fellow say?"

"I don't know?"

"He said, 'It's nice to see you all together'. I noticed Mr William. didn't say anything else but I think I know him well enough now to see a rather proud smile, and another thing Laura that day what a lucky escape that was."

"What do you mean?"

"Well after we looked round that boat, if you remember, we went to have lunch and when we were having coffee he said, 'What do you think Tom, do we want a boat?' And I said, 'No.' I'm sure if I had said *yes* he would have bought one and you may recall at the time you told me to keep my feet on my side of the table."

"Yes I do recall that, but I didn't think of it that way."

# Chapter Twenty-Four

## *Fourteen Years Later*

Where had those fourteen years gone? Tom and Laura had no idea, all they knew was that life had been so good to them, they were still in love as ever. Tom had managed to build a very successful business which put them in a good financial position.

Laura still worked for Mr William. who had become very much part of their lives. His enthusiasm for life was unbelievable, he and Tom had become particularly close, they had many interests in common, sport and technology and most certainly the same sense of humour. He often came to eat with them sometimes bringing a lady friend with him, but he always checked before doing this if it was OK, always filling them in with a little information about her and her name, which was useful as he seemed to have so many strings to his bow.

Effey was still her normal self. They sometimes had to suffer one of her dinner parties together with Conrad. Often, later, the three of them would have a kindly giggle over it all. But Mr William, bless his heart, always had a protective word for her, saying something like.

"Poor Effey, she means well. She cannot help being a snob but she does have her good points, hard to find sometimes nowadays, but we did have good times together though."

The most amusing part for Laura was when Effey came to the office, sometimes just bursting into Mr William's office and most times, if she spoke to Laura, it was always in the category off the office worker.

They had decided to extend the swimming pool with a changing room, barbecue area and a room to eat in if it was not warm enough outside. Mr William. took a great interest in the project and often popped in to see the progress and chat with Tom. One day he said:

"How much do you think this is costing you Tom then?"

"About twenty-five grand I think, by the time we finish."

"Well, I think while you're at it for the sake of a few more bob why don't you make the changing room at bit more?" said Mr William.

"Such as what?" replied Tom.

"Well it seems to me you often have friends to stay. If you made a large bedroom area you could put some comfy chairs in there, a small fridge and kettle for them to make some tea or coffee and somewhere they could go to, a sort of snooze basket. You know how it is when you go to stay with friends the same as it is for them, I expect you know what I mean?"

Tom started to laugh.

'What, somewhere for you to have a dirty night with one of your lady friends when you've had a drink and can't drive?"

"No, no, dear boy, but it's not a bad idea though."

"I'll chat to Laura about it."

The new idea was put into action and, before it was quite finished, there was a knock on the door one Sunday morning and there was Mr William.

"Oh, hi, nice to see you. Come on in, coffee, tea, brandy, glass of wine?" said Laura.

"No thanks. Where's Tom, out by the pool?"

"Need you ask? Yes, go find him."

About three quarters of an hour had passed when the two men came back into the house.

Laura thought Tom looked a little flushed.

"Put the coffee on love I've just had a bit of a shock," he said.

"Why what's up, is there a problem down at the office?"

"No, the problem's here with your boss," he said, holding up an envelope.

"Oh God, have I got the sack? Or has Mr William decided to give up?"

He handed her the envelope.

"Look inside," he said.

She did as she was told only to find a cheque made out to Tom for £30,000. She looked at both men.

"But, but..." was all she could say.

"I know," said Tom. "It's to pay for the pool."

"Are you crazy?" said Laura, looking at Mr William.

"No, it gives me such pleasure to do this. I just don't think you understand how much you guys mean to me, since losing my brothers I realised how lonely my life could have been, but you two have brought such pleasure to me, you have become the family I should have had. I hope you don't mind me feeling this way, but it's the truth."

Laura walked over to him and put her arms around him, and kissed him on the cheek. Looking at Tom, she said:

"Could we have champagne darling just to celebrate the new family member?"

Over the years there were many such times when Mr William. presented them with a cheque, it was what he called 'a little family gift'. He never said 'I'd like to buy this for you' or 'here's a cheque for that', he waited until he knew they had bought something, which he was always interested in. Then he would ask to see it and, if he had a rough idea of the cost, he would say nothing or else he would discreetly find out, and then gives them a cheque or slip it to Laura with her pay cheque on Friday. It did embarrass them both, although they were very thankful and it did bring things to a head when Laura said to Tom she would like to change her car, as it was quite old and a bit shabby. Anyway they found not what they wanted but a very good second-hand bright red Mercedes Sport. It was a bit more than they had intended to spend but Tom could see she was so excited about it and, as they could afford it, he decided that they should get it. Yet not before giving her a hard time by teasing her without her really knowing, saying it was far too extravagant for her just to bomb around in the village, she agreed. But not being able to stand to see her disappointment he couldn't keep it up for long. He secretly phoned Mr William. the next morning before he got to the office and explained that he wanted to pick this new car up for her as a surprise to bring it back to the house, and would Mr William give him a lift to the garage?

"How wonderful, exciting. Of course I will. Are we doing it now?"

"Well if you've got the time that would be great as she's at the office."

"I'll ring her to say I won't be in today, I'm going to see an old client."

So off they went like two little boys and collected it.

"Can I stay and see her face when she gets home? It should only be about half an hour's time when she comes back from the office?" asked Mr William.

"Yes of course you can," said Tom.

They took a little time parking it the other side of Tom's car, blocking the view of it with Mr William's so that, when Laura walked up the hill she, might just see a flash of red but wouldn't really realise what it was. They then went indoors realising by then they had about ten minutes to wait for her. They were a bit like two kids at Christmas, they tried to stand discreetly in the lounge for a good view to see her reaction. It came like a cabaret show: she must've seen it and started to run, throwing down her bag on the lawn. She was screaming and running around it, hands up to her mouth, then she stopped, just stood still, and burst into tears. By this time they had quietly opened the front door and stood there looking at her. She caught sight of them laughing at her and ran to them with her arms open, laughing and crying at the same time.

"I can't believe it, oh thank you so much," she said hugging them both.

"Don't thank me, nothing to do with me," said Mr William. "OK I'm on my way now I've seen the excitement, and no doubt Tom you want to take her for a ride in it, see you in the morning."

Later that evening when the excitement died down Laura said to Tom, "I'm so glad Mr William. said it was nothing to do with him."

"Yes I know what you mean," said Tom. "I just got him to come and pick it up and he wanted to stay and see your reaction. You know he really is a good man, he is always pleased for us."

"Yes, I know what you mean," said Laura.

Friday came, end of the week, Laura put the normal balance sheet on Mr William's desk he gave her a wages cheque, and then held up another one."

"For the car," he said.

"Oh no, most definitely no," said Laura. "I cannot possibly accept this."

Mr William stood up looking very serious, he looked straight at Laura saying with just a hint of a raised voice, "Look here. When you joined us you earned 300 pounds a week. Today, some seventeen-odd years later you still earn 300 pounds a week. In most normal circumstances the pay would've risen in that time. So, once and for all I never want to hear you say no again. Apart from the fact, as I've told you before, from a purely selfish point of view you cannot imagine how much pleasure it gives me to give you both things, if I had a family I couldn't be more fond of them. So shut up and let me have that pleasure. See you on Monday, if not before."

# Chapter Twenty-Five

Laura was woken by the sound of her mobile. They were staying in a small hotel in Devon for the weekend, having driven down on the Friday afternoon to meet up with some old friends on Saturday and returning home on Sunday late afternoon. She glanced at the clock: four fifteen a.m. She nudged Tom, and handed him the phone which she always did if it went in the middle of the night when they were at home. They did seem to be prone to getting wrong numbers, drunks or oddballs and a man's voice so often put paid to them, plus Tom could tell them where to go more effectively.

Pressing the green button he recognised the voice of Effey.
"It's you Tom?"
"Yes, it is Effey," he said, pressing the speaker button so as they could both hear what was being said. "What's the problem?"
"It's William, he's in hospital and he's asking for you both."
They could hear she was in tears.
"Effey, just try and calm down and explain little more," Tom said.
'Well we went out to dinner together last night to Langleys of course."
There was a pause, Tom and Laura looked at one another. Even in a crisis she was a snob.
Langleys was one of the best and most expensive restaurants in town and they knew William often took her there, just to make her feel special.
"So go on," said Tom in a gentle voice.
'We decided to come home for some of my best ground coffee from Fortnum & Mason, and a good brandy, which we drank and enjoyed and then William nodded off, which was fine, but after one hour when I thought it was time for bed, well for him to go home, I couldn't wake him." There was

another intake of breath and pause. "I dialled 999 and the paramedics arrived worked on him for quite a while and then said he must go to hospital. They asked me if he was my husband, and did I want to go with him? I said yes. But I'll phone them later and explained we are not married."

"I wouldn't worry about that Effey," said Tom. "So what are the hospital saying?"

"That he is very seriously ill and in and out of consciousness and asking for Tom and Laura, so you see…" She began to weep again, "I had to contact you."

"Yes, I understand, it's no problem. We will be with you as soon as possible. What hospital is he at?"

"It's the General, do you know where it is?"

"Yes, now try and calm down a little. It will take us about two and a half to three hours to get there, we will leave right now, phone us again with any update."

"Well I shall go back to the hospital now, I can't bear for him to be alone."

"Yes, you be careful driving there, we don't want two of you as patients," Tom said, trying to lighten the situation a little."

By this time Laura was out of bed and dressed throwing things into their cases.

"Tom, we must go right now."

"I know darling, I happen to know the number of the hospital so once we're in the car you ring them and see what we can find out."

There was nobody around as they dashed out through reception, but Tom said, "Not to worry. they've got our card ref and phone number and I can sort it out later."

Speaking to the hospital Laura said, "I believe you admitted a Mr William Manley just a few hours ago. Can you tell me which ward he is in and better still put me through?"

It seemed like an age to Laura, but then a very soft and calm voice said:

"Sister Wallace here, how can I help?"

"I believe you have a Mr William Manley in the ward. Can you tell me how he is please?"

"Oh, are you Laura? Are you his daughter?"

"Yes I am," she lied. "And my husband is Tom."

"Oh good, he is asking for you. Will you come immediately? I think it is not going to be long."

"What do you mean, long?" exclaimed Laura. "We are in Devon and at the very best we may be there in two and half hours."

"Well I have to tell you, my dear, you may be too late. But we will let him drift away peacefully."

"Oh no!" said Laura. "You go to him now and tell him in no indefinite words that Tom and Laura will be there soon and he must be there to speak to us."

"You must realise he is very sick, but trust us we will do our best."

Tom could tell just by the one-sided conversation that things were bad. He glanced at Laura, who looked as white as a sheet. He didn't think he'd ever seen her look so upset. They drove in silence for about thirty minutes, Tom put his hand over hers, gently squeezing it.

"OK, my darling?"

*Yes* she nodded, looking at him with her beautiful green eyes looking so sad.

"Will we make it?"

"We will certainly try," he replied.

She knew him so well and knew that if an answer to a question was no it meant no, and if yes, it meant yes. This time he gave her no false answer.

There was little traffic so early on this Sunday morning. Having broken the speed limit most of the way and probably been caught on every speed camera, especially around Exeter where his camera detector never seemed to stop beeping, they arrived at the hospital. It was six forty-five a.m. It seemed to take ages to get to the ward but, as they walked in, they were greeted by the soft-spoken sister.

"Tom and Laura?" she asked.

They both nodded.

"Please say we are in time," Laura almost pleaded.

"Just I think." She smiled.

He was in a side ward right by the nurse's station. Effey was sitting at the end of the bed, Laura went to him and gently took his hand.

"I'm here," she whispered. "And so is Tom."

Tom walked to the other side of the, bed gently pushing his hand upon the old man's shoulder.

"Come on," he said. "You sure took a good day to decide you wanted to move in with us, we will take you home soon."

Mr William. opened his eyes and smiled at them both.

"Thank you I knew you'd take care of me," he said.

Mr William Manley died at seven ten a.m. that morning with Laura, Tom, and Effey at his side.

The hospital staff were very kind to them, taking them into a small room and gave them some coffee. There was obviously a few formalities to deal with before they left. The sister of the ward came in after little while she went to Effey and took her hand, saying:

"Will you go home with your family now Mrs Manley?"

Effey looked at her for a few seconds and said:

"I'm not Mrs Manley although I could've been. I didn't mean to deceive you or the paramedics, I'm so sorry. I'm so sorry, I'm so sorry."

With that she started to weep.

"Oh it really doesn't matter, my dear. Please don't upset yourself."

She then turned to Laura and Tom.

"But you are his daughter is that correct?"

Tom then took over saying.

"Let me explain, none of us are related, Effey was an old friend and Laura worked for Mr Manley, and she and I have become very close to him over the years and he often portrayed us as family."

At this point Effey was beginning to sob uncontrollably. Tom looked at Laura saying.

"Perhaps it would be a good idea if you take Effey outside. You can sit quietly until I have finished with the details here."

"Yes good idea, we'll do that."

After a while Tom appeared. Apparently Effey had gone to the hospital in a taxi. So he suggested that she went home to their house with them, but she refused and said she would like to go to her own place.

Making sure that she was OK and telling her to ring them if she needed them or changed her mind, they would come and get her.

Once inside their house Laura went to the kitchen and made some tea. Tom came in and put his arms around her, and she cried and cried. Holding her away from him, he said:

"It's OK you had to have some tears and I'm sure you'll have some more. But you must remember he had a good long life and I think, Laura, you extended it for him."

"Yes," she replied. "But I didn't want him to go yet."

He held her tightly saying. "You know Laura, the time is never right for these things; but I know we gave him much pleasure as he gave us. Think of all the laughter and opportunities he gave us, the wonderful memories to talk about for the rest of our lives, so be brave and happy for all of us that we knew one another."

That evening they made a list of all the things that would have to be done on Monday morning.

First Laura would have to phone the London office who she assumed would take care of the funeral arrangements, as for the other Manley brothers. Then Alex Peterson, who was the young solicitor that Mr William. had entrusted his will and final wishes to. He often used the reference library in the office and so Laura got to know him. Mr. B often had long chats with him and got to know and like him always saying he was a bright young spark who would make a very good solicitor, which turned out to be true. So, some years later, when Laura happened to mention to Mr William. about his will she was not particularly surprised to hear that he had entrusted Alex with all his last wishes and will, having transferred it all from the London office, saying "I know he will deal with it very professionally and exactly in the way I have laid out." Then there would be all the clients to inform which she hoped Philip would deal with and, of course, there was the question of what would happen to the practice, which she assumed would close.

"Of course you know within a few months Tom, I shall be out of a job."

"I think we can cope with that," he replied.

After all the normal arrangements together with the funeral having taken place, Laura had a phone call from Alex Peterson.

"Hello Laura how you doing? If it's all right by you I think we need to read Mr Manley's will. So if I may suggest at my office on Friday next, shall we say two o'clock would that be suitable?"

"Yes that will be fine."

"Good, I will write to Mrs Longwait who needs to be present at the request of Mr Manley, together with yourself and of course your husband."

"What about all the beneficiaries? I assume that there must be many?"

"Yes there are, but Mr Manley had very definite wishes as to who should be at this reading and I must carry out all his wishes. So unless I tell you otherwise I look forward to seeing you on Friday next."

Tom and Laura arrived at Alex's office having picked up Effey. As they went Laura felt a lump in her throat, so this was the end of M. M. & M. Little did she know.

Sitting behind his desk Alex said, "Shall I begin?"

"Yes," said Tom.

And so he began:

*THIS IS THE LAST WILL AND TESTAMENT OF MR. WILLIAM MANLEY*

*Well now you are here I hope I have kept my word and popped off quietly without a fuss. If not I'm sorry. I have told Alex that he must read this will in full.*

At that point Alex looked at them all and smiled. "Here we go," he said.

*You three people here today (I'm sure you will have outlived me Effey) have made such fun in my life.*

*I want to thank Tom and Laura, the children I never had who took me into the 20th century. To Tom for all the hard work he put in to build the John and Arabella library. I have set up a trust fund in his name to provide enough money for you to keep library up to date with new books new equipment and improvements with the interests of the new up-and-coming professionals and the young people of our Village in mind, I put no restrictions on this as I know it will be in your capable hands. The trust is £500,000 pounds. I also at this point want to thank you for the wonderful friendship you gave me.*

Tom looked at Laura in shock.

*I now come to the following ladies who are not with you today, but Alex knows how to contact them, who have graced my arm on many occasions and given me companionship and comfort in and out of my bed.*

Laura glanced at Effey, who had drawn breath and was holding one hand to her mouth while clutching her smelling salts to her nose with the other. Then Alex proceeded to read the names of the ladies.

*IN NO PARTICULAR ORDER Joanna, Kate, Isobell, Petra, Madeleine, Anna, Beth, Elizabeth, Dominique, Isla and Natalie.*

As Alex read the names both Laura and Tom recognised some of them as ladies who have been invited to parties in the office and some he had brought to dinner at their house, they also realised Effey was not among them

*And to you, my darlings, I leave £250,000 each.*

By this point Effey realising her name was not amongst those he read out began to cough and splutter.

Laura got up and went to her.

"Would you like some water?" she asked.

"No. No, just a tickle in my throat, thank you," came the rather abrupt reply.

Laura sat back down not daring to look at Tom and hardly able to control a smile.

"Shall we continue?" asked Alex.

*I now come to dear Effey. Emily Longwait. The name you got when you married Mr Longwait. And then when he died you did have a long wait, always hoping I would ask you to marry me, but with your eccentricity and mine I always thought it would be a catastrophic disaster and no good for either of us.*

Tom looked at the floor. He didn't dare look at her or anybody, he knew he would have found it hard to keep his composure. What a character Mr William. was.

Laura barely looked at Effey either, who was now the colour of beetroot.

*And so to you I give my shares and my bonds. The interest on these will enable you to have a Fortnum & Mason hamper delivered to your door by their customised van every week and also to buy you a few new models from some of your favourite classy boutiques, without touching capital. I also leave you £500,000 to enable you to keep your house in good repair and enjoy the rest of your life in comfort. And hope you miss me. All this comes with one proviso which Alex will make sure is carried out and will check regularly.*

*You must buy a cage for that bloody parrot so as it can't shit all over the house and anybody who comes to see you.*

Tom and Laura just began to giggle and realised that Effey was laughing to. Alex had gone back in his chair and was trying to be professional.

"I will get some tea brought in," he said. "I am so sorry Mrs Longwait, but it was my duty as instructed to read all."

Composure reinstated and tea drunk, Alex said, "Shall we continue?"

*And now Tom and Laura who welcomed me into their lives and home together with my friends. Laura I want you to know my brothers and I thought you were a gift from heaven the day you joined M. M. & M. the day you walked into our lives. I was fortunate enough to be with you much longer than they did and if I'd had a daughter, I couldn't have loved her more dearly than I have loved you. When my brothers died I was the sole beneficiary of everything they had, and I know without a doubt it would be their wish that you inherit the practice and the properly. It would be my dearest wish that you continue to run the business but called it B Manley with Laura. But I don't think Tom would approve of this.*

Laura looked at Alex in disbelief.
"Is this correct? I can't believe it," she asked him.
"Yes it's correct Laura and more," he replied.
She then looked at Tom.
"It is a dream?"
She could see he was in shock to, but he just shook his head in a disbelieving manner.
"And now I go on," said Alex.

*And now both of you I leave you all my properties together with everything else I possess including of course the house in Bermuda. I have set up a one-million-pound trust out there in your names so you can make sure the housekeeper and her husband and family who have served me and my family over the years can be looked after in the way they have always been used to. I will not say what you must do with the property, but it is my wish that you will keep it and enjoy the beauty of the island as we all did. There is a set amount of money left with Alex to cover inheritance tax for everybody concerned. (Unfortunately to pay that thieving load of grabbing bastards in the government.) Also enough to cover his account The whole details of which we agreed before my death. Depending on how long I have lived and how flash I have been there probably is about five million pounds left in capital This will help with the upkeep of things.*

Laura found she had tears streaming down her face. She always knew there was Manley money, but never on this scale.

"Are you all right?" Alex asked, looking at them both.

"Just stunned," replied Tom.

"So now I will read the final part."

*And finally my dears don't be sad, I will be with you, you made an old man feel wanted and loved. Remember, in the safe is the story someday to be written with my blessing, I hope by you.*

With that Alex closed the reading of the will. Folding his hands he rested his chin on them and looked at the three people sat before him and thought how this man had changed their lives, and his. He cleared his throat in an almost unnecessary way and, looking at Laura, he said:

"Please excuse me but what is the story, and will you be writing it?"

Laura looked at him unable to collect her thoughts.

"So sorry, I know I shouldn't ask."

"No, no, it's OK," replied Laura. "It is a love story."

Her voice quivering as she spoke. Tom lent forward and put his arm round her and gave her a hug. And with that Effey interrupted.

"Am I in it? I hope I'm in it. Laura please let me be in it, after all it must be our love story."

"Yes, yes," Tom jumped in not wishing to crush her hopes.

By this time Effey was stood up as if preening her feathers.

"Well," she said. "I did love him and he and I, we had our moments and if I have to be on TV I will wear something designer. Just let me know when it will be."

At this point Alex spoke up.

"I'm sure, Mrs Longwait, when things have settled down Laura will give you more information."

"I think I'll go home now. Oh! I don't have a car here. Do I? Of course I came with you didn't I?" she said looking at Tom and Laura.

"Yes you did," replied Tom.

"Never mind, could you phone for a taxi for me?" she said, pointing to Alex.

"Yes I'll get my secretary to sort it," he replied.

"Good, I'll wait in reception. I'm sure you have more things to discuss without me, and don't forget young man my name is Mrs Longwaith to you," she said giving Alex one of her stem looks. "And take my taxi fare out of my inheritance."

The three of them couldn't help falling into the giggles.

"We'll go in and see her in a couple of days," said Tom.

Back home Tom and Laura felt a bit shellshocked and seemed for the first time in their lives together unable to speak. It was Laura who broke the silence.

"I just don't know why we have been given so much, but it's strange. I don t know how I feel, just empty I think."

"I think it's hard to have any feelings at this moment. I think it will take time to absorb it all," replied Tom.

# Part 4

# Bermuda

## Chapter Twenty-Six

It took Tom and Laura a long time to adjust to their inheritance. It wasn't that they just inherited everything, but each month there would be sums of money coming in from different sources, for instance a cheque from the London office, which they felt very embarrassed about as they did nothing to earn it. There was the shock of finding out that Mr William. had never sold his brother's penthouse apartment in Ocean Village in Southampton, and when they got to the big house at Sandbanks in Poole in Dorset they were not surprised to find nice pieces of antique furniture, but a large amount of valuable jewellery together with a new Ferrari and Porsche in the garage, which had never been on the road.

It was now eighteen months later. And the biggest changes they had made were to the practice. They decided to ask young Alex to join them and made him a director together with Paul Irons. They both had secretaries who between them looked after reception which left Tom and Laura free to deal with the general running of the place, the improvements of the library and all the charitable commitments they had also inherited. They now both shared the same office and Tom didn't take on any new work, but from time to time he was still asked to give his old clients advice and, slowly, their life settled down to a little normality.

"I'm thinking, Laura, now Christmas is over and the weather is a bit dismal and cold it would be good to take a holiday."

"Yes, good idea where are you thinking of going?" she replied.

"I think Bermuda, if only just to see what we own, it's sometime now since Mr William. departed, and everything seems to be under control here so how do you feel about it?"

"Unsure," she replied.

'What's that mean?" he asked.

"Well, I know they understand all the details of the will and the trust that takes care of them, but don't you think they might feel a bit uneasy if we actually go there?"

"No. Why should they?"

"Well they know we are not Manley family, and they are true island people. They may think we are just coming to cause trouble," said Laura.

"They'll realise that's not so when they meet us," said Tom.

"I suppose we could stay in a hotel," said Laura.

"Don't be ridiculous. We own the place and they know that when we want to go there it's our right, just as Mr William, his brothers his parents have always done. I know you haven't had any contact with them but I have with, Rio the eldest son. He seems a nice guy, intelligent and very friendly, and he's always asking me when we are going to visit. And don't forget he's a qualified solicitor in the Manley office in Bermuda. He completely understands we are the owners and they are the protected sitting tenants," replied Tom.

"I know all about that, but, but…"

"Come on, I think you're just being ridiculous. It would be lovely to have a holiday and you can hardly use the excuse we can't afford it. I'm going to look at some flights and ring Rio to say we are planning a visit," said Tom.

Laura couldn't quite explain how she felt, was it excitement or fear? She felt very privileged to have known the Manley brothers and in more recent times to have learned more about the whole family story, but she didn't know if she felt comfortable to be in a very private place where so much of their lives were spent. It was almost a memorial to Arabella and John's love.

Tom interrupted her thoughts. "What do you think, two or three weeks? I found some flights," he asked.

"See what reaction you get when you phone Rio," she said.

Tom got up from the computer walked over to Laura putting his arms around her. He said, "You are a funny girl, all the Manleys have given us has never changed you, I love you Laura."

Later that day Tom took the opportunity to phone Rio.

"Hi there, it's Tom. Laura and I are thinking of paying you a visit. How do you feel about it?"

Without any hesitation Rio expressed his delight.

"Wonderful, wonderful," he replied, "we will be all prepared for you and so happy to meet you in person. I'm sure there are many things you would like to know about us as a family and many things we want to tell you about your beautiful house and our wonderful island. When will you arrive?"

"Not quite sure. A few things to sort out first, Laura thinks we should stay in a hotel near you," said Tom.

"Absolutely impossible," said Rio. "This is your house now and we are here to look after you in every possible way and I know everybody will be so excited. You know we and the Manleys go back a long way, we were all as family and we just hope that we can continue that relationship. We have an old grandma who lives with my parents in the house, she is a little confused but often talks about the beautiful Arabella, Mr Manley and the boys. Just let me know the details of your arrival and we will meet you at the airport. Any problems just ring me, I can't wait to tell everybody, cheers for now."

Tom put the phone down feeling a little relief. He had not expected any problems but, for Laura's sake, he was pleased.

It was a cold wet and windy day as the plane took off for Bermuda. Tom squeezed Laura's hand as the plane gained height and they were in the sunshine above the cloud.

"Are you OK?" he asked her.

"Yes fine, a little nervous though," she replied

"Of the flight?" he asked, looking deeply into her eyes

"No, don't be silly. Just a bit nervous of meeting everybody, and the reception we shall get," she said

"Laura, I keep telling you it will be fine, trust me," he said.

It was a very different picture as the plane landed, soon the doors were open and disembarking began. The temperature was perfect, the sun was shining and there was a very warm, gentle breeze blowing.

They collected their baggage and went through customs, Tom pushed the trolley towards the exit. He knew that Rio had said he would meet them, but suddenly he thought how will I know him? He needn't have worried for as they came through the exit doors with the other passengers, there was a large banner saying:

WELCOME TOM AND LAURA.

Before they could take it all in two little people, a boy and a girl, about six or eight years old ran forward carrying huge bouquets of beautiful exotic flowers. With arms outstretched the little girl curtsied to Tom, giving him the flowers and the little boy bowed to Laura. They had the biggest white smiles out of chocolate brown faces, behind them was a small group of people smiling, a good-looking man some six foot tall stepped forward.

"I'm Rio," he said, offering his hand to both of them. "Let me introduce you to everybody. This is my wife Pia, and my brother Joe and his wife Kat, there are many more of us but you will meet all of them later. Come now you must be tired let's get you home. It takes about ten minutes or so once we get away from the airport which always adds time to the journey, but as it's your first visit here you can enjoy the scenery."

Tom and Laura just smiled and nodded in reply, it was all a bit too much to take in.

Once in the car Tom and Rio were chatting away very easily, the two children were kneeling up in the seat beside their father with their chins resting on the back of seat looking at Tom and Laura, and then there was a little lull in the conversation which gave them a chance to get a word in. The little girl nudged her brother who said, "Now Papa?"

He laughed saying, "Yes you may."

Both children sat up very straight and the little boy began by saying as if he was on stage, "My name is Josh, short for Joshua, I am seven years old and the top of my class in school. I am learning about..." there was a pause while he searched for a word, his sister gave him another nudge, which helped him find the word, "England. I am very happy to meet you both and if I can help you please tell me."

With that, a small Black hand with a very pink underside was handed first to Tom and then to Laura.

"Thank you," said Tom. "My name is Tom and my wife is Laura and we are very pleased to meet you and your sister."

He was trying to be very serious as he realised this speech had probably been practiced many times. It was obvious Josh had more to say, but his sister pushed him to one side saying:

"My name is Sophia, I am six years old and am top of my class for knitting, which is better than Josh, he can't knit."

Tom and Laura were trying not to laugh as they guessed that these last few words were not in the planned speech by the look Josh gave his sister; but not to be outdone she continued. "And if I can help please tell me."

And this was followed by a very formal handshake for both of them. The two children then lent very close to their father giving him a kiss with Sophia whispering, "Good Papa?"

"Yes fine, now sit down properly and face the front," he replied.

Just a few minutes later they turned in between two large iron gates to stop in front of a large white colonial house, with a beautiful porch supported by four large pillars.

"This is your house," said Rio. "Something we are all very aware of, we understand the details of the will and trust which we have been given in Mr Manley's will for all of the family from Grandma, to our small children, giving us opportunities that not many islanders have."

Once inside, they sat chatting for about an hour during which time Rio explained the layout of the house.

"Here to the left side my parents live, on the ground floor, they have lounge diner and four bedrooms on suite the kitchen and utility is in the area which returns to the front porch and entrance. Mother's old aunt Bella lives with them but she's known as Grandma, she has great difficulty walking now and has to spend some time in her wheelchair. My brother Tito and his wife Sadie with children Jacko and Carmen have exactly the same accommodation on the first floor above. On the right-hand side it's just the same set-up we live on the ground floor and our younger brother, Zac and his wife Cattie, live above. We are all self-contained with our own entrances. But the courtyard here is a lovely family area to meet and after you have had a rest – shall we say about six o'clock this evening? – the whole family will be here to meet you and our father has a few words he would like to say, and then we would be delighted if you would join us to eat. Your apartment is both ground and upper floor, one bedroom en suite, dressing room downstairs which enables you to step out onto the sand at any time and four further bedrooms en suite upstairs. I think we have prepared the downstairs one for you, but all the others are ready if you should wish to use them. You look right out to the sea. Daddy Man always preferred this. But now it is your house we will do whatever you please. Over the next few days there will be much for us to show you of your whole estate."

All this time the two children were amusing themselves from time to time offering Tom and Laura the dishes with little tasters in. Then suddenly Josh came right up close to Tom looking very serious, saying:

"Is Daddy Man coming soon?"

But before Tom could answer Pia spoke, "No Josh, I have told you Daddy Man has gone to the fairies."

Looking sad with eyes a little bit full he said, "Oh, well if he's happy I don't mind, I expect he'll come and see us when he gets back."

It was all so sweet it brought a lump to Laura's throat.

Standing up Pia said, "Shall we show you to your apartment now? I expect you'd like to get settled."

Tom and Laura stood up and followed her to the two large white doors that opened into their part of the house. The view was absolutely breathtaking, there was a large terrace that ran the length of the building beyond which was pink sand lapped with blue sea. Two young people appeared as if on cue, who Pia introduced as Christina and Pollo "who are here to look after your needs." The two young people bowed their heads to Tom and Laura. And Christina said, "I have unpacked your things. I hope that is correct, would you like anything now or shall I show you to the bedroom, mam?"

"I think that would be nice, but please while we are here will you call us Tom and Laura."

They had been in Bermuda just four hours and it was just impossible to take in everything, particularly to even begin to believe this beautiful house was theirs. Tom put his arms around her.

"Pleased you came now, my darling?"

"Yes. And I must admit if the rest of the family are all like Rio, Pia and the children I'm sure we will enjoy our stay here. Shall we just relax on the bed here and take in the view before we get ready for this evening?"

Tom woke with a start with no idea of what the time was. He grabbed his watch from the side table which was fortunately on local time, which the pilot had given them on touchdown. It was five ten. Laura was dead to the world. He gently gave her a shake.

"Come on Laura it's time to wake up, we've got fifty minutes until we meet the family."

Laura stretched and slipped off the side of the bed. Tom had headed for the shower, she walked out onto the terrace, it really was the perfect paradise. With that Christina appeared.

"Mam, would you like some tea? I have prepared a tray for you, may I bring it to the bedroom?"

"Oh yes, some tea would be wonderful, thank you."

Within minutes she arrived with a tray of tea and little sandwiches and pretty little cakes.

"That looks super, Christina."

'Well mam, I guess it's a long time since you have eaten, and it may be some time before you have dinner so I think it wise for you to have something now."

"How wise you are, and I feel we are so short of time, is there any way you can tell Rio that we may be a little late?"

"Yes, I can tell him but please don't worry. We are not good on time here in Bermuda."

Tom came out of the shower wrapped in a sort of silk bath robe.

"I suggest you don't go out on the terrace in that, you'll be done for indecent exposure," laughed Laura. "Come sit down and have a cup of tea."

They hadn't really realised that they were quite hungry, and they soon tucked into the goodies, and the tea was to die for.

"I think, Laura, you had better get ready you've got fifteen minutes now."

"I know, but I've got Christina to tell Rio we may be a bit late, she says it will be OK. I got the feeling from her comment that everybody is quite laid back with time."

Dressed and ready to go Tom said, "Gosh you look fabulous in that dress, it just falls over your body like skin. Have you got anything on underneath?"

"That's for me to know and you to find out. Later," she replied.

They stepped out into the courtyard to be greeted by what seemed a sea of smiling Black faces and shining white teeth. Everybody stood up with the exception of the elderly lady in the wheelchair, who Laura noticed was much paler skinned than the rest of the family with gingery blonde hair. They all clapped. Rio stepped forward, waving his hands to everybody to sit down.

"This is my father Joe and mother Maria. I am not going to introduce you to everybody individually as I'm sure you will never remember all our names, but I'm also sure you will get to know us all very quickly."

Suddenly a voice chirped up, "They know we are Sofia and Josh and they said we can call them Tom and Laura."

A giggle went round the room.

"Yes. And shush for now please," said Rio to his two offspring. And then he continued, "Father would like to have a few words."

The man who had been introduced as Joe stood up he was six foot tall and very good-looking, he cleared his throat and began.

"As the head of the family I have been asked to tell you how pleased we are you have come to look at your home. We understand from the communications you have had with Rio that you have no wish to change the situation from that we had with the Manley family. We completely understand that we are not the owners and will try always to do as you wish. Whenever you are here, whether it is permanently or just for short stays we will be only too happy to look after you. I expect you have something you would like to say, so please go ahead."

Laura looked at Tom and they exchanged eyes, but she knew he would only be wanting to put them at ease. He stood up saying.

"We are delighted to be here and can reassure you that we have absolutely no wish to change this system that works so well here. I can assure you that you will not have to put up with us on a permanent basis but our visits may get a little more frequent when we get more acquainted with your beautiful island. We must stress we come here as friends and hope you would accept us in time as family as you did with the Manleys. William Manley was our dearest friend and nothing could ever have been more of a shock than when we inherited from him. I will just let you into a secret – my wife here was so reluctant to come and nervous of what your reaction to us may be. I feel over the short time I have known Rio we have a good understanding of each other, and although we have only been here a few hours and late for our first meeting, we feel relaxed happy and welcome already."

Everybody clapped again and Tom sat down, looking at Laura for approval which she quickly gave him with her eyes.

"And now," said Joe, "I think it is time for us to have a drink and celebrate followed by some food."

Then Grandma stood up from her wheelchair and walked unaided to Laura.

A shocked silence fell over the room. Grandma hadn't walked unaided for the last two or three years. She put her arms out to Laura and then took her face into her hands and kissed her forehead.

"My Ari, my darling Ari where have you been? You have not been here to see me for so long?"

Laura was a little bit in shock and she could see teardrops beginning to run down the old lady's face, she gently took her hands saying, "No. But I'm here now."

She didn't know what made her say that but it seemed to please the old lady, who smiled, kissing her on the forehead again. It all happened so quickly that none of the family seemed to realise what was going on, but Maria was now beside Grandma apologising profusely to Laura.

"I'm so sorry. Poor Grandma suffers a little with dementia and her sight is failing and to be honest she took me by surprise by just getting out of her wheelchair and walking to you, I'm so sorry."

"There's no need to be sorry, I understand completely. I expect she just mistook me for someone else."

"Yes, I think so. With your lovely red hair and pale skin it stirred something in her mind from way back and she remembered Arabella Manley. Now come darling, Jo's got your chair here and he's going to push you outside and were are going to eat," said Maria to the old lady.

Calm was soon restored and they all went out onto the terrace. There was a lovely barbecue alight with two very shiny Black boys attending it. Soon there was drinking and chatting and delicious food was served, everybody wanted to talk to Tom and Laura, all discussing who would take them here there and everywhere. The time seemed to go so quickly and suddenly it was two a.m. Rio came over to them, saying:

"I hope you have enjoyed your first evening with us, as I'm sure you have realised we are all eager to show you around, but now I'm sure you would like to go to bed, I'll speak to you in the morning."

Goodnights where made and Laura and Tom made their way back to their apartment. Stepping inside Christina and Pollo were there to greet them.

"What can we get you?" asked Christina.

"Some tea would be nice," said Tom.

"Fine, will you take it here, or will Pollo bring it to the bedroom for you?"

"I think that's a great idea," replied Tom.

They made their way to the bedroom. On the bed lay two housecoats in a pale shade of burgundy. The bed was folded back with a sweet wrapped like a flower on the pillow, and together with the scent of the air it was just so romantic.

Within minutes the tea arrived and Pollo wished them good night. They got undressed and ready for bed. The voiles at the windows were just moving on a gentle warm breeze.

They lay back on the pillow and sipped their tea, they could see the water's edge glistening in the moonlight.

"What a day," said Tom

"I know," said Laura. "And what about Grandma? That was weird and did you hear Maria say perhaps the old lady thought I was Mrs Arabella Manley?"

"Yes, I did. Still, perhaps in the next week or so we will understand more about everybody and learn more about this amazing set-up that is ours, and hopefully see more of the island."

"And more of the Love Island too."

"I don't know that you've got much chance of that Laura, but I think now we've got a pretty good chance of having a long night's sleep."

Laura woke up and looked at Tom who was still fast asleep. Climbing out of bed she slipped on her housecoat and walked out onto the terrace and took some deep breaths of the wonderful clean air. Gosh this place was wonderful. She could quite understand how much the Manleys must have loved it. She felt a twinge of sadness that none of the Manley brothers had any children to inherit it all, and still found it unbelievable that she and Tom were now the owners. She turned to sit down on one of the lounges and Christina appeared.

"Good morning mam, would you like some breakfast?"

"Not just yet thank you, Tom is still sleeping, but some juice would be wonderful," replied Laura.

A few minutes later Rio appeared.

"Good morning and how are you today, did you sleep well?"

"Oh, fantastically and Tom is still doing it," she said.

"I'm not surprised, yesterday was a long day for you both. I'm off to the office today, and I think you two may want to just relax, we have plenty of things lined up for you during your stay, Pollo can take you in the car if you want to do something, and Zac will be bobbing in and out all day if you have any questions. We're all going to eat on the beach tonight, if you feel up to it, please join us."

"That sounds nice, we would love to join you," she replied.

How right Rio had been about their day. When Tom woke they ate a breakfast of luscious fruit, rolls and little sweet cakes, and drank cups of coffee to die for. They dozed on the sunbeds, they swam, and they could see in the distance what Laura was absolutely sure was the Love Island.

At one point they decided to walk along the beach. They took off in the direction of two big sheds, giggling on the way about, if these belonged to them, they were rather big garden sheds. The door to the first one they came to was open a little. They just looked in and could see it was obviously a workshop; the next, one much bigger, was closed. There was a high window on one side which they could just see into: it contained a very big boat.

Laura commented to Tom, "Don't get ideas that it belongs to us."

"Of course not, but do you remember when we were at the boat show with Mr William? At the time he was asking if we should have a boat. Perhaps because we steered him away from it he bought one for here."

They walked on a little more to where the land ended and the water came round. They then walked back past the house and on in the other direction. After a little distance they came across six little bungalows with pretty pointed thatched roofs, they stood back from the line of the house in amongst some tall trees. There was no sign of life and everything was so neat and tidy.

"So what do you suppose this is?" questioned Tom.

"No idea, perhaps we'll find out tonight at the barbecue," said Laura.

They continue to walk and Laura said, "Look Tom, is that the gate in the distance where Arabella and the Black guy had a quickie? Do you remember in the book in John Manley's book when she came back from here and was pregnant?"

"I don't know Laura, don't get too carried away."

They walked to the gate which did seem to be on a line between their land and the next owners.

"Do you want to have a quickie here? There's nobody about and it could keep up the tradition," said Tom.

"Don't be ridiculous," laughed Laura.

They were greeted by Christina when they got back to the house.

"Have you enjoyed your walk, and would you like something to drink?" she asked.

"Yes to both of those questions," replied Tom.

She disappeared returning after a few minutes with a tray of drinks.

"Can you tell us, Christina, what are the little houses just along the beach?" inquired Laura.

"Oh that's where we houseboys and -girls live. Pollo and I live in the second one along. It's really lovely, we are so lucky not many people like us have such good accommodation, most of them just have huts with no facilities and that's how it was many years ago. And then John Manley decided to build them for all his staff, he was such a good kind man our parents loved him and their parents before them He was a good man. God rest his soul."

Silence fell between them for just a few minutes.

"And tell us, is that an island that we can see in the distance?" asked Laura again.

"Oh yes, but that's spooky," said Christina.

"Why?" asked Laura.

"I don't know, but folklore has it that whoever sets foot there never returns, and you know how superstitious we all are so nobody ever goes there," replied Christina and off she went.

"You know why that is, don't you?" said Tom. "That's all to do with Arabella and John Manley, I bet."

"I'm sure you are absolutely right, it's so interesting. I hope we can just find out more during our stay," said Laura.

And so the days passed. Tito, Sadie, Jacko and Carmen took them several times to explore the island. Zac and his wife Cattie took them to the touristy bit for some shopping and some local culture. Rio took them to the Manley Solicitors office and showed them around, introducing them as the new owners. To which Tom quickly added sleeping owners, which made everybody laugh. Then one evening as they were eating Zac said they were planning to go fishing the next day with the big boat, for big fish, and would Tom like to join them? It was a boys' only day so how did he feel about it and would Laura mind? And he went onto explain that they would barbecue the fish for all the family when they got back in the evening

"Sounds great. What time do we take off?" asked Tom.

"About ten a.m. sound OK to you?"

The next morning Tom was up bright-eyed and bushy-tailed, ready for the fishing trip. Christina and Pollo served them breakfast on the terrace. It was the most beautiful morning; the sea was sparkling blue, lapping against the edge of the sand. Tom kept looking at his watch, and Laura could see he was eager to get going. Draining her coffee cup, she said:

"Come on, I'll walk up to the boat house with you, I can see you itching to go," she teased him.

Arriving there it was all hustle and bustle. Rio, Tito and Zac were already there and several of the houseboys were getting ready to put the boat in the water from the slipway. Laura thought they all looked like ants with their beautifully toned bodies looking as though they'd been varnished. It seemed to her it didn't seem to matter what the pecking order was, everybody got on so well; she wondered was it just this family and their workers or were all the local families the same? For a minute her mind went to Mr William. She could understand how he must've loved these people. Then it was time for everybody to get on board, Tom kissed her goodbye, she squeezed him and said:

"Have a lovely day darling! Be careful, you're no fisherman, don't get eaten or fall overboard. Please be careful, I need you back." She laughed.

There was a great roar of the throaty engines as they took off. Laura watched them into the distance, waving goodbye. Turning to walk back to the house she passed the workshop. The doors were wide open and she could see Pollo inside with two other boys. She decided to walk inside: it was stacked full of wood old and new and lots of driftwood, bits of old boats and all sorts of things that looked like rubbish, all very neatly stacked. After greeting them all she sort of wandered round, it was so interesting, and then to her amazement she saw about halfway down a pile a boat with the letters in very faded gold *U. & I. R. 1*. She looked very closely, it was hard to distinguish it clearly – yes it was! As she thought the name of John and Ari's boat she lifted her arm and ran her fingers along the letters. She felt a shiver go down her spine she stood there for a few minutes, just thinking *if only that boat could talk what a tale it would have to tell*. Turning away she said her goodbyes to the boys and stepped out into the sunshine. Walking back slowly to the house she met Joe on the way.

"Good morning, have you been to see them all off on the boat?" he asked.

"Yes I have, I think Tom was quite excited about going if not a little nervous. I don't think he's ever been fishing before, I hope they take care of him," she giggled.

"Yes, he'll be fine. Do you mind if I walk back with you?" he asked.

"No, I'd like that," she replied.

# Chapter Twenty-Seven

As they walked Joe said:

"Glad to have this chance to speak to you alone, mam."

"Please call me Laura."

"Yes mam."

They both laughed.

"But do go on," said Laura.

"I would just like to say how worried my family were when Daddy Man died, and how the new owners would be, but now I know they are happy again and I know they are happy you are here."

"That is nice for you to be concerned for them, but to tell you the truth I was really scared of coming in case you all resented us, but now we are here I know all is well, and I think we will grow to love this island as much as you. Daddy Man did, with its beautiful clear blue sea and lovely pink sand, it's an idyllic climate."

As they walked Laura's mind was in overdrive, and soon they were back at the house.

"Will you come and take a coffee with me on the terrace?" she asked.

"I would be very honoured to do that," he replied.

Christina soon arrived with their drink, and Laura didn't miss the chance to ask a few questions, so pointing out to sea she said:

"Tell me, is that the island that belongs to the house, the one they called the Love Island? And if so is it true that people that go there never return?"

"No, not really that story has just been elaborated over the years because both Mr. and Mrs John Manley are buried there. Do you not know the story?"

"Not exactly. I only know a little about it from Daddy Man. Can you explain it to me?"

"Mr John bought it for his wife for her birthday when they used to come for holidays with the three boys and a nanny. When the boys were tucked up at night they would row over to the island in a boat that he bought especially just for them. They named it *U & I R 1*. They would arrive back early morning before the boys were up, so the story goes. Apparently when they were all here there was always laughter and fun, they say she loved life and lived for her husband and sons. And when Mr John died she brought his body here from England to be buried on the island, in the little stone hut there. I remember it well, everybody here was so sad.

"She had made and arranged all the details with my father, I think he was her most liked and trusted member of staff. He went to the airport with one of the other houseboys to meet her and bring the coffin back here to the house. Father had prepared the boat boarding the bough to take the coffin leaving the seating across the middle and stern. He had fitted an outboard engine to it as to row it would have been quite difficult. Six bonfires had been prepared here on the shoreline and when it was dark they were lit, all the staff were here on the beach and when the preacher came out, followed by Arabella and then the boys carrying the coffin which was covered with beautiful brightly coloured flowers, they all began to softly sing."

He paused for a moment as if reflecting, and Laura was finding it hard to control her emotions.

"And then?" she said.

"Yes I remember it well there was so many tears that night. The singing stopped as the boys walked into the water and placed the coffin on the boat. Everything was silent apart from the gentle lapping of the water on the sand. The preacher said a prayer and gave a blessing. Arabella stepped into the boat helped by my father, and the soft singing began again. My father then came to me and said. 'Come my son, you will come with us'. I was so shocked I just did as I was told, I sat beside him in the stern I was so, so scared. As we crossed to the island singing became fainter. I looked back and I could still see the bonfires burning. Father helped Arabella out of the boat and she went ahead of us to the little hut. The moon was shining so brightly that night that I could see her clearly opening the door. 'Here,' said Father, 'you can help me carry the coffin to the hut.' Although I was quite tall for my age I wasn't particularly strong, but somehow God and my fear must've given me strength. We placed the coffin on the shelf in the hut and Father told me to go back, to keep an eye on the boat in case it drifted. I don't think I have ever run so fast in my life since.

"I didn't know at the time that it had been arranged that she would stay on the island with her dead husband alone. Father had given her a flare gun that she would fire when she was ready to return. He did try to persuade her to come with us but she was insistent that she would stay. As we sat in the boat on the way back Father put his arm round me saying, 'Today my son you grew up.' Somebody day and night was left on guard to look for the flare. It didn't come and I could see Father was very worried.

"After five days Father decided to go to the island going into the hut he could see her lying on the shelf beside the coffin. He went to her fearing the worst, and she was dead. Lying on top of the coffin was two envelopes, one was addressed to Paco, my father, the other one to the Misters H.W. and R. Manley. He ripped open the one for him and read something like, I may not have the words exact, although it is pretty much imprinted in my mind:

*My dearest Paco.*

*Please place my body in the coffin facing my husband. Do not be sad, we are together again for eternity. Please tell everybody at the house not to be sad. We loved every one of you as our family and I know you will continue to look after our sons when they come to stay. I thank you Paco for being such a faithful friend. Please make sure the other letter goes to England.*

*With all my love.*
*Arabella.*

There was a short silence between them. Then Laura said:

"Tom and I were told about the letter some time ago by Mr William. That's what you called Daddy Man, And even then it upset him."

"Yes, I'm sure," replied Joe, "but you can probably understand why the story evolved about nobody returns from the island. They do say that Arabella walks the shore at night here in front of the house, looking for someone, and when she finds them she then can rest, and she and John and the island will disappear into eternity, but who? Nobody knows. I don't really believe it although old Grandma says she has seen her." He smiles. "So it's obviously not her Arabella's looking for. I would've thought if anybody it would be one of her sons, and now that's too late. But of course that gives the believers a chance to keep the story alive."

A little silence fell between them again. And then Laura said, "Please take me to the island, please Joe?"

He looked at her in surprise.

"As my boss I should do as you ask, but are you really sure you want to go."

"Yes, yes I do. Please take me."

"Well, I will have to get the boat and I'll get one of the boys to give me a hand."

"Can we go in their boat?"

"No, we don't have the boat now."

"I think you do. I saw a little bit of it in the boat shed this morning."

"OK, we'll go and look but I think you're mistaken."

Laura's heart was beating so fast she thought Joe must be able to hear it. At the boathouse she rushed in to where she'd seen the name board, hardly stopping to say hello to the workers.

"Look here," she said excitedly.

"Yes I see that, but a name board doesn't make a boat," he said trying to look in amongst the rest of the stack of wood. He said something to the boys which Laura didn't understand, they all laughed and then came over and started to take the stack down. It was all a bit too slow for Laura but eventually they got to the boat. Joe was shaking his head in disbelief.

"Can we go in it? It looks OK," said Laura.

"I don't think it will be seaworthy, it's bound to have shrunk being out of the water for so many years. It needs a few hours in soak to see if it leaks. Come on boys, let's lift it in the water. I can see the Mistress will give me no rest until I satisfy her wishes."

Laura could hardly contain herself. It looked fine. What if it did leak a bit? The water was warm and the sun was shining, if they got a bit wet it didn't matter. She stood patiently looking at it for about fifteen minutes, then said:

"It seems OK can we go?"

"No, we can't," said Joe, looking at his watch. "We will go back to the house, it's nearly noon. We'll come back here at two o'clock and if she hasn't taken on any water we'll risk it. Can you swim well?" he asked, looking seriously at Laura.

"Yes I can," she assured him.

"We will walk back to the house now and just wait," he said in his calm way.

Back at the house once more Laura said:

"Will you sit and have some juice with me now, as I have another question to ask? You seem to know so much about everything here and Tom and I have so much to learn, or do you have too much work to do?"

"I can stay and help you if you wish," he replied looking at her.

"Well it's rather difficult, it's about Grandma. She seems to have a different colouring to all of you, Rio said she was really aunty so, how does she fit in?" asked Laura.

"She's Arabella's daughter but not Mr John's child. It was supposed to be a complete secret to be forgotten, again the story goes that Ari was here alone with the boys because Mr John was busy in England and she made a baby with a young Black man who was working in the Manley office for a short while, he had tragically lost his wife and Ari felt sorry for him. I don't think it was a love affair. But the story says Aunt Bella was conceived on the gate up there as they said goodnight, so if any young couple are having difficulty producing family he brings her along and sits on the gate and that does the trick. I don't know if all of the story is true, these things become embroidered with time. But what I do know from my mother is that the baby was born here in the house quietly one night and by the morning the baby was gone to a young couple who were childless, and they were related somehow to my wife's family. It was all legally binding. But as a child growing up she visited this house often with her mother and played with the Manley boys, and their mother who organised all sorts of fun and games for them and all the children belonging to the staff apparently they absolutely adored her, and so that's why she's a slightly different colour, and has reddish hair. And I think when she got out of her wheelchair and came across to you the other evening when you first arrived, it must have triggered something from her childhood, she never knew that Ari was her mother. But you being white skinned and she being a little confused brought back memories. Does that answer your question?"

"Yes it does. Thank you," said Laura.

"Now," said Joe, "I'm going off to do a few things. I'll be back about two o'clock and we will go to the island, I can't guarantee in which boat though," he chuckled.

Laura sat and pondered for a while about what he had told her, of course it all became clear. Never did she think she would meet the child that nearly broke John Manley's heart?

Laura must have looked at her watch fifty times, had it stopped surely it must be more than half hour since Joe left? She tapped the face of the watch, no it was going. She got up and decided to go and get the clothes ready for the party that night. On the way Christina saw her, saying:

"Can I get you some lunch, Laura, perhaps a little pasta?"

"No, thank you but a little fruit would be nice please, I'm waiting for Joe to come back. We are going to the island."

Christina said nothing but looked horrified as she turned to go to the kitchen.

At last it was quarter to two. Laura was so excited she couldn't sit still, she kept getting up to see if Joe was coming.

Please, please let the boat be watertight she kept praying. Then suddenly Joe was there, she felt she wanted to grab his hand and make him hurry along, although she knew in his world everything was Manyana, slow and relaxed.

"What do you think, will it float?" she asked him.

"We will see, but can you swim well?" he asked, again teasing her.

"Oh yes, I can, I can," she replied, not wanting to put any obstacle in the way, and not able to see he was teasing her.

As they approached the boathouse Laura could see the little boat bobbing at the edge of the shore. She couldn't contain herself any longer, she took off racing to the boat like an excited five-year-old on Christmas morning.

"It's OK, it is OK!" she called to Joe.

"Slow, slow, just let me look, I can't believe after all this time that she will be OK," he said, examining her.

"I do believe you are in luck, she looks sound, climb in I'll go and get some oars, you any good at rowing?"

"I've never done it but I'm certainly willing to try."

"Don't worry I'm only joking with you. I don't think I've ever seen anybody so excited," he said.

It was so beautiful crossing to the island and Laura just sat in the back of the boat, totally mesmerised. She realised she had butterflies in her tummy. Joe jumped out into the water and so did Laura. Just as she imagined perhaps John and Ari did on their moonlight trips. They stood on the sand for a few minutes and Joe said:

"Shall we walk to the hut, would you like that?"

Laura just nodded. Almost from where they had landed there was a path that led to the hut.

"Do you come over and maintain this?" she asked.

"No, I don't, but occasionally I come over and just look really just to make sure the hut is still here, and I've always noticed strangely how the path just stays as you see it today, nothing grows on it."

As they walked Laura noticed the whole area seem to be covered in a beautiful white flower which gave off a most wonderful perfume.

"What are these flowers called?"

"I don't know, but shortly after Arabella died my father said they started to grow and, as you see, they have spread. He didn't know what they were, they are not native to Bermuda, which of course all adds to the mystery of the island. I think the seeds were probably brought here by birds or washed in by the water. I will give you it is a little strange, but I have tried to trace them. Father did bring a small cutting away at one time. It never grew."

"And they never spread onto the path, why?"

Joe just lifted his hands.

By now they were right in the front of the hut.

"Would you like to look in?" Joe asked her.

"Yes I would, do you think it would be right?"

"Yes, I believe so," he replied.

They stepped inside, Laura expected it to be dusty and full of cobwebs, but much to the contrary the coffin, which was large, seemed not to have deteriorated at all over the years. She just stood there for a few minutes in disbelief.

"Come now," said Joe seeing that she was a little overcome. As they stepped back out into the sunshine, he said:

"I will wander on down the path to the boat, you follow when you are ready."

Laura knelt down in the white flowers, with all sorts of things going through her head. Here she was on John and Arabella's Love Island, a place that not even their sons had been to. Was she wrong to want to come? This was the private place of two people who had loved so deeply. And two people that were part of the reason for her and Tom being here, but two people that she felt she knew so well through the wishes of their sons. Two people that she and Tom probably knew more about their private life than anybody else.

She realised she had tears running down her face. She collected herself together and walked back to the boat.

Joe put his arm round her, saying:

"I know how you feel mam, but please don't be sad. It was a place those two people loved."

"I'm not sad I'm just emotional. I've thought about this place for quite some time and just to come here is, is, is unbelievable, thank you for bringing me dear Joe."

He helped her into the boat, pushed it off the shore and began to row back to the house. Laura just sat silently, so emotionally charged with the thoughts of what she knew about Ari and John. And John's book and of course the three Manley sons that had all become so much part of Tom and her lives. She didn't know why but she felt totally drained. She pulled herself together and realised they were at the shore.

"I thought we'd land here instead of going to the boat house which means you don't have to walk back, I think you need a little rest," said Joe.

"Thank you, I think you could be right, and please could you leave the boat here on the shore? I would like Tom to see it," said Laura, stepping out onto the warm pink sand.

"If you wish mam, I'll pull it up on the sand, more so as it's not in the water."

She turned to him and took his hands, saying:

"I'd just like to thank you so much, that was just wonderful, and to be able to go in their boat was a dream."

"I think a miracle, I'm amazed she didn't sink," he joked, waving goodbye as he walked away,

Laura just stood there for a few minutes shaking her head and looking at the boat. She turned and walked towards the house feeling drained. As she arrived at the terrace Christina came out to greet her.

"Where have you been? You look so pale and tired," she asked.

"Joe took me to the Love Island."

"Oh no, you know you must never go there! You're lucky to come back, I told you that the other day."

Laura thought, if you could see a Black girl go white, this was Christina.

"Please go and lie down and I will bring you some tea," said Christina.

Laura did as she was told, her mind just reeling with so many thoughts. She must've fallen asleep, she didn't hear

Christina bring the tea; the next thing she heard was excited voices and realised it was the men coming back from the fishing trip. She quickly looked at the clock, she had been asleep for three hours.

The tea was cold beside her. She got up and walked outside. Some of the boys were carrying a really big fish high on their shoulders, she could see them all walking towards her, children running up and down excitedly.

It obviously had been a good day, as they got to her she could see their beaming faces, Tom's like a Cheshire cat.

"Tom caught the big one! Great fish barbeque tonight," Rio called out, waving to Laura.

Tom shook hands with all of them and they walked on.

"Don't be late, one hour max!" called out Tito.

She could see Tom had had a great day. He was absolutely full of it, telling her all that had happened, even continuing when he was in the shower. Then he said:

"Did you have a good day, did you miss me?"

"Yes I did." She didn't mention where she had been.

The barbecue was super, everybody was invited. Laura found it hard at times not let her mind go back to the Manleys especially when she looked at Aunt Bella. The atmosphere was so warm and she felt this could only have first been born when Ari, John and their boys were here. The fish tasted like no other fish Tom and she had ever had. There was dancing, laughter and lots of drinking, and to feel that they had been expected as the new owners was wonderful. Eventually everybody drifted away and Tom and Laura hauled themselves back to their apartment. You would have thought it was ten miles away instead of a few yards, but Tom with his slurred speech was putting that down to having a very eventful day he told Laura. Nothing to do with too much drinking.

They fell into bed and were asleep within minutes of their heads touching the pillow. Laura half woke up thinking she heard her name being called, yet realising she must be dreaming she turned over and went to sleep again.

# Chapter Twenty-Eight

The next morning they were relaxing on the sunbeds, reading their books when Tom looked up, saying:

"Laura, did I dream it? Did you say, you went to the Love Island?"

"No, I told you, I went to the Love Island."

"You're kidding me just because I did something exciting yesterday," he said.

"Tom, I'm telling you that's where I went."

"How did you get there, did you swim?" he said, pinching her nose and laughing.

"Well it's possible I may have had to swim, but fortunately the boat didn't sink."

"What boat?"

"Ari and John's boat."

Tom was now looking straight at her and laughing.

"You are winding me up you bag, go on make a bit more of the story up, I know you didn't go there," he said.

"Tom, I did. Joe rowed us over."

'What in one of the dinghies from the boathouse?" Tom questioned.

"No, after I waved you off yesterday I walked into the boathouse. A couple of the boys were working in there, it's all full up with wood and old bits of boat and driftwood pushed in a corner, and I saw the letters U. & I. R. 1. about half way down one of the piles and realised it was still attached to a boat. Can you imagine how excited I was? My heart was pounding. Anyway I said goodbye to the boys and started to walk back here and met Joe, I asked him if he would like to come and take a coffee with me on the terrace as I wanted to ask about the island and the family, but most of all the boat. Oh, Tom there is so much to tell you! The island is just so beautiful. It's covered in gorgeous white flowers that smell fantastic. He explained so much. How Ari brought John's body to the island, who Grandma is. She's Ari's daughter Tom and the adoption, together with the superstitions about the island." She didn't tell him about Ari walking the shore.

Once again thinking about it made her cry just a little. Tom took her in his arms, saying:

"Darling please don't cry, it's all right to find out about the family but you should have never gone to the island, and certainly not without me."

"I know, and it was an opportunity not to be missed and in a minute I'll take you down to the shore and show you the boat. I got Joe to leave it there so as I could show you."

"Well, that certainly fills in few gaps," said Tom. "Did you think this about Bella? You did comment about the colouring."

"Yes I know, but I never thought she was Arabella's child."

The plans for the evening, Rio had told them, were to go to a well-known restaurant on the other side of the island so they spent a really lazy day relaxing, chatting, swimming and dozing on the sunbeds, punctuated by little dishes of goodies and lovely fruit juices brought to them by Pollo and Christina.

Just before eight o'clock they went into the courtyard and within a few minutes the three brothers and their wives arrived.

"I'll drive us," said Rio, "and the others will follow on together behind us."

It was the most beautiful alfresco restaurant Tom and Laura have ever seen. There was a steel band playing softly as they walked in, it was obvious the brothers were well known and respected. Rio introduced them to the maître d' as "our new owners", their hands were warmly shaken and they were shown to their table. Tom and Laura noticed there was approximately 50% White and coloured guests, the food, the service, the attention to detail was impeccable.

It was obvious by the number of people that came to the table to greet the family that they were well-known on the island. Each time either Rio, Tito or Dino introduced Laura and Tom as "our new owners", and after a while Tom leant forward to the three men, saying:

"We really would like you just introduce us as Tom and Laura. I'm sure in time as we get to know people more they hopefully will get to understand the situation."

The evening was certainly one to be remembered. Many people danced, some to the steel band and then to the seven piece band that played current hits and romantic oldies. Tom was very aware that many eyes were on Laura and he had to admit she certainly looked fabulous tonight. The band started to play some Barbra Streisand numbers to which they danced together. The floor was packed it was an incredible set-up, half the roof was covered with beautiful silk and the other was open to the moonlight.

Tom held her very tightly to him and after a while she said, "Tom behave!"

"I don't know what you mean," he said.

"Yes you do, you would've thought we were teenagers. I can feel you hard against me."

"Well we are married, you know."

"That doesn't give you permission to make an exhibition."

"No, but it gives me permission to shag the arse off of you when we get back."

She giggled in response saying, "Only once?"

"That's for me to decide, when I see how good you are."

They left the restaurant about two o'clock with Tom having insisted on paying the bill, which seemed to cause the other three great embarrassment. But Tom explained it was a pleasure to be with them all and he hoped they would be able to repeat it whenever they came to the island.

Back in their apartment he did shag the arse off of her three times in total. Once he'd fallen asleep exhausted, she lay there just wanting to take in how much she loved him and how much she loved the feel of him pulsating inside of her, was this how Arabella Manley loved her man? She must've dozed off but was woken by what she thought was her name being called; she listened hard, no perhaps it was in her sleep? She mentioned it to Tom the next morning.

"Too much wining, dining and the other, I think. I'd better cut your rations down," he said, laughing.

Next day Tom looked up from his book and realised Laura was down at the water's edge, stood beside the little boat that she and old Joe had gone across to the island in. He closed his book, got up and walked down to her. Over the last few days he had become increasingly worried about her. She was not her normal bubbly self when they were alone, always wandering to the edge of the shore. As he reached her he put his arm around her, saying:

"What's the matter my darling, you always seem so deep in thought? Are you unhappy or is it something I have done wrong?"

"Nothing's wrong, how could it be? I just like to try to take in all this beauty around us from the many shades of the aquamarine sea to the pink sand, the sky, we are just so lucky. All I hope is our love will last and be as beautiful as Ari and John's was."

"Without those testing times we read of in his book, I hope," he replied, smacking her bottom.

Laura was well aware of how she had been in the last few days, her every quiet moment was taken up by thoughts of the island and Ari and John.

"Come on, let's walk along the shore together," she said, hugging him to her.

As they walked he was aware she kept looking towards the island, and somehow he had an underlying feeling of unease.

The time in Bermuda seemed to be going so quickly but they reassured themselves that it would be only one of regular visits. At this time it seemed everybody wanted to invite them to parties and meet them. Not that they had a problem with that, they were really enjoying it all, and tonight was no exception with a beach party there on their beach. It turned out to be such fun and it was well gone midnight when everybody bade their farewells so, considering it had started around five o'clock, it was quite a marathon. They wandered their way back to their bed, seeming to adopt the way of the true Barbadian.

Tom was woken by Laura, saying:

"Listen, you must be able to hear my name being called just like the other night."

"No I can't and neither can you, it's just the breeze in the voiles and too much rum. Now come on, cuddle down and go back to sleep."

She did as he insisted, but sleep evaded her. She was sure she heard her name, just softly: *Laura. Laura.*

Tom opened his eyes and looked at the clock. It was just after ten a.m., they had obviously slept late this morning. He looked at Laura who was still fast asleep. He lay there for a few minutes more thinking of how she had woken him in the night to see if he had heard her name being called. Of course he hadn't, and he tried to reassure himself that she had been dreaming. He slipped out of bed and pulled on his shorts, walking out onto the terrace; it was yet again another fantastic morning.

Within a little while Laura had joined him.

"Hello my darling, you're a sleepyhead this morning, I've been up for an hour, had a swim and eaten some breakfast."

"Oh," she said, looking at him in surprise, then realising he was teasing her she lent down and pulled his nose.

Pollo then appeared.

"Can I bring you some breakfast, perhaps some nice fresh eggs and fruit and juice?" he asked.

"That will be super," said Tom.

"No egg for me, just fruit please," said Laura.

"Today I was thinking perhaps we would take the Jeep, now we know our way around, and just drive until we found somewhere that looked nice to take a long leisurely late lunch on the beach, just the two of us. Get back sevenish, have a relaxing evening and see what unfolds, what do you think?" Tom asked her.

"Sounds good but what exactly are you thinking in the way of unfolds, may I ask? 'Cause if it's anything to do with sex I won't agree to that."

"That will be the first time since I've known you then, Mrs Nympho."

Pollo arrived with the food just then and they were still giggling.

"You are very happy this morning," he said.

"We are always happy every morning especially when we are here," Laura replied, giving him one of her wonderful smiles that still gave Tom a pleasure to see. Although he thought she looked a bit tired he hoped she would be back to her normal bubbly self, and his whole idea of going off for the day just to get her away from the shore, the boat and the Manleys, would work well.

By the time they left it was midday and they found what turned out to be a truly super and romantic place for lunch. Before even looking at the menu Tom ordered some champagne, which they sipped unaware that they were actually holding hands across the table, chatting and just enjoying one another. It must have been some thirty minutes later when a little cough from the waiter disturbed them.

"Excuse me, sir, we can see you are just so in love are you on your honeymoon?"

They both looked at one another with a smile, and to Laura's surprise Tom said:

"We could be but actually, this is our first visit to your island and our first visit to our house and now we have begun to settle in we thought we would take a little drive out."

"Welcome, welcome," he said, raising his hand to beckon the rest of the waiters, which was followed by much handshaking and smiling.

"Now, you cannot live on love alone you must eat. What can we get you?"

"Just surprise us, but not too much food," Tom said.

"Certainly sir. We will not disappoint you."

"That's a bit dangerous," said Laura,

"Not at all, we don't have to eat it all, and we can afford to pay whatever."

They had a truly wonderful meal of shellfish, fish and local delicacies. They chatted a lot and Tom was delighted Laura didn't mention about hearing her name being called and he had decided he certainly wasn't going to; and to top it all when he asked for the bill they were told it was on the house.

It was nearly eight o'clock when they arrived back and the moon was up.

"Let's take a swim," said Tom, going inside. "We've had such a super day I don't want it to end."

Once inside they slipped out of their clothes, he pulled on his swimming trunks, and she just wrapped an orange silk beach wrap round her, knotting it just above her breasts. They ran to the water like teenagers. The water was so warm it was heaven. Suddenly they were in each other's arms, he undid her wrap and kissed her between her breasts, she could feel his penis stretching against his trunks, he quickly removed them, she wrapped her legs around his waist and within half a second he was inside her, she held him tight with her pelvic muscles.

"Oh God," he moaned,

She released her grip only to tighten it again and again.

"Come, come," he pleaded. They did.

They stayed in the water for some little while just fondling each other, then walked up the shore just a little way collapsing on the sand which was still warm from the heat of the day. Laura found her wrap had floated ashore, which she picked up and put on. Tom just laid there not caring where his trunks where. After they caught their breath back, she lifted up on one arm looking at him.

"That was a first time for me," she said. "Why didn't you teach me that before?"

"Some woman's only just taught me." He said

She ran her hand down his chest to just above his pubic hair. He opened his legs and she continued her journey to gently cradle his balls. Not exactly expecting a response, she was surprised and excited to feel his erection. She knew she wanted it again, she straddled across him taking him in hand he was obviously ready; she raised herself up to take him inside her, but he quickly rolled her on her back.

It was long and fantastic again, he actually brought her to a climax twice before finally allowing himself to join her.

Still lying on top of her completely spent she ran her hands over his backside.

"Your bum's covered in sand," she said.

Back inside Laura made some coffee and they sat together on the sofa quite silent, a silence that is absolutely normal between two people that understand and love one another. Tom was thinking how relieved he felt that things were back to normal. Laura put down her coffee cup and snuggled up to him.

"I love you so much," she whispered in his ear.

"So you should," he said kissing the top of her head.

Within a few minutes they were in bed and asleep.

Laura wasn't sure what had woken her. She lay very still just listening and soon she realised what she had feared there it was, but even more so.

"Come Laura. Come Laura."

She put her fingers in her ears hoping she could still hear it, making her realise she was imagining it; no, she heard nothing slowly removing them there was silence, then:

"Come Laura. Come Laura."

She must have nodded off to sleep again, although very fitfully she kept waking and listening. Then suddenly she was wide awake and was aware of the beautiful smell of the flowers on the Love Island... then she realised there was somebody in the room. She sat up and put the light on, grabbing Tom's arm at the same time.

"What's the matter," he said.

"There's someone in the room."

"Where?"

"I don't know, but I know there is."

"Did you see them?"

"No, but I can smell them, take a big sniff, what can you smell?"

"What am I sniffing for, BO? Garlic? Booze? All I can smell is a delicate flowery, slightly spicy smell."

"That's it, and it's the same perfume as the flowers on the island."

"Yes and that's probably because the breeze has brought it in. Just like it does at home sometimes, if you remember, very occasionally when the wind is in the right direction we can smell the Fawley Oil Refinery and that's right across the other side of the Southampton Water. Laura, there's nobody here, and if there was they would have left by now with all the noise we are making."

"Will you just take a look round please though?" she asked him.

She didn't know why she asked him to do this. She realised by now it was the spirit of Arabella in the room, but she didn't dare say this to him.

Tom took some time to check around not because he had any thought that anybody was there, but just to give himself time to think of what to say to Laura about this situation. Finally climbing back into bed he could see she was close to tears. Holding her close to him he began, in no uncertain way, to say.

"Now ever since you went to that damn island you have been preoccupied by it and this has got to stop or you are going to make yourself ill, and if it doesn't we are going to get the next flight home and that is going to be the end of Bermuda for us."

"We can't go home yet. It's Arabella Manley, her spirit is here."

"Of course it's here if you believe in such things, but you don't. I know you too well, you are to level-headed, I know a lot of things have happened to us both to change our lives, and I think because were now actually here you are just thinking about her and the Manley family and all we have learnt about them. You have let it become part of you, you have let it invade your subconscious mind. I know John and Ari's love story is truly romantic, but so is ours," he said, smiling at her.

When Laura opened her eyes again, Tom was already awake, she leant over him and kissed him.

"I'm sorry about being silly last night, I'm just going to get up now and get showered. I can't bear to think what if I hadn't come home from Canada, what if I hadn't gone to that party, we may never have found each other again, I love you so much."

"I agree with you and now I expect to have my normal Laura back."

She swung her legs over the side of the bed and let out an agonising scream. Tom was by her side instantly thinking she had seen a creepy-crawly or hurt herself in some way. She was clinging to him now, absolutely sobbing, hardly able to breathe.

"Look, look!" she said, pointing to the floor. "Look, foot prints of sand right beside me."

He did look and he could see quite well what she meant.

"I think that was me when I had to go and look round for your bandit last night."

"No. Tom they are not yours. Oh Tom I'm scared, really scared. She's here you know. Don't be cross, you've got to believe me. I didn't tell you all the story Joe told me the other day, 'cause I knew you would think it daft."

She was shaking so badly by now Tom took hold of her by the shoulders, trying to control her.

"OK, when you have calmed down I will listen, now take some deep breaths and make sure you tell me everything."

Still catching her breath she began by telling him how Joe had said that day, even before they went to the island, that the story went that Arabella walked the shore looking for someone. He said he had never seen her, but old Grandma Bella had but she was not the one, and neither were Ari's three sons who she adored, as word had it that when she made contact with that person she would return to the island to be at peace with John and they and the Island would disappear into eternity.

"Tom, I know you think I'm stupid to believe such tales but I think I'm that person! And until you gave me a good talking to last night I couldn't put my finger on it, but I realise now I'm aware of her presence a lot of the time. If we are not actually here in the house, or if we are with other people or I'm alone with you she leaves me. When I go to the shore or the boat alone, I'm even more aware of it."

Trying to lighten the situation a little Tom said, "I hope she wasn't on the shore last night, when you behaved so badly?"

She just shook her head slightly.

"But Tom I'm frightened. When you said about my quiet moments I am just trying to rationalise things, I don't believe in the supernatural, but we own her house, we know so much about her and John's love and life, just think all we found upstairs at the practice, then actually reading John's book, how we got to know her sons, particularly how close we became to William. I have and wear some of her jewellery. We have inherited everything connected to her."

She had stopped shaking now as if talking had helped her, but she was silently weeping.

"Please Tom understand me, I am frightened, what can I do? Help me."

He was quiet for some time, just held her gently rocking her. Then he said:

"Well, we do go home in three days' time. Just don't be alone in that time unless you want to go home today, I'm sure we can get a flight?"

"No we stay, as long as you believe me."

He didn't intend to leave her, although he wanted to find old Joe and just check the Arabella story out.

They had only a few days left now. And today they planned to do some shopping and meet Rio, Tito, Zac and their wives for a meal. There was lots of laughter and truly good feeling between the eight of them and most important to Tom, Laura seemed relaxed and hopefully was having no scary moments. They arrived back about nine p.m.

"Two days to go. How do you feel about going home?" Tom asked Laura as they enjoyed a nightcap together on the sofa.

"I'm looking forward to it in many ways, I love our beautiful home there, but anywhere will do as long as we are together," she said.

She didn't tell him she was thinking *as long as I don't have to take Arabella with me.*

After breakfast they decided to take a swim before walking right along the shore to the point which marked the end of their land. On the way back they stopped at the workshop to have a few words with the boys. Walking on they went right up to their boundary on the other end marked by a gate which they had named 'Arabella's Gate'. They stood for a few minutes just enjoying the view. Laura suddenly held Tom's hand very tightly.

He quickly looked at her saying, "Are you all right, are you on your own?"

"No silly, I'm with you," she giggled.

"OK, OK, there's no need to take the piss. You know what I mean."

Back at the house they sat on the terrace. Christina soon appeared.

"What would you like for lunch?"

"Oh just some juice, fruit and a bun will be fine, we are going shopping in a while and eating dinner early evening," said Laura.

Christina then started to chat about how much she liked shopping and the shops she liked. Tom could hear Pollo in the kitchen, grabbing his opportunity to go and find Joe he ran into the kitchen, saying:

"Do me a favour Pollo, I want to have a quick word with Joe. It's a possible surprise for Laura and I don't want her left alone so as she can follow me, so make sure you two don't leave her alone until I get back, just keep her talking."

Of course this was a lie but Tom wasn't going to go into his reasons. He took off round the side of the house, almost bumping into Joe coming towards him.

"Ah Joe, just wanted to ask you something about this story of Arabella Manley walking the beach. Laura vaguely mentioned it and I wondered if you could tell me more?"

"Yes by all means. They say she walks the shore looking for someone to come and when she finds them she will return to the island to rest in peace with her husband and they and the island will be gone forever. Some of the locals claimed to have seen her, including old Bella, but the island's still there so either they weren't the person she looking for or it's just another of our fairy tales, so to speak. I'm sure you know how superstitious we are."

"So do you believe it?" asked Tom.

"Well, who is there left alive that she could have known? Her sons have all been here, now dead, my old father who she trusted has gone, maybe Bella's true father but he left the island some six months before she was born, probably not even aware that he had fathered a child. Besides I very much doubt if he is alive, he would be a hundred or more now."

"So," repeated Tom.

The old man lifted his hands.

"Ask me when the island disappears," he smiled.

Tom shook his hand, thanked him, and hurried back to his terrace. At least he had established part of Laura's story, and Christina and she where still chatting.

# Chapter Twenty-Nine

After another busy and enjoyable day and night they fell into bed seemingly contented, soon fast asleep.

Laura opened her eyes not wanting to believe her ears.

"Laura come. Laura please come."

Scared but not wanting to wake Tom, she knew she had to deal with this once and for all. She slipped on her robe and stepped outside. It was a wonderful moonlight night she walked towards the shore where the boat was tied up. As she got closer she could see there was somebody sitting in the back of it. As she slowly got nearer she could see the most beautiful woman she had ever seen, her lovely red hair was tumbling to her shoulders and she was wearing what could only be described as a fabulous, turquoise chiffon dress. Laura stood still her heart pounding in her chest.

The woman beckoned her. "Come closer Laura, I won't hurt you. I have waited so long for you to come."

Laura felt as though her feet were embedded in the sand, but with all the strength she could muster she took a few more steps.

"Do you know who I am?" the woman asked.

"Arabella?" Laura whispered.

"Yes and I can see you are wearing my bracelet."

Laura subconsciously put her hand on her bracelet, the one she wore most days. The one the Manley brothers had given her not long after she had joined them. She nodded a reply.

"I can also see you look so like me when I was young. Now I can understand why my boys chose you to help them. They were all very fond of you. Dear Henri, his heart never mended after the tragedy. My baby dear sweet, kind, gentle, Robert. And William, strong like his father, he loved you and Tom like the children he never had. Now Laura, why have I called you? I know you have read John's book and now I want you to promise me you will write it for the world to read."

"But I can't write, I'm no author," said Laura.

"You can and you must, promise me you will, and then we can be free of each other forever. I know I have been a great trial to you, but I want to go back to our island so John and I can finally rest in peace. Now let me hear that promise."

Looking down Laura said, "I promise." She looked up and the vision was gone. She collapsed on the sand absolutely exhausted, it was if all her strength had been sapped from her, she was unable to move.

As Tom turned over in his sleep he put his hand out to touch Laura as normal, she wasn't there. Thinking she may be in the loo, he called out.

"You OK Laura?"

As there was no answer he sat up put the light on repeating his call. Still no reply. He was out of the bed grabbing his shorts and pulling them on.

"Laura, Laura, where are you?"

He ran through the lounge, dining room and on to the kitchen: nothing. Coming back to go upstairs he tried the door into the front courtyard, but it was locked as normal; going up the stairs in great leaps he ran on through the bedrooms and upstairs bathrooms. Nothing. Almost jumping down the stairs he saw the door onto the terrace was open. His worst fears were she had gone, outside.? He rushed across the lounge out onto the sand, calling as he went, not knowing where to look first. Suddenly there was a brilliant flash of lightning and in that moment he caught sight of something on the shoreline, down by the little boat still moored there. Feeling as though his legs were in a dream, he couldn't get there quickly enough.

As he got there he could see it was Laura, unmoving, collapsed in a heap. He turned her to him: she was limp and lifeless. Gently he picked her up into his arms. She was cold. He touched her face, it was damp; but he realised her body was dry. Holding her close to him for warmth, he carried her towards the house.

Christina and Pollo were stood on the terrace, she stepped towards him saying.

"What's the matter, is she dead?"

"No!" he shouted, so loudly it made Christina jump back.

"No, Laura can't die." Tom Screamed.

He laid her on the sofa and dropped down beside her on the floor, she looked so beautiful his eyes filled with tears he gently kissed her on the lips. Thank God she was breathing, but she showed absolutely no reaction to his touch.

Christina and Pollo were still stood there in shock.

"Shall I get the family?" Pollo asked.

"No," said Tom. "But some warm blankets would be a good idea."

They seemed to almost scurry away, almost afraid of the situation. They soon returned with the blankets, which Tom wrapped over Laura, they all looked on in silence for a few minutes. Then Christina said:

"Shall we get the Doctor?"

Laura opened her eyes. Tom held his hand up in protest. Then to all three's amazement she lifted herself up, saying:

"No, no doctor, there's no need for panic, I'm fine but some nice hot chocolate would be fantastic. Perhaps you could make it two? I think Tom could do with one."

Tom said nothing, just held Laura's hand looking at her for any unusual signs.

Christina and Pollo returned with the hot drinks.

"Thank you both," said Laura. "We're fine now, sorry to have caused so much bother, and woken you."

"You didn't wake us, it was the lightning. I think we are in for a storm," said Pollo.

"Please before we go, what was the problem? You scared me." asked Cristina.

Laura looked at the three of them looking at her for an explanation.

"I met Arabella Manley"

There was absolute silence. Tom put his head in his hands, and Christina stood back behind Pollo as if Laura was going to tell them something more she didn't want to hear.

"There's nothing to be afraid of Christina, Arabella will now be at rest, believe me," said Laura. "Now I think you should go home and get some sleep. We will see you in the morning."

Laura picked up her drink, but realised Tom was still silting with his head in his hands. She leant forward and stroked his head.

"It's all right Tom," she said. "Let me explain."

"No Laura."

"What do you mean, no?" she asked.

"You are sick Laura."

"No I'm not sick Tom."

Tom stood up banging the coffee table with his fist, and pointing at her, he said:

"Yes you are and fucking Arabella Manley has made you sick. I tell you Laura, if I hadn't found you on the beach you would have died. Was that her idea? Has she got a place in that coffin on that island for you? I hate bloody Arabella Manley and her island, and her bloody fucking boat, and anything to do with her, and when we get home to England you are going to need some serious treatment. Look at us rowing, is that another part of her plan to come between us? No Laura, I never want to hear another thing about that woman again. Fuck, fuck, fuck Arabella Manley!" he shouted as he stormed across the room out onto the terrace.

Laura was shocked at his outburst. That just wasn't him, she had never heard him swear like that before, she could only assume it was because he was worried about her. Now she felt guilty about having told him about Arabella's presence. She sat quietly for a while hoping he would come back in, he didn't.

She got up went to the kitchen and got a cloth to mop up the chocolate from her cup that had spilt onto the floor. Tom was still outside and now the storm that Pollo had predicted was right over head. She went to the bathroom, washed her hands and splashed her face with cold water, brushed her hair and cleaned her teeth. Going back to the lounge she could see Tom was still on the terrace. She went out to him, putting her arms around him she kissed the back of his neck.

"I'm tired now, I want to go to bed. Please come in."

"Don't go on, just leave me. I'll come when I'm ready," was his reply.

Tom liked the fierceness of the storm, somehow it helped him give vent to his feelings. He was ashamed at his outburst at a time when he should have been more understanding to Laura, but the thought of losing her to something he had no control over had torn him apart. He loved her so much. After sometime with the storm still raging he went back in and slipped into bed beside her. She was still awake.

He lent over her saying, "I'm sorry."

Amazingly enough they both slept deeply and undisturbed until Tom was woken by lots of voices and shrieking coming from outside. He looked at the clock: five thirty a.m. Looking out the window, he could see there was lots of activity going on at the shoreline.

Waking Laura he said, "I don't know what's going on at the shore but it sounds like fun. Let's go and look, perhaps a whale or something has been washed up. They pulled on some clothes and hurried down. As they got closer they could see all the children jumping in and out of the waves with squeals of excitement as it splashed them. Something they didn't normally experience as the water was normally so calm. It seemed as though all the houseboys and -girls were there including the family with much excited chatter going on. The first person they came to was Tito.

"What's going on?" asked Tom.

"Oh, it's the storm last night, it's washed the island away, not particularly abnormal these islands are only shifting sandbanks, although in my experience it is extremely rare for one of this size to be affected, particularly as it had so much root growth on it."

Tom just nodded. Laura didn't know if he had remembered her story about the island disappearing, but she said nothing.

"Sadly too," Tito added looking at Laura, "I'm afraid it took your little boat in its path. Anyway, if you will excuse me I must go, I've got a lot to do today and I want to get this lot documented. See you at your leaving barbeque tonight."

And with a wave he went on his way. Most of the others were beginning to disappear and Tom took Laura's hand. They turned and walked in complete silence to the house.

"It's still only six-ish," said Tom. "I don't know about you darling but I think the best thing for us to do is to go back to bed."

Neither of them were tired or cold, but the comfort of the bed seemed very welcoming.

"Go on then," said Tom.

"About what?" said Laura. "About this morning?"

"No. About last night,"

"Do you mean it Tom? You were so angered last night I'd vowed never to mention it again."

"Yes I agree I was, but I think you must admit this morning's events have put a different light on things."

"OK but only if you don't get cross and tell me I'm sick. Because I'm not and I'm not mad, do you understand?"

Tom nodded an answer.

Propped up on her pillows, Laura began.

"Last night I was being called again, and I thought I've got to get to the bottom of this. Is someone trying to frighten us in view of the Arabella story, or perhaps they don't want us here? So I followed the call. As I got closer to the boat I could see there was someone sitting in the stern. I stopped because I was scared. The figure beckoned to me. It was a woman. She said, 'Come closer Laura I won't hurt you, I've waited so long for you to come. Do you know who I am?' I said, 'Yes I do, you're Arabella.' Then she said, 'I see you are wearing my bracelet.' Tom, I put my hand onto my arm and realised I was wearing it. 'Yes,' I said. Then she said. 'I can understand why my boys chose you to help them, you look very like me when I was young, they all thought so much of you. Dear Henri who's heart never healed after the tragedy. My dear Robert my baby, so kind and gentle. And then dear Willlam, so like his father, so strong in character, he loved you and Tom like the children he never had you know.'"

"She actually said Tom?" Tom butted in.

Laura raised her finger to silence him.

"Yes she did, and then she said, 'I'm sorry to have pestered you so much, and now I will tell you my reason so as we can both be free of each other. And I can return to John and our island to rest in peace. I know you have read John's book of our love together and I want you to promise me you will write it and have it published for the world to read.' 'But I'm not an author I can't write,' I said. 'All you have to do is to promise me and you will have the will to write. Do I have that promise?' Tom, I promised. I sort of bowed my head remembering our conversation with Mr William. and how he had entrusted the book to us and how dear he was to us. When I looked up the boat was empty, the vision the spirit or Arabella whatever you might call it was gone, but the thing that will stay with me forever was her beauty. If her personality was as lovely as her beauty, no wonder everybody loved her."

"And so?" said Tom.

"What do you mean, so?" she replied, looking at him.

"So what happened next?"

"Isn't that enough?" she said.

"What I mean is, you say you looked up and she was gone. I found you in a crumpled heap on the sand. Why was that?"

"Oh, I understand. Well I just felt as if a great weight had lifted from my shoulders, but I also felt absolutely exhausted, my legs felt like lead. I didn't have the energy to move, I just sank down on the sand, and although it sounds silly now I started to cry. I don't remember anymore until I heard Christina say 'Shall I get the doctor?' and I thought, the last thing I want is a bloody witch doctor," she told him.

"Don't be stupid Laura, they don't have witch doctors," Tom said, laughing.

"I'm not so sure. You have to admit they are all a bit hokus-pokus and superstitious here."

"But more seriously you must have cried a lot because your face was quite wet when I picked you up. Laura that was the most terrifying moment of my life, I thought you were dead. I don't ever want to go through that again," he said, leaning over to kiss her on the forehead.

"You know," she began again after a pause, "I'm not one for ghosties up posties eating toasties, Tom."

Which made him laugh saying, "Laura, even in a crisis you make me laugh."

"There is no crisis now, but I didn't say at the time because you would have said nonsense. But from the moment I stepped inside the house I had a feeling of something I wasn't sure of, and as the days went by I became more and more aware of it. I think now it was Arabella."

"And now?" Tom asked, looking worried.

"Oh no, nothing, just nothing. It's completely gone," she said, shaking her head.

"So in view of what's happened with the island overnight do you believe the locals' stories?" Tom asked her.

"I don't know, but it makes you think doesn't it? Although Tito had a perfectly logical explanation, you have to admit. But I know without any doubt in my mind I did have a vision with Arabella, or the spirit of her. What do you think of it all?"

"Well knowing you as I do and now knowing all the circumstances, there has got to be something in it. The only thing I must point out to you is everything you have told me she said were all things you already knew, except we have never thought of Mr William as being strong like his father, because we didn't know the father. We knew they both liked women but I don't think it ever crossed either of our minds to make any comparisons to their character. Let's be honest Laura, we can go on discussing this for ever but as long as you are sure you are absolutely OK, that is all that matters. It's now ten thirty. I think we should get up, have some breakfast and see to a few things before tonight as it's the farewell party for us and I gather from Rio just about everybody we have met since we got here is invited."

"Yes and the little matter of packing to do. That's the worst thing about holidays," said Laura.

Bringing some breakfast for them Christina said, "Laura please, are you all right today?"

"Yes I'm fine," said Laura, not wanting to get into any conversation about last night.

"If you leave out any clothes you will need before you leave tomorrow, Pollo and I will pack for you later," she said.

"That's very kind," said Laura, "but we can't let you do that."

"We are your houseboy and -girl, it is our pleasure and our duty to look after you when you are here, you are our bosses and we like this very much," said Pollo. "We want you to come back many times."

When they had gone Laura looked at Tom.

"That's what I call luxury packing done for us, just like millionaire's life."

Tom looked at her.

"Hard to get used to, but that's us babe."

Sitting over their coffee there was a knock at the courtyard door. Tom got up to open it. It was Joe.

"I hope I'm not disturbing you. Is Laura there? May I come in for a moment?"

"Yes of course, what can we do for you?"

"I just wanted to make sure you were all right after what I hear you experienced last night. As you may well imagine the news has spread fast through all the house staff, who in turn have told all of the family. I hope I have not upset you by taking Laura to the island, Tom?"

"No not at all, she was determined to go one way or another and she's good at twisting people's arms."

# Chapter Thirty

The farewell party was certainly something to be remembered by Tom and Laura. There were so many guests, all people they had met during their stay. All wanting to shake their hand and chat, some Black, some White, but all saying they hoped the two of them would become part of the community just as the Manleys had. The time went so quickly, but towards the end of the evening Joe came over to them clutching what looked like a piece of wood.

"As I walked along the shore this afternoon I found this lying there. Picking it up I realised it may be something you would like, so I took it into the workshop and got the boys to tidy it up and mount it for you," he explained.

As he turned it over they could see it was the name from the little boat, *U. &. I. R. 1*.

Laura shrieked with delight.

"Oh Joe, thank you what a find."

"Well I thought you might like to take it to England with you as a keepsake of your home here in Bermuda," Joe said.

"That is a delightful idea. But if you don't mind I want to keep it here in its rightful home."

"Yes, yes, perhaps you are right. You know one can believe what you wish with these old superstitious stories, but if Arabella was looking for someone I believe it could have been you. Pity you couldn't have asked her what she wanted," he said, winking his eye. "But now the island has gone. For the next generation it will only be a fairy story they will tell their grandchildren."

People began to drift away and soon with just the family and staff were left. To Laura's surprise, Tom beckoned them all around him saying:

"We would just like to say how much we have enjoyed meeting you all, and thank you for making us so welcome. It was quite a daunting task for us to come not knowing how you would receive us after having such a good relationship with the Manleys over all the years. I should add, especially for Laura, it took me quite a bit of persuasion. No doubt you probably had misgivings about us as well, and we hope you will think of us as your friends."

There was lots of clapping and cheering and Rio called out:

"Three cheers for Tom and Laura. Hip, hip?"

There was a resounding Hooray! Each one seeming louder than the last, followed by more cheering.

The flight for England left at two p.m. so they needed to leave the house by eleven thirty a.m. Rio had said if they were in the courtyard a little before it would be nice to say farewell to Joe, Maria and Grandma, as they wouldn't be going to the airport. Despite a late night, Tom and Laura were awake early.

"Let's take a last swim before we have breakfast," said Tom.

"That's a super idea, we haven't got anything to see to. Just get dressed, zip up the cases and go."

The swim was lovely, and Pollo and Christina had breakfast ready when they got back.

"We thought you would leave your swimwear here for the next visit, so Pollo has closed the cases and will get them to the airport ready for your check-in," said Christina.

"Yes that's great," said Tom looking at Laura. "I tell you what, I could get use to this being waited on."

"I tell you what, I love it but it's no different for you, I do it all the time at home for you," Laura said.

Giving a fond farewell and a big thank you to Pollo and Christina they went out into the courtyard. The children were running around excitedly, and Joe was just coming with Grandma in her wheelchair, followed by Maria. Laura went forward to Grandma. Taking the old lady's hands, she said:

"Goodbye Grandma, it's been a pleasure to meet you."

The old lady lifted her head. Taking her hands from Laura and holding them up to clasp Laura's face, she said:

"Come back soon, my darling Ari."

Maria started to correct Bella, but Laura waved her hand saying:

"Please don't worry Maria. It doesn't upset me if she thinks I'm Ari."

She kissed the old lady on the cheek saying, "Yes I will."

Tom kissed the old lady and gently patted her shoulder. Then turning to Joe and Maria, he said:

"Thank you both so much, Laura and I could never have imagined such kindness." He gave Joe a big hug, shaking his hand warmly, then turning to Maria he put his arms around her he gave her a hug and a farewell kiss.

In the meantime Laura was saying goodbye to Joe.

"Thank you for everything Joe. For all the info, and for taking me to the island."

"I'm not so sure I should have done that, I hope Tom will forgive me. I think I told you too much about Arabella."

"No, no, not at all, I persuaded you to take me and who knows? Perhaps she is at peace now." She smiled at him warmly giving him a hug and a kiss. Then turning to Maria she said:

"Thank you is not really enough. You have been so kind." The two women held each other for a few minutes.

"And you to us. Joe and I were very worried before you came despite Rio's reassurances. Now we hope you will come back many times and soon," said Maria.

"Time to go!" shouted Tito.

Outside Rio, Pia and the children were already in the car. Laura and Tom joined them waving as they took off.

As promised their luggage was at the check-in. Suddenly a little Black hand was inside Laura's. She looked down to see Josh with Sofia holding his other hand.

"We want to come to England with you, we don't have to go to school for one week and we want to see Daddy Man."

Laura bent down to them, saying:

"As Mummy told you, Daddy Man is with the fairies still, and it's very cold in England right now. I don't think you would like it."

"We would," he said, with big brown eyes looking for agreement from Laura. Fortunately Sofia saved the day.

'When you come back to see us," she said, "I think Daddy Man will be back from the fairies so you just bring him with you."

"Yes," agreed Laura.

Final farewells were said to all and they went through to departure.

Once in the air with the hostess handing them a glass of champagne, Laura said.

"That was just wonderful, I hope you didn't mean it during one of your outbursts that you hated the island?"

"No. Just heat of the moment. You silly thing, but you must admit you were giving me a hard time at that point. Anyway, more important, what are you going to call this book?"

"Well funny you should ask that. I think:

*U. &. I. R. 1.*"